# my christmas in capri

## TESS RINI

ISBN: 978-1-7376372-7-1 (e-book)

ISBN: 978-1-7376372-8-8 (paperback)

Tessrini.com

Publisher: One Punch Productions, LLC

Cover design and interior formatting by *Hannah Linder Designs*

*For my sister, MaryJo (aka Josepina), who
loves Capri almost as much as she loves me.
Thanks for always being my cheerleader.
XOXO*

# one

Stefano glanced impatiently at his watch for the tenth time. Since he was planning to be in Naples for the day, he had agreed to pick up his sister-in-law's closest friend, Teresa, at the airport. He checked the app on his phone and then the airport's information board. Her flight had arrived. Where was she?

Taking out his phone, Stefano texted again. Frowning, he waited. Nothing. And no replies to his last two texts. Did she miss the flight? Possibly customs could be backed up—the airport was very crowded this time of day. He agreed to meet Teresa where travelers exited customs, so as to not miss each other. Maybe she misunderstood—but there was no other way for her to exit.

It had been a long day, and he was in meetings for most of it. As Executive Vice President of his family's dynasty, Oro Industries, Stefano had worked hard to ascend the corporate ladder. His role now was to ensure their products' distribution lines in wholesale and retail were on target and thriving. Ranging from limoncello to lemon soap, olive oil, and lemon candy, Oro's products were continuing to grow in markets all over the world. And then there were the many local businesses Oro had acquired over the years. He loved his family, but every day, he hated his job a little more. With his brother, Marco, at the helm, he felt guilty for not being more enthusiastic. Marco, who had recently taken over as CEO, needed Stefano to keep a tight hold on things while they navigated through some tough times. Marco inherited his title from their uncle—*Zio* Angelo. But with the role, came managing the corporation's Chief Financial Officer—Angelo's closet friend. Stefano grimaced, thinking back to the fraud they uncovered at the hands of the detestable man. It had caused a lot of pain. The corporation was hopefully through the worst and Marco was finding his feet, but Stefano didn't know what the future held for him personally.

He had taken off his tie and left his suit jacket in the car. Now he longed to get home and change out of his white dress shirt and dark gray slacks. He needed time to unwind, but that probably wouldn't happen. The house was packed with family. At least he could cook dinner and possibly have some solitude while doing it.

If it was anyone but Kate, he would have said no. He was fond of his new sister-in-law, and it wasn't that out of his way. Except, well, he was picking up Teresa. There was just something about her. He met her when she arrived for Marco and Kate's wedding, and she had unnerved him. At first, he was highly physically attracted to her, but then he watched her practically drooling over their cousin, Lucca, a famous movie star. Next came her nonstop chattering with their brother, Nico. Whatever it was about her got under his skin in a way most people didn't.

"There you are!" Teresa came hurrying toward him as if he were the one who was late.

Quickly remembering his manners, he tried to wipe the impatient look off his face. "*Benvenuta*, Teresa," he said to welcome her, kissing her on each cheek.

She accepted his greeting, juggling her purse, backpack, and rolling suitcase. She smiled up at him, her wide mouth showing perfect white teeth—he forgot how petite she was—he was almost two heads taller than her. Her dark head of curls, stopping a few inches below her ears, was perfectly styled, as if she hadn't been on a long plane ride. Her big brown eyes, under their distinct brown brows, were crinkled at the corners, and he noticed a smattering of freckles across her small nose. She was wearing white jeans and a multi-colored top, with big gold hoops in her ears. He blinked a little at all the color before him.

"Sorry if I kept you waiting. Uh, I left my phone on the plane. So stupid—and the crew was nice enough to go get it for me. Then I made a couple of quick stops to buy a few things. Then customs took forever—man, they were thorough. You'd think I was a criminal. But I'm ready!"

"Let me have your bags, and we will go to my car," Stefano said politely, as he grabbed them and headed toward the exit. Teresa was almost running in her sandals, trying to keep up with him, and he slowed down courteously. She was chattering already. *Dio*, it was starting. He realized she asked him a question. *"Mi dispiace?"*

"Have I made you late or something? You seem to be in a hurry. I'm sorry about this. I told Kate I could get a ride. She was already upset with me for not taking Marco's plane, but that seemed silly—just me on a private jet. I mean climate change and all..." Her voice trailed off.

They entered the parking garage, and Stefano made a few small noises to appear as if he was listening. He indicated his large black Mercedes that he used around the city. Opening the door for her, he went to put her bags in the trunk. Getting in the car, he started it and the hard rock music from his deluxe stereo system blasted. He quickly turned it down without comment, but he saw her raise his eyebrows in surprise.

Driving out of the airport's exit, he began to deftly navigate the evening traffic. He realized she finally was silent, and guilt nudged him again. If Marco or Kate found out he was rude, he would get an earful. "Did you have a pleasant flight?" he asked politely.

"Yes, thank you. Though long. It was sweet of Marco to upgrade me. I've never in my life flown First Class. Have you?"

Stefano's lips twitched at the thought of flying anything but First Class or private. He knew he would sound like a snob, but it was his reality. "Well, yes, it is very comfortable."

"They were soooo nice. I slept a lot, though. I worked yesterday, and I was exhausted."

"How is your work at the hospital?" asked Stefano, remembering that she was an obstetric nurse.

Teresa was looking at the window and seemed to be contemplating the question. "Okay," she mumbled.

Sensing she didn't want to talk about it, he decided not to ask any more questions. Instead, he concentrated on his driving, winding through Naples' crowded streets. *Dio*, this was awkward. He shouldn't have offered to pick her up. The silence now was deafening, and he searched his brain for what to say next.

Suddenly, his nose twitched. What was that horrible smell? He glanced over at the rustling to see Teresa shaking a wrapped burger out of a bag onto her lap. She then reached in the bag and grabbed a French fry. He was so distracted, he about drove the car off the road. "What the hell?"

She looked at him with wide eyes, glancing around at his spotless vehicle. "I'm sorry! Do you not allow eating in your car?"

It took him a minute to find his voice. "I do not have rules about eating in my car. I just do not allow that kind of horrendous food in it—or anywhere in my life, for that matter."

Teresa took a big bite of her burger. "What's wrong with it?" she asked after swallowing. She took another bite quickly, grabbing a napkin to wipe a little ketchup off her face.

"Well, it is disgusting, number one. Number two, it is going to kill you."

"What a way to go," Teresa said, smiling at him. "Want a fry?"

"No!" he almost shouted. Taking a calming breath, he asked, "Where did you get that stuff?"

"Oh, it was conveniently right after customs. I was so happy to see it. I was starving. I mean, they kept offering me food on the flight, but it was all plane food, if you know what I mean. And I ran out of the goldfish that were in my backpack and my animal cookies only lasted until we were over Greenland, I think."

He shook his head. "Goldfish?"

"You know, the little cheddar crackers? They are required on any trip—plane, car, train. But I shouldn't have left the other goldfish bag in my checked luggage. And the animal cookies were delicious—I like the pink-and-white ones with the sprinkles. They are mandatory as well."

There were absolutely no words to add, and he decided to stay silent. Finished eating, she put the wrapper back in the bag and crumpled it. She glanced around, looking smug. "Not a crumb in your car. I was careful."

"Except the smell is going to linger forever."

Teresa rolled her eyes, stuffing the bag in her purse. "You'd be so lucky. If they made a car freshener with this scent, I'd buy it for sure!" She settled down now in her seat, almost looking sleepy.

"You can fall asleep if you want," he said quietly. If she slept the rest of the way, it would solve his problem of keeping this conversation alive.

She nodded, not looking at him. But she didn't close her eyes.

They drove for a few more miles, now beginning to leave Naples behind, heading toward Sorrento. They would be at his family's lemon grove in about an hour. The entire family was home, getting ready for his cousin Lucca's wedding. Lucca and his fiancé, Ellie, a renowned artist, were marrying in just a couple of days. Their meeting had been unique, and he almost smiled, remembering their turbulent relationship in the beginning. He realized Teresa was talking again and apologized for the second time. "*Mi dispiace?*"

"No, I'm sorry, Stefano. You didn't need to pick me up. But since you did, let's just take this opportunity to discuss something."

He raised his eyebrows. What could they have to discuss?

"Why do you dislike me so much?"

# two

Teresa looked out the window and bit her lip from smiling. She did not purposely want to needle Stefano, but it was time to find out why he treated her as if she was some kind of parasite. A range of expressions crossed his face, and he obviously was struggling to answer her question. She stared at him, admiring his black hair, which was cut very short, almost spiky in some places. Having the opportunity before to study his face, she thought he was a leaner, sterner version of Marco. His olive skin was so smooth, but now he sported a slight beard along his jawline. A muscle twitched in his cheek.

"Uh, I don't dislike you," came his lame answer.

"Sure, you do. Let's dissect it. We still have some time on this drive—might as well put it to good use," Teresa said, sounding more cheerful than she felt. Deep down, she took it to heart when someone didn't like her—especially Stefano. "Just let it come out, Stefano. What is it about me that bugs you?" she pressed, secretly kind of loving the pained look on his face.

"Teresa, I do not dislike you or like you. In fact, I do not even know you. We have hardly had a conversation. If I remember correctly, you were more interested in drooling over my cousin or laughing with my brother."

"And we have it!" Teresa said triumphantly. "You're upset because it appears I found them more interesting."

"That is not the case," Stefano said stiffly.

"Oh, but it is," she said seriously. "You're a classic middle child, aren't you? You have this handsome and charming big brother and sweet-as-pie little brother, and then throw into the mix a hunky-on-steroids cousin. And you're all twisted."

"I'm NOT twisted!" shouted Stefano. She watched his powerful hands grip his steering wheel more tightly. The sleeves of his white dress shirt were rolled up and his silver watch glinted in the sun. He looked so strong and virile that it almost made her back down. Instead, she went for broke. "Well, calm down. Geez, I'm not eating fast food anymore. Your senses should be lulled. You can relax. Think of this as a therapy session."

"You are not a therapist," he stated roughly.

"No, but I'm like one. I'm a medical professional. And I took a lot of psychology classes at school. For a while, I thought of going into the field. Plus, I've spent years—years—analyzing my family and friends. I'm a great listener. So put that all together, and I'm extremely qualified."

He sighed deeply.

"See, you're longing to get it out. But let's go back to the original question. What else, besides the fact that I'm friendly to your cousin and brother, don't you like?"

"You are...like a hummingbird," he responded quickly, keeping his eyes on the road.

Her eyes widened, not sure if she heard him right. "What?"

"You are like some damn little hummingbird. We have them all over the lemon grove. They buzz around constantly—frenetically, from one plant to another. That is you."

Teresa laughed. "Stefano, I'm going to take that as a compliment. Do you know some people think hummingbirds are the souls of loved ones who have departed? It's good luck to see a hummingbird."

"Then I must have all the luck in the world," he said in a dark tone.

"I have never ever been compared to a hummingbird," she said, a slight smile on her face. "My brothers have called me a gnat, a roadrunner, a whirling top, but never a hummingbird. I think that's lovely."

He looked over at her quickly, almost assessing if she was serious, before putting his eyes back on the road. "You also talk a lot."

"Yeah, well, we can agree on that. I do. I talk a lot, eat junk food, and have a lot of energy. You should see me when I have sugar!"

"*Dio*, don't drink a cappuccino while you're here," Stefano commented dryly.

"Stefano, I believe you just cracked a joke," she teased. Pushing on his upper arm, she felt his warm bicep. She took her hand away abruptly. "Who knew you had it in you?"

"You do not know the first thing about me," he said quietly, not looking at her. Instantly, she stopped smiling. She only meant to tease him a little to see if he would warm to her, but now it seemed to have backfired. He looked almost sad. She stared out the window. As usual, she took it a bit too far, and she mentally kicked herself. She needed to stop teasing men like they were her brothers—the usual verbal rough housing they did was probably not the level of flirting she wanted to attain. Taking a calming breath, she tried another tactic.

"Hey," she said softly. When he glanced at her, she smiled. "I'm sorry if I spoke out of turn. I guess I just wanted to clear the air. It feels cruddy when someone doesn't like you."

He seemed to soften a little. "We should call a truce. It will be a busy weekend, and we will not be around each other much anyway."

She seized on the opportunity to change the subject. "Tell me about the plans. I feel weird being here for Lucca and Ellie's wedding. The timing just worked out better for me to come now, and Kate was being really insistent that I come over."

"She must miss you. I am sure she is probably a little homesick," Stefano said. "But yes, there is a lot going on with the wedding. Lucca is driving us all nuts because he wants everything perfect. It is a small wedding, but you would think it was for the royal family or something. Everyone has been running around trying to get ready for it."

"I'm so happy for them. I spent some time with Ellie at Kate's wedding—she seems really sweet."

Stefano gave her a quick, rare smile. "She is, but she is also tough—which is a good thing. She can handle *mio cugino*."

"Katie told me there's a whole back story."

Stefano nodded and went on to tell her about Ellie's past. Her real name was Eleanor Montgomery, and she was the daughter of Emerson and Miranda Montgomery—Hollywood legends. She grew up in the spotlight, chased by paparazzi her whole life. Ellie had only found a reprieve when she lived in Italy and attended art school. Finding painting to be her genuine passion, she became a sought-after artist before hitting a dry patch. She met Lucca after she delivered a cake to his house. She was then asked to decorate a wedding cake for Marco and Kate's wedding as a favor for a friend. Ellie and Lucca coincidentally reunited again in Tuscany at Lucca's father's villa where they were forced to stay together while the police looked for Lucca's stalker.

His quiet voice softened her frayed nerves. "I didn't know about Lucca's stalker," Teresa said contritely. "I mean, we joked about it and stuff."

"Yes," Stefano said gravely. "It was not too funny, though. We did not know it escalated to that point. It was a relief to hear the

FBI apprehended the man responsible, and it sounds like he will be imprisoned for a long time. That situation—and Lucca's fame —made them decide the lemon grove was perfect for their wedding. We can keep it a tight circle," he added, glancing at her.

Teresa stared at him. Was that a jab at her? She wasn't exactly in the circle. To be fair, she hadn't asked to come. Kate begged her. And the timing in the end was perfect. Why it all unfolded that way was not something she wanted to share with Stefano. "I know I'm crashing the wedding, but it's not my fault," said Teresa pointedly.

"You can be the person who stands up when they ask if anyone objects," Stefano teased.

"Wow, two jokes in one car ride. No, I think I'm good. I can just admire from afar." She felt herself flushing a little. Did everyone think she had a crush on Lucca? If they only knew the man she was desperately attracted to was sitting right next to her.

They soon pulled through the gates of the lemon grove, and Teresa almost sighed out loud. She already loved the family's estate, having stayed there for Kate's wedding. Climbing the gravel hill that turned into a paved road, Stefano pulled the car to a stop on the circular drive. A stone fountain stood in the middle, surrounded by flower beds. The expansive cream-colored house, with its arched windows, brown shutters and covered wraparound terrace was breathtaking. It radiated warmth and looked like a family home despite its size.

Stefano turned to stare at her, a serious look on his face. He appeared as if he wanted to say something, and she stared back. The silence was awkward again. Could he read her thoughts? Maybe he could tell she was so deeply infatuated with him that she thought of no other man since Kate's wedding. She swallowed hard. "Stefano..."

"TERESA!"

Teresa glanced out the car window to see Kate running down

the front steps, Marco quickly following her. Teresa smiled and started to get out of the car, but Stefano was already there, opening her door and helping her out.

Kate flung herself in Teresa's arms and hugged her for dear life. Teresa hugged her back just as tightly, now overcome with how much she had missed her friend. They finally separated, both laughing and dabbing their eyes. "I missed you so much," Kate said, smiling. "I'm so glad you're here."

"*Buonasera*, Teresa," said Marco, coming behind Kate to kiss her on both cheeks and give her a big hug.

"Good to see you, Mr. H," Teresa responded, using the nickname she gave him, which stood for Mr. Hunky.

"Sweet Tea," he said, laughing. He had come up with a silly nickname of his own during their time together. Glancing back, she saw Stefano unloading her luggage from the trunk. She went over to grab it from him. "Thank you for picking me up. I'm sorry if I offended you in the car," she whispered, her eyes trying to meet his gaze. He was busy pulling up the handle of her suitcase, not looking at her.

"*Prego.* Do not worry. Truce, remember?" he asked in a soft tone. "I'll take these up to your room for you," he said more loudly, glancing at her briefly before walking away. "Same room as last time?" he asked Kate, who nodded yes.

Teresa felt oddly deflated. She was hoping they'd have a moment where he would give her a shred of hope. Nothing. There was no time to think about it, though, for Kate grabbed onto her arm and was hauling her into the house, talking without taking a breath.

"Everyone is still up the hill looking at the reception area, and I think Lucca and Nico are stringing lights around the gazebo where the wedding will be," Kate said. "Margherita is running all over the place," she laughed, referring to her mother-in-law, who she adored. "That gives us some time before dinner. Do you want to go to your room and take a shower? Not that you look bad—in fact, you look really nice after that long flight," she said thoughtfully. "I wish you would have let Marco send his plane."

Teresa rolled her eyes, assuring her friend commercial was just fine. She was distracted, thinking back to the extra make-up and hair product she applied when she got off the plane. After receiving Kate's text about Stefano picking her up, she whipped out a new top and jeans from her suitcase and spent some time on her appearance before meeting him. She even put on earrings and her new sandals, which were now pinching her feet. The excuse about customs taking so long was a small fib—she took the time to change since she wasn't about to let him see her all bedraggled with goldfish crumbs and cheese dust on her yoga pants.

She smiled at Kate. "Let me go to my room and at least get settled." Though Teresa was used to telling her best friend everything, she wasn't about to inform her that she was crushing hard on her husband's brother—especially when said brother had no interest in her. It was like they were suddenly back in middle school. The last thing she needed was an eager Kate getting some grandiose idea to convince Marco to ask Stefano what he thought of Teresa. Teresa shuddered at the thought.

Following Kate up the stairs and through the complicated hallways, they finally got to the wing where Teresa had stayed previously. Glancing around at the luxurious room with the big four-poster bed and the colorful comforter, she smiled. "It feels like home. I love this room, Katie."

I know—I saved it for you, though there's a lot more to spare since the wedding is small. Ellie's parents were invited to stay here, but they decided to rent a villa nearby. I think they didn't want to intrude. They are wonderful—wait until you meet them! More celebrities on top of Lucca," she said with a laugh.

Teresa shot her a quick smile, letting Kate tease her about Lucca and the celebrities. It would keep her off the scent.

Kate sat down on the comforter as Teresa disappeared into the walk-in closet to see if that was where Stefano brought her suitcase and backpack. She would unpack later. For now, she wanted to catch up with her friend. Kicking off her sandals, she sat down on the bed crisscross, facing Kate.

"And now, Katie, you can tell me why I'm here."

Kate was looking pale and thinner than she had ever seen her. She looked at Teresa, her eyes full of tears. "I'm pregnant."

# *three*

Teresa put her arms around Kate and let her cry. She didn't ask questions, she just let her sniff and sob for a few minutes. Finally, Kate sat back up and rubbed her eyes, apologizing. Teresa looked around. Finding a box of tissues, she handed it to her friend.

"That's great news, Katie. It is, isn't it?" Teresa asked cautiously.

Kate grabbed a tissue and rubbed her eyes, nodding vigorously. "Yes, it is," she said, giving her friend a watery smile. "But the timing, Teresa. Marco is still getting settled in as CEO, and my company is really taking off. And it's just a lot," she said. "I know I am really fortunate, but I'm just overwhelmed. We're just settling into our lives here, you know? I'm starting to get used to living in Italy, too."

"I know, I know. That's perfectly normal," Teresa reassured her, giving her a quick hug. "You've made a lot of changes, Katie. It's a lot for your over-stimulated hormonal brain to cope with."

"I'm already a terrible mother!" wailed Kate.

Teresa laughed. "Then that list must be really long. Most pregnant women feel overwhelmed at some point."

"I can't stop crying. Marco is so confused. He's never seen me like this, and he doesn't know what to do—he tries to make me laugh and I cry."

"Those pesky hormones will get you every time. What does Mr. H say about all this?"

Kate smiled, as if remembering when she told him. "He's a mixed bag of emotions. He was ecstatic at first. Oh my God, you should have seen him! He was so happy, but then he kind of started freaking out, wondering what kind of dad he'll be. You know his dad left him when he was young. He's had a couple great role models—father figures in his life. But he's worried it's genetic or something."

"I'm sure his mother will set him straight. Marco won't be like his father. He'll be a terrific dad," Teresa rushed to reassure her friend.

"Oh, I know. But he has to figure that out," Kate said simply.

"That's why God gave parents nine months to get used to an idea of a little life-changing bundle," Teresa said with a smile. She was thoughtful as she stared at Kate. "I'm happy to hear this news in person and so excited for you, but why am I here, Katie? Other than nerves, are you feeling okay?"

"I'm so sick, Teresa. I thought it's called *morning* sickness. I'm sick all day and half the night. Remember how I struggle with being motion sick? I can barely ride in a car right now. Do you think that means I'm going to lose the baby?"

"No!" Teresa rushed to reassure her. "That's just the way it is for some women. By your second trimester, you'll be feeling on top of the world. By the way, how far along are you?"

"Just eight weeks," Kate said. "At first, I just couldn't believe it. I must have taken six pregnancy tests. And then I started to worry. My mom miscarried twice. Did you know that? I began wondering if I was going to as well."

"Have you seen a doctor?"

"Yes! Marco insisted right away, and then he made me go

back when I kept getting sick. They gave me some medication, but I'm afraid to take it. I don't want it to hurt the baby."

"Katie, it's important that you're able to hold some food and liquid down so the baby can get nourishment. I'll take a look at it if that will make you feel better. But you didn't just fly me 4,000 miles to do that, did you?"

She looked guilty now. "No, of course not. I mean, selfishly, I want you here the entire time, but I know that you can't do that. I just wanted you here so badly, Teresa. I'm not usually so needy, I know. And when you said you quit your job, it just seemed like it was a perfect time. I thought the change of scenery might help you, too."

Teresa looked down at her hands. "Thank you, it will. I know it will. If you don't mind, I'm not ready to talk about it yet." She swallowed the lump in her throat. "Yesterday was my last day."

Kate nodded and covered her hand with hers. "I get it, Teresa. I'm here when you're ready."

"Have you told anyone I quit?" Teresa asked sharply, really wanting to ask if she had told Stefano.

"Well, Marco, of course..." Kate said, her face turning pink as she trailed off.

"Kate Malone Rinaldi, tell me right now. Who else did you tell?"

"Lucca," she whispered. "For a very good reason! Don't get mad, okay? I'm thinking if you're willing, there could be a job for you here."

"Lucca needs a nurse?" Teresa asked, confused.

"No, no. Completely unrelated. Lucca is going to stay in Italy, and he is forming his own production company. Marco is helping him get it started—as an investor, but also just getting him connected with the right people. You know, lawyers and such.

"What does that have to do with me?"

Kate smiled. "Just hear me out, okay? Lucca has already sold his first series to a new American distributor—they have shopped it to some streaming services. He wants to produce a show where each episode talks about different regions of Italy and the food they eat. Why they eat what they do, the history and the origins of it. He's sold the first season, which would be four episodes to start with."

"I'd watch that! But I'd watch anything about food!"

"I know! Especially Italian cuisine. But here's the deal. He wants to convince Stefano to be the host. Lucca doesn't want to do it. He wants to be behind the camera, and he doesn't just want people to watch it because of him. That combined with the fact he also doesn't know anything about food and cooking, and he wants the host to be an expert. Stefano would be perfect. He has studied cooking and cuisine extensively. Lucca thinks his enthusiasm would come out on camera."

Teresa thought so, too, but she didn't want to give anything away. "What does that have to do with me?"

Kate smiled. "You used to be in television. Teresa, you were a great producer! We think—that is Lucca, Marco and I—think that you could help Stefano get ready for this. Can you imagine him on TV?"

The look on Teresa's face made Kate laugh. "See? Me neither. He'd be a deer caught in the headlights. He needs someone to loosen him up, make him relax and learn how to play to a camera. You're just that person. I saw you transform that last anchorman at the station—he was a wreck on the air before they called you in to prep him."

"Well, at least he was experienced in front of a camera," Teresa said slowly. "Has Stefano had any experience?"

"Well, no," Kate admitted. "But I bet he'll be a quick learner."

"What does he think about doing it? Is he into it?"

Kate bit her lip. "He might not know yet."

"WHAT?" Teresa struggled to keep her voice down. "Katie, he's never going to agree to do it!"

"Oh, he'll agree." Kate smiled. "The guys are meeting tomorrow. They'll convince him. I would put my money on Marco and Lucca."

"He won't want me helping," Teresa said sadly.

"Why ever not?" Kate asked sharply. "Has he been mean to you? Cause if so, I'll go down there right now and deal with him."

Teresa put out a hand to stop Kate from getting off the bed. "Settle down, Miss Hormones. He's not been mean. He just doesn't really like me." She looked away. "Unless you like hummingbirds," she muttered.

"What about hummingbirds?"

Teresa laughed. "Oh sorry, just a joke in the car on the way up." She hurried to continue before Kate could ask more. "Listen, I think you got over your skis. First, let's see if Stefano is even going to do it. And then we'll find out if he will consider my help. If so, we'll talk. In the meantime, we're going to your room and look at your medicine. And I have some ideas on how you can control your nausea by the times of day you eat as well as some other things."

Kate smiled. "I already feel better with you here. But Teresa, don't tell anyone I'm pregnant. Only Marco and I know. And now you. We didn't want to upstage the wedding. We can't wait to tell the family, but not this weekend. I'm only going to tell my sister when she gets here."

"Lips are sealed," Teresa said. "Just give me five minutes to change and wash my face. And then I'll come to you and Marco's room and give you some tips." She hopped off the bed. "And Katie, don't tell anyone about my quitting either, okay? Just between us?"

Kate got up slowly, eyeing her friend. She gave her a comforting smile and then a hug. "My lips are sealed."

*four*

Teresa picked at her food. Carefully separating the vegetables to the side of her dish, she ate just the chicken. At least that was tasty. She took a bite of the rustic Italian bread on her plate and almost moaned. God, she loved bread.

"Teresa, pass the bread," whispered Kate. "It's the only thing that tastes good right now."

Teresa handed her the breadbasket and then continued eating, staying silent. The family was dining at the big wooden table on the stone patio. Even though they were eating outside, everything looked so comfortably elegant, Teresa told Kate when they sat down. It was such a weird combination, but Kate knew what she meant, whispering her mother-in-law wouldn't have it any other way.

Marco was arguing with Nico about how many lights were needed on the gazebo, and Margherita was gently refereeing. Stefano remained silent, eating the dinner he cooked when he got home.

"Where's Lucca?" asked Teresa. She meant the question to be directed at Kate, but her voice carried, and the talking had unfortunately ceased. Stefano's head snapped up, his face impassive.

"He went to dinner with Ellie and his future in-laws," Margherita explained. "Tomorrow night, they are hosting all of us at the rehearsal dinner at a wonderful restaurant."

"Oh, not me. I'll just stay home and hang out with Sophia," Teresa said, giving the dog a pat. Lucca's golden retriever decided she was his new person and hadn't left her side since she came downstairs. Teresa looked over to see Stefano staring at her.

"Well, of course, you're coming, dear," Margherita insisted. "It's a small wedding, and we'll all have a good time. Kate's sister, Meara is flying in tomorrow, and she'll join us, along with a few other friends."

Teresa opened her mouth and closed it again. She'd talk to Kate about it later. Attending the wedding was one thing—going to the rehearsal dinner seemed intrusive. Besides, she wasn't sure how much more teasing about Lucca she could stand. Standing restlessly, she gathered plates to carry inside.

"Teresa, *per favore*, we don't make our guests work," Margherita said and frowned. Teresa smiled at her. "It's fine, Margherita, I need to stretch my legs."

"Call me Rita, honey. And I guess we will let you just this once. Stefano, help her, please."

Teresa quickly walked ahead so no one could see her discomfort at Stefano's help. She stopped as he opened the French door, and she went inside to the cool interior. The extensive kitchen greeted her, and she gently placed plates on the marble counter.

"What's wrong with my cooking?"

Teresa jumped at the quiet voice. Not wanting to turn around so he could see her face, she pretended to be looking for a glass. Out of the corner of her eye, she saw Stefano open a cabinet and grab one. "Do you want water, lemonade, or sweet tea?" he asked. The tone in his voice made her glance at him sharply.

"You don't even know what sweet tea is," she told him severely. "Neither does Marco. What a ridiculous nickname."

"Oh, and Mr. Hunky isn't?"

22

She looked at him, frowning. "How did you know what the H stood for?"

He laughed. "Marco! Of course, he couldn't wait to brag that you thought he was hunky."

Teresa smiled a little. "It's an old joke between Katie and me about guys in high school. But back to your question. I just want some water."

He filled the glass and handed it to her. His fingers brushed hers, and the electricity shot up her arm. She went to walk out of the kitchen to go back outside, but his arm snaked out and stopped her. "Now, back to my question. You didn't like my cooking?"

She felt herself flush. "No, no, it's fine. Why?"

"You left most of it on the plate. Just rearranged it to look like you were eating. And Katie's no better. I do not think she ate much either."

"Well, I can't speak for Katie, but it was great. I just wasn't too hungry."

"Did the fast food you ate for an *aperitivo* fill you up?"

Teresa rolled her eyes. "I knew that would come up again. No, I'm fine. Just probably that my stomach doesn't know what time it is."

He gave her a narrowed look, but indicated that she should go back outside. The family was enjoying being together, and everyone was chatting and laughing. Tiramisu was brought out —Margherita's specialty. Goodness, couldn't these people just have some ice cream? Teresa wasn't a fan of coffee flavor. She accepted a small piece, telling Margherita she was full. She thought about feeding a few bites to Sophia, but chocolate wasn't good for dogs. She swallowed hard, feeling Stefano's eyes on her.

"Are you going to eat that?" Nico asked. He was sitting next to her, and he raised an eyebrow at her untouched dessert.

"Uh...not really. I'm pretty full," Teresa told him.

"Mind if I do?" His fork speared it before she could even nod.

Teresa laughed, thinking there was a human garbage disposal at her fingertips. She should have taken advantage of him earlier!

Listening to the family with half an ear, her mind was reeling from the job offer and information Kate confided earlier. She wondered what Stefano was going to say. Kate told her previously how knowledgeable he was about Italian cuisine and what a great cook he was. She knew instinctively she could get him to a place where he would shine on camera; after all, she'd done it many times before. What she didn't know was if she could be around him that much. It was already tough knowing he didn't like her while she was wildly attracted to him.

Teresa thought back to the first time she saw Stefano. She had arrived with Kate's father, Finn, for the wedding. Stefano was standing on the porch, and she remembered glancing up to see his mocking face as he lounged against a pillar. The whole family was there, greeting them and making them feel welcome. Only Stefano held back. She had felt his penetrating eyes on her and looked up and met his gaze. It was like a thousand little needles attacked her heart. She had almost gasped out loud. He apparently had not felt it, eventually disengaging from the pillar and slowly coming down to shake Finn's hand and greet her with the perfunctory kiss on each cheek.

From that moment on, she avoided him. Sensing there was something he didn't like about her, she chalked her feelings up to a schoolgirl crush. Keeping out of his way worked during the entire wedding. She hadn't even danced with him—watching him with his arms around a multitude of other women had been depressing, though. When she left for home, she reasoned that eventually she'd get over him. Now here she was again, and she almost sighed out loud. There was no way she could work with him. She would break it to Kate tomorrow.

The family eventually headed up to bed and, after kissing Kate good night, Teresa started toward her own room. She whispered to Kate to get some sleep as well to nibble on the crackers they found earlier. "Eat just a couple before you go to sleep and when you wake up," Teresa reminded her.

After taking a long shower, Teresa got into bed and settled down. It seemed like an eternity since she had walked out of the hospital. Now here she was in Italy, feeling so unsettled. After she got some sleep, she'd feel better.

~

"WHAT ARE YOU LOOKING FOR?"

Teresa jumped visibly. She turned a guilty face toward Stefano. "For the love of God, Stefano. Can you not give me a heart attack on my first night here?"

He walked over to her, his gaze sliding down her pajama tops and shorts. It was her favorite pair—pink with little lobsters on them. She was self-conscious, and turned away, facing the interior of the refrigerator, blinking a little from the bright light.

"What are you looking for?" he asked again, only this time more softly.

She shut the refrigerator door and looked at him steadily, trying to ignore her racing heart. "I'm hungry. Happy now? I was just going to make something to eat."

"You are a guest. I will make you something." He put his head in the refrigerator and took out packages of meat, cheese lettuce, tomato, and condiments. Teresa glanced over all the ingredients on the island with a worried look.

He seemed to sense her unease. "Teresa, what would you like to eat?" he asked gently.

"Grilled cheese?" she squeaked out. He probably would think she was about five years old, but since she was a little girl, grilled cheese had been comforting to her. Her father used to sneak it to her when she turned up her nose at her mother's dinner. Her mother remained firm that Teresa would eat what was given to her. When her mother went to work, her father always brought a small grilled cheese to Teresa's bedroom. She smiled now at the thought, blinking aside a couple of tears. She still missed her parents so much.

"No meat? No vegetables?"

"Um, no thank you," Teresa said. She took a breath. "I don't like vegetables."

"You dislike vegetables?" he asked incredulously.

"Shhh! No, Mr. Judgmental Chef, I don't. Okay? And I'm hungry. So, if you'll just point me to the bread, I'll just make myself a little grilled cheese."

He took a breath and stared at her. "I'll make it," he said. "*Un panino al formaggio* coming right up."

He picked up the cheese, and she eyed it suspiciously. "Do you have any other cheese?" she asked, thinking of the individually plastic-wrapped orange slices she bought at home.

"What kind do you want?"

"The orange kind?" she asked nervously.

"You mean cheddar?" he asked with raised eyebrows.

"Well, the label just says American cheese, but yes, I guess you can call it cheddar."

Stefano shook his head. "I am sorry we don't have cheddar. We can order you some for the future. Maybe a white cheddar."

"Cheddar comes in white?"

He gave a rare laugh. "Yes, Teresa, it comes in white, too. But tonight, is it okay if it is provolone? I promise you will like it."

"Well, that sounds fancy. Thank you," she said. She hopped up on a chair at the island and watched Stefano slide out a panini press from the counter. He carefully spread olive oil on the bread, added cheese, and put it on the grill.

They were both quiet as it cooked, and he soon was finished. He cut it and set it before her on a plate. "Do you want anything to drink?"

"Um, Diet Coke?"

He shook his head and sighed. "*Mamma Mia.*"

"Water is fine."

She was surprised when he slid into the chair next to her. He had poured himself a glass of chianti and sipped it as she bit into the gooey sandwich. "This is delicious! What did you add?"

"Just a little garlic salt and *parmesano* to the bread. It's probably the olive oil that you like—it's our family's brand."

"It made it really crispy and delicious. Thank you, Stefano."

"So tonight, my chicken stuffed with feta, sundried tomatoes, basil, and spinach was too…"

She swallowed and looked at him solemnly. "Vegetabley."

He made a sound that almost sounded like a small laugh. "That's not a word, but I get it."

"I ate some chicken. I just didn't eat the inner parts and the side vegetables. Was that squash?" She gave a shudder. "So slimy."

He took another sip, watching her eat, which was making her a little nervous. "For a nurse, you have a remarkably poor diet."

"I'm not a nurse anymore." The words came out before she could stop them. She mentally kicked herself and quickly took another bite, concentrating on chewing. He seemed to be waiting her out. Once she swallowed, he asked quietly, "Really? Want to tell me about it?"

She looked at him. He was staring back at her with serious eyes. He didn't look like he was being sarcastic. She looked away as her mind raced. Should she tell him what happened? He might think she was foolish. Or else he might pity her. Poor Teresa had to be flown to Italy by her best friend because she was too emotional to hold down a job.

Swiveling to face him, she wished she hadn't. He was still gazing at her. She stared back, looking at that fantastic mouth of his. He had beautiful lips. What would it be like to kiss him? Just lose control and kiss him? Stefano probably never lost control. Making a decision, she opened her mouth to confide in him.

"Hey, Lobster Girl, great to see you!" Teresa jumped at the

sound of Lucca's voice. He strolled in, enthusiastically patting Stefano on the back and bent to kiss her cheek. "I didn't know you were here, Teresa."

She could feel Stefano's eyes on her. Why did he always make her feel so guilty? "Hey, Lucca. Yes, just flew in today."

"And is this a private party, or can anyone join?" Lucca asked mischievously, looking at the two of them sitting together at the island.

Stefano got up quickly, grabbing Teresa's empty plate. "I was just helping Teresa with a late-night snack. What about you? Didn't you dine with Ellie and her parents?"

"Yes, I left Ellie there. She's staying there until the wedding. I guess she felt funny being over here with all of you. Frankly, the less exposed she is, the better. I need to get a ring on her finger before she really gets to know this family," he joked.

He turned to Teresa. "My dad and his new wife Madeleine are coming tomorrow, so the volume will definitely go up around here."

Teresa smiled. "I look forward to meeting everyone. I guess I'm crashing your wedding. Katie is insisting."

Lucca smiled gently at her. "The more the merrier. I'm sure Ellie will be thrilled to see you again. The wedding planning has gone quickly. Her mother is ready to come unglued, but an intimate wedding was what we wanted. Though it keeps growing as we realize we should invite more and more family," he said, wincing a little. He pointed at Stefano's glass. "Got any more?"

Stefano grinned. "Ridiculous question." He went into a massive wine cabinet, taking out a bottle. Lucca was looking thoughtful, and Teresa took the subtle hint. She hopped down from her chair. "Stefano, thank you for the grilled cheese. Best one I've ever eaten—fanciest one, too. Lucca, I'll see you later. I think I better get some sleep." And with that, she tried to exit the kitchen with as much dignity as a girl wearing lobster pajamas could.

# five

Stefano took a sip of his wine, his mind a spinning mixture of emotions. The truth was, when he came downstairs to see the back of Teresa's petite frame in her short pajamas, he enjoyed the view. Silly as they were, there was something about Teresa's attire that made him feel a slow, unexpected heat travel through his body. If Lucca hadn't come in, he would have leaned over and kissed her. Thank God for his cousin. He didn't need to start something with his sister-in-law's best friend. His older brother would pummel him. When it went nowhere, Kate would then finish what Marco didn't break on his body.

No, a relationship with Teresa was not wise. They had zero in common. His love of fine food and wine was more than just a hobby—it was a way of life for him. He had been thinking for a while about what to do with his passion. Culinary school was out —he had no desire to be a chef. Doing something around food was his desire, but he wasn't sure what that was. During his travels for Oro Industries, he made a point of building relationships with chefs around the country. These culinary masters were wonderful to him, letting him study their talent, answering his constant questions. Because he was such a good listener, he learned a lot, and he spent hours perfecting his own techniques. Cooking fed his creativity and his soul. He wished he knew what to do with it.

"Stefano, snap out of it. You're not listening to me," Lucca was saying.

"Sorry, I was just thinking. What were you saying?"

"Marco and I wanted to talk with you tomorrow, but since it's just you and me, maybe I could tell you what's on my mind. I didn't expect to have this conversation, but it might be better right now with just you and me."

Stefano furrowed his brow. What could Lucca be so serious about? He was used to his famous cousin and his mischievous sense of humor. He didn't often see a serious Lucca. "Lucca, whatever you want to discuss with me, go ahead. You do not need my older brother to supervise," he said dryly.

"He wasn't going to supervise, just provide a few thoughts. I just wrapped on my last movie and Ellie and I have decided to make our lives in Italy. There's always the chance a film will come along that I want to do, but for now, I really want to start my own production company and produce the content I want to see from Italy."

Stefano stared at him. "Wow, I didn't see that coming. I thought you and Ellie were just going to live here, and you'd still travel and film when you wanted."

Lucca smiled. "I can if I want. Honestly, though, it's just come to a point where I want to do more behind the camera. It's risky. The industry can be brutal. I have to do it well, or it will get instantly trashed. My future father in law has given me lots of expert advice, and Marco has connected me with the right people. I've got a shiny new business plan and have sketched out what I want to do—at least for the foreseeable future."

Stefano smiled at him. "I am sincerely happy for you. That must feel great having the pieces finally falling into place. I am envious, if you want the truth."

"I know you've thought about moving on from Oro. What have you been thinking about doing, or can I ask?" Lucca looked at him intently.

Stefano stared past him, lost in thought. "That is why I am envious. I do not know. I want to do something professionally with food—but not as a chef. I am at a loss. I have spoken to a lot of culinary masters around the country to get ideas. Nothing really feels right. And then I feel guilty for leaving Marco since he has not been CEO that long."

"That was one reason I wanted Marco here," Lucca said. "I needed him to reassure you it was okay to accept my proposal."

"What proposal?"

"Here me out, Stefano. I outlined a creative brief for several episodes of a new show that would travel around Italy and show-case various regions. It would talk about the food and why people eat what they do and the origins behind specific dishes. Get people to understand the significance and differences between regions. The first season would just be an initial four episodes, and it has already sold. Italy is beyond popular right now. I think it could do well for my first production."

Stefano grinned. "Congratulations! It is a great idea! Do you want my help with research? I could certainly do that, *mio cugino*. You do not even have to ask twice. Of course, I would love to help."

Lucca's smile grew wider. "Good, good. Because you wouldn't be the researcher—you'd be the host."

STEFANO LOOKED in the mirror after finishing shaving. He left his usual shadow beard but trimmed around it. Staring at his reflection, he wondered if he had what it took to pull off being a host of a major television production. He was floored when Lucca offered the idea last night. Lucca told him to sleep on it, and he and Marco would discuss more with him the next day.

The three of them spent the morning behind closed doors. Marco and Lucca were steadfast in their belief that Stefano would be an ideal host to travel around Italy and showcase foods of various regions. He admitted he loved the idea, just not his face out front. He had never been a person to seek attention. Teresa hit a small nerve when she called him a classic middle child. It was true he had an older brother who attracted a good deal of attention with his charm and a younger brother who always seemed to be able to talk to anyone. Stefano was an introvert, and now his cousin, who was obviously an extrovert, was thinking this was a great idea.

It was only after Stefano expressed doubts about having the on-camera skills to do the project that Marco spoke up. "We already have that covered. We will hire a producer—someone skilled in getting you prepped. The person we have in mind has had outstanding success in the past, and we are sure you will be ready in time." Marco spoke so confidently that Stefano almost believed him.

He acknowledged his cousin and brother knew how to work him. They planted the seed and told him to think about it. If he was willing to take the first step, they would have him begin his training with the producer immediately. Lucca would be away on his honeymoon, and Stefano could spend the two weeks trying to learn the skills he needed. Lucca was so sure about it that he had already ordered some equipment to be delivered to Stefano's villa on the nearby island of Capri. Stefano and the producer could work there one-on-one and by the end, it would be his decision to make. Stefano had balked. He needed to be at his office in Milan. Marco rolled his eyes, telling him he would get Stefano's extensive staff to cover for him. Anything that needed to be done would be completed. For now, to have two weeks to focus on this work would give him confidence in his final verdict.

Stefano's feelings about the project were complex. Part of him wanted to push himself to rise to the challenge. He already was traveling around meeting chefs and talking about cooking foods of their regions. This show would give him the opportunity to meet even more culinary masters.

On the other hand, he didn't see himself as ever being comfortable on camera. Not a fan of photos of himself, he also winced at the idea of video and the sound of his voice.

Getting dressed, he decided to shelve the idea in his mind and enjoy the rehearsal dinner, which he knew was going to be a phenomenal meal, as it was being prepared by a Michelin Star chef. Glancing at his watch, he realized the rehearsal was probably over. Since Lucca and Ellie were getting married in a small ceremony at the lemon grove, it probably didn't take long. They were all traveling to a restaurant in Amalfi, where Ellie's parents were staying. They had rented out the restaurant for two days so that the staff could create an ideal dinner. Lucca said part of his security team was over there as well.

Straightening his tie, Stefano left his room to join the others, descending the stairs toward the family who was gathered in the entryway and already spilling out to the front terrace. A string of SUVs was waiting to take them.

Glancing over, he saw Marco leading Kate and Teresa into one car. He breathed a sigh of relief. For some reason, he wanted to avoid Teresa. He had to admit the night before he was intrigued, wanting to know a little about her. When he saw how besotted she became at the entrance of his cousin, those feelings vanished like cold water being thrown on him. He got into a car with Nico and his mother, who explained that her brother, Bruno, who was Lucca's father, had just arrived. Bruno was changing quickly, and he and his wife, Madeleine, would join them at the restaurant.

Stefano was silent during the drive, wondering what Marco, Kate, and Teresa were talking about in their car. He ignored the small part of him that questioned why he even cared. His mother chatted about the wedding reception and how Ellie snuck up to decorate the cake with her cousin Brigid, her maid of honor. It was to be a surprise for Lucca, she warned. He nodded absent-mindedly, not caring in the slightest. Soon the car pulled up to the exclusive restaurant, and Stefano politely ushered his mother out of the car and into the restaurant. Tonight, he would enjoy the food, his family, and the scenic view. Tomorrow, he would think about Lucca's ridiculous proposal.

# six

Teresa smoothed down the folds of her emerald green halter dress. She bought it and another dress for the wedding quickly in San Francisco before departing for Italy. Thankfully, she found a helpful saleswoman, since Teresa always felt like she didn't have any fashion sense. Growing up without a mother during her teenage years, she relied on Kate and Kate's mom to help choose her clothes. Her dad and brothers were no help. She still worried sometimes she was wearing the wrong thing, and that's probably why she went overboard with these purchases. They had left an enormous hole in her bank account. Now that she wasn't employed, she would have to be more careful with her money. Still, she wanted to look perfect, knowing Stefano would be present.

Marco and Kate talked for most of the drive. Marco was ecstatic that Teresa had so many ideas about managing Kate's nausea. Teresa told Kate to indulge in her favorite sour lemon candy—easily bought in Positano. A calming lemon candle would also help. Kate, who adored anything with lemon, was excited. She wrote down all Teresa's advice, and Marco insisted they would follow it to the letter. Now Kate survived the winding road well. The driver took the curves at a snail's pace, carefully following Marco's instructions.

Teresa clasped Marco's hand as he politely helped her out of the car and gasped when they entered the building. The restaurant was built on the side of the hill, and the sea lay before them in its stunning glory. Big white pillars and a white iron railing anchored the view and above them was a closed pergola with greenery. Two long tables gleamed with elegant place settings in multi-colored Italian pottery. Flowers were everywhere, from the centerpieces that ran the length of the table to the multitude of flowerpots.

Ellie and Lucca stood with her famous parents, ready to greet their guests. Teresa recognized them immediately. "Katie, I wish you would have let me stay home. I'm not used to this kind of thing. I'm going to say something embarrassing to them," Teresa whispered.

"No, you aren't. They are just people. They put their pants on one leg at a time, my dad would say. They are just like us. Just be yourself. I've never seen you like this before."

"That's because I've never been in a five-star restaurant hob-knobbing with celebrities before." Teresa turned panicked eyes at Kate. "I don't know how to hob or knob," she said and gave a nervous laugh.

Too late. The four of them were approaching. After greeting Marco and Kate, Ellie gave Teresa a big hug. "Teresa, we are so happy to have you here with us," she said with a smile. Teresa returned her smile. Ellie was so authentic and down-to-earth. She was hard not to like.

"Thanks—uh, I feel like I'm crashing your wedding, but it just worked out for me to come during this time."

"We are excited you can join us. I'd like you to meet my parents."

Teresa had no memory of what she had said to Emerson and Miranda Montgomery. Of course, she had seen all their films and stumbled her way through the introduction. The twinkle in Monty's eyes—what he insisted she call him—helped relax her. Ellie's parents were funny and gracious, and she breathed a sigh of relief.

Teresa waved off the server with the prosecco. Kate was worried that people would notice her not drinking. They devised the plan in the car that Kate would take the drinks, but just not sip them. At some point, Teresa would maneuver to take it from her and drink it or Marco would get rid of it.

Another server offered a stuffed mushroom, and Teresa waved him off as well. More canapes came out, and one by one, she took a sniff and smiled at them, but shook her head. She'd kill for some snack mix right now, starting to feel hunger growing. Lunch seemed like a long time ago. She made Kate eat right before they left. Why didn't she have the good sense to eat something as well?

Miranda was announcing it was time to take their seats, and Teresa was relieved to see she was placed next to Kate, and on her left was Nico. That would be good. He could be her wingman if there was food she didn't like. Frowning, she saw Stefano was seated across from her. That was almost worse than having him next to her. Now, she would probably inadvertently keep meeting his eyes. She'd have to make sure she talked with Nico a lot.

Glancing at the custom menu that was printed on her plate, her heart dropped. This would be a long night. Even with all the courses, there wasn't much on it she liked or would even think of eating. And what the heck was an *amuse-bouche?*

Speeches were made, with Miranda and Emerson welcoming everyone and saying how thrilled they were to be part of the family. When the toasting began, Teresa quickly lifted Kate's glass. Kate took the moment to sip her water and held it up. First one down, though she better have something to eat soon, or she would get smashed. The speeches continued and were light and funny. Teresa laughed with everyone else, temporarily forgetting to feel awkward. She was relieved when baskets of bread were placed right in front of her and Kate. "They know us," she told Kate with a small smile.

The amuse-bouche was set before her in a small spoon. She sniffed. Was that bacon? She could get behind something with bacon, but what was inside?

Meanwhile, maybe bacon didn't quite agree with Kate because she looked wildly at Teresa before shuffling hers onto Marco's plate quietly. "It's probably the smell," Teresa told her reassuringly and gave Marco a beseeching look. He downed it quickly, placing the spoon back on Kate's plate. Would he eat hers, too? She turned to Nico—he'd do it. Only, Nico was involved in a heated argument over football—Italian soccer—with Alfonso, who was like a cousin to the men. Teresa made the mistake of glancing over and meeting Stefano's gaze. His black eyes glittered in the candlelight, and he was watching her over the floral centerpiece. He knew. He totally knew she was freaking out. He gave her a subtle nod of encouragement. She glanced down at the spoon and looked up again.

"Try it," he mouthed.

She was a big girl. She could do this. There was a big glass of water in front of her so she would down the bite fast and then gulp her water. It would be like one of those challenges people did on social media. Picking up the spoon, she popped it into her mouth. She was getting ready to swallow and not chew, but she was unprepared for the explosion of flavor in her mouth. She chewed slowly, savoring it. She willed herself not to think about what it was. It was sweet, salty, and cheesy. Was that some kind of date or something? She finally, reluctantly, swallowed. Well, why didn't they just give her a whole plate of those? She took a small sip of her wine and couldn't resist glancing back at Stefano.

He gave her a small smile, almost looking like he was proud of her. Warmed by his praise and with relief coursing through her body, she beamed back. It must have been too enthusiastic because he quickly sobered and turned to his mother to discuss something. Teresa quickly wiped the grin off her face. She glanced back at the menu. Only six more courses to go. She could do this!

IT WAS the slowest dinner of her life. She had been so worried about Kate, but Kate seemed to enjoy everything except the seafood. That was too much, she whispered to Teresa, even though Teresa told her the fish being served was safe to eat. Other than that, Kate plowed her way through the other rich courses. Teresa tried and ate what she could, but she wasn't used to this level of fancy food. At least she was able to have a few bits of pasta, some kind of meat, and the salad was edible. The portions were tiny, arranged to look exquisite. She supposed she should be admiring them but thank God for the menu or she wouldn't have known what she was eating!

She was relieved when they got to the sorbet and then the cheese course. She popped a piece of cheese in her mouth and wildly looked around. There was nowhere to spit it out. She finally swallowed quickly. For the love of God, how did they ruin cheese? She looked it over carefully and realized she must have chosen gorgonzola. She literally just ate mold.

Teresa thanked the dear Lord when dessert came. It was a trio of Italian pastries, including one with chocolate and nuts that tasted amazing. She dove in, eating them all, but still felt empty. Her stomach was swirling with too much wine, bread, and now sugar. She sighed, longingly thinking that if she was back in the U.S., there would be many drive-thru fast-food restaurants for her to choose from. Normally, she could grab a burger, fries, or maybe tacos if she was coming back from some function where the food was unappetizing. Just thinking about it made her mouth water.

Blinking back to reality, she saw Stefano was watching her again. It was like the man could read her thoughts. Scrunching her nose at him, she turned to see if she could get Nico's attention. Finally, she was relieved when everyone began scraping their chairs back to stand. The party soon broke up since the next day would be the wedding. Teresa joined the others in dutifully thanking her hosts. *Best dinner ever. Wonderful cuisine.* She may have laid it on a little thick, but she wanted them to know she appreciated being a part of it. During the drive home, she was silent, letting Kate and Marco talk about the dinner and the next day.

"Teresa, thank you so much for drinking my wine. I don't think anyone noticed. And thank God there was good food there, though there was no way I could eat the fish. It was like a minefield."

Teresa smiled, looking out the window at the inky night and the many stars twinkling. If her friend only knew what a war zone it was for her. Kate had eaten almost everything compared to her.

The family was chatting and laughing as they got out of the vehicles and walked into the house. Teresa entered the kitchen on the pretense of getting water, secretly waiting to see what everyone was going to do. All the men voiced the opinion they would change and take drinks outside. Marco was teasing Lucca that they didn't even have time to have a bachelor party—they should at least hang out together.

"I've been to enough parties," Lucca said, laughing. "I'm eager to get on with it, get my ring on Ellie's finger, and sail away with her." He went on to thank Marco for the use of his yacht.

The women pleaded fatigue, so Teresa climbed the stairs with them. In her room, she changed into her yoga pants and a San Francisco T-shirt and waited. Her room was over part of the terrace, and she heard male voices and glasses clinking. Waiting for a bit, she let them settle in, but her stomach was growling something fierce. She needed to eat.

Not stopping to put on shoes, she silently padded down the stairs. In her calculations, she figured it would take about five minutes to make a sandwich and head back to her room. Sandwiches were portable, and she wouldn't even need a plate. A grilled cheese would be too time-consuming. She'd just make a simple cheese sandwich, and no one would be the wiser. She stopped short at the entrance of the kitchen. Stefano, clad in jeans and a T-shirt, was at the stove. He glanced up. "Grab a plate. It will just be a couple of minutes."

She stood there a minute, her mouth opened in surprise.

"Come on—I am almost ready. Get a plate."

Teresa automatically went to the glass cupboard and got out a dinner plate. She silently brought it to Stefano.

"Pour yourself a glass of wine, if you want one. I think after drinking all of Katie's though, you probably just want some water," Stefano said over his shoulder.

Wide-eyed, she filled a glass with water. Unsure what to do, she sat at the island. He had a kitchen towel over one shoulder, his back to her. She took a deep breath. Whatever he was doing over there smelled darn good. With a flourish, he put a meatball sandwich in front of her. Coated in sauce with parmesan sprinkled on top, she gazed hungrily at it.

"How did you know?" she asked.

"Know that you'd be starving right about now, or that you drank all of Katie's wine?"

"Both," she said, eagerly picking up half. She sunk her teeth into it and almost moaned out loud. She chewed, admiring the fact that he even cut the meatballs in half so they didn't pop out of the bread.

He smiled slightly. "You have a little sauce on your face," he said, handing her a napkin. He walked over and poured himself a glass of wine. "Teresa, never play poker. I saw your face at dinner. You tried, I give you that, but you hated most of what was put before you."

She looked down, feeling tears come to her eyes. "Go ahead, make fun of me."

"What are you talking about?"

"I know I'm not very sophisticated," she said. "And yes, I love junk food, and I eat things that aren't very healthy. So go ahead and let it rip." She put the sandwich down. Despite the gurgling of her stomach, she could almost feel the hunger fading.

"Did I say anything derogatory? I just pointed out you hated the dinner, and I knew you would be hungry. I made you a snack."

"I know, but you're waiting to chastise me. I saw you with the chef afterward, praising him. Talking about some big contest he won."

"The Michelin Star?"

"Yeah, whatever. I'm sure he's fantastic. It's not him, it's me."

"Teresa, look at me," he said gently.

"No."

He sighed and walked over. He put a hand on her chin, forcing her to look at him. She felt a twinge of excitement, staring into his black eyes.

"I'm not going to make fun of you. Tonight's dinner was very extravagant. Your palate cannot be expected to go from beginner to expert in one dinner. It was a lot for your senses to cope. I saw you—you tried things. That is all anyone can ask."

"I felt like a fish out of water."

"You should not feel that way. I saw Kate did not eat some things as well. Which brings me to the next question—the wine?"

Teresa took a big bite. Maybe if she was eating, she wouldn't be expected to answer. She finished a half before looking at him innocently. "Maybe she just didn't want to drink tonight?"

"Is she pregnant?" he asked softly.

She looked down and then focused her eyes on the other half of the sandwich. She was a horrible liar. "You have to ask your brother."

Stefano pumped a fist in the air. "I knew it! I am going to be an uncle!"

She stared at him. She had never seen this side of him. "Shhh—aren't all the guys outside? And I haven't confirmed anything!"

"I can tell by your face."

She took another bite and kept chewing. When she swallowed, she decided to go to a safe topic. "Why aren't you outside, by the way?"

"Because I am in here cooking for you," he said, sitting down beside her. "I hope you like this panino. What is the deal with grilled cheese?"

"What do you mean?"

"I could tell last night that you were so intent on eating a grilled cheese." As she stayed silent, he twirled the stem of his glass, looking thoughtful. "Food is about family, comfort, and memories. Does grilled cheese bring that to you?"

Teresa finished eating, and she carefully wiped her mouth, not looking at him, trying to will the tears away. "Yeah, it does," she admitted.

"Want to tell me why?"

"Not really," she said, thinking about how much she would have to tell him to properly explain. "Thank you for making the sandwich. I'm going to go to bed, and you should go outside and have fun with your family."

She stood and put her plate in the sink, avoiding his eyes. Turning her head at the sound of her name being spoken quietly, she finally looked at him, and he gave her a small grin. "Meatball sandwiches are my comfort food."

She nodded and almost ran out of the kitchen and up the stairs before she did what she really wanted to do: hug him.

# seven

Stefano clapped with the rest of the wedding guests as Lucca and Ellie joyously raised their clasped hands high in the air. Standing before the gazebo, lit up with greenery, flowers, and lights, they were now officially married. They walked down the makeshift aisle with silly grins on their faces and the guests filed out behind them. They all headed up to the reception venue in the lemon grove's large golf carts. Stefano admired the building as he approached. Growing up on the vast estate, it was easy to take things for granted. His family worked hard over the years to add to the main reception venue. With its wrought-iron balconies and colorful shutters, it looked like a castle.

He entered the cool reception hall and took a glass of prosecco off the tray the server was holding. Earlier that day, he nonchalantly went to the kitchen and chatted up the chef, Luciano, and his team of sous chefs about the details of the wedding menu. He was relieved to see there were some things on there that Teresa might like. They were dining on melon wrapped with prosciutto, bruschetta with fresh mozzarella and tomatoes, lemon risotto with vegetables, beef with potato croquettes, sorbet, and many desserts.

He hoped she would like most of it, though she would have to pick around the vegetables. Still, he proactively made a grilled cheese for her, took it to her room, knocked, and ran like he was a ten-year-old boy playing a prank. It was fun to imagine the look on her face when she opened the door. It was an impulsive idea, and he didn't know why he had done it or why he made her the meatball sandwich the night before. There was something about her that made him want to take care of her and nourish her. Though Teresa was usually feisty, there was almost a sadness to her right now. He found that more disconcerting than her constant chatter.

"Stefano, can I get a grilled cheese to go?"

He turned to see Kate, beautiful in a pink flowing dress, looking at him with humor in her eyes.

He felt flustered. "How did you...?"

"Teresa asked me to come look at what she was going to wear tonight and then Room Service knocked," she said and then laughed. She playfully nudged him with her elbow. "That was just about the nicest thing I've ever seen you do."

"I am a nice person," he said, putting an arm lightly across her shoulders. "I hope you are not upset with me."

"Why would I be?"

"Because I wrung the truth out of Marco last night about a certain secret you two have," he whispered in her ear.

She glanced around and then smiled at him. "You're such a terrible liar. Teresa told me you flat out asked her."

He returned her smile. "She was very careful not to confirm, so I could not be a hundred percent until I squeezed it out of Marco. I could not be happier for both of you and for the family. It is going to be wonderful to have a little one running around. Mamma is going to be ecstatic."

Kate gave him a concerned look. "But today it's all about Lucca and Ellie, so not a word. We'll tell everyone when we are ready."

"Is that why you wanted Teresa to come over?"

Kate looked suddenly guilty. "Part of the reason," she answered nervously. "And it worked out, since she's not currently employed."

Stefano turned to face Kate, looking at her seriously. "What happened?" he asked in his point-blank fashion. Usually, he got people to talk by just demanding answers.

Kate seemed to be avoiding his eyes, glancing around the room. "She quit. It's a long story and hers to tell."

"She is fortunate that she can just quit a job and fly to Italy to hang out."

Kate turned suddenly and pointedly looked at him, a scowl growing on her face. "Teresa is the *least* fortunate person I know! She had a rough childhood—nothing that you could ever imagine! I mean, we weren't rich by any means. But Teresa's family had little money. And then her mother died, and then her father worked all the time...and all those brothers! Teresa tried to cook, and she didn't know what to do since they couldn't afford much." Kate stopped talking, looking as if she had said too much.

"Look Stefano, that's all her business. But just know she's the hardest working person I know, and that counts all of you. Teresa worked her way through college to get a degree and took the first job she was offered. She was miserable. It took a lot of guts for her to admit that and go back to school to become a nurse. Unfortunately, she still owes a huge amount of money in university loans. And now she's forced to walk away from her job because of the miserable system. You have no idea." Kate finally stopped, taking a deep breath.

"Katie, I am sorry. I did not mean anything. I had no idea, although I can tell something is bothering her."

"I've said too much. If Teresa wants you to know, she'll tell you," Kate said again, still frowning.

"Do not be upset with me, *mia sorella*. My brother will come over here and hoist me off a balcony if he knows I am making you angry. I promise not to say a word. And Teresa will not be confiding anything in me. We do not have that kind of relationship."

She nodded. "I know. You make her nervous, and I'm not sure why. I'm sorry, Stefano. I didn't mean to snap. These hormones." She rolled her eyes. "But also, Teresa has been my best friend since we were little kids. We have each other's backs, you know?"

He nodded, seeing the fierce loyalty in Kate's eyes. They were interrupted suddenly by some well-meaning cousins. He listened with half an ear, his eyes darting around the room. Dressed in a long gown of coral, Teresa was laughing with Margherita. Not every woman could wear that bright color, but on Teresa it looked enchanting. It left one shoulder bare, and from where he stood, he could see her smooth skin glistening. She wore a gold necklace and gold and pearl drop earrings. Her black curls were out in force. It looked like she tried to tame them into submission, pulling back one side with a diamond clip. She presented a beautiful and vivacious picture. He smiled at the glimpse of ultra-high-heeled sandals under the dress. No wonder she looked taller tonight. She might even come up to his shoulder. His smile grew wider at the thought.

What was happening to him? He shook his head. He was becoming way too interested in Kate's friend, and it needed to stop. The dinner gong sounded at that moment, as if to interrupt his thoughts. Going outside, he found his place card, glanced around, and saw that Teresa was sitting nearby, but not next to him. For some reason, he felt some disappointment; he had hoped to help her navigate the dinner. She was next to Kate again. The two of them seemed joined at the hip. He frowned, remembering his conversation with his sister-in-law. In the future, he would need to be more careful. It was obvious how fiercely loyal they were to each other.

Why was he even thinking about a future? After this wedding, he was going to Capri to think about this project Lucca and Marco were pulling him into. He agreed to work with the producer to get a feel for it, but that was all. There was still a part of him that felt completely out of his depth, and he probably wouldn't even agree in the end. To pacify his family, he would at least spend a few days working at it before he declined. His future was still very murky. One thing he knew for sure—it wouldn't have anything to do with the beautiful, petite, curly-haired woman who was now staring at him.

TERESA QUICKLY AVERTED HER GAZE. Stefano had just caught her staring. He looked so elegant and gorgeous in his dark, perfectly tailored suit. She loved the angles of his face. Sure, he wasn't the smiley type—he was the serious, wonder-what-he's-thinking-type. Frustrating as all heck. She frowned. Then she remembered the grilled cheese sandwich. She answered the door, half expecting Meara to join in the inspection of her new dress. No one was at the door, and she glanced down and found a plate with a linen cloth over it. When she'd lifted the cloth, she had shrieked in delight.

Kate was so curious about why Stefano would leave her a grilled cheese. Teresa fended her off, asking questions about her pregnancy and nausea. Kate was feeling a lot better, though she laughed that she was getting a canker sore from so much sour lemon candy. Mornings were still rough, but Teresa cautioned that might just have to be the way it was for now. Tonight, Kate wanted Teresa to sit next to her again. Kate's worst fear was getting sick and not being able to make a quick exit. With so many people milling about, Kate didn't believe anyone would notice she wasn't drinking. Still, Teresa promised to switch glasses again if needed.

Teresa listened to toasts from all around the table. Monty and Miranda told sweet stories from Ellie's childhood that brought laughter from the crowd. Bruno stood and struggled to talk about what his son meant to him without choking up. She knew Lucca's parents had gone through a bitter divorce and so she wasn't surprised to see Lucca openly crying. Ellie, putting her arm around him, whispered in his ear.

The speeches over, the food started arriving and didn't stop. It started well. Teresa loved the melon with prosciutto and could have eaten a whole plate of bruschetta. She ate a little of the risotto, picking around the vegetables. She was almost full by the time the sorbet arrived. But there was more. The steak was done to perfection, and at least a potato was a potato, no matter what country it was cooked in. Then came cheese and nuts.

Finally, with dinner over, the guests began to stand and mingle before dessert. Maybe she would go talk to Kate's cousin Brigid a little more. Teresa had enjoyed the time when Brigid stayed at their apartment while she was in pastry school. It meant guaranteed treats in the evenings and on weekends. As Teresa skirted the table, she felt a tap on her shoulder and turned to come face to face with Lucca. She hadn't even talked to him the last two days. Flushing a little, Teresa remembered all the teasing she received.

"*Buonasera*, Teresa," Lucca said, kissing both her cheeks. She felt herself turning a brighter red. She never would get used to all the kissing.

"*Buonasera*, Lucca," she answered quickly. "And congratulations. I don't know how to say that in Italian, but I am so happy for you and Ellie."

He smiled. "Thank you. We are so fortunate. We were pleased you could be part of our wedding."

"Well, I didn't give you much choice," Teresa said with a smile. "I hope that's okay."

"More than okay," Lucca said seriously. He put a light arm

around her shoulders, drawing her away from the crowd. "I've been wanting to talk with you."

TERESA SAT ABRUPTLY AT A TABLE, staring at nothing. Her mind was a swirling mess of emotions. Lucca had poured on the charm, describing his project to her. Looking at her with such sincere eyes, he told her how much it meant to him to embark on this new professional journey regarding his country. Lucca was convinced Stefano had the knowledge and expertise to pull off being the host but needed a lot of training to be camera-ready and connect to an audience. He praised Teresa's producing skills and her ability to focus on the details needed to revamp an image. Apparently, he had done his homework, talking to Teresa's former colleagues, who reiterated what Kate told him.

Lucca matter-of-factly informed her of the large salary he was offering for just a few weeks of work. She was stunned. It was more than she ever earned—not when she was in TV and certainly not at the hospital. The salary would allow her to eliminate her school loans and even pay her rent several months in advance. It would mean she could live virtually debt-free and take the time to decide her next move.

Frowning, she realized she was counting her chickens before they hatched, as her dad would have told her. Stefano would never agree to this scheme. Obviously, Lucca was worried about it, or he wouldn't have specifically told her not to discuss it with Stefano. Lucca said he or Marco would bring it up later, and that Stefano would be fine once he learned of Teresa's skills. She had tried not to roll her eyes. There was no way Stefano was going to want to work with her. That was too bad because she knew she could help him, but he would never see that. While he was nicer to her, he probably still didn't think that much of her.

"Would you like to dance?"

Teresa looked up directly at the man she was just been thinking about. Stefano's black eyes stared down at her, his expression serious. Shocked, she continued to stare up at him.

"I believe this is the one time I have seen you at a loss for words," he said, giving her a rare smile.

Teresa rose and took the hand he extended. Wordlessly, she went to the dance floor with him. The band was playing an Italian ballad that she was unfamiliar with. It didn't matter, as she wasn't even sure she would recognize any song at this point. She let her body fold into his, loving the warmth and breadth of him. She resisted the urge to run her hand up and down his strong back and kept her other hand clasped with his strong one. With her high heels on, she didn't have to crank her neck to look at him like she did most times. Despite that, she avoided his eyes, feeling completely out of her depth. She hoped he couldn't hear her racing heart. Time was standing still, and she was unaware of anything but him. She forced herself to take a deep breath, and it came out as almost a sigh. She could go on like this forever.

"What did Lucca say to you to render you this quiet?" Stefano asked in a mocking tone. "Or has depression sunk in because he is now married with a ring on his finger? I guess there's always Nico. He is not famous, of course, but he certainly is rich."

Teresa stopped dancing and stepped back, staring at him. She had gone along with the good-natured teasing about Lucca. It was a distraction with Kate, but coming from Stefano, it stung. He made her feel ridiculous, as if she was pining away for a famous actor. She opened her mouth to blast him but found a lump in her throat. He thought so little of her he even brought up money. Staring at him, she felt tears coming to her eyes. Darn it! She would not cry in front of him. He was gazing at her, a mix of emotions running across his face. Was that a frown, regret, or confusion? It didn't matter. Making a quick decision, she turned and walked away.

Stefano called after her quietly, but she wove through the dancing couples. Most everyone she knew was on the dance floor. She quickly passed by a couple of cousins she had been introduced to and headed inside as if she was going to the bathroom. Instead, she made a snap decision and went through the venue and out the front door.

"Can I help you?"

Teresa glanced over to see Mike Donnelly, Lucca's head of security, standing on the front terrace. "Oh hi, Mr. Donnelly. I have a headache. Would it be possible for someone to drive me back to the house?"

"I'm sorry to hear that," he said, his eyes concerned. "And it's Mike. I can't leave, but I can have someone take you."

He was waving to one of his security officers, who promptly came over and listened to Mike's instructions. Mike opened the door of a black sedan parked in front of them. Teresa smiled weakly at him. "Thank you so much. Can you do me one more favor? Can you let Katie know I left? Tell her not to worry. I think I just probably drank too much prosecco. It always gives me a headache."

"Sure, no problem. Feel better," Mike said, before shutting the door firmly.

Teresa listened to the security officer's small talk as they drove quickly down the winding hill through the lemon grove. Soon they were pulling in front of the house. He ran around to open the door and told her there was a security team around the house in case she was nervous about being there all alone. She assured him she would be fine. But would she?

# eight

Stefano felt like a heel. He deliberately taunted Teresa, and he wasn't sure why. It wasn't like him to be so rude. He had only meant to tease her, but he had taken it too far. It was difficult to admit that it was challenging to watch her flirting with Nico throughout dinner. When he saw Lucca and Teresa walk away from the table, their heads close together and deep in conversation, he was confused. What could they have to talk about? He wasn't jealous of his cousin. *Dio*, he had just gotten married and clearly had eyes for one woman only, and that was his bride. But it nagged at him how easily Teresa smiled at Lucca, her face becoming animated.

He knew he was the serious one and had even been teased about being too intelligent. He'd been called everything in life: stiff, serious, introverted, lacking a sense of humor. To the outward world, he probably presented that way. Internally, he was comfortable with himself. There would never be a time that he could compete with the charming, suave Marco or the joking Nico. While he was growing up, his mother gave him the confidence to just be himself. Around Teresa, that was difficult. He wanted to tease her, to have that easy camaraderie everyone else had. The one time he tried to loosen up and tease her, it awkwardly backfired. She looked at him, hurt registering on her face, her beautiful eyes glittering at him. He felt like he had just wounded a small animal and tried to go after her. Unfortunately, he was waylaid by Ellie's mother, who insisted that he was the one relative of Lucca's she hadn't gotten to know yet. Miranda was very persuasive, and he led her on the dance floor and dutifully answered her questions. He kept glancing at the doors to the venue, waiting for Teresa to emerge. He attempted to look around nonchalantly in case he missed her exit from the venue. Miranda finally asked him who he was looking for, a twinkle in her eye. He was like a school kid who had just gotten caught doing something he shouldn't. Muttering about needing to speak to his mother, he finally slipped away from her probing eyes.

Teresa was nowhere to be found. He couldn't ask Kate if she had seen her or else she'd want to know why. Walking inside, he glanced around and saw only staff, bent on getting their work done. He even glanced through the immense kitchen, but all he saw was the chefs busy making a midnight snack for the guests.

Just as he was passing back through the lobby, he saw Mike Donnelly. "Mike, have you seen Kate's friend Teresa anywhere? Do you know who she is? Petite, black curly..."

Mike was nodding before Stefano could finish. "Yes, she asked for a ride. Said she had a headache, so I asked an officer to take her down to the house. I let Kate know. Did you need her for something?"

Stefano shook his head. "No, no. I was just going to talk to her, but sounds like she needed sleep. Thank you," he muttered, walking away.

He went back outside to the reception, grabbing a glass of wine from a server, and watching the dancing. Romance was definitely in the air, and the couples intertwined on the dance floor were having a wonderful time. Even his mother was out there with Sergio, the grove's foreman, who she recently admitted to dating. He grimaced, realizing he was over this wedding. Putting his glass down abruptly, he strode through the reception area and out front. Climbing into one of the family's vehicles, he drove down the hill.

Opening the door to the house, he heard nothing. The house was silent. He went into the kitchen, hopeful he would find Teresa with her head poking in the refrigerator, but she was not there. Taking off his jacket, he rolled up his sleeves and decided to wait. She was bound to come down at some point. He would make her another meatball sandwich, grilled cheese, or whatever she wanted, and then he would apologize. Though he wasn't sure what he would say yet, he would at least tell her he was sorry.

Pouring himself a glass of wine, he waited, shifting uncomfortably in his chair. Marco finally came in with Kate, but they went upstairs quickly after saying goodnight. Everyone else was still at the reception. He should just go to bed. This was pointless.

Restless, he strolled through the French doors, out to the back terrace. He walked down toward the end, where he could look over the lemon grove. Suddenly, he spotted a small form. Teresa was curled up on the old porch swing his father gave his mother when they were first married. She insisted on bringing it to this house when his uncle built it. It was the one thing his mother wouldn't let go of from his father.

Stefano frowned as he got closer. Teresa was dressed in sweats and a T-shirt, her head on a pillow. She was fast asleep, still clutching a bag of goldfish crackers. No wonder she hadn't needed a snack. He felt himself smiling, and he leaned down and gently kissed her cheek. She stirred, clutching her bag of crackers more tightly.

Should he wake her? She couldn't stay out here all night. On impulse, he bent down and picked her up. She weighed almost nothing. She startled awake and looked at him in the evening light, confusion crossing her sleepy face. "What are you doing?"

"Taking you to bed," he said gruffly.

She started to struggle. "I'm not going to bed with you!"

He smiled, hugging her tighter. "Be quiet, *cara*. I am taking you to *your* bed, where you will get some sleep."

He stopped and glanced down at her. An image of taking her to his bed came to his mind, staggering him. Heat coursed through him.

"I can walk!"

Sighing, he gently lowered her to the ground. This wasn't the time or the place for anything physical, as deeply tempting as it was. No matter what, he had to clear the air. "Teresa, I need to apologize. I was only teasing, and it was not meant to offend you."

She nodded, looking down. "I know, and I didn't mean to be so dramatic. It just gets really old."

"What gets old?"

"All the jokes," she said sadly. Now she gazed up at him. "Stefano, I was never interested in Lucca. I just never met a movie star before. And I don't care how much money anyone has. Nico reminds me so much of one of my brothers. It feels nice to just be with him."

"What does it feel like to be with me?" he asked, instantly regretting the words.

She continued to look up at him, her eyes wide. Slowly, she reached a hand up around his neck and he willingly lowered his head. When their lips met, he felt an electric shock run through his body. He pulled away briefly before descending again and taking her lips in a searing kiss. She dropped her bag of goldfish and leaned up into him. He kissed her with a pent-up passion he hadn't acknowledged, running his hands over her hair, her back, her body. He had no idea how long the kiss went on. It seemed ages before she finally drew away. She looked stunned, her hand flying up to her lips, her eyes wide.

"That's what it feels like," she whispered before turning and running into the house.

# nine

Teresa walked into the empty kitchen. Looking around, she spotted her crumpled goldfish bag on the counter. Stefano probably put it there. Thank goodness—it was still half full, as it was her last bag. She wasn't sure where she was going to get a fresh supply anytime soon.

Kissing Stefano last night was one of the biggest mistakes of her life. How could she have thought that was a good idea? She had looked up at him and been touched by the caring expression on his face when he apologized. For once, he looked unsure and almost vulnerable. Whatever it was stirred her heart, and she had acted impulsively.

This morning, she purposely stalled coming downstairs, knowing there was a planned wedding lunch. Lucca and Ellie had left, but the remaining family was gathering again. She told Kate yesterday that she shouldn't go, but once again, Kate insisted. How was she going to face him? Whenever she got herself in predicaments, she could always rely on confiding everything to Kate, but not now. She had to do this on her own.

"*Buongiorno!*"

Teresa turned around to see Margherita coming into the kitchen. "Good morning, Rita. I'm sorry to come down so late."

"That's perfectly fine, dear. I understand you suffered a headache last night. Are you feeling better?"

Teresa tried not to look guilty. She felt her face growing hot under the older woman's speculative eyes. "Um, it's fine. I just feel kind of wiped out. Probably all the excitement," she said cautiously. She looked at her watch. There was still an hour before lunch. "Where is everyone?"

Margherita smiled, automatically going to the cappuccino machine. She raised her eyebrows, and Teresa shook her head, declining. "Everyone scattered this morning, but we are meeting at Marco and Kate's villa in just a bit. They went home to make sure everything was going to be ready. Kate told me to make sure you were with me! Meara and Brigid went along to help, and I think Nico is showing my brother and his wife the greenhouses."

"Oh, okay," Teresa said, at a loss for words. Margherita hadn't mentioned Stefano. Maybe he was with Nico. Her eyes darted around nervously, as if Stefano was going to pop out of nowhere. She listened distractedly to Rita's chit-chat about the wedding, her family and more.

"Do you want something to snack on until lunch?" Rita asked. Teresa declined politely and continued discussing the wedding. It was a safe topic. She heard voices and sat on the edge of the seat, but it was only Nico who emerged.

"*Buongiorno Té Dolce*!" he called, adopting Marco's name for her but using the Italian translation. He walked to the sink to wash his hands.

"Nico, you're filthy. We are leaving to go to lunch soon," Margherita admonished.

"I know, I know. But *Zio* Bruno wanted to see the greenhouses. I'm going to go shower and I'll drive them over. Why don't you and Sergio take Teresa?" He went to give his mother a hug, but she shoved him off, gently swatting his head.

"Go on with you," she teased, winking at Teresa.

After Nico walked out, she laughed. "He brings me such joy, that one."

Here was Teresa's opening. "Where's Stefano?"

Rita eyed her thoughtfully. "He left very early this morning to go home and isn't coming to lunch. He told Marco he needed to work on some mysterious project. It's fine. Two days of a crowd is about all Stefano can handle." She smiled.

Teresa's heart gave a little lurch. She told herself it was relief, but then a wave of embarrassment swept over her. He regretted last night as well and didn't want to face her today. Once again, she tried to hide her guilty look, and thankfully, was saved by Sergio's entrance. Margherita asked Teresa when she could be ready. She told them she would just a few minutes, running upstairs to grab her purse and meet them in front of the house. Hopefully, her bright pink dress would do.

The drive to Marco's villa didn't take long. They twisted through the hills until they arrived at his breathtaking property overlooking Positano. Teresa had been there before for Kate and Marco's rehearsal dinner. She entered and was immediately swarmed by Meara and Brigid who took her aside. Meara eyed her suspiciously. "We need to talk to you. What is going on?"

"What do you mean?" Teresa asked, stalling for time. Oh God, they knew about Stefano. How was she ever going to face anyone? They pushed her into a nearby bedroom, and Meara leaned on the door, looking at her. Brigid was holding her baby, Norah, and looked more amused than anything.

"Look, Rossi, spill it. I'm Katie's sister. I need to know," Meara said, frowning at her.

Teresa looked confused. Why was Meara entitled to know about Stefano?

"I know something is up with Katie, and I have my suspicions about what it is," Meara said, smiling. "I asked Katie a little while ago, but she was too busy with the staff. So now it's up to you."

Teresa almost dropped with relief. Kate's pregnancy, of course. She made her face look innocent. "I don't know what you're talking about."

Meara started coming toward her, and Teresa held her ground. Meara loved to intimidate people with her height, but Teresa wasn't a pushover. Afterall, she had five brothers.

"What is going on in here?" Kate barged into the bedroom, looking at them confusedly. "We're about ready to sit down!"

They all turned to her, and Kate's face flushed. She shut the door quietly. "Oh, I see, an interrogation. Where's your bright, shining light, Meara?" She beamed at them suddenly. "Fine, I'm pregnant."

Meara shrieked and then boasted, "I knew it!" Brigid thrust Norah at Teresa and threw her arms around Kate. "Oh my gosh, Katie. I can't wait to tell you about what it's like! Or maybe it's better you don't know!"

Teresa laughed. "I already told her that every woman who has ever given birth wants to tell newly pregnant women what it's like."

Meara hugged Kate tightly. "I'm so happy for you, Katie. You could have told me!"

"I tried," Kate said, clearly exasperated. "All day before the wedding, but all you did was work. You had the phone permanently glued to your ear, and then there were people around! Anyway, promise to keep it a secret for a while—we'll tell people when it's the right time. I needed to tell Teresa for medical reasons. That's why she's here."

"You're okay?" Meara asked anxiously. "The baby is okay?"

"Yes," Kate said reassuringly. "But I was losing weight and couldn't keep anything down, and Teresa is helping with that. She's going to help me with a few other things so I'm not so panicked."

"I'm going to be an aunt," Meara said softly.

"Meara, you aren't too fond of kids," Kate reminded her gently.

"I don't dislike kids," Meara said defensively. "Maybe I'm not a big fan, but babies I can at least tolerate. I like to watch them. Just don't make me hold them. No offense, Norah." She smiled at the gurgling baby.

Teresa was holding Norah, rocking her and gently humming. "Katie is going to be just fine. It's just a lot, but I'm going to get her organized medically before I go home."

A knock at the door startled them and Marco stuck his head in. "Katie, everyone is waiting. What is going on in here?" He glanced around and smiled. "Oh, I think I know. Big secrets, right?" He put his finger to his lips. "Come on, *cara*, let's go feed and entertain our guests." He smiled at them all, putting his arm around Kate and leading her through the door.

"I can take Norah back," Brigid offered.

Teresa glanced down. The baby had fallen asleep on her shoulder. "It's okay," she whispered. "I kind of like holding her for a bit."

They walked out of the bedroom and toward the back of the house, where a large buffet was set up with everything imaginable. Teresa made polite conversation with the guests, using the baby as a shield. It gave everyone something to talk about. Part of her waited for Stefano to walk through the door, but she knew deep down he wasn't coming.

"Teresa, let me have her," Brigid said. "Everything is delicious. Now you need to go eat."

Teresa smiled and agreed, handing the still-drowsy baby over to her mother. She went and perused the table that was filled with pastries, cheese, salads, frittatas, bruschetta, Italian meats, and fruit. She filled a plate and stepped outside. The fresh air felt good, and she could be alone with her thoughts.

"Teresa, come sit by me," Marco whispered in her ear. "We

can talk about the project." He gripped her elbow and led her to one of the nearby tables, covered with a white tablecloth with an Italian ceramic bowl filled with flowers. She sat, glancing over Positano below them and the infinity pool that was alongside them. It was gorgeous scenery. She sipped the lemon spritzer Marco set down before her and relaxed.

"Lucca told me last night you agreed to the project," Marco said with a smile.

Teresa choked on the spritzer, coughing. She nodded when Marco asked her with concern if she was okay. "Yes, sorry, wrong pipe. Um, Marco, I'm not sure why Lucca told you that. I told him I'd think about it," Teresa stammered.

He smiled. "*Mio cugino* sometimes gets ahead of himself. I'm sorry, Teresa. Please forgive us. Katie will murder me if she thinks I am pressuring you." At the mention of Kate's name, his eyes searched the outdoor area, as if to reassure himself she was nearby. He smiled, seeing her holding Norah and talking animatedly with Brigid.

Teresa rushed to reassure him. "I don't feel you're pressuring me at all." She looked away, careful to avoid her eyes. "But uh, Marco, I have to apologize. I've decided it's just not something I can do."

"I'm sorry to hear that," he said resignedly.

"I mean, I would do anything for you. Marco, please know that! It's just...I don't think—well, I don't think I'm the right person to help Stefano." She finished in a rush, finally having the nerve to peek at him. His face was thoughtful.

"Teresa, you may have the wrong idea about *mio fratello*. He's a wonderful, loyal brother. I understand he can appear serious, and I guess, stiff. But he is different when he lets himself relax. I think with your help, he would be an amazing addition to this project of Lucca's. He has such a passion for cooking and food and keeping our history alive."

"How did he feel about me being involved?" Teresa asked abruptly.

"We didn't ask him. It seemed pointless," answered Marco. "If he was agreeable, would that change your mind?"

Teresa looked away again, willing herself not to flush. She couldn't let anyone know there was anything between her and Stefano. Well, there wasn't really. What was one kiss, right? She glanced back at Marco, who was leaning forward, his face earnest.

She pursed her lips. Even if Stefano didn't like her—even if she felt humiliated—there was all that money to think about. It could make such an impact on her future. She finally nodded. "If Stefano agrees, I'd be willing to try. But if it doesn't work out, I want to be able to cut it short. Is that fair?"

"Perfectly fair," agreed Marco, flashing his signature brilliant smile. "And here comes my bride, just in time."

"What are you two conspiring about?" Kate said, sitting down and accepting a small kiss from Marco. Teresa sighed without realizing it. They were so perfect together.

"Teresa has agreed to the project and helping Stefano," Marco told her.

"I agreed to *try*," Teresa interrupted. "And only if Stefano says yes."

"Why don't we find out?" Marco asked. He glanced around at all the guests. "Let me go find a quiet place and call him." He stood, his hand running across Kate's shoulder. She looked up and smiled at him before turning and eyeing Teresa thoughtfully. "I thought it would be fun for you, but you seem hesitant. They haven't pressured you too much, have they?

"No, no," Teresa reassured her. "I want to help."

"But...?" Kate looked at her with narrowed eyes. "I know what it is!" she blurted.

Teresa flushed. Kate could always read her like a book.

"You're feeling guilty because you were supposed to be by my side to get over the rough spots. But it's okay. I'm feeling soooo much better, Teresa! And you'll just be busy for ten days or so. I'll be here in Positano since Marco and I are meeting with architects. We're finally going to build a house on his plot of land at the lemon grove." She smiled widely at Teresa. "When you're finished, we can hang out then."

"Katie, you're trying to keep me here throughout your entire pregnancy!" Teresa said and laughed.

"Well, of course. But I know you want to return home. This is a wonderful opportunity, though, right? I'm so excited."

Teresa was forced to smile. If it were up to her, she'd move in with them, but that wasn't going to happen. There was no way she wanted to leech off her friend who needed to be alone with her husband before the baby came. She also didn't want to break it to Kate that the entire plan wasn't going to happen. Stefano would never agree.

"Stefano is on board," Marco said, sitting back down.

"What?" Teresa asked. "There's no way!"

"I admit he was surprised. He did not know that you were in television before nursing."

"What did he say?" Teresa couldn't help the shock registering on her face.

"He just said that it was fine."

"That it was fine?" Teresa echoed incredulously. "He said that it was fine?"

Kate looked at her suspiciously. "Why do you keep repeating that?"

"I just find it weird that he would respond that way," Teresa mumbled.

Marco shrugged. "He seemed nonchalant about it. The only catch is you have to go to him. He's home on Capri. He's getting some work done at the villa and he wants to be there to supervise. It's great timing. By the time Lucca returns from his honeymoon, you'll have Stefano all whipped into shape."

Teresa thought for a minute, remembering when she and Kate traveled to the small island for the day. "Oh, so I can just take the ferry over every day and work with him?"

Marco shook his head. "By the time you catch a ferry—even if I have Luigi take you on our boat, you still have to go up the hill and to the villa. Half the day would be gone. No, it's better if you just stay there."

"I can't stay there!"

"Why not?" Kate asked. "The place is huge. And gorgeous. Wait till you see it. Stefano will cook for you, I'm sure."

"It would just be awkward," Teresa said. "I mean, I don't know him that well."

"Well, you're going to be working closely with him anyway," Kate said, sounding matter of fact. "He has a lot of staff there, so you're not going to be alone with him. He's really sweet when you get to know him."

"I can't believe I'm agreeing to this," Teresa muttered.

"It's going to be just fine," Kate said reassuringly.

"Just fine," Teresa repeated, knowing deep in her heart it wasn't.

# *ten*

The wind blew Teresa's hair all over the place. By the time she got off the boat, she was going to look like some kind of clown, minus the red hair. She frowned, knowing her carefully styled curls were now a wind-blown mess. Nevertheless, she nodded reassuringly when the boat's captain, Luigi, turned to ask if she was okay. Marco insisted on having him take her.

Teresa had waited two days before leaving. She went to Kate's doctor's appointment with her and Marco. Kate sang the praises of her physician already. He was the nephew of the doctor who took care of Kate when she hurt her ankle after first arriving in Positano.

Dr. Alessandro Amato was breathtakingly handsome, Teresa had to admit. Tall, with dark brown, wavy hair, deep dimples and a nice laugh, he reminded her of a famed doctor on a medical TV show she and Kate loved. Teresa rolled her eyes at Kate's obvious matchmaking and remained professional, accepting his offer of a tour of the hospital. While Dr. Amato seemed very up to date on modern methods, he warned her she might be surprised at the state of the hospital. While it appeared to be well run, it looked its age. A sweet nurse, who didn't speak much English, showed

71

Teresa around. It was difficult to ask questions. Teresa wrinkled her nose at the Neonatal Intensive Care Unit, as it didn't seem to have all the modern machinery her hospital at home did. Though Teresa didn't work in that unit, she was familiar with it, having done a rotation there.

When Kate asked her opinion later, Teresa gave it freely. Kate shot a concerned look at Marco, who nodded in agreement. "I wanted to stay down here, but Marco has been determined that I spend my last couple months in Rome or Milan. He said the hospitals farther up north are better equipped," she said. "I didn't want to tell you that because I wanted your honest opinion."

"I haven't seen the hospitals up there, but if they are a step up, then yes, I would feel better about it," Teresa told her. She didn't want to frighten her friend, but pregnancy often came with surprises, and sometimes they were not good ones. And many of those negative outcomes were preventable with the right healthcare. It would be less stressful if Kate was in the best hospital possible.

Teresa had then gotten ready to leave Positano with a lot of trepidation. Kate seemed to sense it, for she took her to a grocery store that catered to tourists. While there wasn't a goldfish cracker in sight, there was American candy and cookies. Teresa selected a package of Oreos and Red Vines and grabbed a few boxes of plain animal cookies. At least that would tide her over. There were some cheese crackers as well, and those would do in a pinch.

The deep blue water sparkled as they approached the island of Capri. Luigi edged the boat into the harbor, his assistant tying it to the dock. Teresa carefully climbed out, followed by Luigi, who was carrying her suitcase and backpack. He made a gesture he would take them for her as they strolled down the dock. Teresa glanced around, wondering how to ask where to go from here. Perhaps Luigi was given instructions. Maybe whoever was picking her up would have her name on a sign like in the movies.

"*Buongiorno*, Teresa," said a familiar voice.

Stefano lounged next to a pole. He wore jeans, a polo shirt, and sunglasses. He looked fantastic from where she stood. Putting a self-conscious hand to her hair, she frowned. She probably looked like a sight.

Stefano apparently wasn't noticing, as he was busy taking her suitcase and backpack from Luigi, who tipped his hat to her before departing.

"Let's go," Stefano said, reaching out to put a hand on her arm. She walked stiffly next to him and queued up dutifully for the tram that would take them to the top of the hill. Neither said a word. They rode the crowded funicular, a vertical cable car of sorts, from Marina Grande to Capri Town up above. Once or twice she inadvertently fell toward Stefano, who seemed to have wonderful balance. "Excuse me," she muttered, not looking at him. He remained silent.

They exited at the top and walked out into the Piazzetta, and Teresa blinked in the sunlight, glancing up at the beautiful clock tower. She dug through her purse for her sunglasses as they walked through the crowds in the square, past designer shops and exquisite cafés. There were no cars on the pedestrian street, and Teresa enjoyed the freedom to swivel her head all over without having to worry about getting run over. She took a deep breath as they passed perfume shops.

Floral displays were everywhere, including pink wisteria and other flowers that were winding up the white buildings. Breathing in deeply again, she now enjoyed nature's perfume as well. The island smelled so good.

As they walked along, Teresa's stomach grumbled, but she wasn't going to say anything. Stefano suddenly veered to the right and led her to a covered patio featuring potted lemon trees.

He gave her bags to the host, who murmured to him, slapping him on the back.

"My stuff..." Teresa stammered.

"Mario will put it in the cloakroom while we dine. It will be safe. Hungry?" Stefano pulled out a chair for her at a table in the corner.

Teresa nodded, transfixed. She quickly ran a hand through her hair, trying to tidy it. He would have to take her as she was. As they sat down, a server came with a bottle of water and a bottle of Pinot Grigio, pouring both for them. Appearing soon behind him was the chef, dressed in a white jacket and black and white houndstooth pants. Stefano stood abruptly and greeted him with a big hug, speaking in rapid Italian. They both laughed a great deal and seemed to be on wonderful terms. Teresa had never seen this side of Stefano, and she watched him while sipping her wine.

"Teresa, *mi dispiace*. I would like to introduce you to my old friend, Carlos. I am sorry. We just needed a moment to catch up. Carlos, my new friend, Teresa," he said.

Teresa tried not to let confusion register on her face, accepting the man's kisses on her cheeks. New friend, huh? This felt like a dream. She gave her arm a little pinch. No, definitely not a dream.

Carlos was speaking with Stefano again and seemed to list things off. Stefano was repeatedly shaking his head. Finally, they seemed to come to an agreement, and Carlos laughed a great deal. Stefano sat and calmly took a sip of his water.

"What have you done with Stefano?" Teresa asked, her face serious. "I'm sure his family will pay handsomely for his return."

Stefano grinned. "He is right here."

Teresa stared at him. "It's just uh, you seem so, so...different," she finally stammered.

"Different how?"

He wasn't going to help her. Stalling, she took her sunglasses off and set them aside. Stefano had done the same, and now his dark eyes were coolly assessing her. Well, at least that seemed normal.

"Um, dare I say happy? Even a little perky?" she finally ventured.

"Perky? I'm sorry I'm not sure of that word."

Teresa laughed. "Of course, you wouldn't know perky. I just mean you're very...happy," she repeated.

Stefano studied her. "Are you making fun of me?"

"No, of course not! I've just never seen this side of you."

"Well, maybe it is time you did," he said.

He seemed to be amused at the bewildered look that was undoubtedly taking over her face. "Um, okay. It's just a little confusing. You're usually so..."

"So..."

"Quiet," she finished, feeling totally out of her element.

"You can say it. Serious, stiff, humorless. I have heard them all. Maybe I am more than that. Maybe I am ready to show you more than that."

"Clearly," Teresa said, her eyes growing wide. "But my question is why?"

STEFANO WAS ENJOYING WATCHING Teresa squirm in confusion. While he spent the last couple of days at his villa doing manual labor, he thought about this moment. He had been working alongside the workers he hired for the renovation, helping them with the demolition work. It felt so good to exhaust himself physically. But he soon learned, his mind continued swirling despite the fatigue. At night, he lay awake wondering what the future held for him. Should he stay at Oro Industries and work alongside his brother in the family dynasty?

They could build something even more significant. Should he agree to this wild idea Lucca had?

When his brain couldn't handle those questions anymore, it shifted to Teresa. It had been some time since Stefano's last relationship. Well relationships, he was forced to admit, considering he spent a lot of years going from one woman to another. Each woman eventually wanted to dig deeper into his psyche, discovering what lay under his exterior. That made him want to erect barriers that even his mother couldn't bypass.

Teresa, small and mighty, didn't seem scared of him. She usually gave as good as she got—until the other night. The look on her face when she backed away from him on the dance floor stayed with him. He admitted to himself he was wildly attracted to her. When he held her in his arms at the wedding, he felt her warmth and energy and wanted more. He was stunned when she had wanted him to kiss her, and he had gotten carried away. Her returning his kiss and then insinuating that she, too, might be attracted to him shocked him. All this time, he just assumed she was attracted to men more like his extroverted famous cousin or even his brother.

When Marco called to tell him he and Lucca hired Teresa to prep him for the show, the puzzle had come together. That was why she was talking so seriously with Lucca. It suddenly all fit, and he admitted to himself he was relieved but also felt even more guilty for teasing her. He was intrigued by the idea of her having the knowledge to do the job—only knowing her to be a nurse.

While he still was undecided about his decision to take part in Lucca's project, he wondered what more time around Teresa would bring. And just what would she do to help prep him? His curiosity was piqued. He had always been an introvert, but in the last year or so, he forced himself to reach out to culinary masters, thirsty for more knowledge. When he talked about food or the family's business, he was fine. Social chit-chat or even sitting down with someone new still challenged him. If he wanted female companionship, he could turn on the charm, but he found it exhausting. From years of experience, he knew to ask a woman questions, let his mind freely wander while she answered and never divulge much about himself. That's why he purposely had no significant long-term relationships, and he liked it that way. Life was less complicated.

In the early morning hours, he decided on a plan to turn that charm on Teresa. For some reason, he wanted her to see a different side of him. He didn't take the time to analyze why, except they were going to be spending more than a week in each other's company. That would be a long time, and he wanted her to like him, even if it was just in the genuine sense of a friend. He still knew there couldn't be anything romantic between them. Every relationship he ever had with a woman ended badly. He wouldn't have Marco and Kate hating him when it was over. And as with all his other relationships, it *would* end. Better to not start anything, but at least they could get to know each other while they worked so closely together. Now he realized she was staring at him, clearly waiting for an answer to her question.

"Why am I ready to show you more?"

She nodded, looking at him speculatively.

"Has anyone ever put you in a box?" he asked.

"You have."

His eyes widened. "How did I do that?"

"Oh no, Stefano, we aren't talking about me. We are talking about you."

He smiled at her. "Caught me. I am going to be honest with you. There is only a slim chance I will even entertain being a part of Lucca's project. I do not think it is anything I would excel at, but I am intrigued by what you plan to do to prepare me. And just possibly," he paused, raising an eyebrow, "it could help me in my future. Maybe I can learn to use those skills elsewhere. But to do so, I must show you a different side of me."

She eyed him thoughtfully. Suddenly, her nose twitched. "Oh my God, that's a burger!" she exclaimed as the server set their plates down. Two cones wrapped in parchment followed. "And French fries!"

"I figured you might as well taste what real burgers and *frites* taste like," he said, and shrugged. "Even if Carlos was reluctant."

Teresa nodded absentmindedly, taking a giant bite out of the burger and Stefano was forced to laugh, knowing at that exact moment, she didn't care if he was sitting there or not.

# *eleven*

Teresa glanced up at the gleaming white villa that lay before them and swallowed hard. She was speechless. She knew the family was extremely wealthy. Shoot, Marco was a billionaire. Stefano probably was, too. But this, this was something. Maybe because the family was so authentic and didn't flaunt their wealth, she had almost let herself relax around it. Now, looking up at the palatial estate, she felt her heart sink. They came from different worlds.

Carefully climbing the stone stairs that lay before her, her mind was still thinking about their lunch together. For some reason, Stefano decided to be engaging and charming. She let him do the talking, telling her about the island and how much he loved it there. It was easy to listen and not interrupt, as the burger and fries were darn good. On the way to the villa, she continued to look all around, as it seemed the incredible views of the Tyrrhenian Sea were endless, and she told Stefano so. He only smiled.

"It is not much, but you call it home," she said as they entered the villa, instantly feeling foolish. He looked at her quizzically, unfamiliar with the joke.

"I mean, this is beautiful, Stefano. It's just...so big," she finished.

His face didn't change expression. "Yes, but it is a home. Come in."

Teresa glanced around at the comfortable couches and chairs and big wooden furniture. They went from room to room—each was different but contained big arching windows. The windows all overlooked fantastic views of the deep blue water beneath them. There were so many nooks and crannies that she couldn't take it all in. She skipped up some stone stairs, following him. "I'm never going to find my way around here," she said and then laughed. "At least point me to the kitchen! Leave some bread-crumbs or something."

"It is easy, I assure you. I will drop your luggage in your room. I hope you will be comfortable."

Teresa glanced around at the large bedroom. The walls were a pale rose, and big arched windows overlooked the sea. She glanced around at the giant bed with its colorful comforter, the big armoire and sitting area to the side that featured colorful pillows. Opening a door to a white stone balcony, she took a deep breath of the island's sweet scent. "Oh, Stefano, it's beautiful," she said with a sigh.

He was watching her, a humorous expression on his face. Running to look at the bathroom, its intricate stone greeted her, and she almost shrieked in delight at the big tub. She came out to see him assessing her, no longer smiling. "I have a lot of work to do," he said abruptly. "Do you mind showing yourself around? Please make yourself comfortable. Go for a swim if you want. I will see you later. *Cena* will be at eight."

With that, he walked away, and Teresa opened her mouth and then shut it again. That was just about the most sudden change in behavior she had ever seen. What was wrong with the man? And why did she still like him so much? Shaking her head, she peered into the immense walk-in closet, wheeling her bag in there. She ran a brush through her tousled hair and washed her face. He made it clear that he wouldn't be seeing her soon so she might as well finish the tour.

For the next hour, she poked around the villa, finding the kitchen—eventually. It was bigger than her entire apartment, she realized, running her hands over the cold marble. She smiled at the all-white plates on the open shelves. Stefano wouldn't allow color to interfere with his food.

Every appliance one could think of dotted the counter and shelves. The kitchen extended farther into a sitting area. It was a wonderful entertaining spot. She walked outside and gasped. The stone outdoor area featured an enormous cooking area. Leave it to Stefano to have a large grill and wood-fired oven. The dining room on the side featured a long table and chairs. Below that level was an enormous pool, surrounded by deck chairs, benches, upholstered chairs, and blue- and white-striped pillows. She smiled at the pool's striped bottom, which featured different colors of blue. All the walls were white, with colorful Italian ceramic pots bursting with flowers. It must take an army of gardeners, she realized.

Back inside, she found a hallway with an elevator. Looking around, she was still alone. She shrugged and took it to the top. The elevator opened to an immense outdoor area, bordered with neutral stone. She found more rooms, which featured a television, game room and more relaxed couches and chairs. Trees were all around them. She felt a part of the natural surroundings that blended with the indoors. One could get lost curled up here, overlooking the sea.

In fact, come to think of it, she was lost. Getting back on the elevator, she headed toward the kitchen. A lot of noise and banging was coming from some undetermined location. Wandering through more rooms, she dragged her hand across beautiful antique furniture. Books and memorabilia crowded some shelves, but she didn't stop to look, as she hadn't yet determined where the sound was coming from. She wandered through several more rooms, her eyes taking in all the lovely pottery and select pieces. It must have taken years to find just the right furnishings. Most of the rooms featured neutral colors. Her bedroom seemed to be an anomaly.

Coming to a study of sorts, she realized she had found the source of the noise. Stefano and a work crew were busy demolishing that area of the villa. Catching her breath, she watched as Stefano in work pants and no shirt swung a sledgehammer, grabbing a piece of wood with his work gloves, sweat dripping from his body. Oh my. She couldn't look away. The best view in the house was right here. Suddenly, he turned and saw her through his safety glasses. Maybe she should feel silly at being caught, but why give him that advantage? She realized a long time ago the only way to deal with Stefano was to hit him head on. Waving as if it was the most normal thing to do while standing there ogling him, she smiled widely, crossing her arms and leaning on the doorframe. He was frowning at her, which made her smile more. Though she should turn and walk away, she continued staring. The workers noticed her and seemed to be asking him something. He answered, but continued staring at her, his eyes ordering her to leave. Finally, he apparently admitted defeat, turning around to continue his work. Feeling triumphant, she watched his lean back, the muscles in his biceps bulging as he worked. It was only when she couldn't take it anymore that she walked away.

STEFANO WALKED out to his pool, his mind racing. Why on earth had he allowed Teresa to stay at the villa? This was his sanctuary, his home. Now it didn't feel that way. He shook his head, trying to clear out the memory of the look on her face while she watched him. She looked—well, attracted to him. This couldn't happen. He turned on the charm at lunch and felt good about telling her about the island he loved so much.

It was only after showing her his home and seeing her there that it occurred to him she would also view a part of him he held so private. She looked so right in that bedroom. He purposely chose it for her because of the pretty rose walls that were original to the villa. Yesterday, he sent his assistant out to buy a colorful quilt and pillows. He had no idea, but he wanted it to look like her. Frowning, he realized he would have to redecorate it when she left. Now that's all he would see.

Why in the world had he thought it was a great idea to dismiss the staff for the week? He told the housekeepers and his assistant that he didn't need them. They had shrugged, used to him wanting solitude when he was home. Now he realized he had solitude with Teresa, except the gardeners and the workers who were carving out a new living area—he wanted something beyond luxurious where he could truly relax.

He took off pants, purposely wearing a pair of swim trunks underneath. It always felt great to finish his day with a swim. Diving smoothly, he swam the length in an easy crawl. The cool water felt fantastic.

"I love your pool," Teresa remarked, as he came close to the wall. Putting out an arm to touch the stone, he stopped, shaking his head. The water fell around his face. She was propped up in the corner, sitting on the stone stairs in a bright red bikini. Her hair, partially damp, was now springing back up to its normal curls. She gave him a wide smile, her face bare of any make-up, showcasing the scattering of freckles on her nose. He chose to concentrate on her face, knowing if he let his gaze fall any farther, he would be lost.

"*Mi dispiace*, I did not see you there," he said, frowning. "I would not have intruded on your time in the pool."

"I think it's big enough for both of us," she said, hoisting herself onto the pool's edge. "It's magnificent, Stefano. In fact, your entire home is breathtaking. It just surprises me."

"Why?" he asked curtly.

"It's just so creatively put together. The way it's furnished. I love all the little alcoves and the way it flows from inside to outside. It's just amazing."

He nodded, not knowing what to say, brushing the water from his eyes as it dripped from his hair.

"Did you have an interior designer?"

"No," he snapped. He sighed internally. He didn't want to talk about the house with her. It was his, and something he held close to his heart.

"Do you entertain much? That outdoor kitchen is phenomenal. I bet it's wonderful to cook there," she said, continuing to probe.

"Not often."

She nodded and bent her head back, her face to the sky. "It's so beautiful here," she said, her eyes closed.

He allowed himself now to let his eyes travel down her petite body. He did not know where she put all that food she devoured. Her body was curvy, but also muscular. He admired the view, finding it difficult to look away.

She suddenly brought her head up, gazing at him. He returned her gaze, just as she had done earlier, but he knew it was time to move on. "If you will excuse me. I am going to swim some laps."

Without waiting for her to answer, he pushed away from the wall, swimming with all the energy that was coursing through his body.

# twelve

After a few wrong turns, Teresa finally made it into the kitchen. She had found even more undiscovered rooms and spent a few minutes soaking in the atmosphere. It almost depressed her how much she loved the villa. She expected to feel uncomfortable by its opulence, but everything had been chosen, almost as if Stefano wanted guests to feel its warmth and at home. That surprised her. For some reason, she pictured him wanting modern and stark surroundings. While there wasn't a lot of color, it still was welcoming. As comfortable as it was, she reminded herself she was going to leave in just a few days, and she had a job to do.

Following the tantalizing smells, she finally walked into the kitchen. Sure enough, there was Stefano, absorbed in kneading pasta, his back to her.

"Hi," she said, feeling kind of shy.

His back remained to her, his biceps working, as he strongly kneaded the dough. She frowned. Was he deliberately being rude?

"Um, hello, Stefano," she said, louder. Approaching him, she had the urge to run her hands down the back of his black polo shirt. His strong back had been so irresistible in the water, his olive skin glistening. Deliberately bringing up the house was her only way of surviving the unexpected meeting in the pool. She finally left when he looked like he wanted to be alone.

Stepping to the side on purpose to avoid any impulsive movement by her hands, she saw he had earbuds in. She waved a little and caught his eye from the side. He nodded and went to the sink and washed his hands before taking them out.

"*Mi dispiace*, I didn't hear you," he said politely. "*Buonasera*, Teresa."

"That's okay. You were definitely concentrating. What are you listening to?" Before he could answer, she picked up his earbuds and put them in her ears. Music blasted through them, and she dropped them on the counter. "Wow, that's a lot. No wonder you didn't hear me." Once again, she found herself surprised. She hadn't figured him for a hard rock fan.

He smiled slightly, putting them in a case. "Can I offer you a glass of wine?"

She accepted the glass of crisp pinot grigio with a smile. Hopping onto a stool at the island, she watched him deftly roll out the dough and then feed it through a machine which cut it into strands.

"Do you ever eat pasta from a box?"

He looked up at her, amusement in his eyes. "No."

"No, like never? You come home after a hard day from work and do this?"

He shrugged. "Sometimes. Or I make a lot to keep and use when I need it. Cooking relaxes me, though. When I was in the states, I did not like boxed pasta. I could not find any made with organic ingredients. I know it sounds weird, but I felt awful after eating it. Maybe it was the flour."

"Organic? Wow, I never knew or even thought about flour. Cooking is stressful to me," Teresa added without thinking.

"It is not for everyone," Stefano acknowledged, taking a sip of his wine, eyeing her. She was glad she changed into the floral wrap sundress. It made the most of her shape. By the way he was looking at her, she was beginning to think he thought so, too.

"What do you make after a hard day?" he asked.

"Reservations," she said succinctly. She laughed. "Sorry, old joke. But I order out if it's really been a hard day."

"What if you cannot? Say you are somewhere, and there is no ordering. What would you make?"

"How did this become about *my* culinary skills?" she asked and then laughed. He was busy cracking eggs into a bowl.

"Is that bacon I smell?" she asked suddenly.

"Italian bacon—pancetta," he said. "A simple carbonara for dinner." He looked up and gave her a slight smile. "It's not very Caprese, but it will do."

"I have no idea what that is, but if it involves bacon, I'm in."

"Somehow I thought you would see it that way," he said and then laughed. "Back to your culinary skills. What would you make for yourself or say a boyfriend?"

"Well, I don't have a boyfriend currently," Teresa replied. "But if I did, he'd have to learn to love grilled cheese, pancakes and scrambled eggs. Anything frozen, of course. Oh, and I can make hardship cookies."

"What are hardship cookies?" he asked, his face inquisitive.

She laughed. "Oh, I'm not giving away all my secrets. But yes, that's the range of my kitchen skills. I don't even want to ask you but go ahead. Bring it on. Let me know all the amazing things you like to cook."

He was busy adding the pasta to the water and stirring. "I like to make almost anything, but even I'm still learning. I was not always a good cook, but I became a passion. Food people questions, watch and learn. Good food I like to eat. But you brings people together. Good food I like to eat. But you provide for better health. A know all that. You are a nurse." He looked slightly embarrassed.

She stared at him thoughtfully. "I do know. I just never had the opportunity growing up and I guess certain foods became a habit. My family...well, let's just say fresh food wasn't much of an option."

"I am sorry about that. But you probably still understand about the memories food can bring back," he said quietly, watching her nod. He turned away, draining the pasta and putting it back into the pan. He added eggs, pancetta and parmesan to the pasta, stirring in some of the pasta water. Finally, he appeared satisfied and ladled it into bowls.

"If you will grab the wine, we can take it outside. I already put some salads and bread out there for us."

Candles were lit at a table and in nearby lanterns, and they sat down at a stone table with chairs. She glanced up at the spectacular sky. The sunset was creating so many bright colors that were her favorites. She wanted to get up and take photos, but stayed where she was. It was a very romantic atmosphere, and Teresa tried to push that aside and concentrate on the pasta. It looked wonderful.

"So, this is carbonara?"

"Yes, it is a poor man's pasta, just bacon and eggs. My grandmother—my *nonna*—used to say most people always have that in the refrigerator. It was a meal they enjoyed, and when I taste it, I think back to sitting at their kitchen table. It brings back those memories of my *nonna* smiling, and my *nonno* cutting the bread, telling me to eat."

She took a bite and moaned. "Stefano, this is so good. It's so simple but amazing."

He accepted her praise with a nod. "The trick is to bring the eggs to room temperature and then add some of the starchy pasta water to make a sauce. The water helps cook the eggs, but not scramble thy sauce. The water helps cook the

She furrowed her brow, trying to figure out how the heck that worked. Then she put her fork down and stared at him, changing the subject. "So, you said there isn't much chance you will agree to be host of Lucca's show?"

He shook his head no, taking another bite.

"You should think about it. Now more than ever, I'm convinced you're right for it."

He put his own fork down and took a sip of wine. He finally said, "I never knew you thought I could do it."

"Oh, I've always thought you could do it," she said, giving him a big smile. "Now more than ever. When you talk about food, Stefano, your whole face lights up. What you said now and earlier when we were inside just makes a person want to learn about Italian cuisine. You can boil it down to the basics. For someone like me who will never ever make this, it still makes me *want* to. That's the key."

"It is not a cooking show," he pointed out, raising his eyebrows. "And I am not a chef."

"No, that's the beauty of it. It's traveling around Italy and showcasing the culture, the food. Talking to chefs, farmers, and grocers. Bringing that warmth and the connection behind it. I couldn't have written a better script just now. Will you at least consider it?"

He twirled the stem of his wineglass, and the flickering candles on the table reflected off his dark eyes. She wasn't sure what expression was crossing his face. Was it uncertainty, fear? He looked at her now, and she suddenly saw a vulnerability she had never seen before.

"Food should evoke all the senses—the smells, the tastes, the textures. It is all one. I am not sure I could impart all that in a television show. What if I agree, though, to keep an open mind? Let me see what you are going to do to me in the coming days."

Teresa's heart fluttered. What she'd like to do to him and with him she could never voice. She looked off into the distance, intentionally avoiding his eyes. The atmosphere was intoxicating, and she nodded, concentrating on eating. It was only when she looked up and met his gaze that she realized she was in over her head.

# *thirteen*

"Let's try it again," Teresa said, smiling widely.

Stefano frowned, pulling at his tie. He was wearing a suit, standing outside in the shade they found on one of his stone patios. Teresa set up a camera on a tripod that Lucca had sent to his villa. This morning, he came down to see her, armed with her electronic tablet, paper tablet, and a lot of energy he wasn't prepared for.

He lay awake for hours last night. To think she was just down the hall in the rose room gave him pause. He would not cross any boundaries. He had promised Marco he had no interest in Teresa for good reason. His protective brother wouldn't have allowed her to come here if he thought that Stefano had any intention of hitting on her. He found himself now thinking about doing that very same thing twenty-four/seven.

Last night he purposely picked up their dishes when they finished and wished her goodnight. He had been a little cold, but he needed to signal to her that their time was to be spent working and not flirting. Teresa hadn't been flirting, though. He found her sincere, an engaging conversationalist, her eyes twinkling and always ready to smile. The sadness he sensed when she first arrived had evaporated, and this morning she literally skipped into the kitchen. He could only grunt at her after drinking three cappuccinos just to wake up.

She had screwed the tablet onto a place next to the camera and they were going to practice reading on it. It mimicked a teleprompter.

"Can I ask you something?" she suddenly broke into his thoughts. "Um, why are you wearing a suit?"

He shrugged. "I thought that is what I would wear on the show, so I was thinking I should wear it when practicing."

She frowned in thought. "My advice to Lucca will be no suit. I see you in everyday clothes. You're going to be traveling around the region. You should look relaxed, and like a normal person."

"A normal person doesn't wear a suit?"

She sighed. "You know what I mean. Stefano, to make this work, you have to look approachable, like someone you want to talk to. A suit lends a certain stiffness and businesslike approach. You wouldn't wear a suit in the kitchen, would you?"

"Well, no, but I'm not going to go on TV wearing a T-shirt and shorts."

"Can we go to your bedroom?"

"WHAT?" he almost shouted.

She rolled her eyes. "To look at your clothes. I assume that's where you keep them. Let's go take a quick look. You've got to have something that is more casual, but not too casual."

He nodded, saying nothing, he led her inside. They climbed the stairs and went the opposite way from her bedroom to a corner room. He pretended not to hear her sigh as they entered the room. Decorating the room had taken some time, as he looked for the perfect pieces. It was done in neutral colors, but he selected accessories that he gathered on his travels. Everything was selected with a lot of care. The massive windows and balcony overlooked the sea. It was a view he never tired of.

Gesturing toward his closet, he stood aside. She looked

around the massive room that was almost as big as a bedroom. Though he had a lot of clothes, they only took up about half of it. She wandered through, the automatic lights coming on as she passed. There were even shelves, tables and chairs in there.

"Oh, Stefano. This closet is amazing. I might just stay in here for a while," Teresa exclaimed, running a hand over his clothes, perfectly lined up.

"Go ahead and tease me," he said drily.

"What are you talking about?"

"How neat everything is. How many clothes I have. Why a man has this luxurious of a closet, I do not know. Just get it done."

"Well, of course you have a lot of clothes. You're an important man. I would expect that," she said reassuringly. "For this show, we just need a more relaxed and comfortable Stefano. And I see you have a lot of clothes that fit the bill."

Teresa wandered over to the section containing perfectly pressed polos, khakis, and jeans. "Would you ever consider a looser shirt, like something untucked?"

He looked at her like she had lost her mind. "No," was his succinct reply.

"Okay, okay." She held up her hands. "Down boy."

"So, for today, why don't you just put on khakis and a shirt? Any shirt. I see they are all solid colors. That will look fine on TV. Let's just start there. We'll talk about your wardrobe with Lucca, but for now, let's get you comfortable."

He nodded, eyeing her. Finally, a slow smile spread across his face. She stood there, looking around, oblivious for a minute, before he saw the slight flush. "Oh, uh sorry. I'll get out of your way. Meet you back on the patio when you've changed."

She almost ran from the room, glancing back quickly. He was forced to smile as he grudgingly loosened his tie. She was something else.

TERESA WENT to the kitchen and filled two water bottles and took them outside. She took deep breaths. Was it obvious to Stefano that she would have spent the day in his room? He looked so right there, and she had glimpsed another side of him. She was longing to spend time snooping over the books on his nightstand, investigate what kind of cologne was in his private bathroom, run her hands over his clothes. Obviously, she was dying to know what made him tick. So far, he kept surprising her. A brief look into his private world might answer a few questions. Yet, he ushered her quickly into the closet, and there had been little chance for exploring.

Before she could analyze the situation anymore, Stefano walked back out to join her, silently accepting the water bottle she offered him. It was mesmerizing watching him take a long drink, his lips raised to the bottle, his strong Adam's apple bobbing. Averting her eyes, she took a deep breath and looked back to see him staring at her.

"Okay, so now we're just going to practice the teleprompter a little. I can control the speed with this app on my phone. I wrote up a little script, just a sample of an introduction you would read to maybe feature a city and their cuisine. And you just practice, and we'll see what speed you read at and how you do at reading and staring into the camera."

Stefano nodded, looking already like a deer in the headlights.

"Stefano, I'm not filming this. Forget that part of it. I'm just letting you get used to the camera. So come on, shake it out."

He looked at her, clearly confused.

Teresa shook her whole body. She danced around for a minute, purposely shaking her arms and shoulders.

He was watching her, his face growing stern. "I'm not going to do that."

She laughed. "I assumed not. Just roll your head slowly. Can you at least shrug your shoulders a little?"

Stefano did so very stiffly, and she laughed. "Okay, now just relax your arms to the side. You don't want your hands clasped in front of your...well, the front of you."

"Why not?"

"That's called the fig leaf pose. You don't want that. You just want your arms naturally to the side unless you bring your hands up toward your abdomen to make a point. But we don't want you talking with your hands, so let's just try to keep them still for now."

He rolled his eyes but did what she told him.

"Okay, I'm going to start the teleprompter, and you just read. You can't screw it up. Let me know how it goes and if I need to adjust the speed."

Stefano's deep voice began. "Each region in Italy features certain pastas, and my favorite is macaroni and cheese, but it has to be the kind in the blue box." He frowned darkly. "I am not reading that. That is not true."

Teresa rolled her eyes. "I told you. I just made stuff up. Just read it. I think I need to just speed it up a little."

He kept frowning, but quickly began to read again. "Naples is known for its Neapolitan pizza—a dough like no other. My favorite is Canadian bacon and pineapple... TERESA!" He broke off, suddenly speaking in Italian. She was sure there might be words she didn't want to know.

"What? I told you it's just for practice. And you were doing great. I think we got your speed set here."

"I cannot read this. If we are going to practice, at least let me write something I would say."

She sighed. "A diva already."

"What did you say?" he thundered.

"I said you're being a diva. For God's sake, Stefano, it's just fake copy."

"Not happening."

"Okay, okay. I'll let you write something to practice this afternoon. Let's talk about your eyes."

"What about my eyes?"

"They're darting all over the place. Like shifty."

"Shifty? I do not understand."

Teresa made her eyes dart all over. "You know, like shifty, sleazy, which won't build trust. Look right at the camera. This camera is your audience. You look right at them. Make love to the camera."

He looked uncomfortable. "I am not making love to the camera."

"Okay, picture some fantastic blonde or something. Make love to her. She's at home watching," Teresa grimaced. Her voice went up an octave. "Oh, that Stefano. He makes me so hot."

"I am not doing that," Stefano stated. "I will look straight ahead, but just so we are clear, there's no blonde and no one inside that camera."

Teresa made another face. "Fine but look friendly. Smile with your eyes. Then look like you're talking to a relative or something. You really want them to understand what you're telling them."

"Smile with my eyes?" He rolled them now.

"I think I've lost you. Can we practice with my copy some more, or do you want to go in and write your own?"

"I'll write my own."

Teresa took down the tablet. "You have thirty minutes, or else you read mine."

"Fine," he said curtly, walking away. He turned around suddenly. "And my favorite pizza for the record is Pizza Bianca."

"Fancy," Teresa muttered, watching him walk away, and suddenly smiled.

# *fourteen*

Teresa skipped down the stairs, her long red sundress flowing around her. Stefano said they were having surprise guests, and she dressed up for the occasion. The afternoon went well once Stefano got the script he desired into the teleprompter. He wrote fake copy about the Amalfi region and lemons. His reading went well, and though he wasn't exactly friendly, she could tell he would eventually loosen up with the camera. It would get tougher when there were more people filming and strangers operating the camera. She was just going to let him practice that a lot and see if his comfort level increased. After that, she would have to help him build emotion. Right now, he was just reading. Then would come interviewing.

She stopped short when she got to the kitchen. Stefano was seemingly using every pan in the place. A long wooden charcuterie tray with various meats, cheeses, and crackers was on the counter, but he was concentrating on something on the stove.

"Wow, you have been busy," she commented as she walked in. He turned around, barely glancing at her. "Yes, sorry, I told you cooking relaxes me." He shrugged, turning back around. She eyed his white shirt and jeans. Who wore a white shirt to cook in? If she did, it would no longer be white.

"Um, can I help with anything?"

He looked at her with a raised eyebrow. "Can you make risotto?"

She rolled her eyes. "No, I already told you my repertoire."

He smiled. "Just testing. Let's go down to the wine cellar and pick out some wine."

She followed him down the stone steps that were inside the enormous pantry, its shelves bursting with ingredients. She hadn't been in there the other day. They emerged into a giant room with shelves of bottles and a massive cooler.

"Stefano, this is for one person? Do we have a problem?"

He smiled and shook his head. "I like to support vineyards in the region, especially small ones. I end up buying too much. I ask a sommelier to come occasionally to clean it out and donate it before it turns. But it is important to have the right wine to pair with food."

He was concentrating now, pulling out a bottle and replacing it. Finally looking satisfied, he grabbed a couple from a refrigerator and indicated the stairs back up.

"Who is coming?"

"You will see," he said. He went back to the stove and returned to her, holding out a spoon. "Taste this."

"What is it?"

"I am not going to poison you. Just taste it."

She stared up at him. He was standing so close that she could smell his spicy cologne. She instinctively put a hand on his wrist to steady the spoon. A jolt of electricity went through her. She met his eyes as she let him glide the spoon in her mouth, feeling the flavors explode on her tongue. "Oh my God, what is that? That tastes amazing."

He smiled. "It's the sauce for the fish."

She looked uncomfortable. "What kind of fish?"

"Why?"

"Why what? I just wondered what kind of fish."

He looked at her thoughtfully. "Teresa, do you eat fish?"

She made a face. "I live in San Francisco. Everyone eats fish."

"What kind of fish do you eat?"

"Fish sticks."

"What is a fish stick?"

"What do you mean, what's a fish stick? Everyone knows what a fish stick is. Breaded fish—you put them in the oven, then eat them with fries and tartar sauce."

He looked at her, confused. "You mean like breaded cod or halibut? Like British fish and chips?"

"Er, not that fancy. They come in a box. I like the narrow ones, not the wide ones."

"What kind of fish are they?"

"I just told you fish sticks."

He shook his head. "I think we have reached the end of the line in this conversation. Tonight, I am grilling some sea bass. I went down to the fish market earlier."

"What else are we having?" she asked tentatively.

"So that's a no," he said dryly.

"That's a 'I have no idea but I'm hoping there's something yummy on the side I can eat just in case,'" she answered.

"I also have chicken because I was not sure what our guests would want to eat. But I promise you there will be something you like." He still hadn't moved and was standing close to her, holding the empty spoon. She could just reach up and bring his head down. She moved a little closer. He seemed to sense it. His head was lowering, his lips inches away from hers.

"Stefano..." she whispered.

"What's for dinner, *mio fratello*?" Marco asked, striding into the kitchen. Kate was behind him, a big smile on her face.

"Surprise!" she exclaimed. "Aren't you excited to see us?"

"Ecstatic," Teresa said, forcing a smile on her face.

SITTING OUTSIDE, they enjoyed the wine Stefano selected. Kate sipped on her lemonade, and they indulged in the charcuterie board. Stefano asked Marco to keep him company while he made a risotto to accompany the sea bass and grilled vegetables.

Watching Teresa eat as many crackers and cheese as she could made him smile. She was worried about choking down the fish. Truth be told, he did it intentionally. He had gone easy on her the first two days, but now it was time to nudge her to be a little more adventurous. She wanted him to get out of his comfort zone so she could do the same. The women were in deep conversation since Kate had arrived. He and Marco caught up on a few business details without them even pausing from their chatting.

"They could talk for days," Marco said, watching them from the kitchen. Their heads close together, the women were laughing. Teresa was wiping the corner of her eyes.

Stefano glanced out and smiled slightly. "Katie is going to miss Teresa when she goes home."

"Well, for now she's here and I'm trying to figure out a way to keep her here for a while. If she would agree to stay through Katie's pregnancy, it would help my wife immensely."

"That is a long time. I am sure she wants to get back and return to work," Stefano said curtly.

"Maybe," Marco said. "But from what Katie tells me, there isn't much to return to."

"No family nearby?" Stefano inquired as nonchalantly as he could.

"Well, several brothers, but they are scattered around the states. I think two are in Canada."

"How many does she have?"

Marco shrugged. He glanced outside distractedly, smiling at

his wife. "I'm not sure. Hey, are you done with that risotto yet? We've been in here forever."

"Good risotto takes a lot of patience and love," commented Stefano.

Marco laughed. "How is it you only wax poetically about food?"

Stefano took a bite of the risotto, a smile growing on his face. "Because food deserves it."

As he arranged the fish that was resting on the plates, he casually continued their conversation. "So, Teresa has no job or anything to go back to. Does she have any plans?"

"I don't know! You're living with her, ask her," Marco said disinterestedly.

Stefano went back to stir the risotto. "I am not living with her. At least not in that way!" Stefano protested. "She does not talk to me about that kind of stuff. I was just interested and am curious about a few things. I just thought you would know is all. And it is your fault that she is here! It certainly was not my idea!"

"Excuse me. I was just going to get Katie some water," said Teresa softly, her face pale. How long had she been standing there? Stefano frowned.

"It's important for her to stay hydrated," Teresa continued.

"I'll bring her some," Marco said, filling a water glass and walking quickly outside.

Stefano stopped stirring and came to stand directly in front of her, his eyes searching her face. "Teresa..."

"I'll just go back outside," she said, turning around.

Stefano gently grabbed her arm, trying to stop her. "Teresa, that wasn't what it sounded like."

Her beautiful eyes, usually abounding with humor, were now glittering with anger at him. "It's Marco's fault. *His* fault I'm here? Like I'm the worst thing that's ever happened to you? I've been nothing but nice to you! Sorry, if I've upset your carefully ordered life. I guess I'll leave with Marco and Katie. You can stay up here in your little Capri Castle and be a hermit for all I care."

Teresa swung around and would have kept walking if Stefano hadn't gotten in front of her quickly. He couldn't let her leave. "*Dio*, Teresa, I am very sorry. I did not mean it that way. I appreciate your work. I have already learned a lot today. I say stupid things sometimes. That was not meant to hurt you."

"Because I wasn't meant to hear it," she said flatly.

"Well, no, but I was trying to tell Marco why..." He stopped.

"Why...?" she pressed.

"Why I was asking so many questions about you."

She fixed him with a stare. "Why were you?"

"Well, it just seems like you know a lot about me, and I don't know as much about you," he said cautiously, as he watched the expressions cross her face.

"Do you want to know more?" she asked softly.

"Yes, I mean, we're spending a lot of time together."

She smiled a little. "Maybe sometime I'll tell you."

He stared at her. "I'd like that very much."

She sniffed. "What's burning?"

"*Dio*, my risotto!" Stefano ran over to it, looking in the pan. "It is ruined!"

Teresa rolled her eyes. "It's not ruined. I'm sure we can still eat some of it."

"I am not serving burned risotto for dinner."

Teresa walked over and looked in the pan. "Are those mushrooms?"

"Well, yes."

She smiled. "No great loss then."

For some reason, it made him laugh. He looked at her now and did something he never thought he would do: He hugged her.

# fifteen

"Stefano, this orzo is fantastic," said Kate, taking another helping.

Stefano rolled his eyes. "You do not have to say that."

Teresa smiled, reaching over to pat his hand. "It's too soon, Katie. He's still mourning the loss of his risotto."

They all laughed at the dark look Stefano shot her. Teresa smiled sweetly back. Despite her cheerful demeanor, she was trying to keep her mind on the present. What happened back in the kitchen? He had thrown his arms around her, but he also held her for a minute. She hadn't known what to do and finally hugged him back. Since then, he seemed to relax a little. During dinner, he even reached over to put a small helping of vegetables on her plate, telling her quietly that it was time for her to be adventurous. She also received a few small smiles from him. She saw Kate watching them and looked away quickly.

"I'm stuffed," Kate said, setting her fork down.

"Really? So, you don't want any gelato?" Marco asked, lifting an eyebrow.

Kate giggled. "Well, I could fit just a little in." She put up two fingers as if measuring.

Marco smirked a little. "I thought as much. We'll clear these dishes and get you some."

Kate reached over, giving Marco a quick kiss. "Really, I need to walk for a few minutes and stretch my legs. Teresa and I will go get it. You guys enjoy some wine."

They gathered their plates and carried them inside the kitchen. Teresa was gently putting her stack down when Kate shot her a glance. "Spill it."

"What are you talking about?" Teresa hedged, not looking at her, and moved the plates around on the counter.

"What's going on between you and my brother-in-law?"

Teresa turned away purposely, opening cabinets, looking for some bowls. "I do not know what you're talking about."

"Oh, Stefano, you're so funny," Kate said, in a singsong voice.

"I never said that!"

"But that's how you're acting! I know when you're interested. And you're interested in that hot man out there." Kate narrowed her eyes. "You know reading people is my superpower."

Teresa stopped and turned then, assessing her friend. It was important she get Kate off the scent that she felt anything for Stefano.

"I know. I know. But you're wrong. It's a job. I have to get him to like me, so he'll trust me."

"So, it's only a job?" Kate asked, still looking dubious.

"Yes, of course. It's part of my job. Get him softened up, get him to like me and then maybe we can get this project done. And at the end, I'll earn a big fat paycheck."

"I just came in to see if you needed help finding things," Stefano said.

Teresa turned, horrified. It was déjà vu—only now she was on the other end. What did he hear? "Stefano..."

"The bowls are over here," he said. "I will get the gelato and bring it out."

Teresa looked over at Kate, her eyes showing her hurt. Kate

shrugged and gave her a speaking look back before leaving the kitchen.

"Tonight seems to be a night of misunderstandings," Teresa said, trying to get the words out.

"I understand perfectly," he said. "Let's serve the gelato before it melts." Without glancing at her, he walked out with the tray, not looking back.

~

TERESA STIRRED the ingredients in the saucepan, watching the sweet butter melt into the brown sugar, creating absolute goodness. She found it oddly relaxing to stir and watch two ingredients become one. Maybe Stefano was onto something. After Kate and Marco left, he simply gathered the dishes, told her goodnight, and went upstairs. Tomorrow, she needed to find a way for him to accept her apology, or at least the explanation why she was so cavalier in answering Kate's questions. It could be mortifying, but if she didn't clear this up, Stefano would never let her continue coaching him. After rolling around in her bed for a while, she decided to come down and make something delicious.

"What are you doing?" Stefano asked loudly from the doorway. Teresa jumped, dropping the spoon.

"Now look what you made me do!" she said, glaring at him. She grabbed some tongs in a nearby crock and used them to get the gooey spoon out, dropping it in the sink. She quickly grabbed another spoon. "This is the technical part!"

She peeped quickly at him. He was wearing faded jeans and an old T-shirt, looking like he hadn't gone to bed yet. For once, his hair was a little disheveled, as if he had been running his hands through it. She quickly gave the concoction her undivided attention. He walked near her, and she was aware of his presence as he loomed behind her, sniffing. "I thought you said you didn't cook."

"I said I didn't cook much," she clarified.

"But you decided in the dead of night to get up and try?"

She refused to bow to his sarcasm. He needed some time and space, and she couldn't take her eyes off the caramelizing mixture to deal with him.

"What are you doing with crackers? Are you making soup?" he inquired, clearly confused. On the counter was a cookie sheet she had readied with foil and then lined up crackers like little soldiers.

She smiled, stirring the mixture. "I'll explain in a minute, but this is really the most difficult part. I can't take my eyes off it."

He came back to loom over her. "Looks like caramel."

She nodded, stirring, and watching the pot intently. "It's done! Get out of the way, Stefano," she barked. Picking up the pan, she gently poured its contents over the crackers and watched with satisfaction as they absorbed the caramel. After dispensing with the pot in the sink and running water in it, she grabbed the chocolate that was melting on a double burner. Stirring it, she drizzled the chocolate over the caramel. Smiling and taking a big breath, she felt accomplished.

"Usually I just use chocolate chips, but I only found these chocolate bars. And these fancy crackers were all you had, but they'll have to do. At least they have salt on them," she said. "This needs a few minutes to cool. I think I'll put it in the refrigerator."

"Now that you are done with your culinary masterpiece, do you mind telling me what you are doing?" He stood staring at her, his arms crossed.

She shrugged. "When I was a little girl, my dad would make this for me as a treat."

"More comfort food?" he asked.

She nodded and went to the sink. "I should clean the pans."

"Leave the pans," he said roughly. "We need to talk."

He silently offered her a glass of water, and she accepted it, following him to a chair at the farmhouse table on the other side of the kitchen. She was suddenly self-conscious of her lobster jammies. Oh well, he had seen them already.

"I think you should return to Kate and Marco's tomorrow," he said quietly. "It was fortunate that I overheard you tonight, before..." He stopped talking abruptly, looking away from her.

Her heart felt like it fell to her feet. "Stefano, please let me explain. I know it sounded bad." Teresa took a deep breath. "The truth is, I'm not trying to soften you up. Sure, I need you to be comfortable in front of the camera. That's all part of the coaching, but there's nothing underhanded."

"You said..." he started.

"I know what I said," she interrupted. "Please don't remind me." Teresa looked down at her hands. She could feel her face growing hot. She finally looked up and met his gaze. "I said it for a reason. I didn't want Katie to...I didn't want her to think there was anything between us. She's so perceptive."

She blew out a breath, running her hands through her curls. She probably looked ridiculous.

"As far as I know, there isn't anything between us," Stefano informed. His gaze was so intense she looked away.

"I'd like there to be," Teresa whispered.

The kitchen was filled with silence. Finally, she peeked at him to see a range of expressions crossing his face. Without him saying a word, she found herself suddenly hauled onto his lap, his lips descending. Opening hers to receive his kiss, she ran her hands over his lightly bearded jawline, neck, and hair. She had waited so long to kiss him again. She hoped he could tell how much she liked him in this kiss.

It seemed they kissed for an eternity. It was heaven feeling his powerful hands through her thin pajamas, running down her back, her hips. Suddenly, he thrust her away, catching her before she would have fallen from his lap. He was breathing heavily. "Teresa, we cannot do this."

"Why not?" she challenged. "We're both adults. If you're attracted to me too, why can't we?"

He gently brought her back close to him, leaning her head on his shoulder. He stroked her curls. "I have been wanting to do that for a long time."

"What?"

"Kiss you again. But also play with these curls. They fascinate me. See, they just go right back in place." He pulled one coiled piece straight out and watched it curl back to its original form.

She made a face but nuzzled more into his shirt. "You should hear the name my brothers have for them."

"Just how many brothers do you have?"

"Five," she said, turning to peep up at him. She saw a slow smile spread across his face. "*Dio,* yet another reason."

This time, he picked her up and placed her back in her chair. "Teresa, look at me."

She allowed her gaze to meet his, which showed regret. "Every single relationship I have ever had has ended badly. You and I would be combustible. It would be a short-term romance and, at the end, would be...ashes. I can't do that to you. I *don't* want to do that to you," he clarified. "And then there would be a long line of people waiting to beat me to a pulp. That includes my brothers, your brothers, and worst of all, Katie."

She gave him a wide smile, and he looked confused. "Why are you smiling? I just told you we cannot have anything."

"I'm smiling because we already do. I want to combust with you, Stefano. More than anything," she whispered.

"But why, after what I just told you? I hope you do not think it will be different for you. It will end," he said firmly.

Teresa nodded as she got up and went back to sit on his lap. She purposely slid against him, running her hands over his strong shoulders. "Stefano, do you know how old I was when my mother died?"

He shook his head.

"I was ten," she said softly. "Ten years later, my father died." She pulled back to look at him, tears in her eyes. "Then eventually, I went to work at a hospital. I've seen so much sadness. Life is short, Stefano. What do you say we grab a little of it for ourselves? Then when it's time, you go your way, and I'll go home. But we'll have something to tuck away in our hearts forever."

He sighed, putting his forehead next to hers. "This is a mistake."

She smiled widely, knowing she had convinced him a little. "No, it's not, you'll see." Smiling, she got off his lap and led him by hand back to the kitchen, getting the tray out of the refrigerator. Breaking off a piece, she held it up for him to see. "I'll make you a deal. If you tell me this isn't fantastic, then we're through."

He speculatively eyed the cracker with its caramel and chocolate on top. "I do not eat that many sweets," he said. "I do not bake."

"Why is that? I mean, you're such a great chef. I bet you could make some amazing desserts." She took a bite and moaned. "Not as good as this, but maybe close."

He smiled gently at her. "I have a theory you cannot be a talented chef and a talented pastry chef. Two distinct skill sets."

"Hmmm," she said, her mouth too full to reply. She chewed and smiled. "Well, I am skilled in baking then. This is soooo good. Come on, try."

She held a piece up to his mouth, and his gaze locked with hers. She could feel the heat as he took the bite. He chewed, and she saw the expression change in his eyes. He opened his mouth. "Give me another bite of whatever that is."

# sixteen

Stefano finished shaving and shook his head at his reflection. Surprisingly, he didn't look too bad, considering he was up half the night trying to justify what he was doing with Teresa. After dutifully walking her to her room, he kissed the heck out of her before thrusting her inside.

"We're taking this slow," he told her before shutting her door. He saw her knowing smile. While he never told her that the dessert was fantastic, he ate half the tray with her.

"Slow," he repeated now, rolling his eyes. The woman had one speed at everything she did, and it definitely was not slow.

"This is a mistake," he said to his reflection and grimaced. Agreeing to start anything with her was beyond stupid. He knew it deep down but looking at her in her pink lobster pajamas last night, he had felt a portion of his hard heart soften. The walls he erected temporarily lowered a little.

Damnit, he wanted to get to know her. She was unlike anyone he had ever met, and everything about her fascinated him. If they just went ahead for a short fling, it wouldn't hurt anybody. Today, he needed to ensure she understood that. When he walked away—and he *would* walk away—there would be no misunderstanding.

Dressing quickly in jeans and a polo shirt, he walked downstairs to find Teresa sitting on the counter eating a roll with cheese in it. She was wearing white jeans and a bright pink top, her big gold hoop earrings swinging as she looked at him. Her curls were very lively this morning, springing to life below her ears.

"Hey, sleepyhead. I was wondering if you were trying to avoid me this morning," Teresa said with a smile, but a look of uncertainty crossed her face.

He walked over to her and stood in front of her, gently appraising her. "We have chairs," he said softly. He couldn't resist leaning in to give her a small kiss. She tasted like butter. Her arms came around his neck, and he found the kiss deepening.

He broke away, staring at her. "*Buongiorno*," he choked out. Turning away from her, he wanted to hide his own uncertainty now. *Dio*, in the light of day, he couldn't keep his hands off her. He strode over to the cappuccino machine and made himself a cup. "Cappuccino?" he inquired politely.

Teresa was busy finishing her roll. "I don't usually touch the stuff. Can you imagine me on caffeine?" She laughed.

He smiled and sat at the island. He took a deep sip and almost choked when she asked, "So second thoughts today?"

"You always get right to the point!"

She shrugged. "Why waste time?"

"No second thoughts, but just a reiteration," he said, eyeing her intently. "Teresa, I like you. I like you very much. I do not want to hurt you. But I have no intention of having a long-term relationship. It is not something that fits into my life. So, when this—whatever this is—ends, I don't want you hurt. Those are my terms, and I need to know you understand."

"Who says I'm the one who's going to get hurt?" she asked innocently.

He frowned but found himself at a loss for words. "I—I have never encountered that."

She nodded understandingly. "But you've never encountered me, either." Hopping down, she stuck out a hand. "We're in it for the short-term, and your rules are accepted."

"And we are going to take it slow," he repeated, stroking her soft, small hand. He watched her nod, her curls bouncing. "Just one thing," he said, eyeing her. "I think we should keep this between us. We have too many interested spectators that would want to weigh in. To the outside world, especially my family, we are colleagues."

She wrapped her arms around his neck. "Kissing colleagues," she said with a smile.

∼

"IT'S OKAY. Reading a teleprompter is really difficult," Teresa said yet again, trying to reassure a clearly frustrated Stefano.

"I cannot do everything you are telling me," he muttered. "Either I read it, or I show some kind of expression. Not at the same time."

"You have to think about what you're reading," she reminded him, but he was shaking his head. He threw up his hands. "I told you, it was a dumb idea."

"Oh, for God's sake, you're not a quitter, are you?" Teresa grimaced, her hands on her hips.

"No, but I feel ridiculous. I cannot master this. I should be able to."

Teresa eyed him for a minute. "Okay, let's just forget about the teleprompter for now. Let's switch to interviewing. Most of the show will be that anyway. You'll be out and about talking to people."

She smiled. "Go get some water or something to drink and let's take a quick break. When we come back, we'll talk about interviewing."

Stefano nodded, but she could tell he was still frustrated. Biting her lip, she knew she needed to get his confidence up. Switching to something different may help. Looking around, she saw some of the workmen sitting on the side of the house, taking a break from the construction project.

"*Buongiorno*," she called, smiling. "*Inglese?*" She thought she saw one man nod, so she started talking, asking if she could borrow him for a few minutes. He nodded emphatically, and she grabbed at his sleeve so he would follow her to the patio. She continued talking, telling him how they were practicing for a television project, and he would be helping. Just act natural, while Stefano asked him questions.

She sat him in a chair on the patio and smiled when Stefano came out with two water bottles. He handed her one and nodded his head toward the man. "Why is Giuseppe here?"

"I thought he could be part of your practice interview. You can ask him questions. Pretend he's a chef of a restaurant, say in Naples, since that's going to be an episode. Ask him how he makes his pizza dough or something."

Stefano chuckled. He broke out in rapid Italian to Giuseppe, who laughed as well, pointed to Teresa a few times. He stood, and Stefano nodded sympathetically before slapping him on the back. Walking away, the man continued smirking.

"Why did you send him away? We needed him!"

Stefano was still smiling. "Teresa, he does not speak English. He just followed you because he thought you were so cute! He also said you talk a lot! I could have stood here and asked him about installing tile, which is what he does for a living. You would not understand if my questions were on target or not."

She sighed. "I really have to learn Italian."

"Well, not really, since you're not staying in the country," he pointed out dryly.

Her heart sank. He was already shoving her out of Italy. Well, she was here now, and she might as well make the most of it. She took a sip of her water and thought for a minute. "Stefano, what do you say we bust out of here? Maybe we can go exploring and find a place where there's someone you can talk to and practice with."

"I am not comfortable talking to a random person."

"It won't be a random person. We'll find someone you would normally talk to. The only difference is I'll bring a camera. Come on, give it a try? Please?" She batted her eyes at him. He rolled his at her. "Fine, but only if we find the right person. Besides, maybe it *is* a good idea. It will give me a chance to show you a little of Capri."

Teresa smiled. She hadn't thought of that bonus. "Great, let me just go grab my backpack. You bring the camera and tripod, and I'll meet you out front."

She walked away and was startled when he pulled her back. He gave her a quick kiss and then smiled, and she felt her heartbeat quicken. Giving him a wide smile, she skipped away, but could feel his eyes on her the entire way to the house.

# seventeen

"This was a great idea," said Teresa, taking in the scenery. "I did not know it was like this on this part of the island," she said with a smile. "The only part of Capri I've seen was all the designer stuff that looks like I landed on Rodeo Drive."

He nodded. "Capri Town is fun, too, but for a different reason. The rest of the island is more about the people and nature. There is always something new around every corner. That is my favorite part, especially here in Anacapri."

They left his car at home. He seldom used it, he told her. Only people who lived on the island and taxis were allowed to drive. She nodded, mentioning that she had seen only vintage convertible taxis or electric cars. They jumped into one taxi and took the quick trip to Anacapri and began walking through the narrow, stone pedestrian lanes that were lined with an abundance of flowers. Picturesque, whitewashed homes dotted the street. Stefano told her there were many walking trails that featured amazing views that they would have to try sometime.

Teresa was only halfway listening. When she looked at him, her heart sped up, and it was as if all sound was muffled. She wasn't fooling herself. When this ended, she was going to be devastated. She didn't care, though. The adage "it's better to have loved and lost" played in her mind. There would never be regret about starting something with Stefano, except for the fact that she'd probably remain single the rest of her life. No man was going to reach his high bar. Sure, he was grumpy at times and too serious, but she glimpsed the real him a few times and she knew he was thoughtful, kind and generous. She wanted to learn more.

They reached the main piazza, and she glanced around, seeing the small artisan shops. He was pulling her over to a nearby produce stand and turned to her. "You wanted me to practice? I will practice here since I know the owners."

He was carrying her backpack with the camera and tripod, and now he handed it to her. "Let me just talk with them so they understand what we're doing."

She followed him over to the edge of the stand. Several tables overflowed with fresh vegetables and fruit. An elderly man emerged from a nearby shed and broke into a wide smile. He embraced Stefano for a long time, talking in rapid Italian. Stefano answered him dutifully, laughing, and submitted to another hug from an elderly woman, who popped her head out to see what was going on. Finally, after much conversation, Teresa faced three sets of eyes. She put up her hand and waved ridiculously.

The woman was the first to approach, putting her hands on each side of Teresa's face and kissing her. The man greeted Teresa similarly.

Stefano grinned. "I explained to Maurizio and his wife, Maria, about our project. They have agreed to cooperate."

Maria ran into the small house, yelling in Italian. "Maria thinks she needs to go brush her hair and put on some make-up," Stefano explained, still smiling.

Teresa bit her lip to keep her from laughing. "Do they know this is just practice? I wasn't even going to turn the camera on."

"Turn it on. They are so excited. You can delete it later if you want," he told her quietly.

Teresa set up the camera and tripod and watched Stefano talking to his friend. She gestured she was ready. "Okay, so on the show, they'll tell you ahead of time what to say. I mean, the producer will have a script, and you'll plan it out. Today, let's just pretend that you're asking him about certain fruit or vegetables of the region and how long he's had this stand. You want his story and to get something personal from him. Get people to know him."

Stefano rolled his shoulders. He looked right into the camera and began talking, introducing Maurizio and discussing his stand. He turned to the man, putting a gentle arm around him, asking him about the stand, why it brought him joy.

Teresa stood, biting her fingernail. After zooming in and adjusting the shot, she watched, transfixed. Stefano was a natural when people were introduced into the mix. He kept the conversation going, picking up a giant lemon and talking about how large they grew on the Amalfi Coast. She shook her head. Who knew he could be like this? This was gold.

Maria emerged and began talking in her broken English. She brought Stefano over to a row of bags arranged in baskets of her dried oregano, basil, and packets of a lemon mixture, she called her own recipe. Teresa quickly adjusted the camera, listening to Stefano and Maria discuss the herbs of the region and how plants were handed down through generations.

Suddenly, Teresa was aware they were staring at her again. "Uh, that was great," she stammered. "I think we have all we need." They smiled and nodded, and she brought the camera over to show them in the viewfinder a quick preview. Maria smiled. "You email us. Okay?" Teresa smiled at her, listening to Maria's use of technology terms as she stood at a produce stand in a rustic piazza. "Sure. I will send you a link to watch it," she said.

Putting the camera in the backpack with the collapsible tripod, she glanced around to see Stefano shopping. He was busy carefully examining vegetables, putting them one at a time gently in a bag. She watched him take out several euros and hand them to Maurizio. The older gentleman was holding up his hands, but Stefano shoved them into the man's pocket, clapped him on the back before coming to join her. He took the backpack and added his bag to it. As they prepared to walk away, Maurizio followed them, still talking. Finally, Stefano submitted to one more embrace, and they were on their way. Stefano grabbed her hand, as if it was the most natural thing in the world. "I think he's still talking," she said, glancing back with a grin.

Stefano smiled a little. "That was a highlight for them. They are wonderful people. Now I am going to show you one of my highlights."

Teresa laughed. "Does it involve food?"

He gave her a sideways smile. "It does indeed."

They climbed stairs toward a restaurant. Teresa stopped every so often on the pretense of taking photos of the sea in the distance and the flora and greenery around them. In reality, it was for her to catch her breath. Stefano, not even breathing hard, stood patiently next to her. She turned to him. "Okay, so honestly, how many more steps?"

He chuckled and pointed. "Just up to that landing right there."

"This better be the best lunch ever," she muttered, continuing to climb. It was disconcerting that from his vantage point, he had a great view of her bottom, but what the heck? She wiggled it a little as she climbed. Let him enjoy the sights! She smirked for the rest of the stairs, finally reaching the top. A restaurant was perched there, the stunning sea below.

"Oh, Stefano, it's magical up here. I bet you never tire of looking at it."

He grinned a little wickedly. "I am definitely enjoying the sights."

'Is it bad that I can tear my eyes away from this stunning glory to eat? I'm starving!" She looked pleadingly at him. He shook his head, smiling, and led her toward their eager host. "Then let's feed you," he said simply.

"STEFANO, what in the world are you making?" Teresa asked as she walked into the kitchen and observed three counters full of kitchen tools, bowls, and pans. They came home after lunch of *Taglietelle Aumm Aumm*. A traditional pasta dish, Stefano told her it translated as "hush, hush." The sauce was made with a fresh tomato sauce that also included fried eggplant, smoked mozzarella, and Romano cheese. Teresa had been a little wary of the eggplant but couldn't resist the warm pleading in Stefano's eyes and she admitted it was delicious.

They had briefly argued over the appetizer of calamari he ordered.

"I'm not eating that," she informed him, her eyes wide.

"It is just..."

"I know what it is," Teresa said and shuddered. "And I'm not eating it."

He only smiled and sure enough, poured on the charm until she at least tried one deep fried piece of squid.

"What do you think?" he asked, his eyes full of humor.

"Tastes like a garlic-flavored rubber band," she said matter-of-factly, before chugging her water.

He rolled his eyes to the sky before diving in and eating half the plate. After they finished, she watched him interview the chef in the kitchen for more practice, and it was even better than before. Stefano was a natural, standing at the chef's side, asking questions, peering into pots. The only issue was his curiosity. She could envision him going off course. That would be something to discuss with Lucca.

Wanting to be comfortable, she changed into her a casual sundress when they got home—a bright sunny yellow floral number that Kate once told her looked great with her hair. She spent a few minutes out enjoying herself on her balcony. She would never tire of the scenery. It didn't seem like she was gone that long, but from the state of the kitchen, she must have been.

With a furrowed brow, Stefano glanced up and shrugged. "It seemed like a good idea—at least I'd be too busy to practice anything with you."

"Practice the teleprompter, interviewing or kissing me?" she asked sweetly.

He stopped and took a sip of his red wine. "There is only one of those I enjoy."

She came up next to him and rubbed her hand over his arm. Just feeling his strong olive skin made her feel warm already. "Okay, don't beg. We'll try the teleprompter later."

He laughed and leaned down and kissed her nose. It was not quite the practice she'd hoped for, but she'd take it for now. Going to the sink, he washed his hands and automatically poured her a glass of wine. She hopped on the counter again, and he raised an eyebrow. "We have chairs."

"So, you keep telling me," she drawled. "What are we making?"

He raised another eyebrow. "*We* are making ravioli."

She surveyed the sheets of dough that were spread on the counter in varying colors—a rich black, bright green, cherry red and regular. "I guess I've never seen all these colors."

"A local school is having a fundraiser, and I promised I would make a few different kinds of ravioli. It takes time, but it is worth it."

He pulled out his phone. Scrolling through photos, he showed her several. "This is what the finished product looks like.

I fill them with different flavors—maybe a caprese, a special sausage, mushroom, crab or whatever is fresh—beet or spinach. All different kinds. I keep thinking of new ideas."

Teresa's eyes widened at the photos that showed large oval raviolis with green, brown or orange stripes as well as solid green or red ones.

"Stefano, these are beautiful! But how do you make the dough so colorful? Food coloring?"

He looked at her in horror. "No, no, it is natural. I use vegetables—beet, kale, mushrooms, or whatever I find. Then I run them through the machine here, and I mix them with the regular dough until I have what I want. The machine does a lot."

He deftly started doing what he described, working with practiced ease. Once some sheets were done, he picked up a bowl and began making dots on the bottom dough. She watched him cover it then and cut the raviolis into oval pillows, using a tool to crimp them.

"They look too good to eat," she remarked.

"Well, that's too bad. You will have to go hungry then," he said dryly. "Because this is what we are having for dinner. I thought tonight we would eat at home, but tomorrow I'll show you more of Capri Town now that you've seen some of Anacapri."

"That sounds fun," she said cautiously. Frowning slightly, she thought of her wardrobe. Did she even have the right clothes? She wished Katie was there to go shopping with. She never knew what to buy. Reading her thoughts, he glanced over at her. "You always look beautiful," he said. "Do not let all the designer stuff fool you. It's still very fun. Though, there may be lots of tourists who remain. Not as many as the summer, but it is still technically the season. We will go to one of the restaurants in the Piazzetta."

She continued watching him deftly moving the dough around. "Can I help?"

He looked at her skeptically, as if deciding.

"Really, I'm not just a pretty face. Will you let me try to feed it through the machine?"

"How about you just put the mixture here in little piles on the dough?"

"But I want to try the machine!" she whined teasingly.

"Teresa, I cannot be responsible for all your fingers. Let us just take baby steps."

She laughed. "Okay, okay." She went to the sink and washed her hands. "Reporting for duty, Chef!"

He rolled his eyes. "You're going to need an apron."

"Why? You don't wear one."

"Well, I do not need one. But if I had to guess, I would say you might." He opened a drawer and took out a red apron, putting the loop over her head and tying it from behind.

She didn't mind—it allowed her to lean into him. Stefano must have liked it, too, because he was busy kissing her neck. She stretched to give him better access. "I like cooking so far."

She felt the laughter shake his body. "We might need some more lessons." Keeping her in front of him, he reached around to grab the bowl. "See? You put little piles this far from each other."

"Hmmm." She sighed.

"Are you paying attention?"

"Why do I have to pay attention when you're doing all the work?" she asked.

"Because the next time I'm going to have you do it all on your own," he said.

"No, you won't! There's no way you'd give me that kind of control," she said and laughed. Stepping out of his arms, she looked at him and saw he was grinning. "I think you're getting to know me really well. How about I set the table instead?"

She tried not to laugh when he looked relieved. Busying herself with gathering plates and utensils, she took them outside to the patio. It was so peaceful overlooking the sea; she couldn't imagine eating anywhere else.

They soon sat down to eat. Admiring her plate, she saw he gave her one of each ravioli. All he used to top them was extra virgin olive oil and fresh parsley and some *Parmigiano-Reggiano*. She took a tentative bite of the sausage, knowing she would love that one and was right. Next was the caprese. How could something so simple—just tomatoes, cheese and basil taste so wonderful? He told her he used fresh and sundried tomatoes, and they were especially sweet. Glancing up, she met Stefano's eyes and knew he was anticipating her trying the mushroom and spinach ones.

She looked down at her plate. "Do you have a dog?"

"Teresa, you know I do not have a dog. Besides, even if I did, you are not feeding my precious ravioli to a dog."

She eyed the mushroom. It looked so pretty with its brown and white stripes. "But mushrooms are so slimy," she pointed out.

"It is not, I promise. I used some breadcrumbs, cheese, and a little sausage in there too, so it's not all mushrooms. You're going to love it."

"How do you say mushrooms in Italian?"

"*Funghi*," he answered promptly.

"See, even the name sounds gross," she insisted. She peeked at him. He was still watching her, not buying her argument. Taking a deep breath, she cut a small piece. Stefano pushed his plate aside and watched her. "I can't eat if you stare at me!"

He laughed and picked up his fork again. "Okay, as long as you're not spitting it out into a napkin." She felt herself flushing since that was her second plan after the dog. Taking a tentative bite, she chewed thoughtfully.

"Well?"

"Truth?" She bit her lip.

He nodded.

"It's not terrible."

Shaking his head, he chuckled. "Not a stunning review, but I applaud your honestly."

Taking a bite of the spinach one, she nodded her head. "Surprisingly, I think I can get behind this one more."

He was sitting back, playing with his wineglass. "Really? But it is a vegetable. Your body might reject it."

"Hilarious. Were you serious earlier about making one with beets sometime?"

He nodded. "Yes, tonight I ran out of time, but I have before. Roasted beets are delicious."

She made a face. "This may be a deal breaker, but I will never *ever* eat a beet."

"Why not?"

She turned wide eyes to him. "I just can't. They freak me out. They are just so...bright. My Dad forced me to eat one when I was little. I thought they'd taste like candy. You know, cause they look like they should. Never again."

"Is this a challenge?"

"Nope. Cause I'm never ever going to eat a beet."

He smiled. "Challenge accepted."

# eighteen

"I cannot do it, Teresa." Stefano walked away in disgust. He turned back. "I hate that teleprompter. It is just not happening. We are done."

Teresa tried not to raise her eyebrows at the expression. She knew he didn't mean they personally were done, but it still made her heart lurch. Watching him pace around outside, she let him calm down. They worked hard most of the morning, doing mock interviews and improving his posture and diction. He had loosened up so much in front of the camera. She knew he trusted her more.

Last night after their ravioli dinner, they lingered for a long time over their wine and watched the glorious sunset. The colors seemed so vivid on Capri—oranges and pinks she had never seen in the sky. He smiled when, yet again, she told him it was breathtaking. She asked him if he ever thought of making ravioli professionally, or even just pasta. He seemed to really enjoy that. He had looked at her astonished, saying he couldn't find a way to replicate the careful quality that was so important.

Finally, they had laid on a nearby double hammock with a blanket in the cooling night watching the stars, just holding hands, and not saying much. She had disappeared inside, only to return with a package of Oreos. He looked at her in horror, but after a while, she felt his hand reaching into her package. Smiling, she said nothing while he munched quietly on them. As the stars twinkled, it seemed like the most natural thing to turn to each other. She never knew a hammock could be so romantic. Her body tingled, remembering the kissing that was done. It had been a lovely night.

He was staring at her now, and she shook her head to bring her back to the present. "Okay, okay. I get it," she said. She looked at him curiously. "What I don't understand, Stefano, is a few minutes ago when it ran out of battery, you kept reading. I heard you when I came back with the charger."

He shrugged, but she watched a careful expression cross his face.

She looked at him, confused. "Is there something you're not telling me?"

"I have a photographic memory," he muttered.

Her mouth dropped open. "You what?"

"You heard me."

She shook her head. "Why is that a bad thing? That's amazing!"

He looked doubtful. "I used to get teased about it a lot in school. People made me feel like I was abnormal."

"Kids are stupid," Teresa said and then laughed. "Stefano, you know what this means? You don't even *need* a teleprompter. You can just say it! Do you think you can?"

"Yes."

"Okay, let's try it. Tell me what you were just reading."

He recited it verbatim, and her mouth dropped open. "That's a little…"

"See, I told you," he said roughly. "It's freaky."

"I was going to say incredible."

"I do not want to be incredible. I just want to be like everyone else."

She went over and gave him a little push. "No, you don't. You want to be like you. So, if I underline words in the script, I want you to punch up can you remember that, too?"

"Punch up?"

She smiled. "You know, use more expression and feeling."

At his nod, she spun around, twirling her arms. "I'm free!"

"What do you mean? I am the one over here doing it."

"Yes, but I don't have to convince you to do it." She smiled widely at him. "This frees up so much time! Want to bust out of here?"

He was clearly relieved. "Definitely."

"THIS IS THE BEST DAY EVER!" Teresa exclaimed as Stefano jumped off the chairlift. He suggested they take the chairlift ride from Anacapri to Monte Solaro, the highest point on the island. The only thing about the ride that disappointed Teresa was that it was singular chairs, and she couldn't ride with Stefano. She kept herself occupied by taking photos on the short ride. Once in a while, she turned around to wave at him with a grin. When she arrived at the top, he jumped off to lead her over and show her the breathtaking sights. It was a clear day, and they could see Mount Vesuvius, the Isle of Ischia, Sorrento, and the Bay of Naples.

"What are those rocks called again? I know you told me," Teresa asked, looking at the arching rustic structures rising from the sea.

Stefano smiled. "The *Faraglioni* rocks—one is called Stella, the second one is *Faraglione di Mezzo,* and the third, *Faraglione di Fuori.*"

She repeated it slowly. "I may have to ask you again," she

cautioned, only making him smile. He let her take a selfie of them before grabbing her hand to catch the chairlift back down. "Come on, I have an idea for lunch. I think you're going to like this."

They headed toward Capri Town in another vintage taxi before getting out prior to the busy area. Stefano led her up some stairs and she saw a restaurant. Assuming that's where he wanted to go, she started to turn into it, but he firmly gripped her hand and continued leading her up to a small alcove.

"HOT DOGS!" she yelled, seeing a vendor with a quaint hot dog stand. "Oh my gosh, like I said, best day ever!"

Stefano laughed. "*Mamma Mia*, I can't believe I'm doing this." He spoke to the vendor, who promptly gave them two dogs, with Stefano handing over a wad of euros.

"Um, expensive dogs," Teresa said, her eyes wide. "Did they really cost that much?"

Stefano didn't answer, calmly adding condiments to his hot dog. Teresa followed suit, and they went to a nearby bench to eat.

"Stefano, seriously. You gave that kid a lot of money."

"Forget it, Teresa."

"But..." She stared at him and smiled at his seriousness. He was looking ahead, calmly eating his hot dog.

"You're very generous to everyone here, aren't you?"

"I think you should mind your own business," he said, calmly taking another bite.

She elbowed him. "You're a softie, Stefano."

He turned to her, gently wiping some mustard off her chin. He smiled slightly. "Don't tell anyone."

They walked to the Gardens of Augustus, where Stefano impressed her with his knowledge of flowers and plants. As they strolled through the stone paths lined with deep colorful flowers, they stopped often at the statues dotting the grass, taking photos of each other.

"How do you know so much about this place?" Teresa asked,

MY CHRISTMAS IN CAPRI

putting her phone away. He looked a little embarrassed. "Mamma likes to come here. I bring her," he said simply with a shrug.

Teresa opened her mouth to tease him and then closed it. He really was sweet. Instead, she grabbed his hand and went back to enjoy the views of the *Faraglioni* from one side. Marina Piccola was on the other side, where Teresa marveled at the number of ships dotting the blue sea. Stefano pointed out the Via Krupp—a winding walkway with hairpin turns built into the rock, telling her it was currently closed. "Too dangerous," he remarked, because of the falling rock. They eventually walked leisurely down another route and through the pedestrian streets toward Capri Town's shops. She was surprised when he suddenly pulled her into a small store. "What are we getting in here?"

"I like that dress in the window," said Stefano, matter-of-factly.

He was greeted by name by the exquisitely dressed saleswoman, who spoke with him in Italian. Teresa uncomfortably shifted behind him. Wearing her white jean shorts and a simple top, she felt underdressed in the boutique.

The girl nodded several times before bringing a dress to Teresa, holding it up. The bodice was a solid royal blue, and the skirt had wide horizontal blue and white horizontal stripes. It was on the shorter side and sleeveless, and Teresa noted there wasn't much to the back.

"*Si*," said Stefano, smiling. He turned to Teresa. "Do you like it?"

"Well yes, but..."

"Try it on?" he asked in a wheeling tone.

"Stefano, I don't need a dress."

"Let me buy you something, *cara*. *Per favore*? He continued speaking in Italian playfully.

Teresa frowned. He knew when he spoke Italian, she would practically do anything for him. Whatever he was saying sounded sweet. "I can buy my own," she said, disregarding the fact that the boutique looked exclusive. She secretly wondered if that was true. It didn't matter because the saleswoman was determinedly leading her to a dressing room where Teresa slipped the dress on, feeling its silkiness against her skin. It fit her like a glove. She twirled around, looking at herself in the deluxe mirrors.

"Do you like it?" Teresa almost jumped at the sound of Stefano's voice right outside.

She cautiously opened the door to show him, feeling her face turning red.

"*Bellissima*," he breathed, looking into her eyes. "Teresa, let me buy this for you, *per favore*." When she frowned at him, he shrugged helplessly. "I like stripes."

She shook her head, grinning at his meek look. "Okay, but this is it. Nothing more."

He agreed quietly as she shut the door, hanging the dress up before putting her clothes back on. He seemed to be awfully friendly with the saleswoman. Was this a thing he did? Bring girlfriends in the store and buy them a dress? She instantly discounted it. While Stefano probably left a lot of hearts broken, he wasn't a player. It had seemed like a spur-of-the-moment idea.

It took just a few minutes for the woman to wrap up her dress in tissue and take the payment from Stefano. She walked around, pretending to look at other clothes, feeling embarrassed. She didn't know of any other time a man bought her clothes. Sure, she dated a lot in college and then men she met through work. No one had ever bought her clothes, though. It seemed so personal.

Strolling out of the shop, Teresa was quiet, soaking in the island's images, intentionally making a memory. Someday when she needed to, she would remember holding Stefano's hand and walking through the floral-lined streets and glancing out toward the water crowded with ships. "I thought we were going to the

Piazzetta," she asked suddenly, realizing they were headed back toward the villa.

"I thought we would go home and relax and get changed. Then return for dinner there tonight," suggested Stefano. "Does that sound good?"

She stopped walking and turned to him. "Stefano, this has been the most magical day. Thank you for my dress, but I hope you know it wasn't necessary."

He leaned down and kissed her softly. She realized he hadn't really done that all day, and she leaned in and let him kiss her deeper. "But this is," he breathed.

# nineteen

Teresa glanced around the restaurant at the elegantly dressed woman and breathed a sigh of relief she had worn the dress Stefano gave her. She had been surprised to see a silky jacket of the same blue in the bag. Leave it to Stefano to think of everything, including the cooling weather. Perusing the menu, she was glad there was food on it she liked. She glanced up to see him staring at her. "What?" she asked, raising her eyebrows.

"You look stunning tonight," he said quietly.

She preened a little. "Oh, this old thing?"

He grinned and then looked down at the menu. "Keeping with our perfect day, I'm not even going to make a suggestion. Order whatever you like."

"But it won't be the same if you don't at least mention vegetables."

He smiled gently. "You make me sound like an ogre."

"No, not at all! If my father was still alive, he'd appreciate it. He sure tried to get me to eat them," she said softly. "But they were usually canned and tasted awful."

"Tell me about him."

She took a sip of wine, stalling for time. She rarely spoke of her parents, finding it emotional. Often, she wished her brothers were around more to reminisce, though.

"He was a great dad," she said. "After my mom died, he was left with six kids ranging wildly in age who were in a sea of emotion. We all had different needs, and he tried really hard to help us all."

"Six kids. That is a lot."

"You're telling me. Anyway, let's not talk about it anymore." She looked away, feeling close to tears. Knowing if she started to really open up to Stefano, he would have even more of her heart, she was eager to keep things on a more impersonal level. "Is it bad if I order *Spaghetti Bolognese*?" she asked. "I mean, I know they just put it on the menu for tourists."

"It's a sound choice," said Stefano, smiling slightly. He ordered for them in Italian, laughing a great deal with the server. Teresa sat back, watching him. When he talked about food, his whole body relaxed.

Soon, a plate of bruschetta appeared, its ripe tomatoes overflowing on the rustic bread. Stefano promised no lectures on vegetables, but he ordered salads, which Teresa enjoyed. "Lettuce doesn't seem like a vegetable," she explained so seriously it made Stefano laugh. Her pasta was delicious, and she ate carefully, conscious to not splash on her new dress. Glancing over at Stefano's pasta with mussels, she shuddered silently, politely declining his mocking question regarding a bite.

Over dinner, they talked a lot about the island. Stefano told her he bought his villa about six years previously. Teresa knew he was two years younger than Marco—making him 31. She did some mental math, realizing he bought it when he was in his mid-twenties. Shoot, she was just three years younger than him —the only thing she owned was her beat-up car.

She tried to concentrate on what he was saying. He tried to get to Capri as much as possible, but he had homes in Milan and Rome as well. There was also the lemon grove, he told her. His mother gave them each a plot of land in case they ever wanted to build something there, and. Marco and Kate were going to break ground soon. Teresa wondered if his other homes were like the one on Capri. She was about to ask when he politely asked if she wanted dessert. She was stuffed for once and declined. Instead, they walked slowly around the Piazzetta, stopping to look at the views of ships—now small little lights in the sea. They sat for some time on a stone bench, just soaking it all in.

"Stefano, I feel like I know all about the island, but not a lot about you," Teresa commented, her head on his shoulder.

"What do you want to know?" he asked guardedly.

"Oh, I don't know. Tell me something personal."

"I am not sure what to tell you."

"I know Marco went to Stanford. Did you go to a university?" She felt his arms go tighter around her.

"Brown," he said finally.

She tried to imagine a younger Stefano in college. "Did you have fun there?" Glancing up, she saw a small smile. "I did. It was a good time in my life. No one knew who I was or who my family was. I was treated just like everyone else. Sometimes this country can seem very small."

Teresa waited for him to continue, but he was silent. Sitting up, she gave him a look. "I'm not trying to pry, you know, just get to know you a little more." She took a deep breath. "It's like you've built this wall around you, and once in a while, I'd just like to climb it and have a little look-see."

He chuckled then. "A look-see. I can guess what that means." He pulled her back into his arms. "What if you don't like what you see?"

"Impossible," she whispered.

He began to talk then, telling her about his college days in Rhode Island. He had loved New England and traveled all over, sailing as much as he could. "I love American beer," he told her with a smile. "And football games. Not soccer, like here, but

American football. And that's where I learned to like hot dogs, too."

She grinned. "Now we're getting somewhere." Feeling his chest rumble, she realized how much she loved that sound. Wanting him to hold her and kiss her, she stood. "Let's go home," she said with a smile.

# *twenty*

Stefano was in the pool, swimming gentle laps, waiting for Teresa. It felt great to stretch his muscles. He kept all his stress in his neck and shoulders, and both were aching. Trying desperately not to analyze this situation with Teresa, he knew they'd have to talk about the future. Kate called to remind Teresa she'd be expecting her in Positano soon and was planning their adventures.

It was almost time to decide if he was going to be a part of this project. Certainly, he'd put forth the work, but he still didn't know if he had it in him. He wanted to get it straight in his head before Lucca put the full court press on him. They were on a tight deadline, and Lucca had a crew standing by to start filming in a week. If he didn't do it, then Lucca would have to step in. Maybe Stefano could just serve as a consultant.

Stefano now knew he could be the host, though. Teresa gave him confidence. They spent the morning working on his posture, diction, and even his facial expressions. Teresa pulled in a gardener—this one spoke English—and made Stefano ask him about Italian herbs and tomatoes. She even put tape on the ground and told him to practice hitting certain marks as he walked so the lighting and camera operators wouldn't have to chase him down. They finally called it quits, and Teresa told him his progress was extraordinary. He realized how much her opinion mattered to him when he felt himself almost burst with pride.

Reaching the end of the pool, he stopped to observe a pair of feminine feet with shiny red nail polish. He looked up and was glad he was in the water. Teresa was wearing two pieces of bright pink cloth. Maybe that was a swimsuit, but it wasn't covering much of her. Swallowing hard, he glinted up into the sun. *"Dio,* you could have warned me. I might have drowned," he told her.

She put her hands on her hips. "You are so dramatic."

"You look gorgeous," he said sincerely.

She nodded, now looking a little embarrassed. "Either your cooking is too good, or this suit is shrinking because I swear it covered more of me the last time I wore it."

"I'll keep cooking then," he promised with mock sincerity.

She rolled her eyes and walked over to the stone stairs and got into the pool. They swam a few laps together, perfectly in sync. Afterwards, as they floated on their backs, she was oddly quiet, which unnerved him. "What are you thinking about?" he asked casually, coming alongside her.

"Tomorrow is our last day," she mumbled.

He nodded, looking over at her pensive face.

"What happens after I leave here, Stefano?"

"With us or the project?"

"Both," she said succinctly.

"To be honest, I am not sure," he said. Suddenly, he felt the pressure. Everything coming at him at the same time. His cousin's senseless idea was messing with his well-ordered life. Teresa, as beautiful and tantalizing as she was, created havoc with his senses. "Let's talk about it at dinner," he said. Swimming over to the side, he climbed out, grabbed his towel, and walked into the house.

TERESA ROLLED over and stared at the ceiling. Today was her last full day on Capri. Stefano had progressed nicely. He interviewed well, and now that he didn't have to read, he didn't even need the teleprompter. She worked with him on posture, how to hold his body and where to put his hands. Interviewing people was his strength. As long as they talked about food, he was charming and relaxed.

She was proud of the work they had done. Though she still worried he would freeze up, she guessed it didn't matter if he didn't have any intention of being on camera. Halfway through their sessions, she turned on the camera without him knowing. She uploaded the digital files because Lucca wanted to see them. Maybe he could persuade Stefano. She doubted it. He was so stubborn.

They didn't talk about anything regarding the future at dinner the night before like he had promised. Instead, he had turned on the charm, cooking her a delicious dinner of something called *Osso Buco*. It was some kind of meat she wasn't sure of, but it was darn tasty. She didn't want to admit it to him, but her cravings for junk food were diminishing. She still had a small stash in her suitcase that she hadn't even touched. Perhaps Stefano was a little right when it came to eating good food.

Throughout dinner and even afterwards while they watched the glorious sunset, he entertained her with funny stories about his brothers and Lucca as kids. They explored the house after that some more. She still got lost in half of it, and they finally settled into an upper outdoor area on a big comfy couch to watch the stars. Well, they glimpsed the stars. That was about it before Stefano's lips descended on hers, and his hands began to rove. She sighed. That was the best star gazing yet.

Now a knock on her bedroom door made her jump. She sat up quickly. "Come in," she called. Was it the housekeeper?

Stefano's serious face appeared at the door. "I am sorry. Were you sleeping?"

She shook her head.

"Can I come in?"

At her nod, he entered, wearing gray shorts and a white polo shirt. He was looking unsure of himself. He stood before her, and she gestured toward the bed. "Sit down."

He sat on the corner stiffly, as if he was scared to touch her.

"What, no breakfast in bed?" she asked sweetly.

He looked uncomfortable. "I should have thought. I'm sorry…"

She put a hand on his arm. "I'm only teasing, Stefano."

He looked down at her hand and then slowly picked it up, holding it, running his fingers down her palm. She felt tingles across her spine.

"I have a better idea," he said. "Why don't you get dressed, and we will grab a quick breakfast? And then we should take the day off. It is our last day. We should explore some more. There is so much you have not seen."

"Take the whole day off…" she repeated. Why not? There really wasn't anything else to do. It was up to him to decide if he was going to take the role. They should have fun on their last day. She had boasted to Stefano about life being short. "I'm in," she said. "What should I wear?"

"Just shorts and tennis shoes. The hike isn't that strenuous, but I want to make sure you see the arch."

She scrambled out of bed, her hand automatically going to her hair. He was staring at her. He cleared his throat. "I'll go get breakfast ready."

She could only nod as he strode quickly out the door. Suddenly, she smiled widely. Her last day was going to be perfect.

STEFANO GOT out two plates and utensils. The oven timer beeped, and he carefully took the frittata out of the oven. He almost made his favorite mushroom and sausage frittata. He smiled at the thought of presenting Teresa with a frittata filled with *funghi*. Taking it easy on her, he made it with pancetta and cheese. It smelled delicious.

He waited for her to appear now before he cut it. Why in the world did he think it was a good idea to take the day off? At least when they were working, he could keep his hands off her. Now they were going to go exploring. It was going to be a tough day and yet, he found himself looking forward to it.

She had looked so sad when she talked about it being her last day. That's why he purposely steered the conversation away from the future last night, aware he was procrastinating. It was just not something he was looking forward to. He went to bed thinking about her. It was in the early morning hours he came up with the idea to spend an unforgettable day together. Why not end it on a great note? Something they both could remember. Then he would take her back to Positano and resume his life. He frowned. Then what? Travel to Milan and work at Oro Industries? What was his future?

"*Buongiorno*," came a soft voice from behind him.

Teresa was standing before him wearing shorts and a T-shirt. He couldn't resist a small kiss before turning around to dish out the frittata. Over breakfast, she kept a steady flow of conversation going, and Stefano was secretly glad. He found her bare legs next to his as they sat at the island almost his undoing. All he had to do was stretch out his hand and slide it up her thigh.

"Are you ready?"

"What?" He looked at her, confused. How did she read his thoughts?

She smiled. "Ready Freddy? Let's get out there and explore."

He smiled and then leaned in and kissed her softly.

"Let's go have fun," he said gruffly.

~

"IT MAKES ME FEEL SO SMALL," she whispered.

"You are small," he pointed out.

They were standing looking at the *Arco Naturale*, a limestone arch in a scenic part of the island. The hike up there was worth it to see Teresa's face.

"I mean, it's so old and so, I don't know—significant. Thank you for bringing me, Stefano. This view right here I will hold in my heart forever."

Teresa gazed out at the spectacular view of Capri and the other small islands. It was a clear day, and Stefano pointed out several landmarks to her, talking about how Capri was only about ten square kilometers. He was like an encyclopedia, she thought, pulling dates and small facts out of nowhere. He explained there were Roman ruins to explore on the island as Capri was where the Roman Empire was run by Emperor Tiberius for the last ten years of his life. Maybe she would see them sometime, he said thoughtfully.

They sat down on a nearby rock and were quiet for some time, just breathing in the beautiful fragrances of nearby flowers and enjoying the view. His quiet question surprised her. "Are you ever going to tell me about the hospital? What happened?"

She sighed. She wanted to tell him, she realized. "I don't want you to think less of me," she mumbled.

"Teresa, I'm not going to think anything bad of you," he said, reaching over to play with a curl. "You can tell me anything."

"Well, the truth is I quit before I got fired," she said. "They were about to fire me." She turned to look at him, expecting him to look shocked. Instead, he just stared at her, his expression bland.

"They were upset with me because I kept breaking the rules. Stefano, the system is so unfair. I watched mothers with good insurance or lots of money have the best rooms, the best of everything—and those who didn't were treated differently. Of course, no one was denied medical care because that's against the law. It was the way it was given. All the conversations and questions. We had to justify everything for the mothers who couldn't afford to be there. I watched mothers with poor prenatal care and limited access to good food. Sometimes they came in with problems related to those issues. But if they managed to make it to full-term when they got ready to go home, you might say I borrowed a few things, maybe a few cans of formula or diapers. That sort of thing to send with them. It was donated—it wasn't from the hospital."

"Who donated it?" he asked.

She looked down. "Well, I did. Most of it, anyway. But they told me that I couldn't bring stuff anymore. This one nursing supervisor really had it in for me. She watched me like a hawk. And finally, she had enough documentation to take it to the Principal Nursing Officer. Some of it wasn't even true. I stole nothing from the hospital!"

"Of course, you didn't," he said.

"You believe me?"

"Teresa, you would never steal or lie. I know that about you at least. So, you quit instead?"

She nodded. "I didn't want them to be able to say they fired me. But the inequity of it all just got to me." She looked off into the distance. Two tears fell, and she roughly wiped them away.

"What else aren't you telling me?" he asked perceptively. He reached over now and put his arm around her, drawing her nearer.

She took a big breath. "My mother might still be alive if it wasn't for the stupid insurance system," she said.

At his raised eyebrows, she began to talk. She told him about her mother's cancer diagnosis, the endless appointments, chemo and then radiology. She was a child, but she overheard her father telling her older brothers the insurance company wouldn't approve of an experimental drug. Without it, there was nothing else doctors could do for her. "There was one nurse, though. This amazing one, Nurse Dee. She tried her hardest to constantly support us and she really inspired me because she was always rooting for the patient. I couldn't stop thinking about her. When I realized I wanted to make a larger impact on the world, I went back to school to be a nurse. I hoped to be like her."

"I bet you are like her," Stefano said, brushing a curl behind her ear. "I am glad you explained everything to me. I am sorry about your mother, Teresa. But you do not know if that drug would have saved her."

"It would have been nice to find out," she whispered.

"*Si*," he said, kissing the top of her head.

"And your father?" he asked gently.

"He never was the same," Teresa said. "Oh, he tried. My brothers went off every which way—to the Air Force, college, hospitality school, trade school. And he was left with this belligerent girl who wasn't the least ladylike and who loved getting into fights on the playground."

He smiled gently, thinking of a mini-Teresa fighting. "I bet you did. What were the fights about?"

"Anything. Everything. One time, one guy made fun of Katie's braces. I creamed him," she said, raising her head to smile at him.

"My dad worked so hard. He drove a truck delivering bread to stores. He picked up other jobs, too. I spent a lot of time with Katie and her family. That's one reason we are so close. And then my dad and I cobbled enough money for me to go to college—with loans and stuff. He died while I was at college. I think he knew he was sick before I went, but he wanted me to go so badly. One of my brothers was with him, so he wasn't alone."

"He sounds like a good man," said Stefano simply.

She sat up and looked at him. "That's funny, because he'd say the same thing about you."

# twenty-one

Teresa walked down the stairs, wearing her long red sundress again. It made her feel feminine, and tonight she wanted to feel that way. Walking into the empty kitchen, she glanced around for Stefano. Nothing. She walked across the expansive eating area to the doors and out to the patio. He was sitting at the table by himself, sipping wine. "Hey," she said softly.

He turned abruptly. "Hey, yourself," he said, standing with the good manners he always showed.

"Where's the food?" she asked, smiling.

"What food?"

"Stefano, every time I walk into this kitchen, you are surrounded by pots and pans and are busy creating something delicious."

He smiled slowly. "Tonight, we will cook together."

"You want me to cook with you? After the last time? You wouldn't even let me put my hand on a spoon to put filling on ravioli!"

He laughed. "I know, and I am sorry. Let me make it up to

you. I think the perfect end to the day will be creating something together."

She winced. "If you say so." She followed him back into the kitchen and he indicated two circles of rolled out dough on a giant wooden spatula. Laughing, she realized what they were cooking. "Oh, I get it. Pizza for the newbie. Well, I've got undiscovered talents. I'm sure of it."

"I'm sure you do," he agreed. He came behind her, tying the apron, dropping a quick kiss on her neck. "Tonight, we make pizza together." He turned around, getting out bowls of ingredients he already prepped.

"The trick is to not overload the dough. Do not put piles of ingredients on since this is a thin crust."

"Do you have any Canadian bacon and pineapple?"

"No," he answered succinctly.

"I thought you could make a Margherita, and I'll make a recipe that has been in my family for a long time. We can trade pieces."

"Hmm, tomato sauce and cheese, right? Some basil? I can do that," Teresa said. She began putting sauce on the dough, using the brush he gave her.

"Good, good, not too much."

"Are you going to oversee my whole pizza making?"

"No, no. Just get that corner over there. We have certain standards here," he said with a smile.

She rolled her eyes, pretending to care about his micromanaging. He could tell her how to make the whole pizza just as long as he stood next to her, looking at her so tenderly. He handed her the fresh mozzarella, already cut into pieces, and she added that. She was busy sprinkling basil leaves and then some oregano when she glanced at his. He spread olive oil on it and was now busy dotting it with something.

"What exactly is that?" she asked suspiciously, her nose twitching.

He shrugged. "Just anchovies."

"There's no way I'm eating anchovies. Just get that out of your head right now."

He smiled. "Teresa, you would never even know there were anchovies. Look, I'm tearing them into small pieces. It will just taste like salt."

She tried not to look repulsed. He was being ridiculous if he thought she was going to eat that. Finished with her pizza making, she watched him place dollops of tomato sauce near the anchovies. He added oregano, green onions, and then sprinkled parmesan over the top.

"Uh, that doesn't look like any pizza I have ever seen."

"Good, right? Tonight is about trying new things," he said, his eyes glinting. He leaned in and gave her a deep kiss. She dropped the brush she was holding and grabbed onto him, reaching up. He picked her up and sat her on the counter, not breaking their kiss. She wound her arms around his neck and through the hair on the back of head. Finally, they came up for air, and he leaned his forehead next to hers.

"We have chairs," she murmured.

He only smiled.

TERESA EYED the pizzas Stefano placed on the table. Once again, they were dining outside. She carefully set the table and nearby area with as many candles as she could find. She had turned on a portable speaker nearby and her playlist was streaming on it. Pouring two glasses of red wine, she sat sipping, waiting for him to come over from the wood-fired oven. The pizzas smelled delicious, and he was busy cutting them into small pieces. Putting one of each on her plate, he smiled at her.

"Try mine," he whispered. "*Per favore*?"

"Why do you care?" she asked. "I mean, it's only pizza. I'm happy just to eat the one I made."

He looked down at his plate and then away from her.

"Stefano...?"

He gave her a tentative smile. "Remember how I told you food brings people together? I just want to share something with you. This was a pizza my family ate at Christmas. Then we loved it so much, we asked ourselves why we did not eat it at other times. We decided it was because we looked forward to it. I guess I am being foolish. I am putting pressure on you to eat pizza. Do not worry about it."

She was oddly touched and put her hand over his. "You tried crackers with some butter and sugar over them. I can try this. But can I reserve the right to leave it at a bite?"

He nodded and watched her. She picked it up and tried not to think about anything but the glittering black eyes that were watching her. Taking a tentative bite, she chewed, before taking another.

"Well? Teresa, I have never seen you this quiet. Please do not eat any more. You tried it, and that is all that matters to me."

She smiled. "It's fantastic."

"Honestly?"

"Really." Cross my heart," she laughed, picking it up again. "It shouldn't be, but it is. Just as long as I don't think about what's on it."

They polished off the rest of his pizza, pushing hers aside, while they talked quietly about their day. Now he sat back, twirling his wineglass. She had noticed he did that when he was pensive.

"Thank you for listening to me today," she said softly.

He looked up and gave her a small smile. "I am glad you told me about it. It explains a lot about you."

"What about me?"

"Just the gaps. Why you are so fiercely loyal. Why you seem

to get such enjoyment about small things. Why you hate mushrooms..."

She laughed. "No, it doesn't!"

They were silent for a moment, lost in their thoughts. Finally, she wanted him to open up a little on their last night. "Stefano, now that you've heard about my job and my family, what about you?"

"What about me?"

"Can I ask about your dad? All I know is Katie said he left when you were little. Do you remember him?"

Stefano frowned into his glass, his face a shadow.

"You don't have to tell me," she said softly. "But it might fill in the gaps." At her same phraseology, he glanced up and shrugged. "It's only fair, I guess. I seldom talk about him. Marco remembers him the best, obviously, since he was older. I sometimes wonder what I remember—if I have seen the photos and filled in the story for myself. I remember him tossing me on his shoulders, and him tending to the crops. He had this big laugh, and it seemed like when he was around, my mother laughed more..." He trailed off.

"And then he just left?"

He nodded. "What I *do* remember is the years following. How sad my mother was. She had these three little boys. If it wasn't for my *Zio* Angelo—my father's brother—I don't know what we would have done. Marco had some learning issues, and so my mother spent a lot of time with him. Nico was the adorable, sweet kid."

"And you..."

He grimaced. "Classic middle child, just like you said. I was happiest with my nose in a book. When it wasn't, it seemed like I just got hurt. Books never hurt me. Numbers never hurt me."

He looked so vulnerable. She wanted to throw her arms around him, but something told her if she did, he would be uncomfortable. "Did anything besides books make you happy?"

He smiled gently. "Food made me happy because it meant that my grandparents or cousins were there or that it was a holiday. Sometimes my mom and I cooked together. The smells, the tastes all brought us together. Just eating this pizza tonight brings back the memories of staring at it in the oven, eating it with sausages at Christmas. Being together with family."

"I get it, I really do," she said softly. "Just like my grilled cheese."

He leaned over and kissed her. She put everything she had in that kiss, thinking of the small boy who suffered so much. The kiss went on and on until he abruptly stood, looking at her. He seemed to be thinking. "Come on, it's getting chilly out here."

She helped him bring the dishes in, and he put them in the sink. "Marta comes tomorrow—she'll put things right," he said. He was staring at her, and she shifted uncomfortably under his gaze. He finally grabbed her hand and led her into a small living area she had passed several times.

He sat down on a massive couch and drew her down with him. She turned to look at him, and he put his hands on either side of her face. Leaning in, he kissed her gently. "I do not want to let you go. Can we stay down here for a while?"

She found her voice. "We could, er, go upstairs," she pointed out gently.

He gazed at her for a long time. "We can't." He took a breath. "If we do, it will be harder to let you go."

# twenty-two

Teresa watched Stefano pilot his ship through the crystal waters of the Tyrrhenian Sea, heading to Positano. They had fallen asleep last night, with her laying her head on his chest. She woke to his gentle breathing in the early morning hours. Sitting up, she stared at him, realizing that he fully intended on walking away from her. It hit her hard. She got up, covering him with the blanket that was thrown over the couch, and then went to her bedroom alone.

The rest of the night she lay in bed awake, mentally kicking herself for even suggesting they take their relationship any farther. He not only slammed that door but made it crystal clear what the day would bring. She went downstairs with her suitcase and backpack. Stefano was just coming in from the construction area and saw them, eyeing her coolly. He informed her he would have brought them down for her, but she only shrugged, heading into the kitchen for a pastry or roll. Her stomach was in knots, and she wasn't looking forward to the ferry ride or Luigi's boat.

They arrived at Grande Marina, only this time, it was Stefano, dressed in khaki shorts and a black polo shirt, who guided her to a small yacht. A man, introducing himself to her as

Remo, was waiting for them and helped Teresa in, going back to retrieve her bags. She was surprised when Stefano left with a murmur about going up to the bridge deck to pilot the boat. She could see him up at the controls, navigating out of the marina and into the waters. Of course, living in Capri, he would have a ship of his own. He never told her he would be bringing her back to Positano and she frowned. Did he have to make everything a mystery? Honestly, he was the worst communicator. Why in the world did her heart ache so much for this man?

Watching him now up at the controls, she lovingly assessed every inch of him. His hair was ruffling with the breeze, his sunglasses on, he stared straight ahead. He looked confident and powerful. None of the vulnerability from the night before was evident. The walls were erected again, and she was on the outside. She longed to go up there, stand behind him and put his arms around his waist. It was apparent that gesture would not be appreciated. It seemed like the farther they got from Capri, the more remote he looked. She could tell even from her long vantage point.

The day was gray and overcast. Occasionally, she felt a drop or two and wasn't sure if it was rain or spray from the sea. She could have gone inside the cabin, but it fit her mood just perfectly, and she didn't mind. She donned jeans and the Capri sweatshirt she bought on impulse on their last day together. He frowned when he saw what she was wearing. Maybe she shouldn't have worn it in front of him. Perhaps he was already regretting starting anything with her. She shrugged. At this point, it was clearly over, so what did it matter?

She watched as he deftly navigated the yacht into Positano. Stefano finally stepped away from the controls and shouted something to Remo and the rest of the crew, who were busy tying up the ship. He came over to her and spoke for the first time that hour. "We'll go up the hill, and then I'll drive you to Marco and Kate's," he said as Remo lifted her bags onto the dock.

She thought about acting remote like him, but something inside her wanted him to squirm. Obviously, he was used to doing the dumping, and maybe he needed to feel a little of the pain. She smiled sweetly at him as if she didn't have a care in the world. "You know you don't have to. I can easily get myself there."

He shrugged. "Marco and I have a meeting scheduled anyway."

She almost rolled her eyes. He was better at this than she was. He singularly let her know he was taking her for the sole purpose of his meeting and nothing else. Deep down, she knew even if he didn't have a meeting, he would have taken her. Stefano was nothing but courteous. She walked beside him, watching people on the waterfront enjoying the day, despite its crispness. He stopped so suddenly she almost ran into him.

"Teresa," he started, closing his mouth as if he was trying to determine what to say.

"It's okay," she said softly. "You told me it was going to end. We both agreed. We had fun, Stefano." She gave him a quick little shove on his arm, like she would do if he was one of her brothers.

He looked at her inquisitively at first, and then a careful expression took its place. He nodded. "Yes, we had fun," he confirmed. He looked like he wanted to say more and stood staring until he finally started walking again.

She climbed the hill with him and then followed him into a small parking area where his black Mercedes was waiting for them. She opened her mouth. She was dying to know how things magically just appeared for him. It was like pulling the curtain away from Disneyland. She closed her mouth just as quickly. It was safer to remain silent. Besides, if a person has enough money, things magically *can* appear. She wouldn't know about that.

She settled into the comfortable leather seats and stayed

silent as they drove, twisting and turning. Finally, they pulled into the wide parking area in front of Marco and Kate's villa. This would be their last moment together with no prying eyes. She turned to him. "Well, thanks again. I had a great time," she said, pasting a smile on her face. "Capri was amazing and thank you for sharing your home with me. I hope I helped you whether you decide to do the show or not." She flashed a brilliant smile and went to open her door.

He made a frustrated sound and came around to open her door. She got out, and he put his hands on her shoulders. He took his sunglasses off and now his dark eyes searched hers. "Teresa..."

"Finally, I've been waiting all morning," said Kate, who was standing at the front door. Stefano dropped his hands as if Teresa's shoulders burned his fingertips. She turned around to see Kate coming toward them, and Marco trailing behind. Teresa walked around Stefano and went to give her friend a hug and kiss. "*Buongiorno*, Katie," she said gaily.

Kate laughed. "Learning some Italian, I see."

Teresa laughed, too. "Well, I got good morning and maybe dinner and food down."

Katie smiled. "That sounds like you. Well, come on in. Speaking of food, our chef made lunch for you guys."

Teresa walked in with Kate, aware that Marco said something sharply to Stefano in Italian. She glanced back. The two were talking intently.

"Don't worry about them," Kate said, as they walked ahead. "I'm sure they are talking business. They always are."

The women walked into the kitchen, where Kate introduced Teresa to Gino, the chef. "He doesn't speak any English, and I'm still learning Italian so it's kind of hilarious," she confided. "I looked up all the words for foods that I shouldn't eat while pregnant and wrote them all down. And when Marco is home, he helps. But it's good because it's making me practice my Italian."

Teresa took the plate Gino held out, her eyes growing wide. "Katie, you didn't!"

Kate laughed. "I did. I told him macaroni and cheese was your favorite. He was a little confused, but I showed him a recipe on the Internet. I think he understood."

"Well, it's not the blue box, but it looks really delicious." She smiled widely at Gino, giving him a thumbs up. The chef burst into rapid Italian, and Teresa just smiled and nodded.

Kate laughed. "Just keep smiling. It works fine. Come on. Let's go into the sunroom."

Teresa followed her and sat down on one of the colorful chairs, putting her plate and glass of lemonade down gently on the table. She took a deep breath. It felt good to be away from Stefano. They could have cut the tension with a knife. Though she was determined to show a brave face, it was the hardest thing she ever did.

Kate was busy talking, filling her in on her eating and how she was feeling. "I owe you, Teresa. I feel so much better. And I started doing the yoga you suggested. Thanks for that link. It's good because it makes me slow down and practice my breathing."

Teresa smiled and nodded. She was beginning to feel like she was back talking to Gino, but it was obvious her friend missed her. She realized Kate had asked a question. "Oh sorry, what?"

Kate looked at her suspiciously. "You're not eating. I thought it was good. You don't like it?"

Teresa smiled. "Oh no, it's really delicious. Sorry, my stomach is just kind of queasy after the ride over."

"Tell me what happened," Kate flatly demanded.

"Nothing happened. Just being on the ship kind of made me nauseous. You know what it's like. You're the one who always gets sick."

Kate put her fork down and looked at Teresa. "Yes, I'm the one who always does. But you're not. Teresa, I've seen you go on roller coasters over and over. Remember that time we went to the fair? You went on every ride multiple times while I stood and took photos of you. So, one brief ride on a ship is not going to make you sick."

Teresa looked down, scared any emotion would be evident.

"I should have known," Kate said.

Teresa looked up now at the tone in Kate's voice.

"You're homesick, aren't you?"

STEFANO TRAILED after Marco into the house. He almost got in his car and left after Marco's rebuke. His older brother was the most observant person in the world. One look and he had known something happened with Teresa. He assured Marco that things were handled. He and Teresa were fine. His brother eyed him suspiciously, but accepted Stefano's explanation without asking for any details.

"Teresa means everything to Katie," Marco stated firmly. "We owe her greatly for coming over when Katie called. You know Teresa never even asked a question? Katie told her she needed her, and Teresa got on a plane. She refused the offer of my private jet. She would have strapped herself in cargo if that's what it took. All because her friend said she needed her."

Stefano nodded, grabbing the leather bag he had brought with him from the car. "Teresa is a very loyal person," he said slowly.

Marco smiled for the first time. "Yes, and so is Katie. I apologize if I jumped on you about it. I just thought I sensed something more, and I can't have Teresa hurt."

"We have an understanding," said Stefano. Marco narrowed his eyes, but nodded and led the way into the house. They grabbed plates.

"Macaroni and cheese?" Stefano asked incredulously. "I haven't seen this since college."

Marco laughed. "Katie's surprise for Teresa."

Stefano glanced around. He wasn't sure where she had gone to. He wondered if she needed comfort food. His stomach was in knots, and he doubted he could eat much of anything. They filled plates and headed to Marco's study. Stefano listened to Marco's rundown of business issues he had missed. Stefano took out his computer and searched for a few emails Marco referenced. He did it automatically, without even comprehending the subject. Taking a deep breath, he tried to slow his mind.

Teresa's behavior was completely disorienting. She acted like the last ten days meant nothing. Did she care for him at all? When he woke up that morning, stiff from sleeping on the sofa, a large part of him was disappointed. He wasn't sure why, but he thought they'd have a moment. That she covered him up with a blanket and left was telling. Obviously, the moment was over. When he almost tripped over her bags, he realized she wasn't wasting time in getting back to Positano.

He knew he could have asked Remo to pilot the boat and spent a few minutes talking to her, but he was taking time to process the situation and had intended to discuss the future when they got to Positano. He was stunned when she cheerfully thanked him, almost as if he had spent the day with her showing her the sights. There was no emotion in her eyes at all. He went back to her words to Katie about it being part of her job. Maybe it all had been. Obviously, she seemed completely at ease with their parting.

He was relieved he decided to not go any further last night. It would be much more difficult to walk away from her. It was far better that she wasn't yelling at him or crying like so many women from his past had done. If that was so, why did it feel so awful right now?

"*Ciao*, Lucca," Marco said, and Stefano looked up to see his cousin on Marco's computer screen.

"Aren't you on your honeymoon?" Stefano asked dryly.

Lucca smiled. He was on the deck of Marco's yacht, the wind blowing through his hair.

"Yes, and if you must know, my bride whipped out her art supplies and is over there right now, painting the Greek isles," he said and laughed. "She begged for some quiet time with her painting, so I'm making a few calls."

Stefano let his mind be carried away. If he was on Marco's yacht sailing with Teresa, the last thing he would be doing is making calls. He could only imagine what he would be doing with her. He swallowed hard just thinking of it.

"But I'm not taking all day to talk to you two. We only have a few days left before Marco's helicopter comes to pick us up and take us to reality. Let's have it Stefano. Are you in or out? How did your training go?"

Stefano frowned. Now was the time of reckoning. He seldom said no to either his brother or cousin. This would be difficult. "My answer is still no. I am sorry. I just do not think I am any good at it," Stefano said firmly.

"Really? Because from what I saw, you're very good at it," answered Lucca with a big smile.

Stefano was confused. "From what you saw? What did you see?"

It was Lucca's turn to be confused. "Teresa didn't tell you? I asked her to upload some of your practice sessions. Honestly, Stefano, your interview skills are impressive. And you seemed very natural. Sure, there's a few tweaks here and there, but you can do this. I was excited."

Stefano stood, intending to go find Teresa. She never mentioned a word. That little spy! All this time, she'd been conspiring with Lucca. He had been completely duped. "I wasn't aware that Teresa was going to send any video," he finally said.

"I know. I think she felt funny about it, but I had to see. Stefano, if you were terrible, it would have put her in a tough spot. She would have to tell you. And she really didn't want to do that, so I persuaded her that I would be the bad guy. But I don't have to be because you were amazing. I couldn't believe it."

Stefano was processing what Lucca said. Did she really send the videos because she had his best interests at heart, or was she again just doing her job?

"Look, Stefano, I am going to play the family card. I have never asked you for anything in my life. But I know talent when I see it and you have it. Just four episodes. Please. It's my first project, and I want it to succeed."

Stefano put his hands over his temple and rubbed. He muttered to himself.

"What did he say?" Lucca asked Marco.

Marco smiled. "He said yes."

"I'M NOT HOMESICK," Teresa informed Kate. "Really, I'm not. It's just been a busy ten days, and I guess I'm tired."

Kate looked instantly contrite. "I'm so sorry, Teresa. Here I keep going on and on about myself, and you've had no fun, have you? What if we go shopping tomorrow? You've just seen bits and pieces of Positano. We'll start there, and then, if you want, we can go over to Sorrento. Or we can relax on the beach, though the weather is cooling. Whatever you want."

Teresa thought about the idea of watching a marathon show on TV and eating a carton of ice cream, but if she suggested that, Kate would know for sure she was trying to mend her broken heart. That was their ritual after every relationship ended. She nodded now, forcing a smile on her face. "That would be great, Katie."

"Mind if I interrupt?" Marco asked from the doorway. He entered and came over to drop a kiss on Kate's head.

"Where's Stefano?" Kate asked. Teresa looked at the doorway, waiting for him to appear.

Marco shrugged. "He's headed to *Milano*. He's stopping by the lemon grove to see Mamma and then taking the helicopter up. I guess he wants to get as much work done before filming starts."

"Wait, he's going to do it?" Teresa asked, her voice anxious.

"Yes. Lucca wore him down, but he agreed." His warm eyes turned to Teresa. "We can't thank you enough, Teresa. Sounds like you did wonders with Stefano."

Teresa could only nod. She had done wonders alright. So much so that he skipped out without even saying goodbye.

# twenty-three

"Teresa, your phone is ringing," Kate said, handing it to her with a twinkle in her eye. Teresa looked at her with wide eyes. Stefano? No, that was ridiculous. Why would he call her? She slowly stopped pedaling Kate's exercise bike and wiped her face with the towel. She probably rode to Naples and back by now, but the exercise felt good, especially after all the pizza Kate made her eat over the last week while they toured the Amalfi Coast. Unfortunately, it tasted like dust in her mouth.

It was also stressful to keep up a cheerful facade in front of her best friend. It was exhausting, pretending that her heart wasn't shredded. She was relieved every day when Kate had laid down for a nap. Teresa would then lie down too, and that's when she could let the tears fall. She wasn't sleeping well, and Kate quizzed her about that also. The charade couldn't go on much longer. Teresa was exhausted. It was during the lonely hours in the middle of the night that she admitted to herself she had given her heart 100 percent to Stefano. She hadn't meant to. She had really thought she could walk away. Obviously, he could.

She took the phone from Kate now and looked at it quizzically. That was when she saw Lucca's name on it. "Hi, Lucca," she said.

"Teresa, thank God. I need you. Listen, we started filming two days ago. Stefano isn't cutting it. He's stiff as a board. He's nothing like those videos you sent. Honestly, if I hadn't seen them for myself, I wouldn't have believed you. This Stefano is completely different."

Teresa climbed off the bike slowly. Kate had walked out, and she sat down now at the weight bench in Kate's exercise room. "Um, Lucca, I'm not sure what I can do to help. If he's not comfortable..."

"But he's comfortable with you! He obviously needs your coaching. Can you get up to *Firenze* tomorrow? Marco will make it happen on his end."

Teresa frowned. She was going to bring it up to Kate tonight that she should head home soon. "Um, I doubt Stefano would want me there," she mumbled. She wasn't sure what she was going to use as an excuse, but Lucca surprisingly supplied it for her.

"I know, I know. He was pretty upset that you sent me those videos of his rehearsal. But I told him you did it to protect him, and then he seemed fine with it."

"Oh, I didn't know you said that." She could already imagine Stefano's anger.

"I told him. I'm sorry. We should have discussed it. But I reminded him it put you in an awkward position if you were forced to tell him he sucked. He got it, and it's fine. I'm sure he'll feel much better when you're here."

She sighed. This was so incredibly awkward. Her mind was racing.

"*Per favore*, Teresa? I know I have no right to ask, and you and Katie are enjoying much-needed time together. I promise to pay you double what we agreed on for the coaching in Capri. I need you."

Teresa smiled for a minute. If someone had told her months ago that her Hollywood hero would beg for her help, she would have busted up laughing. Now it just made her apprehensive. The money did not even make her feel better. "Lucca, you're not paying me double. I will help, but I have one condition. Same as before. Stefano needs to agree."

"He's fine with it," Lucca assured her.

"You asked him?"

"Yes, I brought it up with him last night. He said okay but had the same conditions you do. You had to agree, too. You two crack me up."

Teresa did not know how to answer that and was relieved when Lucca continued. "Listen, Marco will get you on your way. I look forward to seeing you in *Firenze*. And thanks, Teresa."

Teresa hung up and went to update Kate, who frowned at the news. "These men! Don't they get you're *my* friend? You're supposed to be here with me having fun!"

"I know, but I mean, I bet once I get Stefano up and running in Florence, I'm sure he'll be fine for the rest of the series."

"If you have to stay the whole time, you'll be gone for weeks."

"I'm not going to be gone the whole time. Besides, it's not like I'm going to the Outback. You can always come see us wherever we are."

Kate smiled. "That would be fun. I'll be in my next trimester by then and probably feeling great, huh?"

"Yes, it will work out perfectly," Teresa said, smiling. At the beginning of the second trimester, women feel like they can do anything. It hits right before nesting. By the way, did you decide *where* you're going to have this baby?"

"Rome," said Kate. "Marco kind of wanted Milan, but I like the romance of Rome. If I'm not going to be down here, I'd much rather be there."

"That's great," Teresa said. "We'll, go tour the hospital when I get back, and then I'll have to think about my next move."

"You can always stay here with me," wheedled Kate.

Teresa hugged her. "I know and you're wonderful to even suggest it, but reality has to hit sometime."

Kate pulled away and regarded her thoughtfully. "We'll see."

STEFANO PACED THE HOTEL LOBBY. He looked at his watch. The driver texted him more than an hour ago that Teresa was in the car. He knew there was traffic in Florence, but this was ridiculous.

"*Ciao*, Stefano!" Teresa said cheerfully.

"Where have you been?" he asked louder than he meant to. "The helicopter landed more than an hour ago, and Giovanni said you were safely in the car."

"Just a quick stop," she said, waving a fast-food bag.

He groaned. "I should have known." Motioning to seats off to the side of the lobby, he nodded to Giovanni, who was taking Teresa's bags to the hotel's porter.

She glanced around at the opulent hotel, the polished gold mirrors, and Persian carpets. "Nice! Lucca's budget must be better than most."

Stefano frowned. Now was not the time to tell her that he was paying for his own lodging and food, as well as Teresa's. It felt ridiculous having Lucca's new production company pick up the tab, especially because he was the one who needed Teresa. Besides, he didn't want to stay at the touristy hotel with the rest of the crew and their prying eyes.

She took out her burger and fries, setting them on a napkin. "Mind if I eat? I didn't have anything this morning. I was a little nervous about the helicopter."

He inclined his head but looked at her quizzically. "Really? I would have thought you were looking forward to it. You assured me you loved that sort of thing when we took the chairlift."

Her cheeks were becoming pink, and he wondered if he had inadvertently discovered something. Was it possible she was nervous about seeing him? He crossed his legs and stared at her. She was intently picking out the pickles on her burger. "Every time," she muttered. "I say no pickles every time, and yet here they are."

He couldn't resist smiling at her. "How long has it been now since you ate fast-food? Your body must have gone into withdrawals, but I guess the detox is over," he said dryly.

She was chewing so she couldn't smile, but her eyes were amused. She nodded, taking a sip from her drink. "And Diet Coke, too. Man, it's a good day."

Stefano rolled his eyes before leaning forward. He regretted choosing the lobby for this talk, but he thought a more neutral place than a hotel room was appropriate. He glanced around to ensure their privacy. "Teresa, we need to talk. Obviously, this is very awkward. I want to apologize that you needed to come. It pains me to say this, but I need your help."

She was staring at him now. Pushing a fry into her mouth, she simply chewed. The silence made him uncomfortable. He finally continued. "I know things ended abruptly, but you must know that was the best way."

She picked up another fry and put it in her mouth.

"I probably should have talked to you a little more and told you what I was thinking," he muttered.

She slurped her drink, setting it down. "And we have a winner."

"What?"

"You finally said something worth listening to."

He frowned. No one ever talked to him like that. "*Mi dispiace*?"

She rolled her eyes, stuffing the rest of her fries in the bag and rolling it up. "You heard me, Stefano. You finally got to the bottom line. I've been sitting here waiting for that little nugget."

"Little nugget? I do not understand you sometimes," he said and sighed.

She laughed. "Join the club. Most people don't. Stefano, I'm not angry with you. We're adults. You told me things were going to end, but I didn't expect you to just throw me off the cliff—metaphorically," she added at his raised eyebrows. "I thought we were friends, at least. You just seemed so remote, and I wasn't sure why."

He couldn't keep her steady gaze. It unnerved him. He had been wrong. A crowded lobby was not the place to have this conversation. "This isn't…"

She interrupted him quickly. "If you're about to tell me this isn't the place to have this conversation, I swear to God I will pin you down and make you eat the rest of these fries."

He found humor bubbling up, and he couldn't hold it in. Laughter rang out—both him and her, and he shook his head. She could make him laugh like no other person. Finally, he found the right words. "If you try to poison me, Lucca is going to retaliate. My body would react violently to those disgusting oily sticks that they claim are potatoes."

"Oh please, quit with the 'My Body Is a Temple Act.' You'd love them. That's why you don't want to try. You'd be more addicted than me!" she said. She stood and held out her hand. "Truce? Let's get back on track as friends. Let me go to my room and get my stuff, and we'll head to the studio Lucca's renting. I need to see the dailies and see what you've been up to."

He accepted her small hand, holding it for a minute. It was a fight to hold off his desire to wrap his arms around her and kiss her senseless. He needed to keep her as a friend. How was that going to even work? He had no choice. "Friends," he agreed quietly, knowing deep in his heart that it wasn't going to be possible.

# twenty-four

Teresa looked into the mirror and sighed audibly. She looked awful. Quickly, she washed her face, brushed her teeth, and re-did her make-up. She wanted to stop somewhere when Giovanni picked her up, but he rushed her into the waiting car. It was all she could do to convince him to stop for a snack. As it was, she hadn't even really wanted it. It was just her way of inciting emotion from Stefano. It took all of her strength to nonchalantly brush his apology aside from downstairs. Wait. Did he apologize? She frowned. Not really. He had only admitted that he should have taken more care in...well, dumping her.

There was no way he was going to witness her broken heart. She had too much pride for that. Lucca was relying on her to do a job, and that's what she was going to do. Whatever it took to get Stefano ready, she would do, collect her ginormous paycheck and go back home. This was business. Things didn't work out sometimes, she reasoned. He warned her in the beginning. And now he needed her. Sure, she could tell him to go fly, but where would that get her? A twisted part of her wanted to show him she could do this—that he meant so little to her it was easy for her to show up and get him on track.

Squaring her shoulders, she gave herself one more appraisal. The new colorful top and floral skirt she bought in Positano looked nice on her. It felt good to splurge and buy a few new things, considering she hadn't brought that many clothes with her. Who knew she was going to stay this long? And now that the weather was changing, she would soon need a few sweaters.

Riding the elevator down to meet Stefano, she gave herself one more pep talk and exited. He stood near the doors, wearing dark blue pants and a white dress shirt. She swallowed hard. He looked very handsome and impatient. Both were normal.

"There you are," she said again and watched him frown. She loved saying that in a sing-songy tone that always made it seem like he was the one that was late.

They walked through the hotel's front door, and he signaled to Giovanni, who was waiting in a nearby car. Stefano held the car door open, and she slid in and then realized he was coming in behind her, forcing her to slide over as close to the door as she could.

"I won't bite," he whispered.

"I know that," she said more curtly than she intended.

"The studio isn't that far away," he said, changing the subject. "I think you will like the crew. They all seem good at their jobs and very professional. Some are Italian and some American. Lucca said he already blew some of his budget by hiring who he thinks is the best. He is so desperate for this to be successful."

She nodded. "He sounded a little panicked on the phone."

Stefano was looking out the window. "I have never seen him like this. He is usually so relaxed. This means a lot. I feel like I am letting him down."

Her heart melted. Before she could think about it, she picked up his hand, which was lying on the seat. "Oh, Stefano, you're not. Really. I'm sure it's nothing we can't fix."

He was looking at their clasped hands. She felt him squeeze hers suddenly. "Thank you for coming."

TERESA LEANED over the Director of Photography's shoulder and watched the dailies on the screen. There wasn't much to watch. Lucca obviously saw the handwriting on the wall and directed the crew to spend more time getting B-roll—the shots they would need without Stefano in them.

Normally, she would think getting paid to watch Stefano on video would be a win-win, but this was cringy. What happened? He was so awkward and stiff. Even during his interview with a cheese monger in the *Mercato Centrale*, a public fresh food market in Florence, he stood awkwardly, asking a question, and then looking like he was not interested in the answer. His eyes darted all over, watching crew members move around. She shuddered internally, carefully to keep her face a mask since he was watching her reaction intently. She had seen enough and turned away, making a motion to stop.

"Okay, well, I see you picked up some bad habits, my friend. We'll get those cleaned up, and you'll be good to go."

Stefano stared at her, clearly tense, a muscle twitching in his cheek. "This was a stupid idea," he said quietly. "I should never have let them talk me into this."

She smiled reassuringly. "Stefano, it isn't that bad. It's nothing we can't fix."

"How fast can you fix it?"

"Well, considering that Lucca wants you on set this afternoon, I would say that it's going to have to be really fast!"

"What?" he thundered.

"He emailed me the call sheet. You have a call time this afternoon. You're talking someone named Franco who owns a famous *panini* shop."

Stefano grimaced. "I saw that, but I didn't think it was still on the schedule. I thought he would give us some time to rehearse. Lucca told me about Franco. He's a good friend of Ellie's and wanted to give him the publicity. This episode is going to be about the Florence *panini* and then, of course, the famous *Bistecca alla fiorentina.*"

Teresa glanced around and saw a small office. "Let's go in there and sit down. I have an email with the show notes and script, but do you have a hard copy?"

He pulled them out of a leather portfolio, and she quickly reviewed them. "It seems to be a straight-forward interview. You can glance over the intro and do that on your own. Let's go over the interview with Franco. I'll be Franco, and you ask me questions. They want you to ask about his background and why he does what he does, but then it looks like you can ask more detailed questions about what makes Florence sandwiches so unique." She quickly got up and stood next to him, showing him again what his posture should be.

"Franco, what do you think makes a panino in *Firenze* different from anywhere in the world?" he asked Teresa solemnly.

"Well, it's the mayonnaise. You have to have good mayonnaise," Teresa stated.

Stefano threw up his hands. "It is not the mayonnaise. I cannot practice with you if you are going to make up stuff, Teresa!"

She sighed. "You asked the question perfectly. Very conversationally, just a little too stiff." She picked up the paper and scanned it. "Let's pretend that I go on and on about these various sauces that sandwiches in Florence have. What are you doing while I'm answering?"

He nodded, smiling a little.

"Stop nodding!"

"Why?"

She tried not to show her exasperation. "Remember, we went over this on Capri? Don't keep nodding. You'll look like a bobblehead!"

"A what?"

"Just don't nod, okay? You can smile slightly but look like you're really listening."

"How does one look like they're listening?"

"Well, you keep eye contact. You don't glance back at the camera or look around at the crew. Forget about the camera. It's just you and Franco having this talk. And if you think you're messing up, like stumbling over a question, just take a breath and ask it again. This isn't live television. They can easily cover it with B-roll and then cut out your next question if they don't like it."

"What's B-roll? I was too embarrassed to ask anyone," he admitted quietly.

"I'm sorry, I should have explained that. The camera crew will get all kinds of shots—people eating sandwiches, the sandwiches themselves, Franco preparing a sauce, cutting up meat, whatever. Then they can cover the edits that way."

Stefano nodded. "Oops, sorry, head nod."

She smiled. "It's okay, Stefano. We aren't on camera.

LATER THAT AFTERNOON, after the lunch rush was over, they arrived on set in front of Franco's shop in a popular area in Florence, near the Duomo. Teresa glanced around, watching the crew setting up. A few sprinter vans lined the narrow street and were wedged as close to the café as possible. What appeared to be a customized van was off to the side.

"Thank God," came a voice Teresa knew well. She turned to see Lucca coming toward her, wearing jeans, an old T-shirt and a baseball cap. His security was standing discreetly behind him. She accepted his kisses on each cheek and beamed at him, ignoring Stefano's dark look he shot her. What was with him? His cousin just got married, for goodness' sake!

"Hey, Mr. Director, I'm reporting for duty," Teresa said.

Lucca smiled. "I appreciate you coming out. We need to nail this today. Third time is a charm," he said, glancing quickly at his cousin. "Stefano, you can go to the trailer and check in with wardrobe and hair and make-up while I show Teresa around and introduce her to everybody."

Stefano frowned. "I thought what I am wearing is fine. And do I have to put make-up on again? No one," he said, enunciating the words, "told me I would wear makeup."

Lucca smiled and whispered to Teresa, "Diva, already." Turning back to Stefano, he spoke to him in Italian. Stefano finally nodded and left to go into the trailer.

"What did you tell him?"

"Mostly threats," Lucca said and smiled, but then his face turned serious. "Do you think he can do it, Teresa? We honestly tried everything. You saw the dailies?"

She nodded and winced. "I get it. Look, I don't know if I can wave a magic wand. This shoot might take a little longer than normal, and we may have to just keep rolling until we get what we want. But I worked with him for a couple of hours, and I think he can do it. If nothing else, we may have to do it in smaller shoots. I hope you have plenty of B-roll video to cover him if we don't."

Lucca rolled his eyes. "We do. But my hope is the viewer would connect with Stefano. I wanted his knowledge and passion for the way we eat to come out. Instead, I got Mr. Cardboard. I'm really nervous about this project. I want everything to be perfect."

Teresa smiled and put a comforting hand on his arm. "We'll get there. By the way, where is your new bride? I know she calms your nerves."

He smiled at the mention of Ellie. "She's in Tuscany. We ended up buying her parents' villa. Of course, they wanted to just give it to us, but we bought it from them and she's having to sort through their stuff. Some movers were coming today to get some of their furniture out so we can make it more of our place. She may join us at some point, but she's tied up at least during this shoot." He sighed before putting his arm around her. "Come on and meet the crew."

Entering the shop, Lucca introduced her to the Production Manager, Ian, and Assistant Director, Autumn, who were going over the call sheet. They both shook her hand distractedly before returning to their tasks. A sound guy hurried by and waved a greeting before going into the equipment van. Lights were already set up, and the café was ready.

"Teresa, is that you?"

Whirling around, her eyes widened. "Andy!" she said, flying into his arms for a bear hug.

STEFANO WALKED INTO THE CAFÉ, readjusting his shirt. Wardrobe chose a sage green shirt and off-white pants for him to wear. Both were more casual and made with lighter material. It felt very different from the tailored clothes he normally wore. He felt a little uncomfortable, but he was doing his best to adapt and not touch his perfectly styled hair or face. Feeling ridiculous, he looked over to see Teresa in the arms of a giant of a man who was intent on squeezing her to an inch of her life.

"Andy! What are you doing here? Oh my gosh, it's so good to see you!" she said and then laughed.

Andy's arms were all over Teresa. Stefano kept his hands to his side, clenching his fists. He'd like to pry those arms right off of this guy. Andy finally pulled back from her. "You, too! I can't believe it. Wait till some of the guys hear. This is amazing!"

Stefano stood awkwardly while Teresa and Andy caught up. Apparently, they'd worked together in San Francisco for a couple of years. Teresa was telling him about her nursing, as well as the parts of television she missed. They discussed a former co-worker and some scandal when Stefano finally cleared his throat. Teresa turned around, giving him a smile. "Andy, have you met Stefano yet?" she asked politely.

They both nodded. "We met a few days ago at the first shoot," Stefano said. "You two used to work together?"

Andy grinned and put his arm back around Teresa. "Teresa was one of the best producers at the station. She ran a tight ship. It was always great when she was at the helm. I left a little after she did. Hey, T, we'll talk later. I can see Autumn waving at me. I better get finished setting up."

Andy hurried off, and Teresa turned back to him now. "Lucca really picked the best. Andy is great at his job. Okay, let's take a look at you," she said.

"I can't believe I have to wear make-up," he muttered. "They sprayed it on with this small device. It's unbelievable."

"Stefano, it's just some base make-up. Everything is shot in such high definition these days that everyone has to wear makeup. Or else the viewers are distracted by every little mole or freckle. Believe me, when you see yourself on television, you'll be glad you wore something."

He grimaced. "I doubt I will ever watch."

"Stefano, we're ready for you," Autumn said from behind them.

Teresa beamed at him. "It's time. Okay, roll your shoulders."

Stefano frowned at her, but Teresa was insistent. "Come on, roll your shoulders like we used to do. Now push them toward your earlobes and hold and down. Okay, roll them back again and put your head to the side. Now smile wide at me."

He gave her a large fake smile. She grinned at him. "You're ready."

Stefano went to stand by Franco, towering over him. The older man, slightly balding and heavy-set, was rubbing his hands together nervously. They listened to Lucca describing the shots he wanted and how the interview should go. It was pretty much what they had practiced. Stefano listened but was distracted watching Teresa deftly skirt a light and walk to the back, obviously keeping out of the way.

They began the interview, and Stefano talked with Franco about his beginning, his family's roots and why he liked owning the shop. A couple times, Stefano glanced over at Teresa, and she frowned so fiercely at him, he realized he was doing what she said not to. He carefully re-asked the question then and stared straight at Franco. Doing everything he could not to nod, Stefano found himself asking some follow-up questions that weren't in the script. Soon, he realized he was enjoying talking to the older man. Lucca stopped them a couple times to give them a little direction and to beg Franco once again to keep his answers a little more succinct. Stefano was reminded not to look over at the boom operator. "Just talk, Stefano. We have a mic on you as well, so you don't have to worry where he is."

They changed course then, and Stefano stood by, watching Franco assembling a favorite panino of Florence—filled with beef, and then cooked with onion, parsley, celery and tomatoes. Franco told Stefano it was the salsa verde—a green sauce that made it so delicious.

The filming stopped for a minute to adjust the lighting, and Stefano glanced over to see Teresa conferring with Lucca, who soon strolled forward. "Stefano, why don't you slice up tomatoes or dice some celery or something? We need you doing something, or else you're just kind of looming over Franco."

Stefano was relieved. He'd much rather be working in the kitchen. He donned an apron and cut tomatoes and joked with Franco. This was more fun now. Together, they built a giant panino.

Lucca and Autumn conferred for a few minutes and were finally satisfied. "Stefano, take a break. We're going to get a few more shots of the ingredients and of Franco. You can practice your intro outside."

Stefano and Teresa went outside, and she handed him the script. "Have you read over it?"

He frowned. "Yes, I made a few changes, though. I don't know who these writers are that Lucca hired. They don't seem to truly understand Italian cuisine."

Teresa laughed. "Okay, well, do what you have to do. Now just walk toward me and talk. It would be good if you smile occasionally, too."

"When do I smile?"

She tried not to laugh. "Let me see it." Teresa read it over again, grabbing a pen from her pocket. "Here, here and maybe here." Just give a small smile. Can you remember to do that?"

He nodded. She gave him a look. "Don't nod." At his glare, she held her hands up. "Just getting you in the mood. Knock 'em dead."

"Aren't you supposed to tell me to break a leg or something?"

She rolled her eyes. "Just get it done, okay? Those sandwiches looked pretty good. I really want one."

He smirked and walked over to where the crew set up frames with light diffusers, ready for his intro. "Franco Cavalli began making sandwiches at his grandfather's elbow. His family has operated this small panini shop for three generations, and it has become a popular place for students who study abroad. They flock to Franco's because of his presence on social media but also because he has never altered the way he makes the famous sandwiches of *Firenze,* in which he uses…"

TERESA'S SMILE GREW WIDER. This was the way they had practiced. While Stefano wasn't as relaxed as he was on Capri, he was loosening up. Lucca made him do it four times, and some of her wondered if he was just messing with Stefano. The fifth take seemed to satisfy him, though, and Stefano disappeared into the trailer and came out in his original clothes. "Franco's is closing—that is why we did it now when he was not busy. What about if we..."

She bit her lip. If he was going to ask her to go out with him, she would have to refuse. Spending even more time with him was not a good idea for what little of her heart he had not broken.

"Teresa!" She turned around at Andy's voice. "What do you say we go grab something to eat? I know you. We'll find pizza or something. I'm dying to talk to you. We have so much gossip to catch up on."

Teresa looked quickly at Stefano and then back at Andy before nodding. "I'd love to, Andy. Stefano, do you want to join us?" she asked politely.

There was a dark look on his face, but quickly his expression went back to his usual neutral self. He shook his head. "No thank you. You should catch up with your...er, *friend*."

She ignored his small jab. "Then I'll see you tomorrow. Sounds like we have some kind of steak first thing. I'll text you, and maybe we can meet before your call time." She quickly walked away with Andy, trying to look like she was happy. Part of her felt relief, as it was all she could do to keep up her nonchalant attitude. It was wearing her down. She turned to Andy and gave him her full attention.

# twenty-five

"God, that smells delicious," Teresa said, sniffing appreciatively. She walked into the kitchen, and one of Florence's most renowned and oldest restaurants known for their *Bistecca alla fiorentina* –a rare beef steak on the bone that she was told was one of the most famous dishes in Tuscan cuisine.

"How can you want to eat steak at seven in the morning?" Stefano grumbled. "I can't believe we needed to do this so early."

Teresa shrugged. "Lucca said the restaurant wanted to be involved, but they are booked solid with reservations. There's no way they can close, and it would be too chaotic while they are serving. So, morning it is. You'll feel better once we get a little protein in you."

Stefano winced. "It smells delicious, but it is going to be hard to eat *Bistecca* this early. Especially since I got so little sleep."

"Well, you're going to have to Cranky Pants," said Teresa matter-of-factly. "It's in the script. We've been over this, Stefano. After all the chit-chat we practiced, you need to take a few bites." She ignored his glare and kept walking into the set. Stefano already got dressed and was in the dreaded make-up trailer, and they were ready to go.

Teresa knocked on his door at five in the morning, just as she promised in her text the night before. Truth be told, she and Andy found some pizza as promised, and she was back in her hotel room early the night before. In a twisted sense of rebellion, she decided Stefano didn't need to know that, so she waited to text him a few hours later. He had opened the door this morning with his hair still ruffled, wearing just jeans. She swallowed hard, watching him quickly put a shirt over his head, his muscles rippling. Wisely, she had sent coffee and pastries to his room, and she chomped on a *cornetto,* an Italian version of a croissant, while Stefano practiced some of his lines.

He seemed even more versed in the Florentine steak, telling her all about it on the walk over about how it was important the meat be aged for two weeks and grilled over charcoal embers with oak or olive added. The meat, served rare, must be thick enough to stand on its side, he explained earnestly.

Watching him interview the chef, Teresa felt a renewed sense of confidence in Stefano. The interview segment went well. It helped that the chef was young and already award-winning. He had been interviewed many times and knew exactly what to say. This time, Lucca started with them cooking together. Stefano was so much more relaxed with a knife in his hand and moved around the kitchen with confidence. Lucca only stopped him twice because he either spoke with his back turned or moved too far out of the shot.

"I can't cook and think about all this film stuff," grumbled Stefano, but Teresa noticed he never made the same mistake twice. She watched as the steak was almost finished, and the chef drizzled olive oil and added fresh herbs to it.

They took a quick break while the steak rested to grill some vegetables. Those were not needed in Teresa's opinion, but the chef was insisting on it. Now it was time to try it, and the chef expertly cut a section off and he and Stefano took a bite.

Her stomach grumbled. That looked delicious, but then she grew concerned, realizing she hadn't practiced with Stefano how to eat on camera. Hopefully, he wasn't going to take a big bite, or else he'd be chewing and there would be dead air. Her heart sank. They chewed and chewed. Lucca called cut and shot her a look. She shrugged and approached them.

"That smells delicious," she said enthusiastically, giving Marcello, the chef, a big smile. "But we need you to take a small enough bite without it being obvious. That way you can chew it quickly and then swallow it or else we just have dead air. And then Stefano, you have to start talking immediately, telling him how good it is." Beaming at both, she walked away and gave Lucca a nod.

The two repeated the shot, and this time Stefano chewed quickly, except he praised Marcello in Italian, going on and on. He must have realized what he did because he quickly changed to English, slapping Marcello on the back.

Lucca yelled cut. "I think we're actually going to use that, Stefano. It was real. We'll subtitle you, but it's authentic. Take a quick break, everyone, while we get some more cutaway shots."

Stefano walked over to her. "I can't believe I spoke in Italian."

She laughed. "It must get exhausting, always having to speak English. It's fine. I think Lucca is right, and it is more authentic. People will love it. Italian is such a beautiful language." She sniffed. "But right now, if someone doesn't give me a bite of that steak, I'm going to lose it."

STEFANO WATCHED Teresa inhale several bites. Fortunately, Marcello had three platters of the meat sitting on the side for the cameramen to film. Once they were done, everyone took a sample. Teresa was going in for her fourth, if he counted right. He watched her expressive face, loving how much she obviously was enjoying it.

"I am glad you get to taste what real beef is like," he commented dryly.

"Okay, okay, it's not my usual fast-food burger. I get it, but now is not the time to rub it in. I can't spend time talking. I have to eat."

He laughed and went over to the front of the restaurant where he was going to film an intro. Once again, he glanced over the script, changing it in his mind. Lucca hadn't minded his edits so far, even encouraged him. He glanced back at Teresa, who was joking with Andy and taking another bite, saying something about stabbing him with her fork if he got in her way.

Part of him should be relieved she was busy last night. Today, he noticed the wedding ring on Andy's finger, but that only made him feel marginally better. Late last night while he was waiting for her text, he admitted to himself he was wondering if they ended things too early. Of course, he didn't have any idea they would be thrust together again. The realist in him told him to keep it strictly business and then move on with his life. Still, he was finding it difficult to resist the tug to spend more time soaking in Teresa's happiness and enthusiasm for everything—well almost everything. There were foods that she was definitely not enthusiastic about. He admitted his heart felt lighter around her, but he knew he was treading on uneven ground.

"Ready, boss?" Andy asked Lucca, as they all moved into position. Stefano rolled his shoulders and put them up to his ears a few times. He glanced over at Teresa, a small smile on his face.

This time he didn't have to walk. He was supposed to stand in one place and say his lines. He did so several times and looked over to see both Lucca and Teresa shaking their heads. Teresa was whispering in Lucca's ear.

"Stefano, we need some kind of movement. I think we're

going to set back up at the market, and we can try there again. You can walk by the butcher's case. We probably need to get a few more shots there anyway." Lucca turned to the crew. "Let's just say two hours from now, everyone."

Lucca approached Stefano. "Teresa is right. You were great, but the market just makes it livelier. Why don't we grab Teresa and go to lunch? Then we can head down to the market and resume shooting."

Stefano sighed, knowing that meant changing and putting make-up on all over again. "That sounds good," he told his cousin. "Though I'm not sure if Teresa is hungry anymore."

# twenty-six

Teresa gratefully stretched out on the bed. It had been a tiring day. Thinking it over, she admitted the fatigue was probably from having to keep up a charade in front of Stefano and now Lucca. She longed for the days in Capri where she could lean over and kiss Stefano or just grab his hand. Today, she found her nails tightly pricking her hands as she kept them in fists. Her job was to watch Stefano and yet she was finding that to be very difficult. Keeping a poker face was not something she was known for or particularly good at.

Ignoring her stomach grumbles, she wondered how the last shoot went. The crew needed Stefano to stay and film a few more scenes in the market. Since he was doing so well, she walked away, looking at the cases of meats, pasta, cheeses, and rows of produce. Not a goldfish or Oreo in sight. She'd kill for a red licorice rope right now. Her old cravings were back in force—probably emotional eating, she reasoned. Finally, she bought a box of chocolate cookies, but they hadn't staved off her cravings. At some point, she would have to get up and find a room service menu, though when she looked at it the other day, it was uninspiring.

Lunch was more fun than she thought. She went with Stefano and Lucca to Franco's, and they shared his delicious panini. Teresa sunk her teeth into the meat and cheesy goodness and never wanted to stop eating. Lucca amused them by telling stories about how he and Ellie went there on their date in Florence, and Franco gave him the evil eye like a father. Lucca laughed, but his face clouded for a minute, as if he was remembering something negative about the day. Franco joined them at one point, and Teresa listened to the three men discuss food as if it was a religion.

Stefano was in his element at the market, walking amongst the stalls. She was impressed, as he pointed out different things to the crew during breaks. His demeanor was growing friendlier with them. It probably helped that they were all soaking in his knowledge, asking him a lot of questions. Autumn seemed to really be warming to him, and Teresa frowned at the thought. At first, she hadn't paid much attention to the tall blonde with the beautiful blue eyes, but now she was having second thoughts. Autumn came up to Stefano's shoulder, and she had seen her smiling into his eyes. Turning over, Teresa closed her eyes and tried to shut off her mind.

Two hours later, Teresa blinked her eyes open. It was astonishing to see the time. She must have been more tired than she realized. Picking up her phone, she thought about looking for a restaurant nearby and picking something up. She was surprised to see a text from Stefano. Maybe that was what woke her up. The text was simply an address. It couldn't be another shoot. The crew was already on their way to Rome, their next location. She quickly texted a question mark back.

Stefano's answer was immediate: *Cena at eight. Text me when you arrive.*

Well, he might invite her rather than just ordering her to come to dinner. Should she go? Lucca was probably going to be there, too. It would be nice to have dinner with them even if she needed to keep up appearances. She wasn't used to hanging out in a lonely hotel room and though she knew she could always reach out to Kate, she didn't want to interfere with her friend's time with her husband.

Glancing at her watch, Teresa yelped at the time and went to take a quick shower. Exiting the hotel shortly after, she ran her hand down the silky black and white polka dot dress Kate helped her buy in Positano. She didn't know how fancy of a restaurant it was, but she felt good in her new dress.

Waving to the valet, she smiled when he instantly got her a taxi. She showed the driver the address, and he nodded, winding through Florence's narrow cobblestone streets with break-necking speed. When they pulled up in front of a building, he pointed to it.

"This can't be it," Teresa said, looking at the building.

"*Si, si,*" he insisted, gesturing toward the fare box. She handed him some euros and got out quickly, watching him speed away. Oh, it must be where Lucca was staying. After all, he couldn't very well stay in a hotel without being bothered by fans. Dutifully texting Stefano as instructed, she stood, tapping her foot in its high-heeled sandal.

"You found it," said Stefano from the door. "Come on in." He led her to a small elevator, and they wedged themselves in. She was tightly pressed up against him and took a big breath. God, he smelled fantastic. Instead of cologne, she smelled garlic and maybe onions. She smiled into his chest, thinking about how much that scent was better than a men's cologne. They were so close she couldn't even lift her head.

The doors opened into an apartment. "Where's Lucca?" she asked, as they exited the elevator. Glancing around, she saw big wooden Italian furniture and luxurious Persian carpets. The room was very old-fashioned, but beautifully furnished.

"He's not here. Did you expect him to be?" Stefano asked dryly.

She felt herself flushing. "Oh no, sorry. I guess I just assumed this was where he was staying. What are you doing here?"

"Cooking you dinner," he told her. "This was my *nonni's*—my grandparent's apartment when they came to the city. It has been in the family forever."

"You cooked me dinner?"

He smiled. "I told you. Cooking relaxes me and, well, it's hard to eat alone. Lucca drove back to Siena to see Ellie, and the crew left for Rome. So, it is just you and me."

Teresa swallowed hard. Put like that, she found her mind going in a million directions.

"Come on," he was indicating stairs. "We're going upstairs. I'm glad you brought your jacket."

She climbed the narrow winding staircase, and they entered another smaller area that contained an efficient kitchen. Strands of pasta were draped over the small island, and pans were bubbling on the stove. Beyond the kitchen, sliding doors opened to a rooftop.

Stefano handed her a glass of pinot grigio. "Let's go outside. I want to show you something."

They walked through the doors, and he smiled at Teresa's gasp. "Stefano, it's beautiful."

Before them lay all of Florence, lights sparkling throughout the city. They walked around, and Stefano pointed at the domes, patiently telling her what they were, as well as even more landmarks.

"I could look at this forever," she said.

He laughed. "I think you said the same thing in Capri." He pointed to another small staircase. We're actually going to eat up there where we will have a 360-degree view of *Firenze.*

"I would offer to help with dinner, but something tells me this is your show," she said. "No pun intended," she added with a smile. Walking back into the kitchen, she watched him as he went to the sink and washed his hands. He was wearing khaki pants and a blue and white striped dress shirt with the sleeves rolled up. She smiled at the memory that surged forward—he liked stripes. Now he slung a towel over his shoulder.

He gave her a small smile. "Thank you for your offer, but everything is almost done. He went to a small oven and took a flatbread out. She watched him move around the kitchen, boiling the fresh pasta quickly and then draining it and stirring it back into a saucepan, flipping it around.

"Stefano, why don't you ever get dirty?"

He looked at her quizzically, and she continued. "I mean, you never get a spot on you, but you're working in flour and flipping that pan all over."

He shrugged. "Practice?"

She shook her head. "I could practice for the rest of my life, but I still go through at least two aprons when I cook."

He grinned a little at that, and she watched as he put two bowls of pasta and the wine glasses on the tray. He handed her a basket where he put the pieces of bread he cut into triangles.

Back outside, she eyed the small stairs. Kicking off her sandals, she followed him up, carefully holding the basket. Before them lay another breathtaking view of Florence. She put the bread on the table and walked around the entire roof, soaking it all in. "This must be the best view in Florence."

"I agree. But it will be here all night. We should eat before it gets cold," he said, gesturing at the table. On the stone table was a small vase of flowers and two candles on it. She smiled. He had obviously put them there if the apartment was empty.

"What is this?" she asked, eyeing the pasta that looked like fat spaghetti.

"Pici," he said. It's just flour and water, but it's a pasta of this region. The sauce is a simple tomato and garlic. We call it *Salsa all'aglione*."

She took out a piece of the thin bread first. "This smells delicious. Is this some kind of focaccia?"

"*Schiacciata*," he informed her. "It literally means smashed."

She took a bite and moaned. "Stefano, this is life-changing bread. Seriously." Taking another bite, she tasted the olive oil and salt.

He laughed. "I can't take credit for it. I bought it at the market. It needs to be baked in a wood-fired oven, and we don't have one here. I made everything else, though."

She took a tentative bite of the pasta and nodded. "That's delicious."

He smiled, and they ate in silence for a minute. She looked over at his dark eyes that were watching her. She swallowed and put her fork down. It was time to ask what had been on her mind since she arrived. "Stefano, what am I doing here?"

HE SCOOTED his chair back and took a sip of his wine, stalling for time. He should have known that Teresa would be direct. She always was. They were similar in that way. He never understood what power it was to ask simple questions. "I could tell you I wanted to thank you for all your work. I have a lot more confidence going to Rome and this next shoot."

"Yes, you *could* tell me that, but it wouldn't be the truth, would it?" she said, studying him, her head to one side.

He sighed. She looked so beautiful tonight. Her black and white dress was low cut and showed off her curvy petite body. Her black curls were extra bouncy, and he resisted the urge to reach over and pull one. He watched her bite her lip. She acted unsure, just as he was.

Walking around the market after the shoot, all the fresh ingredients called out to him, and he desperately wanted to cook and relax. The next thing he knew, he was selecting cheese, bread, and ingredients with a half-formulated idea of inviting Teresa. He texted her before he could change his mind.

Now she was here, looking at him with those big, beautiful brown eyes. She deserved an explanation. The only problem was he wasn't sure what it was. He met her gaze. "You are right. To be honest, it started out as just the simple desire to cook. And when I thought about who I wanted to cook for. It was you."

"Why me?"

He swallowed and stared at her directly. "You want the truth? I have missed you."

"I've been with you every day for the last two days," she pointed out.

"I have missed us," he clarified. "I missed... everything we had in Capri. Teresa, I want more. I want you, and I am not sure how you feel. You seemed to be able to easily walk away when we parted."

"It wasn't easy," she said curtly. "But it's what we agreed. We had a deal. I kept the deal."

He frowned. "I guess I did not look at it as a deal, but I understand that is what it might have seemed like. I cannot tell you where this will go. But it is not just about me either. You will be leaving soon to go home. There are no good answers, but I want to be with you."

She gave a small laugh. "At least you're honest."

Taking a deep breath, she looked at him seriously. "So, you thought you could cook me this wonderful dinner, bring me up to this breathtaking spot, be all romantic and sweet, and I'd just fall into your arms? Do I have that right?"

"I bought dessert, too," he said seriously.

She laughed. "What kind of dessert?"

He raised his eyebrows. "Do you like donuts?"

She smiled widely at him and then nodded.

"We don't nod, remember?" he teased, making her giggle. He reached over and put a hand over hers. "I don't want to pressure you. If you want to think about it, I get it. To be honest, I want to kiss you so badly right now, and so maybe I better go get the plate of *bomboloni* instead."

He stood and found her right next to him. She put a hand on his chest. "Stefano, I can't," she whispered.

He avoided her eyes, putting the dishes on the tray. "I understand," he said stiffly. "You have gone to great lengths to help me, and now I am asking too much. I apologize for even asking."

"Stefano," she said softly. "I meant I can't eat the *bombo* thing or whatever you just said, because I'm going to be busy." She reached up to his neck and brought his head down. He dropped the dishes back to the table with a clang, and his hands slid around her waist, kissing her with all the pent-up passion he kept reined in since Capri. Meanwhile, all of Florence lay twinkling at their feet and neither cared.

# twenty-seven

"Are we almost there?" Teresa asked in a pretend, whiny voice. "How much longer?"

"Eat your snacks and be quiet," teased Stefano, as he drove his Ferrari toward Rome.

"Okay, okay," Teresa grumbled. Reaching her hand into the bag, she pulled out a package of M&M's. It was exciting to find snacks waiting for her in the car. She didn't have any idea where Stefano unearthed American candy and snack mix, but she was touched.

Last night, after they finally got enough of each other, they reluctantly drove back to the hotel. She had laid awake second-guessing herself. Was she being a doormat, returning to his arms after he made it clear he was not aspiring to have a long-term relationship? Should she have made him work harder for it? These were questions for a best friend to help answer. Only there was no way she could involve Kate. While she loved her friend dearly, she also knew Kate wouldn't want to keep anything from Marco. She and Stefano agreed in the early morning hours, they would still keep their relationship a secret. Part of Teresa didn't want to. She wanted the entire crew to know—including Autumn—that Stefano and she were together. Teresa wanted to shout it from the rooftops, and she admitted it hurt her a little that he didn't. Her practical self reminded her it was much better this way; if everyone got involved, she and Stefano would lose the precious bubble they were in.

Glancing over, she watched him confidently handling the powerful car, concentrating on the busy roadway. His short hair was blowing in the breeze, and his dark sunglasses shaded his eyes as he turned to her, giving her a small smile. He seemed looser and happier. She was hoping she had something to do with it.

"Did you see the call sheet and script?" he asked, breaking into her thoughts.

"Yes, tomorrow and the next day are going to be busy. I love the concept of Roman street food. It sounds delicious. I hope we get to eat some."

"I'll save you a few bites," he joked.

"You have the best job ever."

"I'll switch places with you in a heartbeat," was his dry comeback.

"Come on, you have to admit you're having *some* fun."

He thought for a minute and then nodded. "I guess I am. It seems like it is going better."

They were entering the city limits now, and he pulled up to a light. She watched in fascination as mopeds zoomed past them from every direction. He seemed nonplused, glancing over at her. "I couldn't have done this without you, Teresa," he said sincerely.

She swallowed a small lump in her throat. She was feeling emotional. "Of course you could have."

He shook his head. "No, I do not believe so. You are a great producer. You should even direct. Sometimes you have been telling Lucca what to do," he pointed out.

"I know. I need to hold my tongue. I've always been able to see small details, you know? Read people's faces. It helps me in nursing now. Lucca is just lacking confidence. I need to remind myself to let him take the lead."

"I think he welcomes your input if it is going to make a better product," Stefano said seriously. "Speaking of nursing, have you thought about what you are going to do when you return home? Are you going back into nursing?"

"I'm not sure," she mumbled. Why was he already bringing up her leaving? She cleared her throat. "I mean, I've worked too hard to just leave the field. But I know it's not healthy for me to be back locked into a system that doesn't treat people fairly."

"I'm sure you will find something," he said reassuringly.

She frowned. She didn't want reassurance. What she wanted was for Stefano to say he couldn't live without her, or at the very least, suggest she should move to Italy so they could see where this thing between them went.

They finished the rest of the drive silently, both lost in their thoughts. Glancing up in awe at the opulent hotel he pulled in front of, she realized she should be grateful she was here now. At least she should make the best of it.

THE NEXT TWO days were a blur for Teresa. She stood by and watched Stefano discuss *Carciofi alla Giudia*—Jewish fried artichokes on the street corner with a vendor. Their season was just beginning, and Teresa saw them everywhere. After the crew started breaking up the set, she walked up to Stefano, who held a piece of an artichoke up for her to take a bite. "Try it. It's not a vegetable technically. Artichokes are a flower."

She tentatively took a bite and smiled. "It almost takes like chips. It's good!"

"Do not act so surprised! I love these. I could eat a hundred of them," he said.

They ate their way through triangular sandwiches filled with meatballs and another with lamb. They also tried two *biletti di baccalà*—which Stefano swore to her was cod, and similar to a fish stick. Wrinkling her nose, she agreed, though no tartar sauce was to be found. She washed that down with a traditional pastry of Rome, a *Maritozzo*, which was an oblong-shaped delicious soft bun filled with sweet cream. She grabbed a second to store in her purse for later.

Despite their daytime eating, she still had an appetite. At night, they dined at small cafés and then shared gelato as they strolled through the streets, enjoying Rome at night. Even though their schedule was packed during the day, they went to St. Peter's Square, the Colosseum, and the Trevi Fountain. They dined one evening in front of the busy Pantheon.

Lucca disappeared each evening—watching the dailies and making calls to America, or so he said. Chances were good he was on the phone with Ellie. Teresa didn't mind—it left them blissfully alone. Stefano inquired hesitantly one night if she wanted to go with the crew. Andy had invited her to join them for dinner. She reached up and gave Stefano a kiss in response and he only smiled.

She longingly looked at the Colosseum now as they drove past, on their way to Naples.

"You didn't get to see as much of Rome as you should have," Stefano remarked. "We didn't even have time to go inside anywhere."

"I know, maybe next time. So much to taste, though. That creamy pasta with black pepper yesterday was amazing," remarked Teresa.

"*Cacio e Pepe*," said Stefano. "Did you not hear my intro about it? Its birthplace was Rome."

"I know, I know. Just testing you," she teased.

"And I loved that pizza we had in Travestere."

"Teresa, I was talking about sights—not food," Stefano said, glancing over at her.

"It's fine," she said. "I'm sure one day I'll be back. I threw a coin over my left shoulder at the Trevi fountain."

"I'm sure that will work," was his gentle reply.

PULLING INTO NAPLES, Stefano went directly to the set. He and Teresa discussed pizza on the drive down to the point that Teresa felt like she could make it. She learned the birthplace of Neapolitan pizza required specific flour to make the dough, which then needed to be refrigerated for a few days. Stefano talked about the need to cook it in a very hot wood-fired oven, but the most important part was to use simple but exquisite ingredients.

As he talked, Teresa realized how self-assured he had become. It was almost as if he was filming now while telling her about the pizza. Though she stepped in a couple of times in Rome with some direction and thoughts, Stefano had gained confidence and didn't really need her input.

"Stefano, I don't think you need me in Naples," she said. "You're doing great. I can probably go back to Positano now."

He parked and turned to look at her, and she was surprised to see the vulnerability in his eyes. "You still have a lot of good ideas, Teresa. It was you who thought to have me in the food cart serving people. That was fun."

She smiled. "That was an excellent shot. I know it was rough for the Production Manager. He had to get everyone to sign releases. But it showed how popular that cart was."

"Teresa, I meant what I said. I want you with me, not just to help me with filming, but because it feels good to be with you. Do you want to go back to Positano?"

She looked at the sincerity in his eyes and swallowed hard. Shaking her head, she gathered her sweater and purse. His hand came down to stop her. "So, you will stay?"

She could only nod, the lump in her throat was growing.

# twenty-eight

Stefano pulled up to his family's estate in the lemon grove, parking his car near the front door.

"Are we just stopping here before you take me to Kate's?" Teresa asked.

"No, I thought we would stay here," Stefano remarked before getting out and coming around to open her door.

"But, Stefano, I should go back to Kate's. I don't need to burden your mom with an extra person."

"It's no trouble," he murmured.

She reached her arm out and stopped him, trying a different approach. "Stefano, your mom is pretty sharp and she's going to guess we are together. In fact, I'm already worried about Lucca. He was watching us pretty closely."

They filmed in Naples for three days, tasting various pizzas. Teresa, who counted pizza as one of her top three favorite foods, didn't care if she saw another slice for a while. Stefano proclaimed the one topped with Salame Napoli—a local salami —his favorite and convinced her to try it. He fed her a bite, holding the cheesy goodness up to her lips. She smiled up at him, not realizing until later when she turned around that Lucca was watching with narrowed eyes. They finally wrapped in Naples, and now they were taking a couple of days before production would begin at the lemon grove. Lucca's idea was to use the lemon grove to showcase a Christmas celebration.

Stefano was looking at her intently. "Mamma will love having you. It is easier for you to be here then come back each day." Before she could argue any further, she was led up the stairs to the house. The door flung open.

"*Buonasera.*" Margherita was already reaching out to embrace her.

"*Buonasera*, Rita," Teresa repeated, still uneasy.

"Stefano, no one has told me how it has been going. I've only heard bits and pieces. How has filming gone? Is the crew nice? Is Lucca happy?"

"Mamma, let us in the door, and we'll submit to your interrogation," Stefano said.

Rita rolled her eyes but turned and led them into the kitchen. Stefano disappeared with the bags to take upstairs, and Teresa watched as Rita poured three glasses of wine. "Let's all go out on the terrace, and you can catch me up on everything, Teresa. I trust you to tell me more than my son," Rita said with a smile.

Teresa tried to keep her face expressionless. Catch Margherita up on their relationship or filming? If his mother only knew! Sitting down, Teresa bit her lip. While Rita was chatty and sweet, she knew there was an observant mother behind those twinkling eyes. She even heard through family lore how Margherita carefully extracted information from Kate early on. Rita knew Ellie was really a famed artist, and caught on to secrets, even if she was not directly told.

"Filming has gone very well. Stefano is doing great," Teresa started. "He's gotten better with every shoot."

"I am hardly a natural," Stefano said from behind her, coming to join them. She noticed he sat across from her and not next to her. His eyes gave her a speaking look, and she realized he understood his mother's skills.

"That's wonderful to hear," Margherita said. "Tell me, Teresa, how did you get him all primed and ready? I can't wait to hear your techniques."

In the midst of taking a sip, Teresa choked, coughing a little. "Sorry, wrong pipe," she said. "Um, well, just general practice, I guess," she said, feeling her face flush.

Fortunately, Stefano saw her discomfort and launched into a tale about the teleprompter and their interview practice. He even made light of the head, nodding. Margherita was laughing, asking more questions, and Stefano took the lead in answering. Teresa gratefully sipped her wine.

"Before you arrived I just started to think about dinner and realized you'd probably want to cook," said Margherita. Turning to Teresa, she added, "It relaxes him."

"Oh, really?" Teresa muttered, analyzing the contents of her glass.

"Did you have anything in mind?" Stefano asked.

"No, dear, whatever you like. You probably know what Teresa likes by now."

"Oh, yes." Stefano smiled a little at Teresa. "No mushrooms, no truffle oil, eggplant is a maybe, and pretty much anything resembling a vegetable should be carefully discussed prior to introduction."

"That's not true," Teresa said and laughed. "I ate salad. You saw me!"

"Oh yes, an *insalata* that may or may not have had a ton of dressing and cheese on it," he remarked.

"Well, I didn't make it, I just ate it," argued Teresa.

"I'm surprised you did not add some goldfish crackers to it," said Stefano with a laugh.

"Well, I would have if I had any more," Teresa said defiantly.

"Mamma, you'd never believe what Teresa does with salt crackers," Stefano challenged.

Teresa rolled her eyes. "Please, you are dying for me to make that again!"

Margherita was watching the entire exchange silently. Now she patted Stefano's hand. "Well, go inside, dear, and find something that we'll all like."

He laughed and got up, dropping a kiss on his mother's cheek. "I am going to go take a shower, and then I will cook something even the most finicky eater will love," he said with a smile.

"Just no pizza," Teresa called after him. He turned, laughing, remembering the amount of pizza they ate in Naples. She watched as he disappeared through the doors to the kitchen. Teresa turned back around and realized she still was smiling. She looked over to find Margherita studying her, her head to the side.

"How long have you and my son been an item, as we used to say?" she asked.

Teresa felt the color creeping back. Margherita looked at her sympathetically. "It's okay, dear, as it is none of my business. You don't have to answer. But I will tell you this. It's seldom my son acts like that."

"Acts like what?" Teresa asked.

"Happy."

～

"IT'S NOT HAPPENING, Lucca. So save it. You will just have to find another place!"

Teresa winced at Stefano's firm words. While not shouting, he was close to doing so. Walking into the kitchen, she observed Stefano and Lucca standing a few feet apart, clearly facing off. Margherita was sitting at the big farmhouse table, sipping a cappuccino, clearly not affected by the yelling.

"*Buongiorno*, Teresa," she said, now frowning at her son.

Stefano's head whipped around to look at Teresa. He gave her a small smile and said good morning, as did Lucca. Teresa went over to the table to join Margherita, figuring that it was too late to withdraw, but it was safer out of the way.

"Stefano, you didn't even ask Teresa if she wanted a cappuccino," Margherita admonished him.

"She does not drink coffee," said Stefano matter-of-factly. "And it is all I can do to get her to eat breakfast."

Teresa tried not to wince. The fact that he admitted he knew that in front of Margherita and Lucca did little to dispel their closeness.

"What are we fighting about?" she whispered to Margherita.

"*We* are not fighting," Stefano stated from across the room. "I am merely informing *mio cugino* that we are NOT filming at my villa. It is my home, and it will stay private."

Lucca turned away, nonplused. He was ignoring Stefano and making a cappuccino.

"Well, you're informing him kind of loudly," Teresa pointed out. "And why would we film at your villa? I thought the last episode was to be here at the lemon grove. The crew is coming tomorrow."

Margherita made a gesture. "A simple miscommunication. We are getting ready for an extravagant fiftieth wedding anniversary. The couple is flying in family from all over the world. We need time to prepare for the event. My assistant inadvertently switched the dates."

"Can't we just push filming back a week?" Teresa asked, looking at Lucca's solemn face and Stefano's stubborn one.

It was Margherita who answered her again, the concern registering on her face. "We have a wedding after that and another after that. It is still the season for us."

"I've tried to rent every villa around," said Lucca glumly. "They're booked solid."

"What about a restaurant? Or is there a commercial kitchen?" asked Teresa.

"No, the premise of this is a family Christmas. What Italians in our region eat for Christmas. It's going to look weird if we're at a restaurant."

"You can use this house," offered Margherita.

"Thank you, *Zia* Rita," said Lucca. "But you have enough work to do here."

"Look, Stefano, we can find a restaurant where we can prepare the food. Thanks to *Zia* Rita, we have a contingency of Italian mammas to help us cook. But when we sit down, we have to have a family table. It has to be a home. No viewer is going to know we are filming at your villa. They'll think it's a set or a place we rented."

"I will know," Stefano grumbled. "Film at Marco's then."

"I don't want to stress Katie in the slightest, and I think filming at her home may do that."

"What about Nico? He can be talked into anything."

"We aren't all going to traipse down to Sicily. That's more time and expense," Lucca said firmly.

Stefano made a face. "Fine. One day, Lucca. One day is all you get."

Lucca inclined his head seriously, almost as if he said another word, Stefano would change his mind.

"I'll get everything organized. It may take a day or so. Are you returning to Capri?" Lucca asked.

Stefano nodded. "I was planning on leaving tomorrow. Let me know what is needed."

"You won't have to do anything. Our Production Manager will handle it. I promise you we'll be in and out, and you won't even know it."

Teresa glanced at Stefano's face. Chances were, he would know it.

STEFANO EXCUSED himself soon after Lucca left, saying he needed to spend some time looking over work at Oro Industries that he had been ignoring. He told Teresa he would see her at lunch or later. Ignoring the speculative look from his mother, he went to the study and shut the door. Sitting in the big leather chair behind the desk, he felt himself breathe easier.

Just as he was getting comfortable in front of the camera and possibly not regretting the decision to cooperate, Lucca sprung this on him. He knew how important it was, but just the thought of the entire crew at his house, invading his privacy, made him uncomfortable.

He acknowledged another concern he had, and that was his relationship with Teresa. During dinner last night, both he and Teresa were careful to keep topics neutral. They talked a lot about the coming baby, even laughing a little over names. That led to a discussion about his siblings' and Margherita's own pregnancies. She asked Teresa about her family life, and Teresa opened up a little about her brothers and childhood. Stefano listened intently but wondered why she had never shared these stories with him. He realized the show consumed them, and admittedly, a lot of it was focused on his own self as he navigated this new challenge. In the process, he realized he hadn't ever pressed Teresa for more details about her life.

He felt like a heel but tried not to show any emotion in front of his mother. Instead, he wanted to gather her in his arms and beg forgiveness. While he knew their relationship would soon come to an end, that was unforgivable of him. Other than her confiding in him about how she left the hospital and a little about her parents, he knew so little. Why did she leave television? Did she enjoy nursing? What were her options when she went home? He suddenly tried to picture her at the hospital and then going home. He knew from Marco she used to live in an apartment with Kate. Did she still live there? By herself? He frowned.

Last night, she told them about her brothers. Anthony was a successful real estate agent in New York. Bennett was in the Air Force and moved around a lot. The twins, Cameron and Derek, were living in Eastern Canada, where they ran a small inn, and Edward owned a vineyard in Oregon. When Margherita asked when was the last time they had all been together, Teresa shrugged and looked away. Margherita hadn't pursued it. Maybe they weren't a close family.

When she went home, he would suggest to her that she spend some down time visiting her brothers, at least a few of them. That gave him a sense of ease to think she wouldn't be alone. He frowned for a moment, realizing the names were in alphabetical order. Why did they skip from E to T? He would have to remember to ask her that.

Opening his laptop, he tried to concentrate on the multitude of emails he received. His executive assistant called him when there was something urgent. Stefano knew there was nothing too important, and he could spend the day showing Teresa around the lemon grove or doing something fun. He just needed the space to think. He sensed his mother guessed there was something between him and Teresa. When Teresa warned him that Margherita would figure it out, he brushed it off, though he knew deep down she was right. He never let his family become involved in any of his personal relationships. He didn't need their opinions or his mother growing close to anyone. Every relationship was temporary, and he couldn't risk them getting involved. He shook off his thoughts and tried to concentrate on the emails. It was only an hour later that there was a tentative knock at the door. Teresa's smiling face soon peeked in.

"There you are! I don't mean to disturb you. I know you probably have a ton of work, but I just wanted to tell you I'm going to Katie's."

Stefano stood when she opened the door. Now he motioned her inside. She was smiling, shutting the door, but staying near it.

"Are you going for lunch? I was just about to come and talk to you about an idea."

"No, actually, I packed my bag. I'm going to go there for a couple of days."

He gave her an appraising look. "Is there a reason?"

"No, not at all. I can see you need to work, and your mom is busy. Katie wants to spend time with me, and I'm just sitting around. You're going back to Capri, so I might as well spend some time with her and get out of your way."

"You are not in my way," he murmured.

She smiled a little wider at that. "That's just a figure of speech."

"I know I said I was going to Capri, but that was a figure of speech, too, in from of Lucca. I was hoping *we* were going back to Capri."

She gave him a speculative look. "But don't you have a lot of work to do? I mean, will I just be in the way there?"

He shook his head. "Teresa, I apologize. I should have talked to you about this sooner. I just needed some time…"

"I get it. You needed time to breathe," she interrupted.

He gave her a small smile. "How did you know?"

She shrugged. "I could just tell."

He walked over and put his arms around her, gazing at her. "Well, I've had that time, and now I was looking outside at this gorgeous day and wondering if perhaps we take a little escape until we start filming."

She grinned at him. "What do you have in mind?"

# twenty-nine

Traveling over the sea in Stefano's boat, Teresa smiled. Once this man made up his mind, he moved at lightning speed. She found herself hustled out of the house after he sent a quick text to Margherita that they were headed to Capri. He stopped at a restaurant and picked up an order, and a delicious aroma was coming from the bags.

They arrived down at the dock, and Stefano piloted his boat toward Capri. This time they were taking a sleek speed boat that raced across the waves, leaving her almost breathless. As they got closer, Teresa realized they weren't going toward the Grande Marina. She glanced over at Stefano, who had changed into a pair of khaki shorts and a white polo shirt. He was smiling and humming a little, looking so relaxed. They passed tall limestone cliffs, and Stefano pointed out several items of interest before piloting the boat toward an inlet that was so bright, its grays and pinks looking almost like there was a light shining on it. Cutting the engine, Stefano came to stand by her.

She squinted at the rock. "Is that a...?"

He smiled. "Looks like a heart in the limestone, does it not? This is one of my favorite places. I thought we could have a picnic," he said, already opening the bag and setting out containers on a table. He had ordered *Panini Caprese*, salads and even potato chips. Crunching on a chip, she smiled. "This is perfect, Stefano."

"The chip or the day?"

"Everything," she said. Suddenly, she reached over and gave him a quick kiss. He pulled her back, kissing her again, deepening it. It was only when they heard voices that he pulled away. Other boats were coming by.

"Hold on to the food. I will anchor a little farther from here so others can visit our heart."

She smiled a little at his referral of *their* heart.

Quickly moving the boat, they continued eating their lunch, and Stefano told her more about the island, the grottos and natural attractions. "Do you want to go through the Blue Grotto?" he asked.

"Would that be super boring for you? I know Katie and Marco did it, but we don't have to. I mean, it's touristy, I know."

"Want to know a secret?" He gave her a thoughtful look. "I have never been."

"Really? Why not?"

"I don't know. I guess there was never anyone I wanted to go with," he murmured.

"Well, if you're up for it, I would love to." Teresa fought to keep her voice even. She was oddly touched that he would choose her to go through the Blue Grotto with.

They finished their lunch and dutifully waited in line for a rowboat to take them through. Stefano quietly handed several euros over to an operator, and they climbed into a boat along with others. He told her it wasn't as crowded as usual, given that the season was ending.

The rowboat operator steered them toward the Blue Grotto, and Stefano tugged her down, so her head rested on his chest. Everyone else was doing the same, and Teresa realized why

Stefano had hesitated about going with just anyone. It was a strangely intimate experience, given they were in a boat with so many people. She could feel his heartbeat, and his arms came around to squeeze her. She gasped as they entered the Blue Grotto, watching the shimmering bright blue water.

"It's magical," she breathed, and Stefano bent his head and kissed her cheek. She held onto his hands, never wanting the moment to end, but it did quickly. They transferred back to their own boat with Stefano promising more sights.

They went past the Green Grotto. Its intense emerald green water was breathtaking. "We should have brought bathing suits," Teresa said, wanting to dive in. Stefano smiled. "Next time. The sun is out, but it is too cold."

Would there be a next time? Before she could ponder that, they kept going all around the island, with Stefano showing her so many things, the White Grotto, the Punta Carena Lighthouse and more. She watched him speed past an arch.

"Does that have a name?"

"The Arch of *Faraglioni di Mezzo*," Stefano said, as he guided the boat through it slowly. He turned quickly and gave her a small kiss, an odd expression crossing his face. Before she could question him, Stefano began piloting the boat faster, gathering speed as he talked about Marina Piccola, where beach clubs were usually bursting with tourists, but not this time of year.

"How do you know all this?"

He shrugged. "It is my home."

Finally, anchoring in the Grande Marina, Teresa sighed. He looked at her inquisitively. "I don't want the ride to be over," she explained.

"Oh, we're just getting started," he promised, grabbing her hand.

AFTER GOING to the villa and changing in her beloved rose room, Teresa was happy to hear they were going out. Strolling hand-in-hand through the Piazzetta, they stopped to watch the vivid sky turn shades of pink and orange. Looking around the square, she was astonished at how much had changed. Lights were already being strung for Christmas, though Stefano told her that the large light display probably wouldn't be in place for a couple of weeks. Stalls were erected for the Christmas market.

"I bet it's magical at Christmas," Teresa commented.

Stefano smiled gently at her. "Things are very magical for you, aren't they? It is, I guess. I have never been a big holiday person, but I enjoy hosting Christmas here. There is a calmness. There are not a lot of tourists, and it is simple. And New Year's is very special with a concert in the Piazzetta and fireworks. I have spent the last five New Year's here because of it."

Teresa felt her heart sink. She would be long gone by New Year's. Thinking of Stefano drinking prosecco and toasting in a new year without her stung. Before she could contemplate that for too long, Stefano was pulling her into a nearby restaurant to leisurely dine. When they exited, the lights were twinkling in the square, and she stopped to take it all in. Stefano leaned down and gave her a lingering kiss. "Magical?"

"Yes, that's for sure," she said. They walked silently through the square until Teresa breathed in deeply. Her nose twitching, she glanced at Stefano. "Do you smell that?"

"Yes, cinnamon."

She took a deep breath. "Why does this island smell so good?"

Stefano laughed. "Because we're standing in front of a patisserie," he pointed out. She followed him in, but for once turned down his offer of cookies. The vast assortment of Italian cookies included lemon-ricotta, sprinkle cookies, chocolate *biscotti*, anise pizzelles, and *Torcettis,* sugar cookies that were twisted and covered in powdered sugar.

He bought several cookies, tucking the box under his arm. "I know you said you were full but try this one. My *nonna* used to make them every Christmas," he said, showing her one he called a *Cuccidati*. She took a bite of the plain cookie with a little frosting on top. Inside was a mixture of fruits and nuts. "That tastes just like a fig newton," she exclaimed and laughed at Stefano's furrowed brow. "That's a good thing," she explained. "But I can't eat anything else, even though they all look amazing."

"Well, this way you'll have breakfast," he said with a grin. She gave him a little shove, but he was probably right.

# *thirty*

Teresa carefully stepped between the lights and over the wires. Stefano went early for wardrobe and makeup, and she was proud she found where they were filming all by herself. She was starting to know her way around the island. The old-fashioned restaurant featured a large kitchen. Teresa smiled as five older women in aprons were moving frenetically around the kitchen, laughing and yelling at each other in Italian.

"Where's our host?" Lucca asked Autumn.

"He's out back," said Autumn. "I think he's been in wardrobe and makeup, but he might be adjusting the script."

Lucca turned to Teresa. He held up a coin. "Flip you for it? Tails, you go, heads, it's me."

She laughed, laying a quick hand on his arm. "It's okay. I'll go." As she went toward the back door, she heard Ellie asking what that was all about.

"I think he'd rather see Teresa than me," Lucca said quietly. Teresa winced. They could definitely add Lucca to the list of family members who had guessed about their relationship. She should probably tell Kate soon, at least when it was over.

She found Stefano sitting at one of the restaurant's outdoor tables with the script in front of him.

"There you are!" she said in her usual greeting.

He looked up, his face serious, but a small smile tugged the corners of his mouth. That was encouraging.

"Whatcha up to?"

He shrugged. "The script is all wrong. I have crossed half of it out. It is like the writer went online and just copied material. There is no feeling, no emotion. There are no reasons for *why* we eat what we eat."

Teresa smiled a little. She sat down and picked up a sheet. "Wow, you murdered this. I mean, there's nothing left. Are you re-writing the whole thing?"

He shook his head. "I thought I would wing it."

"Wing it? Stefano, wing it?"

His eyes were amused. "I know, not my usual self, am I? But since I know all those women in there, I would rather we all just cook and talk."

"What about all this info about Christmas on Capri? That's all going to be a voiceover—something you read later."

"I already talked to Lucca this morning. Since the Christmas decorations aren't completely set up—they have filmed what they can, but the rest will have to be stock footage."

"I wish I could see the island at Christmas," she said without thinking. She wanted to take the words back as soon as they left her mouth.

"Teresa," he looked at her uneasily. "We have to talk…"

"Stefano, we're set. Are you ready?" Lucca called from the door.

"*Si*," Stefano said, but his gaze never left Teresa's.

TERESA THOUGHT the shoot would never end. She felt that her presence was valued, though, when Lucca consulted her a few times, asking her opinion. The women were all talking at once, and it was like herding cats. She and Lucca finally separated them with their dishes, and they were gently told not to speak unless Stefano was asking about their dish.

The women discussed the history and meaning behind the Feast of the Seven Fishes. They made dishes that included baked and salted cod, *insalata di mare* (cold seafood salad) crab legs, *fritto misto di pesce* (Fried fish), fried calamari, muscles with white wine and *Spaghetti alle vongole* (spaghetti with clams).

With fish not being her favorite, it was her nightmare for Teresa. She thought she even heard something about squid being stuffed and baked with cheese. Shuddering, she needed to go outside once or twice because of the smell. She thought longingly of the early years of turkey and all the trimmings and then later, lasagna at Kate's house when Teresa's mother died. This was just...fishy. She wrinkled her nose.

When Lucca finally called a wrap, she was relieved. Glancing around, she saw a lot of tired faces, as it was a long day. Ellie left in the afternoon, muttering something about it being too good of an opportunity to paint. Now Stefano and Lucca were walking toward her. "Why aren't you staying at my place?" Stefano asked Lucca.

"Ellie chose this amazing hotel. Sorry, *cugino*, but we still want to be alone," teased Lucca.

Stefano made a face. "I think my villa is big enough that you can be alone."

Lucca only smiled and shook his head. He whispered something to Stefano which she couldn't hear. If it was about her, unfortunately it had put a dark look on Stefano's face. Lucca slapped him on the back. "Early call time tomorrow. You guys get some rest, and we'll see you up there. One last day of filming."

Teresa, I'm going to need your help. Tomorrow has a lot of moving parts."

Traveling leisurely up to the villa, Teresa was glad for some quiet. Normally, she would chat about the shoot, but something told her that Stefano wanted silence as well. She remembered back to his statement about having a talk and wondered when that was going to happen. He must have sensed her discomfort because he turned and gave her a small smile. "You're uncharacteristically quiet."

She shrugged, but her stomach betrayed her. A large grumble bubbled up.

"Teresa, did you eat anything today?"

"I ate some bread," she muttered.

"What about all the fish? The crew was digging in, but come to think of it, I did not see you."

She smiled and dug a package of cheese crackers from her purse. "I ate these."

"*Dio*, that's it?"

"Well, the bread, too. But to be honest, I just went outside. The smell was horrendous."

He shook his head, muttering to himself and leading her inside. "We will have an early dinner. In fact, we better also get to bed early tonight, since filming begins almost at dawn."

"*Signore* Stefano!" called a voice. They turned to see a petite older woman in an apron hurrying their way. She broke out in rapid Italian, her arms flying. Stefano put a leisurely arm around her small shoulders in a calming way. He turned to Teresa. "Teresa, this is Marta, my housekeeper and friend." Teresa reached out a hand, but the older woman grabbed her, kissing each cheek. She broke out in more Italian.

Stefano laughed. "She says she likes you because you can look her in the eye! Marta is anxious because crews have been here decorating all day. She is very protective of me. I guess we better go see the damage."

They followed Marta toward the kitchen and living areas and stopped dead in their tracks. "It's like a Hallmark movie exploded," Teresa said.

At Stefano's confused expression, she added, "I mean, it's a lot."

He agreed, walking around, his face expressionless. They went through the doors to the outside area, where rows and rows of lights were strung.

Teresa smiled, twirling around. "This is so pretty," Teresa said. "It's like a fairyland."

Stefano was silent, shaking his head slightly and walking back to the kitchen. "Marta said she made lasagna and then purposely stayed out of everyone's way. I will put it in the oven, and we can have dinner in about an hour. Can your stomach wait that long?"

Telling him that would be fine, she felt dismissed and climbed the stairs to the rose room, hoping its color would cheer her. Exactly an hour later, Teresa strolled downstairs. She had decided to spend the entire hour in her room. At least the dreaded talk he hinted at earlier couldn't happen with her sequestered. Instead, she spent time on her little balcony and tried to make a mental memory of the magnificent beauty below her. It would be something sacred to keep in her heart.

Stefano was standing near the sink, his back to her.

"Hey, something smells good," she said nonchalantly, walking into the kitchen. If nothing else, she learned to stick to food when she felt uncertain about what to say.

He dried his hands and turned toward her. "I thought maybe you would be down sooner. We could have eaten an *aperitivo*. I know you are very hungry."

Ignoring his comment about being gone for so long, she smiled brightly. "I am. Let's eat."

Instead of going out to their usual table by the pool, he led her into a smaller living area. "Since they decorated everything in the kitchen and dining room, I thought we better stay clear of those areas."

"Oh, I thought we'd sit outside under all the lights."

"It is starting to get cool at night," was his quick reply.

Teresa regretted they couldn't go outside. It looked so romantic with the lights. She was suddenly uneasy, maybe that's not what Stefano wanted. They sat on comfortable chairs, and she took a grateful sip of wine that was placed at a table in front of them. It was easy to talk about the shoot while they ate. Stefano was giving her the complete biographical history of each of the women who he filmed with, almost as if he didn't want to leave room for any genuine conversation. Teresa occasionally nodded and smiled, but she continued to eat. At least the lasagna tasted good. Sitting back and pushing her plate away, she looked at him. "So, tomorrow is the last day of filming. All you will have to do is some voiceovers and post-production work."

Stefano smiled slightly. "*Si*, thankfully. Once again, I could not have done it without you, Teresa."

She grinned. "It's been fun."

He was looking at her seriously. "You're good at what you do. Why did you leave that for nursing?"

"What's wrong with nursing?"

"Absolutely nothing, of course. But you are so talented at producing, and obviously you would also make a talented director. Lucca consulted you many times. That is a pretty big compliment from my perfectionist cousin."

"Television just got to be too much with the egos, the constant negativity of the business, always vying for ratings and clicks. I wanted to go into something more meaningful, somewhere I might make a difference. I told you I had a role model, and she stuck with me. I guess I kept thinking I wanted to make her proud."

"And then you quit," he said.

She narrowed her eyes. Was he trying to make her angry? "Yes, I quit...again. I guess I'm a quitter."

He shook his head. "I did not mean it like that."

"Well, what did you mean?"

"I am just wondering what your next move is. Are you going to find another job in a hospital? Do you still want to be a nurse?"

She shrugged. "To be honest, I'm not sure what I'll do next. Something in nursing for sure, but I hadn't thought about it."

She frowned. Was this his way of easing her out of his life? Planning her future? She decided to turn the tables. "So, what are your plans?"

He looked at her, confused, so she continued. "Are you going back to Oro Industries and just exist like before?"

"I didn't just exist. I was helping my brother and the family. The corporation is our legacy and it's important to him and our family," he said roughly.

"But what's important to you, Stefano?"

He avoided her eyes and took a sip of wine, not immediately answering. She decided to keep pursuing the subject. "Stefano, when are you going to do something for you? First, you slog away at a job for your brother, and then you do this project for Lucca. But when is it your time?"

He raised his eyebrows. "Slog?"

"Yes, slog. That's the perfect word for it."

"I appreciate your concern, but this is my decision to make," he replied in a dangerous tone.

"Is that your polite way of telling me to mind my own business?"

At his slight head nod, she stood abruptly, pacing restlessly. "So, I'm not allowed to ask questions or encourage you to pursue whatever *you* are dreaming about?"

He frowned and stood as well. "You know nothing of my dreams."

She threw her hands in the air. "That's it! Thank you, Stefano. You're right. I know nothing about your dreams. You've never shared them because you button them away and build this wall around yourself so no one will ever figure you out. I barely was able to have a look-see. That way, you can't try and fail. Am I right?"

"What do you know about it?" he exploded. "We are exactly alike, aren't we? What have you shared with me? In fact, other than the circumstances around your departure, and a little about your family, what *have* you shared at all? You have five brothers. I finally learned about them only because you felt compelled to tell Mamma. Why don't you see them? Why did your parents skip from E to T? What makes your heart race? What are *your* dreams?"

Teresa took a few steps back. She turned, looking away from him. Her mind was whirling. Why was he reciting the alphabet? What makes her heart race? Him. Should she tell him that? The timing couldn't be worse. "Don't turn this around on me just because you don't want to admit anything," she retorted.

"Teresa, I am not," he said, frustrated, running his hand through his hair. He looked at her suspiciously. "Have you told Katie about us?"

"No!" she said curtly. "I haven't. I have purposely kept this— whatever this is—from my best friend. It's almost killed me. I'm sure your mother and Lucca have guessed, though. I'm sorry if you find being with me so embarrassing."

"I am not embarrassed. I just thought it would be easier if only we knew about us. I will set them straight."

"What will you tell them?"

"I will tell them the truth," he finally said.

"Am I part of any future? Any dreams?"

He avoided her eyes, walking toward the window.

"I guess that's a no," she stated quietly.

"The answer is I don't know." He turned around to look at

her. "I care for you—more than I have for any other woman. But..."

"But not enough."

"It is not like that, Teresa." He shrugged. "I am not sure I will ever be able to care enough to share my life with anyone. That is who I am."

"Can you change?" she asked hesitantly.

He stared at her, his eyes pleading with her. "Please go home, Teresa. Please go home and go back to nursing or whatever makes you happy. I want you to be content, and to keep the joy you always radiate. I cannot give you that."

"And what about you?" she asked softly.

"What about me?"

"Are you going to be happy....ever?"

He looked vulnerable for a minute, and then the expression was gone. "I do not know."

# thirty-one

"That is a wrap," said Lucca to widespread cheers. Prosecco flowed, and the crew hugged and kissed each other, toasting with their glasses. Lucca threw his arms around Ellie, giving her a long kiss. He approached Teresa. "Thank you, Teresa. We could not have done this without you. Of course, we couldn't have done it without Stefano, but you made it happen."

Teresa smiled weakly and could only incline her head. The giant lump in her throat made it difficult to speak. She took a cautious sip of her prosecco.

Last night, she left Stefano standing by the window, looking out into the inky night. He simply let her go upstairs. Today, they carefully avoided each other. She knew Lucca was eyeing each of them in a thoughtful manner. He almost seemed aware he should keep them apart. Stefano was a pro now, and there wasn't any reason for her to even be on set, except Lucca seemed to really value her opinion.

Lucca had asked Stefano to find two families who he was friendly with. They lived on the island, and as they ate, they talked about their Christmas traditions. The crew served the dishes from the day prior, using them almost as a prop. In another scene, Stefano helped some of the family members bake Christmas cookies in his kitchen. It was big enough for all of them to gather, and Lucca was thrilled with the authentic sweet moments he was able to capture. Teresa couldn't take her gaze away from Stefano. He bent down to pick up a little girl and place her on the counter so she could help roll out cookies. Teresa felt tears in her eyes, remembering Stefano teasing about sitting on the counter. She realized she was jealous of a little cherub-cheeked five-year-old. Maybe Stefano also remembered because he glanced over at her and then looked away.

Watching Stefano charm the mothers and grandmothers, just as he did the day before, was even more difficult. It no longer seemed to bother him that they were filming in his home, and he followed all Lucca's directions perfectly. When they wrapped, the crew began indulging in all the food Lucca had ordered. Teresa avoided all the delicious goodness that was laid out, as her stomach was in knots. It was a rare moment that she couldn't eat. She realized Lucca was still speaking, and she turned to him. "I'm sorry, Lucca. What did you ask?"

He narrowed his eyes and glanced back at Stefano, who was deep in conversation with Alfonso, their family friend who came to watch for the day. He turned his head back to her. "I was wondering how long you're staying on the island or if you even know."

She seized the opportunity. "Actually, Katie really wants me to come back and spend a little more time with her before I leave for home. I know the crew is leaving for Positano soon and I was going to ask Andy if I could go with him."

"I'm sure there's someone who is going back," Lucca replied. "Andy and a few crew members are staying tonight through one last sunset and then getting night shots. We need some cutaways outside for the opening of the show. I'll call Marco and he will send someone for you."

"No, that's fine. I can leave with whoever is going back."

"Do you know when you're returning to the states?" Lucca asked.

She shook her head. "I need to see how Katie is feeling, and then I'll decide. Soon, I'm sure."

Ellie joined them, linking her arm through Lucca's. Obviously, she had been listening. "We are so excited for Katie and Marco. I wish they had told us at our wedding. We would have celebrated them as well."

Teresa smiled at her. Ellie had such a great heart. "That wasn't going to happen. They would never take your day away from you. If you guys will excuse me, I'm going to go ask Andy if he knows who is leaving tonight and get my bags."

She stopped at the table of crewmembers and whispered in Andy's ear. He assured her a few of his crew were leaving shortly and would be happy to have her join them. With that problem solved, she slipped out of the kitchen and ran upstairs. She had packed her bags early that morning just in case. Leaving the door open, she went in and quickly glanced around to make sure she didn't leave anything behind.

"You're leaving," came Stefano's deep voice from behind her. Teresa jumped a little, turning.

"God, Stefano, you practically gave me a heart attack. Don't creep around like that."

"I seldom creep," he said mockingly before turning serious. "You do not have to run off, you know."

"Why would I stay?" she asked, in her usual direct manner.

He looked so uncomfortable that she took pity on him, despite the fact her heart was shredded. Walking over, she reached up, one hand on his neck. When his lips descended, she gave him a small kiss on his cheek, avoiding his lips. "Thank you for everything. I'll never forget your island. As you know...it's magical."

Stepping back, she grabbed her backpack. "I'm ready to go now."

"THANK GOD, YOU'RE BACK," Kate said, tossing a spoon into the massive farmhouse sink and rushing over to hug Teresa. Pulling back, she saw Alfonso.

"Alfonso! How are you? I'm so sorry I haven't been able to get to the ceramics shop," Kate said, beaming. Teresa knew Kate was fond of the young man who ran a shop in Positano. She had helped Alfonso in the shop there when she first arrived in Positano and twisted her ankle. It was something to do while she couldn't sightsee.

"That's okay, Katie," he said, grinning at her, his smile as big as his head of windblown curls. "I apologize, but I must go quickly now. I brought Teresa home, but it's time for football practice.

"You're still playing?" Kate asked.

"Just local games here." He smiled. "*Ciao.*"

"*Ciao,* Alfonso," both women said automatically, watching him leave.

Kate turned to her. "He's the best soccer player. Seriously, I'm so happy you're here. You have to save me from myself. Teresa, it's true what they say about cravings. I can't stop eating gelato. Like I need to just inject it." She looked closely at her friend. "Looks like someone else needs some, too."

Teresa smiled weakly. Glancing around, she asked, "Is Marco here?"

Kate shook her head, going to the freezer to get out more cartons of gelato. "He went to the lemon grove to see his mother about a few things. We thought we would take you up to Rome tomorrow. Marco has opened a satellite office there. He already has a flat in Rome, and we'll stay there during my third trimester."

Teresa automatically sat down at the massive table. Grabbing a carton, she pried the lid off. "What flavor is this?" she asked after a bite.

"Pistachio," Kate answered.

"Ew."

"What do you mean, ew? It's delicious. Here's chocolate with nuts or lemon. Take one of those if you want."

Teresa gratefully took the carton from Kate and dug in.

Kate was smiling. "It's been a long time since we sat together eating ice cream or even junk food. Probably when Marco and I were on the outs."

Teresa nodded, looking down and taking another bite.

Kate set her spoon down quietly. "Want to talk to me?"

Teresa swallowed the rest of her gelato. Glancing at Kate's face, she felt a flood of memories return—them swinging at the park as kids, their first day of school, the day they both got braces because their parents figured they would be happier if they did it together. They were side by side during almost every significant event in each other's lives. Teresa felt her emotions bubbling to the surface.

She took a deep breath. "I fell in love with him," she whispered.

Kate stood, bringing back a box of tissues and setting it on the table. Teresa gratefully grabbed some, as the tears flowed freely.

"Stefano?"

Teresa nodded, looking at her hands.

Kate moved her chair closer. "Thank God! Finally, you're ready to talk! I've been waiting forever for this. Start at the beginning," she said simply.

"AND THEN I just left with some of the crew, and Alfonso offered to drive me here," Teresa said, sitting back.

"So, how did you leave it?"

"I just said goodbye," said Teresa. "He couldn't offer me anything else."

"I'm going to kill him," Kate growled. "I'm going to torture him first, and then I am going to murder him."

Teresa burst out laughing, drying her tears at the same time. "Oh, cause the pregnant lady is going to go to an Italian prison. That's a good idea."

"Okay, what if I stop short of criminal? Like really just make him pay?"

Teresa rolled her eyes. "We're not back in middle school. We can't prank him."

"He's acting like he's in middle school," Kate muttered.

Teresa frowned. "Katie, listen. You can't tell Marco. He will be furious that you're upset, and then it *will* be like middle school."

"I can't lie to my husband," Kate said. "He deserves to know."

"Deserves to know what?" came Marco's voice from the other side of the room. As he approached, his eyes took in the cartons of the melting gelato and the grim expression on Kate's face. He walked over to give Kate a quick kiss and then went to Teresa, kissing her on each cheek. "*Buonasera*, Teresa. We are thrilled to have you back."

Marco sat down and eyed them both with a serious expression on his face. There was a knowing glint in his eyes. "Is this gelato party only for you two, or can I join?"

Kate smiled. "We'll let you join, but I have to warn you we ate almost all the gelato."

"*Dio*, I'm going to have to buy a gelato company so I can at least keep the earnings in the family," Marco said and laughed. He looked from one woman to the other. "And now you can both tell me what is going on," he said quietly.

MARCO WASN'T GOING to be persuaded to let the subject go. As succinctly as possible, Teresa informed him she and Stefano were more than friends. She glossed over much of the story, ignoring Kate's expression. Kate would undoubtedly inform her husband later and that was fine.

"I'm so very sorry, Teresa. Had I known it was more than Stefano admitted to me, I would have warned you." He looked contrite. "Of all of us, Stefano is the most stubborn, and he's never sustained a significant long-term relationship."

Marco sat back, gazing at her thoughtfully. "Let me ask you a question. You said you went on a boat ride around the island. Did you go through the arch of the *Faraglioni di Mezzo*?"

At her nod, he smiled slightly. "If you don't mind me asking, did he kiss you?" he asked gently.

She looked confused and then a little embarrassed. "Well, yes, but why is that important?"

Marco's smile grew. "It's called the love arch. Legend has it if a couple of kisses underneath it, they will be together forever."

Teresa rolled her eyes. "Marco, I love your Italian legends, but your brother was very clear this was a short-term relationship and not forever."

Marco continued smiling, his eyes glittering. "We shall see. This gives me a little insight into what my brother really feels. I know it doesn't help, but he's trying to figure himself out right now."

"Aren't we all?" Teresa muttered.

Marco looked over at Kate quickly and she nodded. "Teresa, since you brought it up, maybe this is the time we all talk," he said. "Katie and I both want you to come with us to Rome and evaluate the hospital. I want her to have the best care."

Teresa smiled a little. "I want Katie to have the best in the world, too. You are very fortunate to have excellent medical care. Not everyone has that."

Marco looked grim. "Katie has shared with me a little about

what happened in San Francisco. I'm sorry you went through that. You know in Italy we struggle as well, even though we have a different system. Different regions have varying healthcare accessible to them. And of course, those of us with money are privileged, and I recognize that."

Teresa shrugged. "At least you understand that. So many people I took care of just take it for granted. Others struggle not only with getting the right care but also paying for it for years to come. Marco, I don't mean to be rude, but you're a billionaire. I mean, how can you even relate?"

"I can't pretend to completely relate," he said sadly. "But I spent a lot of time in hospitals when my uncle died and earlier, when my father was dying. I saw the difference in treatment of patients there. I can only imagine the large bills people must face with your insurance system. But what can I do? I am sincerely asking."

"Well, the U.S. has a lot of problems. I think that's a large issue to tackle. But here in Italy, I guess you could improve the health care in places that need it. Like that hospital you took me to."

Kate smiled a little. "I bet Meara would have some ideas. A foundation maybe?"

Marco grinned widely at her. "Katie, have I ever told you that you are brilliant?"

"Not today," she clarified, and then grinned smugly.

# thirty-two

"I don't understand what's going on," Teresa said, trailing behind Kate into a boardroom in Rome at Oro Industries' satellite office. "Sit down, Teresa, and we'll explain," Marco whispered.

Teresa glanced around at several people in suits, laptops open. She immediately recognized Kate's physician, Dr. Amato, and gave him a small wave. He smiled broadly at her and pulled out a chair next to him.

Sitting quickly, she watched as Marco took over the room with his presence and charm. His assistant handed him a remote and Marco pressed a button. Cabinet doors slid open to a screen. For the next thirty minutes, he went through a series of slides regarding the launch of Oro Industries' new foundation: Angelo. Marco explained that their *Zio* Angelo was a presence in their lives, and he and his family were indebted to him. However, it was Angelo's sense of service to his community and how much he helped those around him that was the inspiration for this foundation. Angelo, meaning angel in Italian, was perfect. There were many murmurs around the room. Marco had them eating out of his hand.

Marco asked everyone around the table to introduce themselves. There were attorneys, physicians, accountants, and when it came to Teresa, she flushed. "Teresa Rossi, R.N.," she said simply. "And the second inspiration for this venture," Marco added as Kate beamed. "I always knew that Angelo would want us to start something that gave back to our communities, but I never knew what until Teresa brought me the idea to improve medical facilities and build clinics within our own region. And that will be the mission statement of Angelo."

He went through some additional slides regarding timelines and studies to be done, concluding with an appeal that it would certainly take all of them to build something extraordinary. There were some questions following, including who was leading the charge. Marco nodded, as if he anticipated that question. "We will conduct an executive search for that position, but in the meantime, we need to lay the groundwork and I have a few ideas about that."

Teresa couldn't stop smiling. Even just seeing some initial ideas and composites about the foundation gave her chills, and she felt honored that Marco and Kate included her as an inspiration. When the meeting ended with another one scheduled soon, Teresa stood.

Kate was watching her from across the table, her eyes twinkling. "Teresa, stay here," she whispered. Teresa sat back awkwardly and watched everyone leave the room but Marco, Kate, and Dr. Amato.

Marco stared at her steadily. "Teresa, Katie and I have a proposal for you. We would like you to stay in Italy for a few months and work on building this foundation. You have a vision that I don't know if any of us can completely understand. I've asked Dr. Amato to also be a consultant. We need to focus on all aspects of healthcare, but for obvious reasons, I want to start with obstetrics." He turned and gave Kate a loving smile.

"But I don't have any expertise in Italian healthcare," Teresa began.

"You know what a state-of-the art OB wing should look like," Kate said firmly. "Plus, we need more clinics to provide prenatal care. This may take a while and I know you probably want to go home. But Teresa, think about how many lives you could influence?" She adopted a wheeling tone. "Even if you just help us get the initial studies and gather the information we need."

Dr. Amato sat next to her silently, and Teresa turned to him. "Dr. Amato, do you have time for this? I mean, I don't even know where we'll start."

He nodded seriously. "I have personal reasons for seeing this get off the ground, and I would welcome your advice, Teresa. Certainly, I can provide a physician's perspective, but we all know that nurses are the innovative ones. They are the medical professionals who most affect patient care."

Teresa beamed at him. That one line about the importance of nurses sold her. She thought back to Nurse Dee who would be so proud of her if she helped build something that helped patients. She turned to Marco and Kate. "I accept, but only for a few months."

Marco nodded gravely. "Thank you, Teresa. I hope you know that although my wife is desperate to keep you in the country with her, this is a legitimate request. We truly feel you have the passion for this job. I'll handle the paperwork regarding a visa or anything we need to do."

Teresa felt overwhelmed. She spent the days following her departure from Capri trying to put up a brave front, but her heart was broken. While she knew it would be safer to put miles between her and Stefano, there was something oddly comforting to know she was still in the same country as him. It didn't matter, though. She realized they might as well be oceans apart, as he was gone from her life. After everything seemed so bleak, she suddenly felt a small surge of hope regarding her future.

"Welcome to Angelo," said Marco, his eyes dancing.

STEFANO LEFT CAPRI shortly after filming wrapped. His villa, chock full of people, felt surprisingly empty after everyone left. He traveled to Milan and dove back into work with earnest. He took part in several teleconferences with Marco, who was busy opening the satellite office in Rome. It was only at night when he let himself into his penthouse flat that he poured himself a glass of wine and allowed himself to think about Teresa. Her words of him "slogging away" at Oro Industries stayed with him. He acknowledged that's how he felt most days. Get up, go to work, come home. Hit repeat.

Thinking of his brothers, his uncle and even Lucca, he wondered if he was the only one who didn't have a passion for something. Sure, he loved cooking, but he wasn't going to be a chef or any kind of culinary genius. If Lucca's show got picked up for a second season, he may opt to do it, but it would be nothing that truly fulfilled him. He went to bed and had laid there staring at the ceiling like he did most nights.

He purposely sent Teresa home and yet, his heart ached for her. Knowing he probably deeply hurt her made him feel even worse. When he berated himself for beginning a relationship with her, he admitted he didn't regret one single second. Those memories were close to his heart. He knew from the beginning he would have to let her go. Insecurities from his youth about feeling awkward and humorless flooded back. Teresa deserved the best, someone who was joyful and made her laugh. She needed someone who would be devoted to her and would get her to truly open up, which was something he wasn't able to do. He wanted to be honest, too, and tell her about his feelings for her. In the end, it was better for her to just think he was a heel.

Stefano knew he looked terrible. Even his executive assistant asked if he was considering taking a holiday. Maybe it was time. He could accomplish some work at his villa and enjoy the solitude.

He wondered what Teresa was doing now. For some reason, he felt easier knowing she was back in the United States. Better for them to be separated and on two different continents. Time and space, he reminded himself. Still, he constantly wondered where she was. Had she found a job, or was she traveling? It was the early morning hours before he closed his eyes.

# thirty-three

Stefano smiled for the first time in days. Arriving at his villa, he instantly sent his staff home, cranked up the music, and proceeded to go on a pasta terror. He made all different shapes of pasta. Then he turned to his raviolis, making dozens of batches. Some he would freeze, but most he would give away to families on the island. Kneading, folding, and creating, he finally felt at peace.

At night, after making several deliveries to grateful friends, he walked around the Piazzetta, feeling little joy at seeing the growing amount of Christmas decor. He remembered how thrilled Teresa was at just the small amount she had seen. Now they were adding more, and everything looked...magical. He frowned darkly. He missed her so much. Walking past a patisserie, he smelled cinnamon and spices. If Teresa was here, she would tug him in to survey the cases of Italian cookies.

It wasn't doing him any good to think about it. He walked home quickly, trying to put the memories to rest. Maybe tomorrow he would take some raviolis over to his mother. She could put them aside for when the family was home.

The next morning, Stefano loaded up multiple containers

and jumped into his boat for a quick ride, and then he got into his car and headed to the lemon grove.

His mother was surprised to see him. "I thought you were in Milan," Margherita said, smiling as he came into the kitchen.

"I decided to come home for a few days," he remarked nonchalantly, unloading the containers of pasta.

"It looks like you've been busy!" Margherita got up from where she was sitting at the island to come over and peek into his containers. "You know, Stefano, these are remarkable. The colors are so vibrant," she said, surveying the colorfully striped ravioli.

"I brought a bit of everything, sausage, mushroom, caprese, crab. Oh, and I brought some pasta, too. You can put it in the freezer."

"You make better pasta than I do," Margherita said and laughed. "It's not natural you know to out-do your mother."

He reached over and gave her a quick kiss. "Thank you, Mamma. How have things been here?"

She smiled. "Very busy, but you know I like that. Now that things are winding down for the season, I'll relax a little more. Bruno wants me to visit them in Tuscany. I may take a trip there in January."

Stefano listened to her with half an ear. He was thinking about a sauce he would make for dinner. He could at least stay and dine with her.

"So that's my plan," she concluded. "What are yours?" she asked, regarding him.

"What do you mean? I am just working." He shrugged.

"Have you given any more thought to leaving Oro?"

"Why does everyone keep asking me that?" Stefano asked in frustration. He took a long sip out of his water bottle, avoiding his mother's eyes.

"Maybe because we see how you need more," Margherita replied.

"I don't know what more is," Stefano acknowledged softly.

"Well, I can tell you, honey," Margherita said with a smile, sitting back down at the island. "It's cooking. Feeding people is the way you show your love, Stefano. It's your passion."

"But I don't want to be a chef or responsible for a restaurant."

Margherita was staring at him, a light in her eyes. She waved at the containers. "What about making this? Is there a way you can streamline it to take it to production?"

Stefano frowned. "What makes it special is that they aren't made in large quantities."

"Well, at least the pasta, dear. I mean, even organic dried pasta would be something. We don't have any products like that at Oro. It would be nice to offer it."

"You mean oversee some kind of pasta line?" he asked, as he got out a cutting board and gathered ingredients for a sauce.

"I'm not sure. You would have to think about it. But yes. Something you're truly interested in. Combine your skills of what you currently do with a product you feel passionate about."

"I will think about it," he said. "My mind has been on other things."

Margherita nodded. "Teresa," she stated.

Stefano turned from her, washing his hands in the sink. Margherita was not going to be deterred, though, and continued talking. "She is a very engaging person. I can see why you've fallen for her."

He turned around, feeling the color drain from his face. "Mamma, I have not fallen for her. We became good friends." He saw the speculative look from his mother and added, "Okay, so maybe more than friends, but not anything that can be long term. I am not like Lucca or Marco."

"I know you're not like them, sweetheart. You're my Stefano."

She got up and walked toward him, her face registering concern. "We never talk about it, and maybe I've been wrong ignoring this subject. Is it because of your father and me? Is that why you don't ever want to be with anyone for very long? Oh, I've seen the photos in the tabloids. The endless ladies at the social events you go to in Milan, but you've brought no one here."

"Of course, I have not done so, Mamma. There has never been anyone to bring."

He sat down at the island and took a long breath. "Please do not analyze me. I do not know why. I just dislike anyone that close."

"What happens if they start to get close?" she asked gently.

"I feel like I cannot breathe."

She put her arm around him. "Stefano, I know your father's departure from our lives made you very angry. But I hope by now you have understood that it wasn't you. It wasn't me either. He thought he couldn't give us what we needed."

"What if I am like him?" Stefano asked, his eyes searching her face.

"You aren't! Stefano, I see how much you give to your family. You worry about me, encourage Nico, and you're still working hard at Oro Industries because you want to support Marco. You have a lot of love to give if you would just let someone be a part of your life."

"I am not sure I can," he responded. "Mamma, Teresa deserves more than me. You know what I am like. I am not social or the life of the party. Teresa needs someone who will bring her happiness."

"How do you know you don't?

He shrugged. "She seemed okay with our parting ways. I know she cares about me, but also, she has gone home. So that settles that."

"Home to what?"

"I am not sure. But I could not ask her to stay if I did not know what I even wanted."

Margherita sighed. "Oh, Stefano. Maybe you shouldn't think so hard about it. One of these days, you are going to have to let your heart lead you."

She got up and went over to give him a kiss. "I have to run up to the venue. I'll be back if you're staying for dinner. I assume you're cooking?"

He nodded. "I will be here. I think I will spend the night."

Margherita left then, and he automatically began cutting vegetables. His mind was back on Teresa after shifting her to the side. He understood what his mother was trying to say. Possibly he did let his father's abandonment affect him. Moreso, he never met a woman he truly wanted to spend forever with, until Teresa. And now he wanted to do the right thing. He wanted her happiness with every fiber of his being.

He also admitted Teresa, and now his mother, were pushing him toward something bigger for a reason. The idea for a pasta line wasn't completely wild. Though pasta factories in Italy were widespread, most didn't have the global reach Oro did. He could possibly work with an existing one to expand Oro's brand. And as for the raviolis, maybe there was a way to expand production of them. He could streamline them and sell them at least in Italy.

He was mentally running numbers in his head; the possibility was there. This idea might be something to bring up to Marco. Distracted, he didn't know how he did it, but the knife slipped, suddenly, deeply gauging his finger and part of his palm.

Swearing forcibly, he grabbed a kitchen towel and applied pressure for a few minutes. He never cut himself. What a careless and ridiculous accident! Pulling the towel away, he saw his hand bleeding profusely. He was feeling a little lightheaded. Grabbing his belt, he swung it off, trying to make a tourniquet. He strapped it around his arm the best he could.

Picking up his phone, he thought about calling his mother, but this would send her over the edge. Instead, he called Sergio, who answered promptly and expressed concern. He'd pull up in a minute to pick Stefano up and get him to a doctor.

Stefano walked outside, trying to hold the towel over his head. What a fool he was! Now he would waste time getting stitches. Maybe he could avoid that. One more peek at the cut told him the hospital or clinic was his only choice. He was grateful when Sergio pulled up quickly.

An hour later, Stefano looked away as the doctor sutured his hand. He swallowed hard, feeling queasy. He hated hospitals and everything about them. A bright light was shining down on his hand and the doctor and nurse, though they were being kind, were hurrying to get it done. There seemed to be so many people waiting.

"Busy night," he commented.

They nodded. "Every night is like this. There are a few clinics, but they have limited hours. There isn't anywhere else for people to go, especially those who can't pay for private care."

Stefano felt guilty. He panicked when he saw the blood gushing out and just told Sergio to get him to the hospital. It was fortunate that he was even able to be seen. As it was, his hand was being stitched at a make-shift area in the hallway.

Keeping his eyes averted to avoid watching, he glanced down toward the end of the hallway near the desks where nurses were busy charting. He glimpsed black curls and a bright pink sweater. His heart lurched a little, thinking of Teresa's curls. She would wear a sweater like that. Suddenly, he got another slight glimpse. It couldn't be. There was no way! He moved to try to see better.

"*Signore*, we need you to stay still," the nurse admonished him.

He mumbled his apologies, trying to just move his head. And then he saw her. It was Teresa! His heart began racing. What was she doing here? There was someone with her. He narrowed his eyes, and then his beating heart almost stopped. Alessandro? She was with Dr. Alessandro Amato?

Stefano let out such a burst of Italian, the doctor stopped suturing, asking if he was in pain. He shook his head, still staring down toward Teresa. The nurse appeared shocked.

Teresa was laughing at something Alessandro said, and he put his hand on her arm. Stefano started to stand.

"*Signore*, we need you to stay still," the nurse said, coming over to stand over him.

"*Mi dispiace,*" he muttered again. He watched as Teresa and Alessandro walked down the hall. Teresa was taking notes on an electronic tablet. She stopped and said something to Alessandro, who nodded. They disappeared behind two electronic doors.

Adding a bandage, the doctor was finally done. Stefano thanked him quickly and stood. He walked toward where he had seen Teresa.

"*Signore*, that area is for staff only," a nurse called after him. "You need to exit this way."

He nodded absentmindedly. Looking over his shoulder, he willed her to appear. She was gone. He walked out to where Sergio was waiting, his mind racing. His phone rang and he fished it out of his pocket with his uninjured hand and saw it was Marco. "*Pronto*," he answered automatically. "*Si*, I'll be right there."

# *thirty-four*

Teresa waved goodbye to Alessandro as he shrugged on a jacket to leave. He was going to some kind of gala and was already running late. Saturday night and where was she? Working in a makeshift office in a hospital. Oh well, as soon as she captured their last notes, she would return to Positano. Marco sent a driver to take her to their villa, but she wanted to finish a few last notes and email some photos.

She traveled south with Marco and Kate for just a few days. Teresa wanted to stay in Rome, but then realized it was a good opportunity to do more work surveying the hospital and its needs.

The team Marco assembled made incredible progress in just a few weeks. They already hired multiple people to help with sourcing equipment, and in a few days, they would interview various companies about expansion efforts. Her phone lit up with Kate's photo flashing on it. "Hey, I was just going to call you," Teresa said. "I'm sorry I'm so late." She listened for a minute and felt the blood drain from her face. "I'll be right up."

Teresa ran, pushing the elevator button several times as if it was going to make it go faster. Finally, the doors opened, and she ran in. A voice called out in Italian, and she impatiently put her hand on the doors to prevent them from closing. No matter what language, "hold the door" sounded the same. The voice appeared in front of her in the form of Stefano. She dropped her hand and backed up. "Stefano," she squeaked.

He didn't look as surprised to see her as she did him. She glanced down at his bandaged hand. "What did you do to your hand?"

"Cut it," was his terse reply. "I assume you are on your way up to Katie?"

She nodded. "I'm sure everything is fine. But it's good she came in to get checked out."

The doors opened, and Teresa flew through them. She would deal with Stefano and the effects of seeing him later. Now she just wanted to see her best friend. Knocking quietly, she entered the small room. "Katie! What happened?"

Kate was sitting up in bed. A monitor was beside her and another was strapped around her abdomen. An IV drip was in her arm. Marco was pacing alongside the bed, looking worried. Kate rolled her eyes and smiled weakly. "I'm sorry, Teresa. You leave me for five minutes, and I freak out. I got this pain, and it just panicked me." She bit her lip and looked past Teresa. "Oh, hi, Stefano." She looked confused. "Are you two here together?"

"No!" Teresa almost shouted. Taking a breath, she went to Kate's bedside and asked a series of questions lightly. While she did this, she snuck a peek at the monitors' numbers. Reassured, she smiled at Kate. "Have they given you an ultrasound?"

"They just finished," Marco said, stopping to put his hand on Kate's shoulder. "They said the baby looked fine, but they are waiting for the doctor to review it."

Kate nodded. "I guess it was just a gas bubble. At least that's what they say."

Teresa's eyes narrowed. "Katie, did you eat that pizza again? The one with the Calabrian chili paste on it?"

Kate flushed a little. "It's just so good," she muttered.

Teresa rolled her eyes. "Katie, we've talked about this. No more! I'm making you a list! There are certain foods you just can't eat right now or you're going to end up here."

Marco inclined his head seriously. "I'll take care of it. Do the baby's numbers look okay to you, Teresa? And what about Katie's?"

She reassured them everything looked fine and then continued to rub Kate's arm comfortingly. Her friend was looking a little shaky. "Why don't you guys go out in the hall for a few minutes? Let me talk to Katie."

She watched as the door shut and turned back to her friend. "I'm glad you called me. I was just downstairs going over some notes."

Kate adjusted a little, looking uncomfortable. Teresa automatically grabbed a pillow, nestling it behind Kate, who sighed. "It just feels so much better having you here. Marco was a wreck. Can you imagine what he's going to be like when I give birth?"

Teresa laughed. "He might surprise you. It's these false alarms that are more difficult."

"I feel like an idiot," Kate said.

Teresa sat down, staring at her friend. "Listen, I've taken care of mothers who came in with the same problem. Ninety percent of these trips aren't anything. It's okay. Truly. It can be scary."

Kate looked sad. "I miss my mom, Teresa. And why am I so weepy?"

"Those pesky hormones again," Teresa answered automatically, picking up Kate's hand. "Of course, you do. I miss her, too. She was like a mom to me, too, you know."

Kate wiped the corners of her eyes. "If I don't stop crying, Marco will think there's something wrong with me. Talk to me about something else. Distract me! What in the world is Stefano doing here?"

Teresa told her about her elevator ride, and Kate's face grew dark. "I want to just wring his neck. Honestly, Teresa, I'm so sorry you guys even got together. I don't know what's wrong with him!"

Teresa shrugged. "Clearly I'm not enough."

Kate started to sit up.

Teresa pushed her down gently. "Hey, lie back down. They need to monitor you for a while."

"I want to go pummel him!"

"Well, not right now. We want your numbers to stay low," Teresa said and smiled. "But thanks, Katie, you always have my back. Promise me, though, you won't say anything? It's awkward enough."

Kate opened her mouth to answer when the door swung open. Dr. Amato came strolling in wearing a tuxedo that fit him like a glove. "Dr. Amato, you look dashing," said Kate. "Doesn't he Teresa? Oh my gosh, I feel horrible you left whatever you were at because of me."

Dr. Amato smiled gently at her, coming over to look at the monitors. He was very tall and bent over to ask Kate a few questions. "Please don't worry about that. It was just another boring event. I'll just do a quick exam, and we'll probably send you home, Kate. I read your chart on my way in. It sounds like there are a few foods you need to cut out of your diet for now."

Teresa admired his dark good looks as he examined Kate, asking her several questions, and evaluating the ultrasounds on his electronic tablet. He looked like a model tonight, and normally Teresa realized she would be giggling with Kate later about how swoon-worthy he was. Now she felt nothing. He didn't hold a candle to Stefano. She had spent considerable time with the man in the last few weeks and, though he was charming and kind to her, she didn't have one spark of attraction.

"I'll speak to Marco on my way out. Let's have you finish that bag of fluids we are giving you, and then we'll send you home," he said. "You were a little dehydrated. Make sure you drink enough water," he added before leaving, giving her a small smile.

Teresa watched his broad back disappear out the door and turned back to eye the bag on the metal pole. She gave Kate a reassuring smile. "Well, that's all good. I'm going to go back down to the office and grab my stuff, and by the time I'm back up, that fluid will be done. Then you can be discharged."

Walking into the hall, she saw Dr. Amato quietly talking to Marco. Stefano stood by, looking uncomfortable. She walked down the hall toward the elevators.

"Where are you going?" Stefano asked from behind her.

She turned around. "I'm going to get my stuff."

"Why weren't you out with your boyfriend?" he asked roughly.

She looked at him quizzically. Was he talking about himself in the third person?

"Stefano, did you lose consciousness and hit your head, too? What in the heck are you talking about?"

"Your boyfriend. He sailed in wearing his fancy clothes, but you were still here."

"Alec?" she asked, her eyes growing wide.

"Oh, it's *Alec*?" he rolled his eyes. "Please, his name is Alessandro. How long has that been going on?" he spat. "Give me a break. Really Teresa? You can do better than that guy! He is not to be trusted. He makes me look like a choirboy when it comes to women."

Teresa stared at him. "You have lost your mind! And you know Stefano, it's really none of your business."

"You were supposed to go home!"

"Well, I didn't! Sorry, but I think Italy is big enough for the two of us for the time being." She walked over and pushed the elevator button.

"Are you staying because of *Alec*?" he said the name with a sneer.

She looked at him coldly. "You really can be a jerk, Stefano," she finally said. "And no man would be the reason I stay in Italy."

The elevator doors opened, and she walked into the small space. Pushing the button, she waited for the doors to close before she crumbled next to the wall.

# *thirty-five*

S tefano arrived at Marco and Kate's villa the next morning. He left the hospital shortly after his confrontation with Teresa, slipping out quietly when Marco went back into Kate's room. Sergio drove him home, and he was admonished by his mother for a solid hour about not letting her know. "I shouldn't have to find out my son is in the hospital through Sergio," she told him repeatedly. It got worse when he stupidly told her about Kate. He reassured her Kate was fine, and no one was keeping anything from her.

After much debate, he decided to stop by the villa on his way back to Capri. There were one or two matters to discuss with his brother. Why should Teresa's presence stop him? Deep down, he admitted to himself that he wanted to see her. Apologizing to her would be the least he could do. Seeing her with Alessandro really rocked him the night before. He was awake all night thinking about her in Alessandro's arms. It tore him up.

Growing up, there was only one person in his classes smarter than him, and that was Alessandro Amato. Alessandro transferred from Rome to Stefano's school at the age of ten. A constant thorn in his side, Stefano competed with Alessandro at every level academically. Everything seemed to come so easily to him. Then they matured into men and continued their rivalry from afar. There was a time Stefano thought about being a doctor, but realized quickly there was no way. He shuddered at the sight of any blood or a medical procedure. When he returned to Italy, he heard information occasionally about Alessandro going to medical school and eventually building a flourishing OB/GYN practice. He also heard that Alessandro was even just as accomplished with women. While Stefano never lacked for female company, he saw the models and actresses Alessandro went through and almost found it humorous. That never bothered him until yesterday. Alessandro could have all the women in the world—just not his. He swallowed hard. Teresa wasn't his, and the sooner he moved on, the better. It would undoubtedly be better for her, too, just as long as she didn't end up with the likes of Alessandro. Frowning, he knocked on the villa's front door, and it was immediately opened by their housekeeper, Anna.

"Stefano, come in, come in," she said with a wide smile. "What a frown! You don't frown at Anna that way," she admonished him. He apologized, kissing her and sweeping her into a hug. She had been with the family in one capacity or another for a long time, and she was always a fan of his.

"What are you doing here?"

Stefano looked up to see his sister-in-law staring at him coldly. It was worse than he thought. Clearly confused, Anna disentangled herself, looked at both their faces, and mumbled about finishing cleaning. She swept off without a backward glance.

"*Buongiorno*, Katie," he said, walking forward. He was about to bend and kiss her, but she turned around and walked toward the kitchen. "If you've come to see Marco, he's not here. You should have called first."

Stefano grimaced. "Katie, maybe it's a good thing that he's not here. I guess we should talk." He glanced around. "Is Teresa here?"

"No," came the icy reply.

"Katie, can we sit down? I want you to relax. Marco will kill me if you get worked up."

Kate indicated a pair of comfortable chairs off the kitchen and sat down, glaring at him. "Well guess what, Stefano? I am worked up. *Very* worked up."

"I know things with Teresa didn't end...well, they didn't end the way you may have wanted, but we are both adults and it is our own business."

"Your own business!" she exploded. "That is my best friend. My *very* best friend. Why, of all the women on this earth, did it have to be her whose heart you broke?" Kate got up and began to pace.

"Katie..."

"Don't Katie me. Why wasn't the best person in the world good enough for you? She's never been in love before! Not real love anyway." She eyed him with a fierce look. "There's got to be something loveable about you, but frankly, right now I'm not seeing it."

"Please sit down," he pleaded.

Kate perched on the edge of a chair. She took a deep, calming breath. "I'm sorry," she breathed. "I feel better now."

He gave her a weak smile before his face lost all expression. "First, Teresa is not in love with me. I know she cares for me, but she has clearly moved on."

At Kate's raised eyebrows, he continued, "Teresa *was* good enough. She is far better than me." He stopped and swallowed hard, running his hand through his hair. "I do not know how to explain it. Teresa lights up a room. She can go into a crowded party and leave knowing everyone, as well as the names of their significant others, kids or even their pets! I watched her with our crew. They adored her. I am the opposite. I am stiff and uncomfortable, and half the time I would rather be in the kitchen than out mingling." He looked down at his hands. "It is all I've thought about the last few weeks. *She is* all I've thought about. Teresa needs someone different from me."

Kate was eyeing him, looking calmer. "Stefano, you're such a bonehead."

"*Come, scusa?*"

"You heard me. You're an idiot. Capital I. I should learn what that translates to in Italian. Why do you think Teresa needs someone different? Did she tell you that?"

He made a frustrated gesture. "Well, no. I just assumed. I mean, she is so self-sufficient and independent. She does not truly need anyone."

"I'm wracking my brain right now trying to find a more polite word of a name to call you," said Kate in a cold tone. She took another breath. "Stefano, you're my brother-in-law, and I truly love you, but honestly, right now, I want to smack you so hard."

"Katie, you're getting worked up again."

"I'm sorry. It's just that you're talking nonsense. You don't know the first thing about her!"

"That is just it. I tried. She does not confide in me. She did not tell me much about her life. Just odds and ends. If she really cared about me, why would she not tell me?"

Kate frowned. "No, actually she wouldn't. Teresa doesn't even open up to me half the time. I have to pry it out of her. Look Stefano, she lost her mother as a kid. Her Dad and her brothers tried, but they're a bunch of guys. She spent a lot of time at my house with my mom, but it wasn't the same. Teresa learned to hide her feelings because it was better than upsetting everyone. She knew her dad was trying, and she could see how disappointed he became when he thought he was failing. Her brothers were all older. They tried too but left to go to do their own thing."

"She's not close to them?"

"She talks to them, and they see each other now and then. But after their dad died, it was like the family sort of fell apart. Teresa has suggested different times when they all might get together, but someone always has an excuse. I guess it's another reason she doesn't put herself out there emotionally."

Stefano stared off into the distance. His mind was processing the information Kate was giving him.

"Stefano, can I ask you a question that's none of my business?"

He nodded, already dreading what she would ask.

"Are you in love with her?"

"*Si,*" he admitted simply. "I didn't think I was. I put it down to just caring about her. But when I saw her with...well, I just knew."

"Then fight for her! Fight for what you have."

"I don't know how to show her," he muttered.

"Excuse me?"

"You heard me."

Kate leaned forward and grabbed his hand. "Stefano, I've seen you. You know how to love. You are very nurturing, feeding those around you. That's my favorite thing about you!" She laughed. "But seriously, you bring us all together. Sure, it may be because you planned a dinner or something, but you're the one to suggest it. You're the glue, Stefano. Even with your mom around, you're still the glue. You force us to sit down and be a family and eat your good food. You remind us of your—I mean *our*—family's heritage."

He let go of her hand and stood, walking over to the window and looking out.

"Stefano, remember that ancient cookbook you showed me? It had all the old recipes in it. We laughed over some of them. A pinch of this, a handful of that."

He turned and gave her a small smile. "The one that said to go to the butcher and use a five lire coin to buy the meat."

Kate laughed. "Yes, exactly. Who kept it? Who treasures it? Stefano, you do because that's how you pass along love to your family. You can share that love with someone—someone very special. You just have to let her in."

"She climbed the walls for a look-see," Stefano said, remembering Teresa's words.

Kate looked confused. "Maybe let her use the door this time."

STEFANO LEFT SOON after his talk with Kate. Despite her willingness to talk about Teresa, Kate did not offer any information about where Teresa was. He hadn't asked, as he wasn't sure what he was going to do. Her words stunned him, and he needed time to think.

Traveling back to Capri, he walked past everything Teresa loved, trying not to smell or see all the wonder she found on his island. Arriving at his villa, he walked directly upstairs to the rose room. He sat by the chairs near the balcony watching the vibrant sunset, remembering a different time.

Was he enough? Could he be enough? He had thought he was doing the right thing. The thought of Teresa with someone like Alessandro twisted his gut. What if Alessandro was a rebound romance, and Teresa turned to him because she was feeling rejected and hurt?

He wanted her so badly. Maybe Kate was right. They could make it work. Teresa understood him better than anyone. It was she who first suggested that he pursue his passion for pasta making. He frowned and then slowly smiled. It was so obvious now. He realized Teresa must have planted that seed with his mother. Their words were ironically almost the same. At some point, she must have put the bug in his mother's ear, maybe thinking he would trust her more. That made his heart sink. Teresa probably felt he didn't trust her, when in fact, he trusted her more than he did anyone. Her opinion meant everything.

Kate was right. What an idiot he was. Why hadn't he realized how good they were together? He would go to Teresa and hope she would believe him and understand he broke it off because he thought she would be better off without him. He needed her back—again. She should be here with him right now on their island. Squaring his shoulders, he picked up his phone to call his brother.

Marco's face came on the screen. Stefano purposely video called him so he could see his face and determine if he was being honest.

"Are you alone?"

"Why? That's a weird way to start a conversation."

"I just need to talk to you privately."

"I'm alone," Marco confirmed. "Kate is upstairs taking a nap, and I wanted to get some calls out of the way so I can be with her the rest of the evening without this phone in my hand."

"Did she tell you about our talk?"

Marco grinned. "Yes, she did. Sounded like she verbally beat you up. She felt pretty smug about it."

Stefano winced. "Your wife is no wilting flower. She let me have it and, well...she is right."

"About which part?"

"I believe she called me an idiot. That part."

Marco laughed. "Well, I could have told you that."

Stefano rolled his eyes. His brother's teasing should be expected. "Where's Teresa? Is she upstairs?"

"She's not here."

Stefano frowned. Was she out with Alessandro? "Where is she?" he ground out.

"Calm down. She went back up to Rome."

"With Alessandro? You let her go? Come on, Marco. We both know what he is like with women. He may be a brilliant doctor, but how could you encourage him to be with Teresa?"

Marco was smiling, obviously enjoying himself. "Jealous?"

Stefano took a deep breath, trying not to send his phone flying.

"Okay, okay, I could drag this out, but I want to join my wife. Teresa's in Rome, working for Oro's new foundation. Alessandro is just assisting with some of the logistics as a consultant. There is nothing between them. Teresa hasn't even looked at him in that way."

At Stefano's confused look, Marco explained about Angelo. "We just wanted to get it off the ground. It was wonderful for us because Teresa has been able to be with Katie too, but I truly wanted her passion for this project. It means a lot."

Stefano was blown away. "Why didn't you tell me or Nico? Does Mamma know?"

"I was going to tell everyone in a few weeks once we had more plans and everything was a little solidified. It's moving quicker than I thought. I should have known with Teresa involved," Marco said and laughed.

"Unbelievable," Stefano said. "It is perfect, Marco. It really is." He was silent for a moment. "And I may have an idea to contribute."

"What?"

"I will tell you after I speak with Teresa. Tell me where she is staying in Rome."

Marco frowned a little, eyeing Stefano. "You're sure? Because I have to tell you, if you hurt her again, Katie won't go as easy on you. Or me, for that matter. She's already told me as much. You need to be absolutely certain that you not just love her but will be with her."

He paused, smiling a little. "I guess the arch hasn't lost its magic."

Stefano looked confused until a light dawned, and he grinned. "*Si.*"

# thirty-six

Stefano traveled up the elevator of one of Rome's most exquisite hotels, rehearsing what he would say to Teresa. He practiced it on the helicopter ride to Rome, and now he was about to deliver the most important words of his life to the love of his life.

The elevator doors opened directly to the suite. He blinked. Standing before him, looking him straight in the eye, was Meara. It reminded him of the first time he met Kate's sister when she had walked confidently into Marco's apartment in Milan. A force to be reckoned with, she was now eyeing him narrowly. She pushed the mass of wavy red hair behind her shoulders. Her arms were crossed over her usual business attire. Today it was a navy suit, her fabulous legs shown off by the short skirt, her feet in high heels, making her as tall as him.

"*Buonasera,* Meara," he said politely, kissing her on each cheek.

"What are you doing here?"

"You must have authorized me to come up. I gave the desk clerk my name."

She rolled her eyes. "I know *how* you got here, but I'm wondering *why* you're here."

"To see Teresa. I didn't realize she's staying with you."

Meara continued to look at him as if he was something crawling that should be stepped on at any moment by her fine Italian sandals. "And you think you can come here just like that? Haven't you done enough?"

He sighed. "No, I haven't done enough. That's why I'm here. Is she home?"

"She ran out for snacks."

He smiled then. "That sounds familiar. Let me guess. There was not anything on the room service menu she liked."

Meara didn't return his smile. "She'll be back in a few minutes."

"Thank you for letting me up." He looked at her earnestly. "Meara, I have been through Kate, and then Marco, and now if I have to go through you, I will. But I am staying here until I see Teresa. I apologize for my rudeness."

Suddenly, Meara's face broke out in a rare grin. "You didn't think I would just let you up here, did you? I heard the entire story from Kate and then Marco, who called and said you were on your way. Kate's right. You are such a…"

"Fool," he finished firmly. "And a lot more words your sister used and is probably coming up with right now. Listen, Meara, I promise I am here because…"

"Why *are* you here?" a voice asked from behind him.

Stefano turned around to see Teresa emerging from the elevator. She was wearing black yoga pants and her Capri sweatshirt. Her curls were in disarray, and she wore no make-up, causing the freckles across her nose to be more prominent. She was holding a white plastic bag in one hand and a bottle of Diet Coke in the other. He thought he had never seen anyone so beautiful.

Suddenly, he felt rushing in his ears. He swallowed hard. He wanted to throw his arms around her and hug the life out of her.

The relief he felt when Marco told him she was not with Alessandro overwhelmed him, and now she was standing before him.

"Well, I know when I'm not needed," Meara said, gathering her purse. She walked past the two of them and got on the elevator. Facing Stefano, she made a signal with her hands, pointing to her eyes and then to him. It clearly said she was watching him.

Teresa walked farther into the apartment, putting down her bag. She turned around. "Why are you here, Stefano?" she asked again with no warmth in her voice.

"Can we sit down?"

She looked at him for a minute and finally started walking toward the balcony. "We can sit out here."

Stefano stepped onto the wide balcony and looked at the spectacular view. Rome literally lay at their feet, the domes majestically rising. The sun was setting, casting a golden glow over the city.

"Beautiful view," he breathed. "It reminds me of so many others we enjoyed."

She took a sip of her Diet Coke and waited, not acknowledging his comment.

He took a deep breath. "Can we sit down?"

She waved at the stone patio table and its chairs on the side. "How's your hand?"

He looked confused for a second. "Oh, it is fine. I actually forgot about it."

"Have you looked at the wound? You need to make sure it's not getting infected or anything."

He nodded solemnly. "It is not."

She took another sip, clearly waiting.

He looked out toward the Rome sky. "I met you in the evening when the sun was setting. Do you remember?"

She looked confused for a second. "Of course, I remember,

but I'm surprised you do. I arrived with Katie's dad, and everyone was warm and welcoming. Only you stood on the porch and just...well, just looked at me."

He turned to her and stared at her. "I was mesmerized. You were laughing and talking and were so full of—joy, I guess. I could not take my eyes off you."

"Stefano, I annoyed you. You even told me I was like a hummingbird."

"Aren't hummingbirds amazing? I think so. Teresa, it was not that you annoyed me. You are unlike anyone I have ever met, and certainly as different from me as anyone could be. It made me feel uncertain."

She screwed the lid on her bottle, setting it down with a thud. "If you've come to tell me that again, I get it. You really could just have texted me that if you felt compelled to tell me again."

He smiled gently at her. "No, I needed to come here in person to say this. And if you kick me out because of it, so be it. Teresa, we are very different in so many ways. I love fish—any kind. And you love...well goldfish crackers. I love to cook, and you love to pour sugar over crackers and top it with chocolate."

"You have to admit, that tastes fantastic," she muttered.

He grinned even wider now. "I admit it. You light up a room and I...well, most of the time I prefer not to even be *in* the room unless it is a kitchen. l wanted you to go because I thought I was not good enough for you. I *made* you go because I wanted you to have the best. I am profoundly sorry, Teresa. Especially about my assumptions about you with Alessandro. I am such an idiot."

Her eyes searched his face, and then she looked out over the scenery. She frowned. "Don't call yourself that. You're not an idiot."

He smiled a little. It was touching to hear her defend him to himself. She turned and looked at him. "For how long? I sat looking at a view just as beautiful as this one when you asked me to still be part of your life. And I fell for it. I fell for you...hard.

So, for how long this time? You broke my heart, Stefano," she said softly.

He watched her face, the range of emotions crossing it. Swallowing the lump in his throat, he stood and walked to her chair. He plucked her out of it, his arms holding on to her tight. "If you love me even half as much as I love you, how does forever sound?"

She looked at him now, tears in her eyes. "Like a long time." She sighed. "I don't know if I can do it. She broke away from him. "If we get back together and you dump me *again*, I'm not sure what will be left."

"I understand," he said gently. "I think I knew deep down I wanted forever when I piloted the boat through the Arch of Love. You may not believe in those legends, but I do. At least deep down. So, I am seizing that legend, and I walked through these doors tonight to ask for a chance. Will you let me prove myself to you? I have a lot to tell you and more apologizing to do but let me prove myself to you. I won't touch you unless you want me to. We can spend some time here in Rome together if you have time—as friends."

She stared at him seriously. "I have missed you, too, Stefano. More than I want to admit." Her eyes searched his face. "I want to try. My father once told me never to live my life with regret, so I need to give you a chance."

Giving him a tentative smile, she looked up at him, a small twinkle in her eye. "Frankly, the only regret I have so far is that calamari you made me eat.

He threw his head back and laughed.

TERESA CHANGED into the blue dress Stefano bought her in Capri what seemed like ages ago. Standing back, she surveyed herself. She wanted to send him a signal. She gave herself a self-satisfied smile.

Holding Stefano at arm's length all week was difficult. He held to his end of the bargain, though, and now she was frustrated. She wanted him to touch her, she *craved* him touching her. It had been important for her to establish herself as someone who wasn't just going to cave to his every whim. He truly hurt her, but over the last week, they spent some afternoons and every evening together. Slowly, she felt the ache of her heart mending. Opening up to her, he talked a lot about his childhood, what formed him and why. She found herself doing the same, quietly talking over dinner about how she struggled as a teenager. It was too hard to see the hurt in her father's eyes, so she pretended she was just fine. Her brothers ranged from overprotective to seemingly disinterested, and she navigated them as well. She told Stefano how much she wanted to be all together again, but it seemed impossible. Maybe she was the only one who wanted it, she told him sadly.

Stefano reached over and grabbed her hand but didn't kiss her. She was aware of his every touch, the hand on her back, guiding her into a restaurant, the feel of his hand on hers as she balanced on the cobblestones. Every night, he saw her to the hotel suite and left her with a brief hug. She almost grabbed him several times to kiss him, but she knew once that occurred, she would be lost.

Tonight, he texted her to meet him outside. He always came up to escort her out for the evening, and it made her curious what he was up to. Glancing at her watch, she realized she was going to be late if she didn't get going. Descending the elevator, she didn't see him in the lobby and headed for the doors. As she exited, she looked up to see Stefano grinning. Dressed in a gray suit, he looked very handsome, adjusting his bright blue tie. Did she tell him she was going to wear blue? She looked past him to see he was standing in front of a golf cart.

"*Buonasera*, Teresa," he said.

"There you are," she said, her past greeting that used to frustrate him. Now she saw seemed to make him smile.

"What are you up to, Stefano?"

"You've seen very little of Rome. Just a few landmarks, some restaurants and *piazzas*. I thought tonight we would try to see more."

He ushered her over to a seat. "Meet Matteo. He is our tour guide for the evening."

She smiled widely at Matteo, who nodded to her. Stefano got into the seat beside her, and she noticed his approving glance at her dress. She smiled to herself. It was having the desired effect. Before she could think about that, they were off, traveling first past the Pantheon. For the next hour, Matteo wound through the streets of Rome, skirting motorbikes, cars, tourists, and other golf carts with ease. He drove them past Rome's famed monuments, all lit up for the evening. Most they had seen already, but it was fun to zip through the streets and get out every once in a while to take a quick selfie. Matteo took a more formal photo of them at a spot with a majestic view of St. Peter's in the background.

They wound up a hill, and Matteo told them he was taking them to the beautiful Borghese Gardens, where they could see all of Rome. At the top, he parked and they wandered away, while Matteo went to join the other drivers. Stefano grabbed her hand, and they walked down the path. She stopped several times to take photos. "This is breathtaking up here," she said, smiling over her shoulder.

He returned her smile. "Almost magical, one would say. This is a first for me. I have never been up here."

They continued down the path, finally sitting down on a bench. "Stefano, thank you. It's beautiful," she said, looking up at him.

"It's beautiful from my view as well," he said, looking down at her. "You look stunning tonight, Teresa."

She gave him a shy smile. "This old thing?" she teased.

"It is not the dress," he said, his eyes traveling over her. "But it is a *very nice* dress that I liked instantly. It is you. You look... happy."

"I am," she answered honestly, looking out at the view, watching the city turn golden in the sunset. "This week has been fun with you. I'm sorry I've been tied up during most of the day, but I promised Marco."

"No, you need to work on the foundation. I am very proud of you," he said, gazing at her. "Have I told you that?" At her head shake, he frowned. "I am sorry for that, too. I am proud of you, no matter what you do. You were wonderful working with me on Lucca's production. But I know how much you are contributing to Angelo, and it makes me so in awe of you. I hope that kind of service is something I can do someday."

He looked away. "This week has also given me time to work on my own idea about the future."

"You have an idea?"

"Yes, I didn't want to tell you before because I wanted to make sure it was something that really made sense. And there was also another reason, but we can talk about that later."

"I have all the time in the world. Matteo will just have to wait. You can pay him double," Teresa said, lifting an eyebrow. "Tell me now, Stefano."

"Do you remember our fight in Capri? Well, of course you do. Sorry, that was a stupid question. Obviously, you saw my unhappiness in my role at Oro. I knew I was unhappy, but it felt disloyal to leave my brother and I convinced myself I could keep doing it. You called it slogging away," he said dryly.

"I know. I apologize. I shouldn't have said that."

"Well, I am glad you did. You taught me a new word, and it is very descriptive. That is exactly how I felt. When I was not thinking about you, I spent a lot of time thinking about what I *did* want to do. That is professionally," he added, his hand stroking hers.

He told her quietly about his talk with his mother. "You had such faith in me. You believed I could do something with my passion. Did you possibly hint your idea to her?"

"Me?" she asked innocently. "Okay, well, maybe I might have mentioned it."

"The idea got a little bigger since your discussion, but that is my mother. I have been running the numbers and talking with some local factories, and I think there is a way to combine some of my ideas and create an entire pasta and ravioli line for Oro, both locally and in the states. I'd like to make it organic and include lesser-known pastas, such as *chitarra*." At her confused look, he added enthusiastically, "It's pressed into a wire and has an edge. It has a great texture. There are others too, like *manfredi lunghi*. It has long ruffled edges. Or even *pici*. Not every box has to be spaghetti or fettucine. I want to showcase the pastas of the various regions. It means a lot of development to get it right, but I am willing to dive in."

"Oh, Stefano, that's amazing. I'm so glad you decided to do it," she said. She wanted to throw her arms around him, but she held back. "I don't understand, though. Why didn't you want to tell me about it?"

"Because I decided that all the profits would go to fund Angelo," he said quietly. "This isn't a business venture to make me money, but if it could affect someone's life, then it would be worth it."

"But..."

He put his finger over her lips. "That was the missing link, Teresa. I was wondering why I would start another business. What would that serve? I mean, it might fulfill me creatively, but I do not need to make any more money."

"Why didn't you want me to know that?"

He looked away. "When and if you decide you want me back in your life—permanently—I want it to be because you are in love with me and trust me. I do not want you to think that I am doing this to win you over."

She grinned at him. "That wouldn't have happened."

He shot her a concerned look. "Because you already have won me over," she whispered.

He gently kissed her, almost as if he was worried she would change her mind. He pulled away abruptly. "Teresa, why did your parents skip to T?"

She looked confused, and he continued. "Your brothers' names are alphabetical, and then it skips from E to T."

She smiled. "My mother wanted to name me something else that began with an F, but my father said they needed to name me Teresa after his mother. So my mom made it my middle name."

"What is it?"

"Faith."

# thirty-seven

"Katie, how much time do you need for the stuffing? My potatoes still have to go in," asked Teresa anxiously. She blew a lock of black curls out of her face as she carefully layered marshmallows over sweet potatoes.

"That looks...interesting." Stefano teased, as he walked into the kitchen, stopping to kiss her on top of her head.

"You're going to love them," Teresa said. "Hey, come back here, give me a real kiss," she demanded and felt his lips on hers, long and lingeringly.

"Oh, get a room," Kate said, frustrated. "Teresa, come here and taste this. It doesn't taste like my mother's stuffing at all."

"I'm sure it's delicious," Teresa replied distractedly. "Ellie, can you turn that second oven on?"

Teresa gave Stefano a little shove. "Go check on the turkey. It's still on the grill, isn't it?"

"It is. Along with me."

She laughed. "What do you mean?"

He grimaced, grabbing a bottle of wine and some glasses. "My brothers and Lucca are asking a few questions about us, as you can imagine. Not to mention my mother," he said dryly.

"Well, go out there and face the music," she said and laughed. "You deserve it after staying out all night with your little secret last night. Are you going to tell me what all you guys were up to?"

Stefano grinned. "Patience is not one of your virtues."

"Oh, enough about my virtues! Get out of here. I've got enough on my hands."

"You are like a chef, directing your staff," he whispered. "It is very sexy. I could stay and help..." he added in a wheedling tone.

She rolled her eyes. "Out. I'm letting you cook the turkey. Be happy with that."

Teresa turned away and popped her potatoes in the oven. "Who was the brainchild of this idea to give this Italian family an American Thanksgiving?" she asked.

"Wasn't mine," Meara answered, coming through the door with bakery boxes.

"Meara, where have you been? You were supposed to be here making pies," Kate said.

Meara raised a carefully coiffed eyebrow. "Have you ever known me to bake anything? It took me a while, but I finally found an American pastry chef here. And look, two pumpkin pies and an apple. I forked over a lot of cash, declined an offer of a date three times, but I got them!"

Ellie was carefully taking a green bean casserole from the oven. "Do you know what it took to find crispy onions here? I finally found someone in the states to send them over."

Teresa grinned. "You guys, thanks for making this happen. I always loved Thanksgiving. My brothers watched football, and no one would eat at the table. It wasn't like a traditional Thanksgiving, but we were all together," she said wistfully.

"Well, we're all together today," Kate said, coming to put an arm around her. "So, are you going to fill us in on how it's been going?"

Teresa smiled. "It's been an amazing few weeks. I mean, it's been a lot of work during the day, but with everyone's help, the foundation is really becoming a reality. Alessandro has been wonderful and has brought up so many good ideas. He's such a great guy."

Meara was eating a carrot off Kate's crudité platter. "Alessandro this, Alessandro that. What's with this guy? Between you and Kate, I hear his name more than anyone."

Teresa rolled her eyes. "You do not. I'm just giving him credit. I had a small dream, but he truly sees what is needed. It will be so exciting to see it become a reality someday."

Kate smiled. "It will, thanks to the Angelo Foundation. And now Stefano's new venture after he gets it up and running. I know how it's going with the foundation," she said and rolled her eyes. "What I was referring to was how it's going with our turkey chef?"

"Even more amazing," answered Teresa, feeling herself growing hot under the speculative eyes.

"You need to give us more than that," Kate insisted. "Or I'll bring Margherita in here to grill you under the lights."

Teresa giggled. "I told her to stay outside and enjoy the guys. What do you want me to say? It's just different this time around. He's let down the walls, and I've had more than a look-see."

At their confused looks, she grinned. "It's just going great. That's all you need to know."

"I wish someone would explain this whole wall thing to me," Kate muttered.

They all turned as Stefano brought in a large platter with the turkey on it. "He needs to rest for a little before we cut him," he told them.

"I'm not sure how you know the turkey is he, but he's beautiful," Teresa said admiringly at the golden bird.

Stefano gently placed the turkey on the counter and Teresa took a deep breath. "It's Thanksgiving."

He smiled tenderly at her. "Almost. Come here."

She followed him to the French doors leading out to the back terrace. He put out an arm, stopping her for a moment. She looked at him inquisitively.

"Thanksgiving is not just about the food you have been busy cooking. It is about family."

She smiled. "I know and I'm so glad everyone is here."

He nodded. "Yes, everyone." He gently prodded her out the door.

Teresa blinked in the sunlight. "Oh my God, there's no way."

Standing before her were five very familiar faces. Her brothers' grins were all in force. They faced her, standing in a semicircle. Her eyes swam with tears as she looked at them. She glanced back at Stefano, who was standing at the door, watching her intently. Her oldest brother, Anthony, stepped forward first and she finally felt her limbs able to move. She leaped into his arms to give him a long hug. He pulled back, smiling. "Happy Thanksgiving, sis."

TERESA SAT BACK with a big smile, looking down the table. They were in Margherita's formal dining room, one they used for only the most special occasions she told Teresa. Ellie had worked her magic on the table, arranging fall flowers in Italian ceramic vases. She even found chocolate turkeys from somewhere. They ate and laughed and ate some more. After the first few tentative bites, Stefano dove into her marshmallow potatoes. Since he tried it, she reciprocated, biting into a beet he had roasted with other vegetables. It wasn't so bad, she admitted.

There were multiple conversations going on, with most everyone talking at once. For once, Teresa was the quiet one, looking around, soaking it all in. She nudged her brother, Bennett, who was seated on her left. "You guys act like you haven't seen food in a week!"

"Hey, I've been eating military food for a long time," he said, eagerly grabbing another helping of potatoes.

"And I'm still growing," Edward said, reaching for more stuffing.

Cameron reached over and helped himself to some more turkey before grinning. "Yeah, growing is a nice way of putting it," he said, patting his brother's stomach. He smiled at Teresa. "We sure surprised you, Slinky. The look on your face was hilarious."

Teresa rolled her eyes at her brothers' pet name for her, which was after a popular coiled toy. She couldn't keep from grinning at him, though. Outside, after she hugged each of them two or three times, she dried her tears and pronounced it time to eat.

Between bites, the truth came out that Stefano sent a plane to pick each of them up. "We should have all made you a priority before now," Derek told her earnestly. Of all her brothers, Derek was the most serious, but also had the biggest heart. She realized now that Stefano reminded her a little of him. She smiled at him. "It's okay," she murmured. "We're all here now."

"We all wanted to come," Cameron assured her. "And even if we hadn't, something tells me Stefano would have come over himself to make sure we got on that plane."

Teresa smiled up at Stefano, who was gazing down at her. He looked so handsome in his gray cashmere sweater and jeans. She ran her hand across his back, loving the soft feeling. She wanted to reach up and drag him down for a kiss but realized that was probably not a wise idea in front of her brothers, who would whistle and yuk it up.

Margherita's voice broke into her thoughts. "I think we should take a long break before dessert. This is like Christmas. Thank you all for the lovely meal."

"You haven't eaten your chocolate turkey yet," Stefano whispered.

"I'm stuffed. I think I'll save him for later," she said and laughed.

"Let's take him and go for a walk outside then," he continued, picking it up. "Your brothers are definitely occupied."

Dying to be alone with him, too, she willingly agreed.

They strolled outside, and she looked over the vast lemon grove, the vista going on beyond where she could see.

"Stefano, I don't know how to thank you for getting my brothers here and for putting up with my idea for an American Thanksgiving. It feels so right somehow," she said. "I don't know why, but it meant a lot to me."

"You are the glue," Stefano said. "That's why."

She smiled at him. "I don't understand."

"Kate explained to me that I was the glue. I was the one who liked the entire family to be together. The way I show my love is through cooking and food, bringing the old recipes to life and sharing them so no one forgets those who came before us."

"But what does that have to do with me?"

He smiled down at her. "You wanted to have everyone together today, to sit at a table and share with them the dishes that you celebrated as a child. Those smells, the tastes. It brings back everything, doesn't it? And now you are sharing them with your new blended family."

Wiping the corners of her eyes, she realized he was right. "I wanted everyone to be here, and I guess I wanted them to experience Thanksgiving. But I mean, I'm not a part of your family." She looked up at him. He was serious, his eyes searching her face. Reaching over, he touched her cheek gently and then handed her the chocolate turkey. She desperately wanted him to kiss her, and she knew the confusion showed on her face. Why did he want her to eat chocolate?

"Look at the turkey," he whispered.

Teresa's eyes grew enormous. Hanging on the ribbon around the turkey's neck was the most beautiful ring she had ever seen.

A diamond band with an emerald-cut sapphire in the center, was surrounded by diamonds. The bright blue of the sapphire reminded her of the waters of Capri.

He untied the ring and bent down on one knee, almost eye level with her.

"I figured if I wound it around chocolate, you would notice," he said with a smile before growing serious. "Teresa, with this ring, I am asking you to join my family, to join my life. Will you be by my side until the end of our days and share everything with me? We will bring people together, whether they are related by blood or not. And we will be a family. We will celebrate, and we will work hard at helping those who do not have the same opportunities we have."

Tears were running freely down her face. She could only nod. She dragged him over to kiss him, and he whispered, "*Ti amo.*"

"*Ti amo,*" she answered. As he stood, she jumped into his arms. It was only then she glanced back to see the entire family standing in front of the window, watching. All of Stefano's family were obviously thrilled. Kate was crying her eyes out and Marco was comforting her. Cameron and Edward were mimicking them, hugging and kissing, while Anthony and Bennett raised their hands in the air in a fist pump. Derek simply nodded approvingly.

She sunk into Stefano's embrace as he continued to kiss her. She pulled back. "Did they know you were going to ask me?"

"Do you mind? Last night, I asked your brothers for their blessing. That led to a full-on interrogation lasting hours and, well, many drinks. Thank God, I brought my brothers and Lucca as back-up. Finally, I received their unanimous approval," he grinned before becoming serious. "You once were upset because I was trying to hide our relationship. I wanted both of our families to be a part of the moment you accepted my request for a forever with you. After all, we are all family now," he said before his lips descended on hers.

# *epilogue*

"You look so beautiful, Teresa." Kate sniffed. "I know I'm selfish, but I wish I wasn't looking like I swallowed a basketball."

Teresa glanced over at her best friend in her bright blue gown. "Not quite a basketball yet, just wait. You look gorgeous, and I couldn't wait to marry Stefano. Besides, I've always kind of wanted a Christmas wedding," she said, a dreamy smile on her face.

She looked back at her reflection and admired her Italian lace dress. It was a simple cut, given she was so petite. But it flowed around her, draping down to a small train. Francesca, who Teresa met at Kate's wedding, had assisted. Francesca was an expert at shopping and had scoured Rome with her to find it. The tall blonde had been tireless in her quest for the perfect dress.

Margherita lent her the same veil Kate had worn as her something borrowed. For something old, Kate produced a bracelet Teresa had given her many Christmases ago. "I can't believe you still have this," Teresa said, teary-eyed. Her something new was the stunning sapphire rope necklace Stefano gave her as a wedding present, saying not only did it match her ring, but it was also their color—the color of Capri.

The night before at the rehearsal dinner, they had escaped outside to have a few minutes alone. The family gathered at the villa where Stefano agreed they could have dinner catered by a local restaurant instead of cooking. He was relaxed, holding onto Teresa the whole time. The wedding was to be intimate. They had only invited the family, some people from the foundation and a few friends. Kate laughed that it would be the most intimate wedding in a public square anyone had even seen.

They discussed getting married at the lemon grove, but they both agreed they wanted to have the ceremony on Capri. "It's our home now," Stefano said, gazing into her eyes. But he looked at her like she had lost her mind when she told him she wanted to get married in the Piazzetta right before sunset. They walked there every night since her return to Capri. The fairy lights were up in full force, strung throughout the square. The clock tower had a Christmas scene projected on to it, and a large extravagantly decorated Christmas tree as well as a hand-carved Nativity scene stood in the center.

Now, the day before Christmas Eve, they were to be married. "It's so public," Stefano argued gently. She only smiled and shrugged. She didn't care how many onlookers there would be.

"What if it rains?" Stefano asked nervously.

"Then we'll just get married at the villa," Teresa said matter-of-factly. "I don't care, Stefano. I just want to be married to you." That brought a smile to his face, and he kissed her so passionately, she felt it in her toes.

Ellie came in wearing a long green gown. "You guys aren't crying in here, are you? Cause if so, I'm going to leave, or else you'll take me down. I never used to cry before I met this family."

"Well, I'm certainly not crying," came a voice from the doorway.

"Oh, Meara," Teresa said and laughed. "Someday, someone is going to make you cry. Hopefully happy tears." She glanced at all of them. "It feels so good to have you all here. Last night was so much fun." They all stayed at a glamorous hotel in Capri Town, where they laughed and cried, telling stories until Kate finally fell asleep, her spoon still in a carton of gelato.

Grabbing her white stole, Teresa went with her friends out to the Piazzetta, with Ellie holding her train. Her flowers arrived from Stefano this morning. She breathed them in. They smelled of Capri, their perfume so well-known to her now.

Lucca agreed to walk her down the aisle, as her brothers went home after Thanksgiving following lots of hugs. Marco was the best man, and of course, Kate was her matron of honor. The chairs and runner were set up near the large Christmas tree. She heard the string quartet begin to play, and she gratefully clung onto Lucca's arm as Kate walked up the aisle. There were several people in the square, but they watched respectfully from a distance. Now it was her turn. Though she was beyond happy, suddenly she felt a wave of grief wash over her. Oh, why today? She blinked back the tears, determined to be the radiant bride she wanted to be.

"Excuse me, I believe this is my honor," said a voice. She turned to her right to see her brother Anthony standing there, a light in his eyes. "Anthony, how did you get here?" she whispered. "Oh my God."

He handed her a handkerchief, and she stopped and patted her eyes. Taking a breath, she whispered thank you and began to walk, holding on to his arm.

They walked three rows before they stopped. She looked over at Anthony, who was smiling as he handed her over to Bennett.

"You came! How did the Air Force give you more time off?"

He kissed her cheek. "They knew nothing would keep me from being here tonight."

A few more rows, and she found them pausing. No, it

couldn't be. "Oh, Cameron, I'm so glad you're here," she whispered.

He kissed her cheek. "Just keep walking, Slinky," he said, his eyes suspiciously moist.

Three more rows and they stopped, and this time, she let the tears flow. Derek gave her a rare smile. "I love you," was all her serious brother said.

Finally, they arrived at Edward. By now, she was shaking. "Oh, Edward," she said. "I can't believe this." He grinned. "Saved the best for last, Slink."

She arrived at the altar, smiling tremulously at Stefano, with tears now running down her cheeks. Edward wiped them gently and then kissed her cheek, and each brother stood behind her for a moment. She felt their hands on her shoulders. It was a small sign her parents were with her as well. She gratefully took Stefano's arm, feeling unsteady.

His smile was tender and full of love. "Welcome home."

TERESA'S SIDES hurt from laughing. She and Stefano decided on a less formal dinner at a hotel bordering the Piazzetta. Rather than a traditional dinner, they selected a series of foods they both loved. The guests would be completely confused by dining on sliders, fries, pizza, caprese ravioli, bruschetta and *risotto alla pescatora*, Stefano's favorite. More and more plates kept coming out. That was the way it was to be.

Teresa kicked off her high heels and sat at a round table with her brothers, eating an Italian version of what looked like a churro.

"I still can't believe you are all here, again," she said.

"Slinky, there is no way we'd miss this," Anthony remarked, the corners of his eyes wrinkling just like their father's used to.

"Stefano sent the plane again," Edward informed her. "He made it easy because he knew we wanted to be here again."

She smiled, watching her husband across the room, holding a toddler belonging to one of his friends from the island. "My husband is a family man."

"He better be good to you," Derek warned.

"He is, don't worry. And if he's not, you all know I'll whip him into shape," Teresa replied and laughed.

Bennett reached over and tweaked one of her curls. "Twice in a month. Must be some record. Slinky, I'm really sorry it took us so long to realize how important it is for all of us to be in one room at the same time. I know you wanted us all together many times in the past. We just didn't make it a priority. I don't know, I can't speak for these lug nuts, but for me, it made me sad to think of us together without dad. Or mom even."

"I know, but they would want us to be together," Teresa said. "You guys mean everything to me. You promise you'll come visit? Or I'll come back to the U.S. as often as you want me to."

"The scenery isn't bad here either," Cameron said, looking around. "Did you see how Meara has grown up?"

Teresa rolled her eyes, glancing behind her and seeing Meara and Alessandro talking. It seemed like they were disagreeing about something. She wondered what they were talking about—Meara didn't look too happy. "Cameron, she's off limits, you know that. Not my best friend's sister!"

"Oh well, I could get used to this life, though," he said. "The food isn't bad either, especially the sliders."

Teresa burst out laughing, thinking of Stefano's face when she told him that. She didn't have to. She felt two hands on her shoulders and glanced up to see his head shake and a defeated smile on his lips. He leaned down and gave her a thorough kiss.

Edward whistled, and Teresa broke off and glared at her brother. She stood and put her arm around Stefano's waist. "Come on, Stefano, let's go cut our cake that Ellie decorated. If we stick around here, they are apt to tell you any embarrassing story about me they left out at Thanksgiving."

"Oh, we've got more stories," Anthony promised.

Instead of going to the cake, Stefano pulled her out to the dance floor under the twinkling lights of the restaurant's decorations. "Let's do this first," he whispered, his lips trailing from her cheek to her ear. "I want to dance with my stunning bride."

She slid tightly up his body. "I haven't had time to thank you. You brought my brothers to be here for the most important day of my life," she whispered.

"It didn't take any convincing. They all wanted to be here. They know you are the glue," he said, his eyes glinting, before he leaned down and kissed her softly.

"Merry Christmas, Teresa."

She smiled up at him. "*Buon Natalie.*"

# *upcoming books*

Looking for your next sweet romance from Italy?

Check out the next in the series—
Meara and Alessandro's story: ***My Adventures in Rome***

E-Book Available Now!
Paperbacks available at Amazon or your favorite bookstore
**Continue on to read the first chapter!**

## My Adventures in Rome: Chapter One

Gelato. Lots of gelato. She was going to stuff her face with gelato. All different flavors. Pints and pints of the creamy sweet goodness for which Italy was known.

Meara Malone closed the door quietly behind her with a small click. It was tempting to slam the heavy mahogany door until it shook off its hinges, but that would display her temper. And Meara never showed her real feelings, especially in business. That would give her opponents a window into her emotions. As a woman in a corporate man's world, she had been forced to claw her way to the top. As she did so, she learned the game well. Early in her career, she naively thought people were promoted and recognized because of their hard work and success. It soon became clear to her that advancement was not always based on merit.

She squared her shoulders now and straightened up to her impressive height of almost six feet, even taller in her high-heeled Italian custom-made shoes. Impatiently brushing her long, wavy red hair back from her face, she strode out of what had been her executive suite for the past year.

She had just been fired.

There was no need to linger. There were no personal items in her office—no framed photos of loved ones, not even a roll of mints in the desk drawer. Watching how ruthless the corporate world could be, she learned a long time ago to leave as small a footprint as possible just for this reason. Though she had never been terminated, she had seen others' demise. She wasn't about to lose her dignity with employees watching their former Chief Executive Officer carry a box of belongings out the door.

Meara's phone buzzed, and her younger sister's photo flashed on the screen. She should probably take the call, but she had to mentally compose herself first. Kate would have to wait.

Walking out into the gloomy December day fit her mood

perfectly. Rome was not as picturesque when the sun was not shining brightly. Not that she had noticed the Eternal City very much, considering she had worked most of the time during her tenure there.

As she headed to her hotel, Meara shook her head slightly at her driver who was standing at the door of a luxury black sedan, ready to chauffer her anywhere. He would find out soon enough that he was excused. She had an overwhelming amount to do, including packing and moving out of her place quickly.

Graham, the chair of the board, had a smug look on his face as he offered to allow her to stay in the company's penthouse in one of Rome's best hotels. He appeared to be inordinately pleased with his own graciousness, telling her she could continue occupying the apartment for thirty days. Though he was quick to point out it wasn't technically part of her significant severance package. While staying would make it easier for her, Meara was not inclined to take him up on his suggestion. That would mean being beholden to him, and that was the last thing she wanted to do.

She entered the hotel and rode the elevator, using her keycard to her apartment. After a brief moment of concern, she was relieved it still worked and that Graham hadn't pulled a sly one on her. Automatically, she kicked off her heels and walked barefoot across the exquisite carpeting to sit down on the plush sofa in the enormous room. Tucking her long shapely legs beneath her, she stared straight ahead. It wasn't that she had been fired; it was more that she hadn't seen it coming. She always saw what was coming. It was her strength. What had changed? She had gotten soft, letting herself slide in the last several months.

During the last decade, Meara had made a name for herself in Silicon Valley, working her way through the tech world. She was a rising star, a strong independent woman. While not vain, she acknowledged she was attractive. Unfortunately, in her world, it ultimately was a barrier that forced her to work even harder to be taken seriously. Now, in her early thirties, she felt like a failure.

Her phone on the coffee table buzzed, and she saw it was Kate again. She let it go to voicemail. She pushed down the guilt because she needed time to just breathe.

Meara had grown closer to her sister over the last several months, and now she lived in Italy as well. Kate had traveled to Italy on vacation in the summer and ran smack into a billionaire who had literally swept her off her feet after she injured her ankle. Marco Rinaldi was beyond handsome, charming and had just taken over as CEO of his family's dynasty. As the largest exporter of lemon products and olive oil from Italy, Oro Industries was a well-known powerhouse in Italy's corporate world. On the surface, Marco had seemed like the worst match for Kate. In fact, Meara had warned her repeatedly to stay away from him, believing everything she had heard and seen about the playboy billionaire.

Meara had even appeared at the family's estate in a vast lemon grove to show Kate photos of Marco with his ex-fiancé. They eventually learned the photos had misrepresented what was truly occurring. Meara still had a twinge of guilt about how easy it was to convince Kate to pack her things and leave abruptly.

It was only after their father's heart attack that the sisters—never very close—had formed a bond. Meara finally realized Kate had a fine-tuned intuition and possibly Marco could be trusted. On Kate's urgent appeal, Meara agreed to assist Marco and his brother, Stefano, unravel the complex corporate fraud by Sal, the company's Chief Financial Officer. Worse yet, Sal had been the best friend of their beloved late uncle. Meara had relished in watching the forensic accountants and lawyers expose his misdeeds. He was now awaiting trial in prison, and

Marco was finding his way as CEO after Sal's constant undermining.

Meara had made good on her own interference and convinced Marco that Kate loved him just as much as he loved her. Marco had flown to San Francisco on the evening of Kate's book launch, and they had married shortly after. Kate had become pregnant quickly, and while the couple was thrilled about it, the surprise came at a time when they were still adjusting to their new lives. They were living in Positano but planned to move to Rome shortly to ensure Kate was near a modern hospital.

Her sister's photo appeared again on her phone, and it snapped Meara out of her stupor. Her heart began to race. Why was Kate calling her repeatedly? What if something was wrong with her or the baby?

"Katie, are you okay?"

She heard her sister's musical laugh. "I'm fine! Why does everyone ask me that all the time?"

"You called me three times! I was worried!"

"Well, if you're so worried, answer your freaking phone," Kate grumbled, but then her tone changed, sounding excited. "Didn't you get my text? We are in Rome, and Marco and I want you to come to dinner tonight."

"What's going on? You sound perky."

"I am NOT perky!" Kate said with an exasperated sigh. "I hate that word. I...we just want to talk to you."

"I already know you're pregnant," Meara said dryly. "What more news can there be? Twins? Triplets?"

"Oh God, bite your tongue! I think one baby is about all Marco and I can handle at this point. At least emotionally. We just want to discuss something with you. Marco is insistent that it be soon. And with all the wedding plans and Christmas coming, we thought it should be sooner than later. And tonight works well."

Meara sighed, leaning her head back on the sofa. Kate's best friend Teresa was getting married soon to Marco's brother, Stefano, in Capri. Kate was thrilled that Teresa would join her in Italy and also be part of the family. No one had seen this romance coming, as Stefano and Teresa were as different as night and day. Stefano, who had amazing culinary skills and loved fine dining, was an odd match for Teresa, who craved fast food. They had been brought together when Stefano had agreed to star in their cousin, Lucca's streaming television show about Italy's cuisine. Strikingly handsome like Marco, the resemblance stopped there. Stefano was quiet and withdrawn. Lucca had hired Teresa, a former television producer, to help draw Stefano out so he would be personable on film. While they had fallen in love, it appeared something must have happened to separate them. Teresa had remained in Italy because Kate was desperate to have her friend, who was now a nurse, close to her during the early weeks of her pregnancy.

Stefano and Teresa eventually made their way back to one another and decided to get married on Christmas Eve, which was now just weeks away. Meara had her doubts until she had seen them at Thanksgiving when Stefano had proposed. They were obviously deeply in love, and somehow it just worked. Kate was now in nonstop planning mode, helping Teresa with the wedding. Meara was happy for them and looking forward to it. All this romance, though, and finally establishing a closer relationship with her sister had distracted her. She had put her work second on some days. That was something she never would have done in the past.

"Are you still there? Can you come over?" Kate interrupted Meara's thoughts.

"Katie, it's not really the best time," Meara responded, examining her manicured nails. She didn't want to admit to her sister her plans were to change clothes and then pop down to the nearby gelateria where the staff knew her by first name.

"Why not? Do you have a hot date?"

"You know I'm not seeing anyone," Meara answered sharply. She swallowed and tried again. It wasn't fair to take her mood out on her sister. "I just had a horrible day. I was thinking of taking a bath and then going to bed."

"Meara, it's five o'clock," Kate protested. "Pull yourself together and head over in an hour or so. We're casual. You can wear sweats if you want."

"When have you ever seen me wear sweats unless I'm in a gym?" Meara asked incredulously. Even then, she only wore chic workout gear. Meara took a deep breath. Kate could be even more stubborn than she was, and it may be difficult to shake her off this idea. "Okay, fine," she said resolutely. "I'll change and come over. But only for dinner, and then I'm coming back home. It will be an early night."

"That's fine. I know how hard you've been working, and you're probably tired and want to get to the office early tomorrow as usual. See you soon!"

Kate hung up with what seemed like a satisfied click, and Meara groaned. She closed her eyes for a minute. If only she could cry. She hadn't been able to since she was younger. Somewhere along the line, she had convinced herself crying was a sign of weakness. It would help if she could release this energy. Picking up a pillow from the sofa, she threw it as hard as she could. It bounced off the wall and slid to the floor with a quiet thump, a less than satisfying result. Reluctantly, she stood to go get changed and see whatever this mystery evening her sister had planned was all about.

Something was up, but she couldn't put her finger on it.

Get your Kindle copy of My Adventures in Rome!
Paperbacks available at Amazon or your favorite bookstore

# author's note to the reader

Dear Reader:

Thank you so much for traveling to Capri with Stefano and Teresa. This was such fun to write! How could anyone not love writing about food? It was hilarious to think of foods that Teresa would adore and Stefano would abhor!

My friend, Lee played a role in my research—helping to describe what filming in Italy would be like. And thank you to my writing idea partner, Mary for all of her details regarding junk food!

If you want more...there is! Tour through more regions of Italy in this series: From Italy With Love. We'll travel all over, but we'll always swing by the Amalfi Coast to say hi to the family.

Grab some delicious Italian food or a gelato and enjoy more from Italia! Remember to sign up for my newsletter at Tessrini.com/newsletter to read a bonus chapter from *My Secret Positano.*

*Cin Cin!*
XO, Tess

# about the author

Tess Rini has spent her professional life focused on non-fiction writing, from her journalism degree to her editing and writing magazine articles and content for local government. She has published one non-fiction book under a different name.

Tess was raised on a self-induced steady diet of Harlequin romances and so it was inevitable that she should try her hand at romance writing. The idea took off when she combined her love of Italy with her love for romance novels.

When not writing, she can be found relaxing in her Oregon home, traveling or cooking Italian cuisine (her specialty!) for her husband, four daughters and son-in-law. Keeping her company while writing or watching Hallmark movies is her adorable, but anxious, golden retriever.

Sign up for her newsletter at Tessrini.com/newsletter to read a bonus chapter from *My Secret Positano* and stay up on all the latest Italy news.

Website: tessrini.com
Or follow her on social
Facebook @tessriniauthor
Instagram @tessrininauthor

Made in United States
North Haven, CT
23 June 2024

53974220R00181

# 01

# CORPSE BLADE

# CORPSE 01 BLADE

## TITAN COMICS

**Assistant Editor** Louis Yamani / **Designer** David Colderley
**Group Editor** Jake Devine / **Senior Creative Editor** David Manley-Leach
**Editor** Phoebe Hedges / **Editorial Assistant** Ibraheem Kazi / **Art Director** Oz Browne
**Head of Production** Kevin Wooff / **Production Manager** Jackie Flook
**Production Controllers** Caterina Falqui & Kelly Fenlon
**Publicity Manager** Will O'Mullane / **Publicist** Caitlin Storer
**Publicity & Sales Coordinator** Alexandra Iciek
**Digital & Marketing Manager** Jo Teather / **Marketing Coordinator** Lauren Noding
**Sales & Circulation Manager** Steve Tothill
**Head Of Rights** Rosanna Anness / **Rights Executive** Pauline Savoure
**Head of Creative & Business Development** Duncan Baizley
**Publishing Director** Ricky Claydon / **Publishing Director** John Dziewiatkowski
**Chief Operating Officer** Andrew Sumner / **Publishers** Vivian Cheung & Nick Landau

## CORPSE BLADE - Vol 1

SHIKABANE GATANA Vol.1
©Hajime Segawa 2020
First published in Japan in 2020 by KADOKAWA CORPORATION, Tokyo.
English translation rights arranged with KADOKAWA CORPORATION, Tokyo
through TUTTLE-MORI AGENCY, INC., Tokyo.
This translation first published in 2024 by Titan Comics,
a division of Titan Publishing Group, Ltd. 144 Southwark Street, London SEI OUP, UK.
Titan Comics is a registered trademark of Titan Publishing Group Ltd.

10 9 8 7 6 5 4 3 2 1

First edition: December 2024
Printed in the UK
ISBN: 9781787743526

A CIP catalogue record for this title is available from the British Library.

# CORPSE BLADE

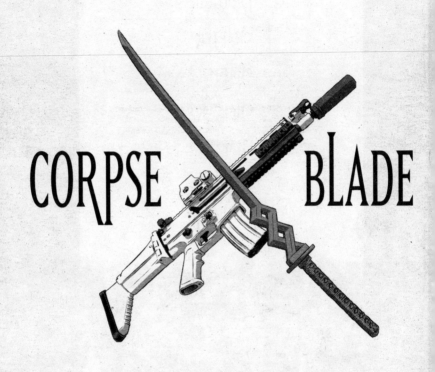

## SHIKABANE GATANA VOL 1
### CREATED BY HAJIME SEGAWA

## TRANSLATION: MOTOKO TAMAMURO AND JONATHAN CLEMENTS
### LETTERING: CALE WARD

# CONTENTS

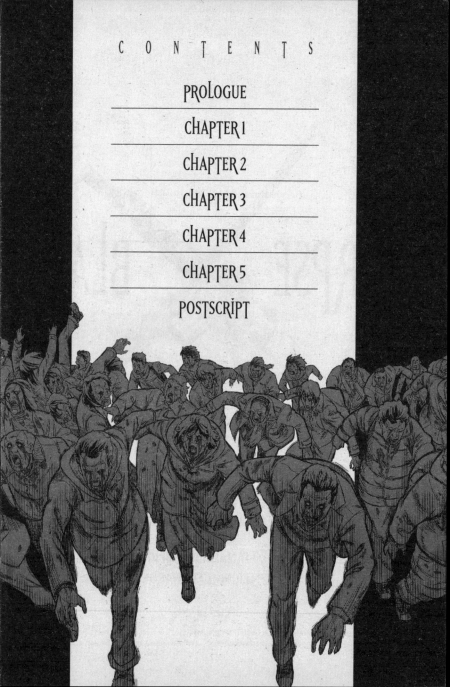

# PROLOGUE
## CORPSE BLADE - REINCARNATION

THIS PANEL APPEARS IN THE FIRST EPISODE.

屍刀　シカバネガタナ

01

CORPSE BLADE

CHAPTER 1

CORPSE BLADE

BLAM

BLAM

A NORMAL HOME DOESN'T USUALLY HAVE A FIRING RANGE IN THE BASEMENT...

WHY DO I HAVE TO DO THIS TRAINING?

BLAM

COME TO THINK OF IT...

...OUR FAMILY WAS KIND OF STRANGE.

IT'S A VIOLATION OF THE FIREARM AND SWORD CONTROL LAW ANYWAY.

YOU'VE REALLY IMPROVED, TSUTSUKI.

STILL...

HUH? WHO'S *NORMAL*?

I'M GLAD I'VE GOT A SISTER.

IF I DIDN'T HAVE SIBLINGS, I WOULDN'T HAVE GROWN UP NORMAL.

...I NEVER IMAGINED...

AREN'T I?!

POW!

THAT DAILY LIFE WOULD...

FOOOM

...COME TO AN END SO SUDDENLY.

CRUNCH

STAGGER

COLD...

A MONTH LATER.

DAMN. I FEEL SLUGGISH.

TREMBLE    TREMBLE

HAVE I GOT A COLD?

WHAT HAS HAPPENED TO THE GOVERNMENT?

GRR... WHY HASN'T ANYONE COME TO RESCUE US?

SLIDE...

CRUMBLE...

ガラ...

CRUNCH

ザ

ACHOO!

IT WAS AS IF THE WORLD CAME TO AN END.

ヨ゚゚

ヨ゚゚
*TUMBLEWEED*

ヨ゚

AN UNKNOWN CATA-CLYSM...

...RIPPED TOKYO APART...

...AND TURNED IT INTO A *GHOST TOWN.*

BUT THE POWER IS STILL ON.

IT MAKES NO SENSE.

FLICK 千力

FLICK 千力

CH-KI

NO SIGNAL, AS I THOUGHT--

THE SITUATION IS ALREADY BAD, BUT...

STAGGER...

池袋駅
Ikebukuro Station

IF THIS FREEZE GETS ANY WORSE, I'M A *GONER*.

BUT BEFORE *THEY* FIND ME, LET'S FIND MEDICINE.

JUST TO MAKE THINGS WORSE...

HELP!

DASH 夕゛

TAP TAP 夕 夕゛

URGH!

UR...

ZOMBIES AREN'T SUPPOSED TO BE REAL.

DASH

WHAT THE HELL?!

POP

...AND THE NUMBERS KEEP GOING UP.

UGH-EE!

TWITCH

BITES INFECT PEOPLE...

HOW CAN I SURVIVE?!

WHERE ARE THE POLICE?!

WHERE'S THE ARMY?!

DASH

SOMEONE HELP ME!

HELP!

...IN A PLACE LIKE THIS!

HUFF

I DON'T WANT TO DIE...

HUH?

THIS WAY!

CHAK

SLASH

UGH!

GRR.

FWIP

BSHOO

SHE'S... POWERFUL!

SCRATCH SCRATCH

UGH!

RUUMBLE

SLAM

I'VE MANAGED TO HIDE FOR A MONTH, BUT I CAN'T DO THIS ANY MORE!

I LOST MY FAMILY. CAUGHT A COLD.

HELL NO.

*KOFF*

...

*KOFF*

*SOB*

*SST...*

EH, EXCUSE ME...

BUT ARE YOU TSUTSUKI TSURANUKI...

...MR. TSURANUKI'S SON, BY ANY CHANCE?

Y-YES, BUT WHY DO YOU KNOW MY NAME...?

SECOND YEAR OF JUNIOR HIGH?

AM I *FAMOUS* OR SOMETHING?

HUH?

HUH?!

WHAT DO YOU MEAN?!

MY PHOTO?!

ALL I HAD WAS YOUR PHOTO.

I'VE BEEN LOOKING FOR YOU.

SLIDE...

Sigh.

OH GREAT! I'VE FOUND YOU AT LAST...

MY FAMILY OWNS A SLIGHTLY *DIFFERENT*...

EH.

...MARTIAL ARTS DOJO.

SST...

TO PROTECT...

YOUR FATHER ASKED ME...

...YOU AND YOUR TWIN.

BOOM

WHAT THE HELL?!

MY... FATHER?!

CRUNCH...

....

THE ROOFTOP SEEMS TO BE SAFE.

MY NAME IS KARINA KARINA.

YES, BOTH NAMES ARE THE SAME. I'M A SOPHOMORE.

NICE TO MEET YOU.

GACHAK

YES, THAT'S RIGHT.

"PRO-TECT"?

DO YOU MEAN LIKE A BODY GUARD?

WELL, I DON'T KNOW WHAT TO SAY...

HUFF

BUT WHAT DOES IT MEAN?

HUFF

HUH...?

OH, SORRY...

IT'S JUST THAT I'VE LOST FAITH IN HUMANITY THESE DAYS.

I'M GUESSING IT'S BECAUSE I'M YOUNG AND INEXPERIENCED.

ARE YOU WORRIED?

SURE, SOME HUMANS ARE SCARY.

YOU'RE DEAD!

EEK!

GIMME YOUR GUN!

CAUSE EVERY TIME I'VE BUMPED INTO HUMANS ...

THEY'VE TRIED TO KILL ME!

I WAS TOLD TO PROTECT BOTH OF YOU.

BY THE WAY, WHERE'S YOUR SISTER?

WHERE DID YOU GET THE GUN?

I FOUND IT! MAYBE IT'S EX-ARMY (IT'S A LIE).

It's his family's, actually.

TSURARA AND I GOT SEPARATED IN ALL THE CONFUSION.

...

SO, I'M TRYING TO...

REACH MY FAMILY'S RENDEZVOUS POINT, WHICH WE SET UP IN CASE OF EMERGENCY, BUT...

BECAUSE I KEEP HAVING TO MAKE LONG DETOURS...

HU FF

HU FF

...I CAN'T MOVE FORWARD AS FAST AS I WANT.

LET'S FIND HER TOGETHER.

GACHAK

I SEE.

SHE SEEMS NICE...

...BUT CAN I *TRUST* HER?

...

AW...

BUT SHE'S USED TO SLAYING ZOMBIES, AT LEAST.

IT'S LIKE HER PERSONALITY DOESN'T MATCH THE WAY SHE LOOKS.

...BUT SHE'S A WHOLE NEW LEVEL.

PEOPLE CALLED ME ODD...

EH...
I'M FINE!

EH...

...YOU SURE YOU'RE OKAY?

I MEAN, A MONTH AGO I HAD NO IDEA.

NOT MUCH.

HOW MUCH DO YOU KNOW ABOUT THIS PLACE?

BY THE WAY...

TREMBLE TREMBLE

I WAS GOING OUT WITH MY FRIENDS...

...THERE WERE MOVIES TO SEE.

I WAS STUDYING FOR NEXT YEAR'S COLLEGE EXAMS.

I WAS LIKE ALL THE OTHER KIDS.

Would you like one?

I LOVE THAT SERIES, TOO!

WOW! YOU WATCH WESTERN FILMS.

YES, I WAS LOOKING FORWARD TO **WORLD WAR DEAD 2** COMING IN THE SPRING.

MOVIES? DO YOU LIKE THEM?

I KNOW, RIGHT? BECAUSE OF THOSE DELETED SCENES.

I THOUGHT THEY MIGHT RECYCLE THEM IN THE SEQUEL.

YEAH, THE FIRST ONE WAS GREAT, BUT I WAS WAITING FOR THE SEQUEL.

WORLD WAR DEAD

WORLD WAR DEAD 2

IF YOU'D LIKE, LET'S GO TO SEE THE FILM TOGETHER ONE DAY...

...WHEN THINGS GET BACK TO NORMAL.

CRUNCH CRUNCH

AWW... IT'S BEEN A WHILE SINCE I COULD TALK *NERDY*.

...EVER GET BACK TO NORMAL?

CAN THINGS... ...KET OFFICE

OOOOOOOOOO

Central Entrance 1

DOOM

COLD AIR.

GACHAK

WAFT...

GUR-GH!

CRASH

KARINA!!

....!

BLAM

DAMN!

BLAM

GRO-AN...

ROAAR

K-KARINA...

HUFF

UGH...

HUFF

HUFF

HUFF

HUFF

...SHE'D LITERALLY *SHIELD* ME.

I DIDN'T THINK...

DRIP

DROP

HUFF

DISAP-
POINTING...

HUFF

SLUMP...

IT WAS
A ZOMBIE
COMMANDER.

I'VE
NEVER
MET
ONE SO
STRONG.

A CORPSE
PUPPETEER.

HOW
...

...DO YOU
KNOW
THAT?

HU FF

HU FF

MY FAMILY...

...HAS BEEN FIGHTING AGAINST ZOMBIES FOR A LONG TIME.

WE ARE HUNTERS OF THE UNDEAD.

CALLED *CORPSE BLADE.*

FWIP

THAT DOESN'T MAKE ANY SENSE.

NO TIME TO EXPLAIN.

CORPSE B--?

URGH...

WE NEED TO GET AWAY QUICKLY.

HOLD ON TO ME.

SLIDE...

...I CAN'T...

...LET YOU DIE...

HU FF

HU FF

SORRY...

GO... AHEAD OF ME.

WHAT...

KARINA!!

SHE'S WILLING TO DIE TO PROTECT ME...

OH, NO!

RUUUMBLE

GA SHA
RATTLE

KAA

THE EXPLOSION ATTRACTED THEM!!

HU FF

HU FF

DAMN IT.

GACHAK

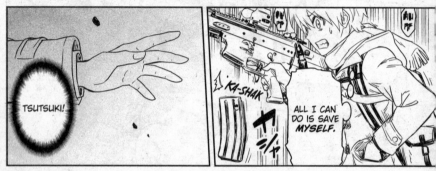

DON'T RUN AWAY.

RA-TAT-TAT-TAT

DON'T YOU EVER RUN AWAY AGAIN!!

THWACK

THWACK

FLOP

RA-TAT-TAT-TAT

THUD

URGH!

WHAT SHOULD I DO?!

DAMN! I'M SANDWICHED.

DASH

YAA

STOMP!

ズ

KARINA!

SLUMP...

ズ

...

SWAY...

SHRR

SHE'S INFECTED...

OH...

NO...

SPUTCH

...FROM THE WOUND SHE RECEIVED EARLIER?!

...!!

GA-CHAK

I DON'T WANNA DIE...

SWISH

...KARINA?

...

K...

KO-FF!

HU FF

ARE YOU ALL RIGHT?

HU FF

SNAP...

TSU- TSUKI...

I DON'T THINK...

...I'M CLEAR.

I DON'T KNOW...

IS YOUR BODY...

...ALL RIGHT?

SHE'S STILL CON- SCIOUS?!

A- ARE YOU OKAY...?

KO-FF!

WHAT'S GOING ON...?

SPLASH

KOFF!

KOFF!

HASN'T SHE TURNED INTO A ZOMBIE?!

...HAVE DIED!!

ALL THE OTHERS...

...

THERE ARE STILL LOADS OF THEM OUTSIDE.

THERE ARE MANY OTHERS...

HUFF

HUFF

THAT WASN'T THE ONLY CORPSE PUPPETEER...

HOW LONG BEFORE SHE TURNS...?

UGH ...

HOW DOES SHE KNOW...?

...

...

AREN'T YOU...

...AFRAID OF ME?

SHOW ME YOUR WOUND.

LET'S STOP THE BLEEDING AND HIDE SOMEWHERE.

CRUNCH

I AM, BUT...

...

I DON'T WANNA LEAVE...

...THE PERSON WHO RISKED HER LIFE FOR ME.

CRUNCH...

I'M GONNA FIND HER, BY ANY MEANS.

BUT TSURARA IS STILL ALIVE SOME- WHERE.

A TWIN CAN ALWAYS SENSE IT.

EVERYTHING IS STILL A MYSTERY...

HU FF

HU FF

...WHY ALL THIS HAS HAPPENED.

...EVERY-
THING
CAN GO
BACK TO
NORMAL.

SO
ONE
DAY...

I'LL
TRY...

PLEASE
DON'T BITE
ME.

# CHAPTER 1 - END

CORPSE BLADE

CRUNCH

HUFF

HUFF

CHAPTER 2

SHE NEEDS TO REST SOMEWHERE SOON, BUT...

HER BODY IS ALREADY COLD...

AND HOSPITALS ARE CLOSED.

ZOMBIES ARE *EVERYWHERE*...

DING
DONG

DING
DONG

A&E
Entrance

HELP US,
PLEASE!

EXCUSE ME,
ANYONE
THERE?

...

THERE'S
NO DOCTOR
HERE.

WE
CAN'T LET
YOU IN!

GZZ

I
CAN'T
TAKE HER
ANYWHERE
WITH
PEOPLE.

GO AWAY
ALREADY!

BASTARD...
SHE'S INFECTED.

UGH...

ヂ"CREAK ヂ"

CRUNCH ヂ"

IS IT OKAY TO TAKE HER TO A *LOVE HOTEL*?!

BUT THERE COULD BE KEYS AT THE FRONT DESK.

HOTEL LOVEHO

REST ¥48... STAY ¥78...

HUFF

HUFF

TSU-TSUKI...

IF I TURN INTO A ZOMBIE...

...YOU HAVE TO SAVE YOURSELF.

...TIE ME TO THE BED.

HUFF

HUFF

I DON'T KNOW...

...HOW LONG I CAN STAY HUMAN.

I BEG YOU.

WHAT THE ?!

KARINA.

SST...

...

HU FF

HU FF

CREAK

I'VE NEVER SEEN ANYTHING LIKE THIS BEFORE.

IS HER ZOMBIFICATION *SLOWED* FOR SOME REASON...?

ABA

...AND WAKE UP SOON AFTER AS A ZOMBIE.

RISE

USUALLY, THEY'RE DEAD WITHIN MINUTES OF INFECTION...

Ugh

GAPE

AAA-RGH!

HUH? WHY AM I LYING ON THE BED?!

UGH...

A DREAM?!

STARTLE

TADA

OH, TSUTSUKI...

GOOD MORNING!

ARGH!

WHIP

Sorry, it's unsightly...

I'M SORRY TO HAVE WORRIED YOU.

CHIRP CHIRP

KARINA... DID YOU HAVE A BATH?!

HOTEL

!!

SST

YOU MAY NOT BELIEVE IT, BUT MY WOUND IS FINE. LOOK.

I'M FINE NOW.

HOW ARE YOU FEELING?!

IT'S CLOSED AND ALMOST GONE?!

SHE WAS SERIOUSLY WOUNDED...

THUMP

THUMP

SHE'S RECOVERED ALREADY?!

I FOUND YOU ON THE FLOOR AT DAWN.

YOU PUSHED YOURSELF DESPITE HAVING A FEVER, DIDN'T YOU?

HUH?!

YOU CALLED THAT ZOMBIE A **CORPSE PUPPETEER**, DIDN'T YOU?

EH...

CAN YOU TELL ME A BIT MORE ABOUT YOURSELF?

WHAT DOES THAT MEAN?

ONE THAT CONTROLS OTHER ZOMBIES.

HOW MUCH DO YOU KNOW?

Y-YES...

ANYWAY, LET ME DRESS FIRST.

AND I'M SURE MY STORY WOULD SOUND CRAZY, BUT...

MY KNOWLEDGE IS LIMITED...

...

SST

ズッ

REMEMBER THAT ZOMBIE WE CAME ACROSS YESTERDAY...

ITS BODY STITCHED UP WITH SEVERAL BODIES?

...WITH AN ARTIFICIAL LOOK AND A REINFORCED SKULL?

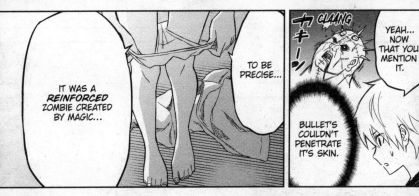

IT WAS A *REINFORCED* ZOMBIE CREATED BY MAGIC...

TO BE PRECISE...

CLAANG

YEAH... NOW THAT YOU MENTION IT.

BULLET'S COULDN'T PENETRATE IT'S SKIN.

...TO SPREAD COMMANDS FROM ELSEWHERE.

IT'S LIKE A RELAY ANTENNA...

SO, I'VE BEEN STRICTLY TRAINED SINCE I WAS A SMALL CHILD.

MY FAMILY - THE DEAD HUNTERS - HAS BEEN FIGHTING AGAINST THEM FOR A LONG TIME...

THERE ARE *REVENANT* STORIES ALL OVER THE WORLD.

I SEEM TO REMEMBER ZOMBIES ORIGINALLY CAME FROM MAGIC FROM HAITI OR SOMEWHERE...

HANG ON A SECOND.

*MAGIC?* THAT'S SO UNEXPECTED!

...DIFFICULT TO BELIEVE, BUT...

YEAH, IT'S...

WOULDN'T IT HAVE BEEN ON THE NEWS?

HAVE ZOMBIES REALLY EXISTED FOR SO LONG?

ARE YOU SURE...

...YOU'RE OKAY?

YES. I'M FULL OF BEANS NOW.

It's a beautiful day!

YOU'RE THE ONE WHO SHOULD LOOK AFTER YOURSELF...

...IS IT SAFE TO BE WITH HER?

I'M GLAD SHE'S BETTER, BUT...

NO... I'D LIKE TO HEAD TO MY FAMILY'S RENDEZVOUS POINT, AS SOON AS POSSIBLE.

THIS UNUSUAL RECUPERATIVE POWER, TOO.

HER SUPER-HUMAN ABILITY SCARES ME.

I'M ANXIOUS... IS SHE REALLY NOT GOING TO TURN?

THE MUTATION SEEMS TO HAVE STOPPED.

OH YEAH. I HAVEN'T ASKED YOU WHERE THE MEETING PLACE IS.

WHERE ARE YOU GOING?

And I'm feeling better now.

BUT SHE'S STILL CONSCIOUS.

YOUR HOME IS IN HIKARIGAOKA, RIGHT? WHY IS IT SO FAR FROM HOME?

TOKYO DOME?

HOME

ITABASHI-WARD

NERIMA-WARD

WE ARE HERE

TOSHIMA-WARD

BUNKYO-WARD

NAKANO-WARD

SHINJUKU-WARD

TOKYO DOME

CHIYODA-WARD

USUALLY, AN EMERGENCY RENDEZVOUS WOULD BE IN AN EVACUATION SHELTER CLOSE BY.

SUIDO-BASHI...

NEAR THE TOKYO DOME.

I CAN'T SEE THE BOTTOM...

THESE FISSURES ARE SERIOUS OBSTACLES.

...ZOMBIES ARE NOT THE ONLY PROBLEM.

TOPOGRAPHY CHANGES AT THIS SCALE...

...ARE NORMALLY IMPOSSIBLE.

IT'S NOT LIKE WE HAD A MAJOR EARTH-QUAKE...

...IT'S STRANGE THAT POWER AND WATER ARE STILL WORKING.

SPLOSH

SPLASH

CRUNCH

BUT THAT'S WHEN I REALIZED...

POWER LINES AND WATER PIPES MUST'VE BEEN SEVERED...

WHERE DO THEY COME FROM?

IF I FALL, I'LL DIE.

IT'S A BIG-SCALE **SUPERNATURAL PHENOMENON**.

NOTHING MAKES SENSE.

INVESTIGATORS AND RESCUE TEAMS FROM OVERSEAS WOULD BE INTERVENING.

SURE, IF IT WERE A NORMAL DISASTER...

IF TOKYO IS THIS DESERTED, THEN...

I DON'T WANT TO THINK ABOUT IT, THOUGH.

THE SCALE OF THIS DISASTER MAY BE FAR BIGGER THAN WE THINK.

IN THE LAST MONTH OR SO...

I HAVEN'T SEEN A SINGLE AIRPLANE OR HELICOPTER.

I'M TALKING ABOUT MERE POSSIBILITIES, THOUGH.

OR EVEN THE WHOLE PLANET.

IF THIS ISN'T JUST TOKYO, OR ALL OF JAPAN...

IT KIND OF MAKES SENSE...

...

...THERE IS A LEGITIMATE REASON WHY THEY CAN'T RESCUE US.

OR...

YEAH... THERE'S NO POINT IN DISCUSSING THIS.

IT'S TOTALLY HOPE-LESS.

BUT NOTHING'S LEFT ON THE SUPERMARKET SHELVES...

YEAH...

BY THE WAY, AREN'T YOU HUNGRY?

NO, SURELY WORCESTER SAUCE WOULD BE BETTER THAN SOY SAUCE.

THE DEEP *UMAMI* AND FRUITY SWEETNESS IS THE BEST.

HEHE. DO YOU LIKE WORCESTER SAUCE WITH DEEP FRIED MEAT?

I WANT TO EAT TONKATSU. HAVEN'T EATEN IT FOR A WHILE...

RUUUMBLE...

THAT'S NICE. I ALSO LIKE CITRUS SOY SAUCE.

I LIKE SOY SAUCE.

...MY SISTER USED TO MAKE THAT... TONKATSU.

TSU-RARA...

ARE YOU ALL RIGHT?

...SO SHE WASN'T GREAT AT COOKING, BUT...

...SHE LEARNED HOW TO MAKE MY FAVORITE FOOD.

IT USED TO BE JUST THE TWO OF US AT DINNER TIME...

YET I ABANDONED HER.

SHE HELPED ME SO MUCH...

I BELIEVE SHE'S SAFE...

...BUT I HAVEN'T FOUND HER YET.

I SPENT DAYS SEARCHING OUR NEIGHBORHOOD...

GRIP
ギュ

I MAY BE ABLE TO FIND FROZEN TONKATSU...

IN A SHOP THIS SMALL, THERE SHOULDN'T BE MANY.

キラ

キラ

...

CLATTER...

...

OH ...

FS-HOO

CHAK

IS IT...

A SUMO WRESTLER ZOMBIE?!

WHICH DOESN'T MAKE THINGS EASY...

SHIT. THEY ARE SUPER POWERFUL.

KARINA, GET DOWN!

WHIP

UGH!

POU

NO WAY SHE HAS SUCH STRENGTH...

SHE STOPPED...

...A SUMO WRESTLER'S ADVANCE?!

HFA
....

A *SWORD* CAME OUT OF HER HAND...!!

AGAIN...

ARGH!

CRAAASH

RUN. THEY HEARD THE NOISE. THEY'RE COMING.

QUIVER

QUIVER

UGH...

THIS...

SMASH...

ALL

ガシャア...

SHRR KO KO

BA-SHA

...GONE BACK INTO MY BODY?!

IT'S...

TAP

KARINA, LET'S GO TO A BACK STREET!

UGHA

HU FF

KA-CHA

THIS ROOM IS UNLOCKED.

JUDGING FROM THE MESS, ZOMBIES BROKE THROUGH THE WINDOW AND THEY FLED.

HU FF

HU FF

WHERE ARE THE RESI-DENTS?

THERE MAY BE SOMETHING TO EAT.

JERK

GI...

YOU NEED TO EAT NOW, OR THE NOODLES WILL GET SOGGY.

SLURP ず" ず"

...

YESTERDAY I FELT SO FOGGY...

...I COULDN'T REMEMBER WHEN THE BLADE CAME OUT. WHEN WAS IT UNSHEATHED?

THAT MAY HAVE SOMETHING TO DO WITH WHAT HAPPENED.

OH YEAH. DIDN'T YOU SAY SOMETHING ABOUT CORPSE BLADE?

I WAS TOLD **CORPSE BLADE** WAS A SPECIAL TITLE...

...BUT AS I'M A DEAD HUNTER TRAINEE, I WASN'T TOLD ABOUT THE DETAILS.

I WISH I COULD BUT...

...I CAN'T.

THEN...

...PERHAPS YOU SHOULD FIND YOUR FAMILY.

INCLUDING MY GRANDFATHER, WHO KNEW THE STORIES.

BECAUSE ON THE DAY OF THE COLLAPSE...

...MOST OF MY FAMILY MEMBERS DIED.

...KILLED THEM ALL.

SOMEONE...

KARINA...

WHAT HAPPENED?!

GRAND-FATHER!

PLEASE... ...THESE CHILDREN...

BY THE ZOMBIES...?!

OH NO...

THAT'S ...

...WHAT I WAS THINKING, BUT...

COMPLETING IT WOULD BE...

...THE ONLY THING I CAN DO TO HONOR THE DEAD.

BUT, GUARDING YOU IS AN IMPORTANT MISSION INHERITED FROM MY GRANDFATHER.

I DON'T KNOW WHO DID IT.

NO.

SOMETHING *WEIRD* IS HAPPENING TO ME.

AND THAT SUPER HUMAN STRENGTH EARLIER.

BUT SURELY THINGS CAN'T BE...

ズ ズ ZU
ズ ズ ZU
ズ ズ ZU

I DON'T THINK...

...I'M HUMAN ANY MORE.

...SO CONVENIENT.

I'M JUST SCARED OF MYSELF.

SNAP... ピキ...

I MIGHT TURN INTO A ZOMBIE AT ANY MOMENT, TOO...

FOR STARTERS, SHE GOT THAT ABILITY...

...BECAUSE SHE SHELTERED ME.

IT WAS ME WHO WAS SAVED.

I'D BE MORE UPSET.

AND IF I'D LOST MY FAMILY AND THOUGHT I WAS TURNING...

...MUCH MUCH MORE ANXIOUS THAN ME.

SHE MUST BE...

I WOULD'VE BEEN DEAD THREE TIMES ALREADY.

WITHOUT YOU...

...EVEN IF YOU TURN INTO A ZOMBIE.

I'M READY...

I DON'T KNOW WHAT I'LL DO...

WHEN THE TIME COMES...

I'M BETTING ON YOU!

AND THAT YOU WON'T BECOME A ZOMBIE.

I'M BETTING ON THE CHANCE...

BUT...

THERE'S STILL HOPE.

TRY TO BE YOURSELF. AS LONG AS YOU CAN.

SO, DON'T JUST GIVE UP.

I TRUST YOU.

WHOOSH...
ヒュゥゥ...

TREMBLE
ブルッ

IT'S STILL COLD HERE...

ACHOO!

DO YOU MIND IF I SIT BY YOU?

SST
スッ

...WARM.

YOU ARE...

ザリ…
CRUNCH...

オオ…
OO...

THAT'S
...!

CHAPTER 2 - END

CORPSE BLADE

# CORPSE BLADE

...SO CLOSE, BUT...

DOOM

OH NO...

THE TOKYO DOME IS...

CHAPTER 3

DOOM

I CAN'T SEE THE WHOLE PICTURE, BUT...

...IT SEEMS THE CITY IS DIVIDED...

...INTO SEPARATE AREAS.

...

CROSS THAT?

HOW CAN WE...

CRUNCH

...

THOUGH I KIND OF KNEW IT...

DAMN!

...THAT WE DIDN'T GO STRAIGHT HOME ON THAT DAY.

IT WAS OUR FAULT...

THE DAY OF THE COLLAPSE WAS MY FATHER'S BIRTHDAY...

SO WE SAID WE SHOULD GET HIM A PRESENT.

AFTER SCHOOL, WE POPPED INTO TOWN, WHICH WE SHOULDN'T HAVE...

LEAVE YOUR VEHICLES WITH THE KEYS INSIDE.

THERE ARE CRACKS IN THE GROUND AHEAD!

ROAAR

CHATTER CHATTER

...

HOPE WE WEREN'T HIT BY A MISSILE...

SIGNAL DISTURBANCE?!

NO INTERNET...

WHAT HAS HAPPENED?!

COME TO THINK OF IT, THAT WAS THE FIRST TIME I SAW ZOMBIES.

I WONDER HOW MANY SURVIVORS THERE ARE IN TOKYO...

IT'S BEEN A MONTH...

...

IT'S NOT YOUR FAULT.

YOU'RE DOING REALLY WELL IN THIS SITUATION.

I RESPECT...

...YOUR STRENGTH.

DESPITE HOW *DANGEROUS* IT'S BEEN, YOU'RE STILL LOOKING FOR YOUR FAMILY.

IKEBU-
KURO

SUGAMO

?

TOKYO
DOME

BUT,
AS WE MOVE,
I'M NOTING THE
FISSURES ON
THE MAP.

I'M SURE
THERE'S A
ROUTE IN.

TOKYO
東京

HUH...?
OH NO...

IF YOU
HADN'T SAVED
ME, I'D--

I'M SURE
THAT'S WHAT
TSURARA
WOULD DO.

LET'S WORK
THROUGH THE
DIFFERENT
ROUTES.

I
HAVEN'T
BEEN MUCH
HELP.

I'LL
BE WITH YOU
UNTIL THE
END.

SO, DON'T
GIVE UP YET.

THEY'RE WALKING IN A LINE.

THAT'S FUNNY. THEY'S USUALLY MORE RANDOM.

CRUNCH...

DOOM ゴゴ

ゴ

ゴ

ゴ

FWIP FWIP

DON'T,
IT'S DANGEROUS!
OBVIOUSLY THIS
BUILDING ISN'T
NORMAL!

DO YOU
MIND IF I POP
IN AND CHECK
INSIDE?

HAVE YOU
SEEN THIS
BUILDING
BEFORE...?

IT'S
AN ODD
BUILDING.

THERE IS NO DOUBT THAT THEY ARE INVOLVED IN THIS COLLAPSE...

AND PROBABLY... THE ATTACK ON MY FAMILY...

WHAT...

YOU MEAN THE ONES WHO CREATE ZOMBIES...?!

BUT THIS WEIRD ATMOS- PHERE...

THE *MAGES* MIGHT BE IN THERE.

...IT MAY GIVE US A CLUE HOW TO PROCEED.

IF I CAN FIND OUT WHAT THEIR PURPOSE IS...

YOU STAY HERE AND GUARD THE ENTRANCE.

SO, LET ME GO.

I'LL DO MY BEST TO AVOID FIGHTING AND BE BACK ASAP.

CLUE...

...YOU THINK?

WHAT'S THIS BUILDING FOR?

NO DOORS ON EITHER SIDE.

CHIIIIING

WHAT A LONG CORRIDOR... MY EARS ARE RINGING.

SPLASH

SWISH

?!

RUSTLE

AU...

THOSE ARE THE ZOMBIES WE SAW EARLIER.

A cherry tree?

WHAT IS THIS PLACE...?

SLUUURP

SIP

PLUNK

SLICE

GRAB

ZCHA...
ズチャ...

LICK

MUNCH
MUNCH

SQUELCH

SHUDDER

SHE'S EATING THEIR BRAINS...

A REINFORCED ZOMBIE...?!

SHE'S NOT A MAGE!

SHE'S A *CORPSE PUPPETEER.*

...

SPLASH

WHAT ...?

WRIGGLE

THUD

THAT PILE OF BODIES IS HER FOOD, HUH?

...

DOOM

*Free-zing...*

BUT IT'S ONLY BEEN FIVE MINUTES.

SHE'S TAKING HER TIME...

FEELS LONGER.

CHI-K!

BUT...

THERE ARE TOO MANY MYSTERIES AROUND THE COLLAPSE.

MY PRIORITY IS TO FIND A PATH ACROSS TO THE DOME SIDE.

IT'S TRUE THAT WE ARE STUCK DUE TO A LACK OF INFORMATION.

THIS BUILDING IS JUST A DISTRACTION.

WE SHOULD REALLY AVOID UNNECESSARY RISKS.

I don't have much ammo left.

...WE MAY NOT BE ABLE TO PROCEED IF WE KEEP AVOIDING RISKS.

AS KARINA SAID...

SHE SEEMS RELIABLE...

...BUT MAYBE SHE'S TOO HASTY.

BUT SHE JUST SAID WE SHOULD KEEP GOING.

HOW ARE WE SUPPOSED TO DO BOTH?!

IF I GET PULLED INTO THE WATER, I'M FINISHED.

SLASH

UGH!

ALL I CAN DO IS HANDLE THEM EACH IN TURN...

WHIP

CHAK

HOW CAN I FIGHT AGAINST THIS MONSTER?!

HUFF

TSUTSUKI'S AT THE ENTRANCE.

IT'S TOO DANGEROUS TO DRAG HER OUTSIDE...

HUFF

CHAPTER 3 - END

CORPSE BLADE

IT WAS TWO YEARS AGO.

CHAPTER 4

I WAS 15...

...WHEN I FIRST FOUGHT AGAINST ZOMBIES.

ONCE EVERY THIRTY YEARS OR SO, THERE'S A MINOR ZOMBIE OUTBREAK.

BACK THEN, THIS IS WHAT I HEARD.

CRUNCH

AS FOR CLEANING IT UP, THEY OUTSOURCE IT TO US.

...SHUTS DOWN MEDIA ACCESS, AND CONTAINS THE PROBLEM.

THE GOVERNMENT LOCKS DOWN THE AREA...

UGH...

KAA!

DON'T THINK.

DING DONG

SOCIETY WOULD COLLAPSE.

...IF PEOPLE KNEW THE *UNDEAD* COULD RISE?

CAN YOU IMAGINE WHAT WOULD HAPPEN...

...I AM NOT ALLOWED TO TALK ABOUT IT.

THEY DON'T KNOW OUR 'FAMILY BUSINESS' AND...

SOMETIMES IGNORANCE IS BLISS.

READY TO GIVE MY LIFE FOR THEM.

THE SAFETY DEVICE IN SOCIETY.

I AM 'THE SWORD' AND 'THE SHIELD' TO PROTECT EVERYDAY LIFE FROM THE SHADOWS.

...THEIR SMILES...

BE-
CAUSE
...

...MAKE
ME...

...FEEL
WARM.

I'VE LOST COUNT OF HOW MANY I'VE CUT OFF.

DAMN! JUST HOW MANY TENTACLES DOES SHE HAVE?

HOW CAN THAT HAPPEN SO FAST?!

THEY'RE GROWING BACK?!

WHERE'S IT COMING FROM?!

SHE'S GOING TO ATTACK FROM UNDER-WATER...

SHE'S INTELLIGENT AND ACCUSTOMED TO FIGHTING.

EXHAUSTION ALONE IS GOING TO WEAR ME DOWN.

I DIDN'T EXPECT SUCH A MONSTER TO EXIST...

GLUG

HU FF

...

HUFF

CAN'T AFFORD TO MAKE MISTAKES.

KEEP ANALYZING THE SITUATION.

KEEP COOL AT ALL TIMES.

I WAS BORN TO FIGHT AGAINST ZOMBIES AND RAISED AS A WARRIOR.

I'M HEIR TO GENERATIONS OF THE DEAD HUNTERS.

DON'T GET OVERWHELMED.

TRUST MY OWN POWER.

THUK

SHRR

HU FF

I ENDURED STRICT TRAINING.

...TO BE WORTHY OF MY HERITAGE.

I PRACTISED EVERY DAY...

SPLASH.

AH, THE ZOMBIES WHOSE BRAINS GOT EATEN BY THE MONSTER.

SORRY GUYS...

GRAB

DASH—

GLUB

I'M GONNA USE YOU AS DECOYS!

WHOOSH

SWISH SWISH

SLASH SLASH

WRAP

SNAP SNAP

CALM DOWN. I'M ALSO A MONSTER...

MY PHYSICAL ABILITIES HAVE BEEN IMPROVING.

GLUB

GLUB

GLUB

THE SCARS ON HER FACE HAVEN'T HEALED.

SPLAASH

AND NOW SHE LACKS TENTACLES ON HER BACK...

WHOOSH

WHIP

WHIP

UNLIKE HUMANS, THEY ONLY HAVE ONE VULNERABLE POINT.

SLASH

SLASH

SLASH

SLASH

THEY ARE MONSTERS, BUT AT THE END OF THE DAY THEIR BODY CONSISTS OF FLESH AND BONES.

IF YOUR SWORD CAN'T REACH THE NECK, YOU NEED TO IMMOBILIZE THEM.

THOSE FEW SECONDS UNTIL HER LEGS REGROW...

...ARE CRITICAL.

SWISH

LOCK

WHACK

THUD

WHAM

...I'M A DISCIPLE OF THE KARINA GROUP OF THE BICHU SCHOOL OF SWORDPLAY.

EVEN IF I'M THE LAST OF US...

KARINA THE **DEAD HUNTER.**

UGH...

THE DEAD HUNTER'S TECHNIQUES...

SNAP

ボッ CRACK

...DON'T WORK.

TURN

WHAP

I'M NOT GOOD ENOUGH, HUH?

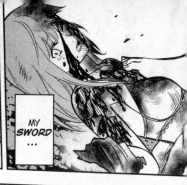

MY SWORD...

CRUNCH

AFTER I TRAINED SO HARD...

PEW

PEW

CLANG

WRIGGLE

CRUNCH

DRAG

UGH...

CLANG

CLANG

CLANG

CLANG

CLANG

MOVE, BODY!

MOVE!

SCRAPE

NOT JUST MY FAMILY...

WHEN THE CITY COLLAPSED...

BUT ALSO THE PEOPLE I WAS SUPPOSED TO PROTECT.

...I LOST EVERYTHING.

DRAG

...!

HUFF

HUFF

IF I CANNOT PROTECT ANYONE...

...I HAVE NO WORTH AS 'A SWORD', EITHER.

...A PURPOSE IN LIFE.

I NO LONGER HAVE...

BLAM

BLAM

CREEAK

STILL...

I'M NOT SURE HOW LONG I CAN HOLD ON TO MY HUMAN MIND.

NOT TO MENTION, I MIGHT HAVE BEEN *INFECTED*.

...HE WOULD TRUST ME.

HE SAID...

...HE'S THE LAST THING...

SNAP

SNAP

SNAP

FOR ME...

SNAP

TANGLE

URGH...

WRING

ガリ
TWIST
リヨ

ノ

ゴ
GLUB

ボ

...

グ PSH

ズ

ゲ
WRING

グ

I
WILL...

...NO
LONGER...

KARINA!!

PHUUF

SPLASH

KA-

SPLATTER

HUFF

HUFF

CHAPTER 4 - END

CORPSE BLADE

CORPSE BLADE

# CHAPTER 5

WELL DONE...

HMM...

VSHHaboo

...FOR SLAYING THE 'WELL' GUARD ON HER OWN.

HUFF

HUFF

SORRY...

WHY DIDN'T YOU CALL ME WHEN YOU FOUND AN ENEMY?!

I TOLD YOU IT'D BE DANGEROUS!

I'M FINE...

HU FF

I JUST NEED REST...

HU FF

...WANT TO DRAG YOU INTO A *BATTLE.*

I DIDN'T...

HU FF

HAVING SAID THAT...

HU FF

...

I'M STILL INEXPE- RIENCED.

...I COULDN'T HAVE SLAIN HER.

...WITHOUT YOU...

WHAT ARE YOU TALKING ABOUT?

YOU'RE RIPPED TO SHREDS.

PROTECT SOMEONE - SOMEONE DEAR TO ME...

I WANT TO BECOME ABLE TO...

I DON'T WANT TO BE JUST PROTECTED.

...PROTECT THE WORLD.

I WAS RAISED ONLY TO...

NO ONE HAS...

...EVER SAID THAT TO ME.

PFFT

CHING

THUMP

!

SPLASH

LOOK AT THE WATER SURFACE!

WHAT ...?

GURGLE

...ALREADY
IN THE CLUTCHES
OF THE ENEMY.

ARGH!!

SPLAASH

WHERE ARE WE?!

WHAT HAS HAPPENED?!

VSSHH

THE SHAPE OF THE ROCK IS DIFFERENT FROM BEFORE...

UGH

GK-OFF

WHAT?!

SOAKED

KARINA, GET ON MY BACK...

DRAG

...IT'S DANGEROUS TO STAY HERE.

ANY-WAY...

....!

OOOOOO

WHAT DOES HE MEAN BY "THE ENEMY"?

HUFF

HE WAS TALKING ABOUT TSURARA.

HUFF

WHO WAS THAT MAN?

WHAT ON EARTH WAS HE TALKING ABOUT...?

THIS CITY'S CONNECTED TO ANOTHER WORLD...?

....!

CRUNCH...

A BASEBALL STADIUM?

POKE

!! THUD THUD

ALI...

KAA!

DASH

SHIT!

IT MAKES NO SENSE!!

DAMN!! ZOMBIES...

WE COULDN'T REACH IT BECAUSE OF THE HUGE CRACK IN THE GROUND.

WHY ARE WE IN THE TOKYO DOME?!

THWACK

THOP

THUCK

WHAT THE...

THOP

THUCK

THEY'VE BEEN SHOT!! BUT FROM WHERE...?

TOK

CLOMP

WHO ARE THEY?!

FWIP

...

BRRT

RA-TAT-TAT

THERE'S MULTIPLE PEOPLE!

THE SELF-DEFENSE FORCE?!

STARE...

THEY'VE SURVIVED!!

THEY ARE THE MILITARY!

CAN YOU HEAR ME?! ANSWER!

ARE YOU WOUNDED? WHERE ARE YOU FROM?!

RA-TAT

DOES IT MEAN...

THEY'RE POWER-FUL...

...WE ARE SAFE?!

THOP

THOP

UGA!

FWIP

Y-

ARE YOU ALL RIGHT?! ONLY TWO OF YOU?!

YES.

CHAK

THE WOMAN'S INFECTED!

UGH...

!!

SHE'S TURNING INTO A ZOMBIE!!

SNAP...

!!

I STILL DON'T KNOW...

...WHAT HAPPENED...

....TO THIS CITY.

BUT...

NO MATTER HOW MUCH THIS PLACE IS DEVASTATED BY THE DEAD...

NO MATTER HOW MUCH THE CRACKS HAVE CHANGED THE LANDSCAPE...

...THAT ONE DAY...

...WE COULD GO BACK TO...

AT THE BOTTOM OF MY HEART...

...I JUST HOPED...

...IF I CAN FIND MY FAMILY.

...NORMAL LIFE...

KARINA...

CHAPTER 5 - END

TO BE CONTINUED IN VOL 2.

CORPSE BLADE

# CORPSE BLADE - POSTSCRIPT

I USED UP ALL THE PAGES FOR THE MAIN STORY, SO HERE IT IS, ON THE BACK COVER*!

A POSTSCRIPT SHOULD REALLY BE AT THE END OF A VOLUME BUT...

THANK YOU VERY MUCH FOR YOUR SUPPORT!

HI! I'M HAJIME SEGAWA!

*ON THE ORIGINAL JAPANESE VERSION, THE POSTSCRIPT WAS PLACED ON THE BACK COVER.

ALSO, ERM, I HAVE A DOG AND A TORTOISE. I LOVE MOVIES, BUT PEOPLE DON'T UNDERSTAND MY TASTE (SAD).

Editor

BOTH OF THEM ARE FALSE.

WIKIPEDIA SAYS MY AGE IS 70, BUT IN FACT, I'M A 20-YEAR-OLD FEMALE COLLEGE STUDENT!

LET ME INTRODUCE MYSELF TO THOSE WHO DON'T KNOW ME.

OH?

I APPRECIATE MY EDITOR WHO SAID THAT!!

KABOOM

**SEE YOU IN VOLUME 2!!**

AAARGH!!

AM I SOUNDING WEIRD?

...

YES, BUT IT'S VERY LIKE YOU.

Also sword fights and gun battles!

I LOVE ZOMBIES, BUT I TRIED NOT TO MAKE THIS A CLICHÉ. I WANTED TO DRAW SOME YOKAI STUFF, TOO.

YEAH, AND, AS NATURAL DISASTER IS INVOLVED AS WELL, IT'S DIFFICULT TO CATEGORIZE MY WORK.

# EXCITING, NEW MANGA!

**SHADOWS OF KYOTO: VOL 1**

**ATOM: THE BEGINNING: VOL 1**

**KAMEN RIDER: KUUGA VOL 1**

**AFRO SAMURAI: VOL 1**

**ALPI THE SOUL SENDER: VOL 1**

**WITCH OF THISTLE CASTLE: VOL 1**

**"TENGEN" HERO WARS: VOL 1**

**THE GREAT YOKAI WAR: GUARDIANS: VOL 1**

**THE POETRY OF RAN VOL 1**

## FOLLOW TITAN ONLINE HERE!

f facebook.com/comicstitan   ✗ @ComicsTitan   ◎ titancomics

# FAN FAVORITE MANGA!

# STOP

This manga is presented in its original right-to-left
reading format. This is the back of the book!

Pages, panels, and speech balloons read from top right to bottom left,
as shown above. SFX translations are placed adjacent to their
original Japanese counterparts.